CATHERINE COOKSON

◆

The Love Child

◆

A Novel

SUMMIT BOOKS

New York   London   Toronto   Sydney   Tokyo   Singapore

SUMMIT BOOKS
Simon & Schuster Building
Rockefeller Center
1230 Avenue of the Americas
New York, New York 10020

Originally published in Great Britain by Bantam Press, a division of
Transworld Publishers Ltd. as *The Gillyvors*.
SUMMIT BOOKS and colophon are trademarks
of Simon & Schuster Inc.
Manufactured in the United States of America

1   3   5   7   9   10   8   6   4   2

Library of Congress Cataloging in Publication data
Cookson, Catherine.
The love child: a novel/Catherine Cookson.
p.   cm.
"Originally published in Great Britain by Bantam Press . . .
as the Gillyvors"—T.p. verso.
$20.00
I. Title.
PR6053.0525L63   1990
823'.914—dc20   91-20676
CIP

ISBN 978-1-4516-6015-9

To Jack, with my warmest thanks
for keeping me on the straight and
narrow – legal-wise. May you
continue to sing in the mornings
to Kathleen

If you are the bastard of a king, an earl, a lord,
Although the shame will still be there,
You'll get a cut from the world's fare;
Your mother too will have her share.

But if you spring from the loins of the poor,
Your mother will be classed a whore,
A Strumpet, a Gillyvor or a sot,
And her bread will be dearly got.

As for you, the stain is red,
And qualifies you for any man's bed.
But should you rear and stand aside
And demand to be a virgin bride,
Prepare for ridicule and disdain.
Base-born, a child of Cain,
A bastard,
And that you will remain.

The fairest flowers o' the season
Are our carnations and streak'd gillyvors,
Which some call nature's bastards.

From *The Winter's Tale* by
William Shakespeare

PART ONE

The Family

1

'I tell you, Dada, that's what I mean.'

Her face bright with merriment, the young girl read again from the magazine: 'Ladies and farmers' wives will benefit equally from the scented sachets on their pillows. The fragrance is derived from rose petals, sweet briar blossom–' At this point the dark, bright eyes lifted from the page and swept over her family before she went on, gurgling now, 'Cow pats, well ground, as in Farmer Cox's boxings, sold by the pound and dampened, for poultices on the chin, and boils where boils have never bin . . . '

Her voice trailed off and joined the peals of laughter as, dropping the magazine on to the low oak table, she turned and clung to her sister, the while her two older brothers, their bodies bent forward, made guttural sounds and their younger brother, Jimmy, lay on his back on the mat before the open fire, his legs in the air treddling as if he were on a mill; the youngest of them all, a nine-year-old boy, leaned against his mother's side, and she drooped her head until it touched his, and they shook together.

The father hadn't openly joined them in their laughter; but rising from his seat at the side of the fireplace, he slapped his daughter playfully on her bent head, saying, 'One of these days, Miss Clever Clops, that tongue of yours will get you into mischief. Now come on, all of you! It's half-past eight and bed is calling.'

Slowly the laughter subsided, as one after the other of the family rose to their feet and wished their mother good-night. First, there was Oswald and Olan, the eighteen-year-old twins, like her, both dark but different in stature, Oswald being almost half a head taller than his brother, and broad with it, and he, bending and kissing his mother on the cheek, said, 'Now, I've told you, Ma, you're not to get up to see us out. We're big enough and daft enough to cook a bit of gruel and heat a pan of milk.' But to this Maria Dagshaw answered, 'You see to your business, my boy, and I'll see to mine. So, go along with you both.' When, however, her son Olan bent towards her, she gripped his arm, saying, 'D'you think you'll be able to stick that driving and the winter coming on?'

'Don't you worry, Ma; anything's better than the mine; I would drive the devil to hell twice a day rather than go down there again. And the smell of the bread, anyway, keeps me awake. A wonderful new idea, isn't it, Ma? To send bread out and about to the houses?'

'Well, they do it with the tea, why not the bread?' said Nathaniel.

The two young men turned and looked at their father, and Oswald said, 'You're right, Dada. And Mr Green said there'll be other commodities on the carts before long. If they can carry stuff into the market on a Saturday, why not carry it round the doors, Monday, Tuesday, Wednesday, Thursday and Friday.'

'Well, there's something in that.' Nathaniel smiled on his sons and there was pride on his countenance. 'Good-night,' he said. And they both answered, 'Good-night, Dada.'

14

Nathaniel now turned to his daughters, saying, 'You two scallywags, get along with you into your bed before trouble hits you.'

'Oh, you wouldn't whip us, Dada, would you? Oh, you wouldn't! Oh, you wouldn't!'

'Stop your antics, Cherry, else you'll see whether I will or not. And you, Anna, stop your jabbering in bed. And don't shout up to the boys else I'll be in there with a horse whip; you're not too old to be skelped. D'you hear me?'

'Yes, sir. Yes, sir. Three bags full.' At this the two girls joined hands and were about to run down the long room when they turned again and doubled back to their mother, whom they kissed on both cheeks, while she smacked playfully at their bottoms.

When the door had closed behind them Nathaniel turned an unsmiling face towards his wife, saying, 'Those two are so full of the joy of life it frightens me at times.'

As Maria said, 'Oh, don't say that,' her fifteen-year-old son, Jimmy, looked at his father and asked him a question: 'Why does it frighten you, Dada? Because they laugh, and sing, and Anna can make up funny rhymes and stories? What is there in that to frighten you?'

Nathaniel walked towards the fair-haired boy, who was a replica of himself when young. 'I'm always afraid they'll be hurt eventually,' he said. 'And you know why, don't you? I've explained it to you.'

'Yes, Dada, I know why. But as you said, the boys have weathered it, the girls are weathering it in their own way and I in mine, because I have learned to fight like Ossie has taught me. Nobody insults Ossie, either in the village or in the market. And they won't me either, because as I grow I'll become stronger. Anyway, I can use my fists and feet to match any two . . . '

15

'Jimmy! Jimmy, quiet. You've heard me say the pen is mightier than the sword and from that you can gather the tongue is mightier than the fist or the foot.'

'No, Dada, I don't, not when you're dealing with Arthur Lennon or Dirk Melton.'

'You should keep away from them.'

The boy now turned to his mother, saying, 'How can I, Ma, when I have to pass through the village to get to the farm?'

'Well, I take it back in the case of Arthur Lennon.' His father smiled down at him now. 'Being the son of a blacksmith, he's tough. But still, as I've always said, if you can use your tongue, it's better in the long run, because you know you can confound people with words. Only' – he smiled now – 'you've got to know what your tongue's saying and not let it run away with you.' And his voice now rising, he looked down the room and cried, 'Like my dear daughters do!'

'Oh, Nat.'

'Well, they are listening behind the door.'

'They're not; they'll be in bed.'

'I know them.' He now turned to his son, saying, 'And I know you, young fellow. Off you go; and take Ben with you, if you can drag him from his mother's arms.' He bent down and ruffled the brown-haired boy who, when he turned his head and looked up at him, caused a strange pang to go through his chest as he asked himself again how he had come to breed this boy, who had the look of an angel in a church window and the manner and gentleness of a female and the questing mind of someone twice his age. He was the seventh child and a seventh child was always different. But Ben was so different that every time he looked into his eyes he thought the gods must be jealous of such as he, and he feared their decree that the good die young.

16

The boy kissed his mother on the cheek and drew himself from her hold, then put his arms about his father's hips and laid his head against his stomach; and for a moment there came on the kitchen a silence that lasted while Nathaniel led his son up the room to the ladder that was set at an angle against the end wall. And as he helped his son onto it, he said softly, 'Don't let the boys get you talking; they've got to get up in the morning. You understand?'

'Yes, Dada. Good-night, Dada.'

The boy turned from the bottom rung and laid his lips for a moment against his father's cheek, and Nathaniel watched him climb, then disappear through the trap door and so into the long roof-space that held four beds, but which allowed standing-room only down the middle of it.

When he turned from the ladder it was to find Maria standing at the far side of the long trestle table, which was already set for a meal with wooden bowls, wooden plates and a wooden spoon to the side of each plate. In the middle of the table stood a china bowl of brown sugar, and at one end of it was set a bread-board with a knife across it, while at the other was a wooden tray holding eight china mugs.

Maria was looking towards them as she said, 'We'll have to go careful on the milk until Minny is back in working order again. What d'you think she'll have this time?'

'Well, if William's done his duty it could be twins. Let's hope triplets, but that's too much to ask. If she comes up with one nanny we'll be thankful. Come and sit down.'

He went round the table and put his arm across her shoulders and led her back down the room towards the fire. And there he pressed her into the seat he had recently vacated, and with the liveliness of a man half his forty-four years he twisted his body into a sitting position at her feet, and laying his head on her knee he remained silent for quite some time before he asked quietly, 'How long d'you think

17

it can last from now on? The twins are near men, the girls near women.'

'Oh Nat. You mean, our way of life?'

'Yes, just that, Maria, just that; our way of life and this present happiness that has grown and matured in spite of everything.'

'It'll last as long as we're together, and nothing can part us except death. And then if you were to go I wouldn't be long after, and I know it's the same with you.'

He put up his hand and placed it on hers where it was resting on top of his head, and in a low voice, he said, 'It's been a strange life, hasn't it?'

'And it'll go on being strange,' she replied; 'it's the way we've made it.'

'Yes. Yes, you're right. And consequently they'll all have to fight their way through it, each one of them. Yet they know where they stand, even down to Jimmy. He's a wise boy, that one. And then there's Ben. He doesn't somehow need to be told, he knows it already. He's imbibed it, whether from the others or the atmosphere in the house, but he knows he's one of a family that lives apart . . . You know what tomorrow is?'

'Yes, I know what tomorrow is, dear. It's the seventh of September, eighteen hundred and eighty and the anniversary of the day we first met. As if I could ever forget it!'

There was a pause now before he said, 'I can see you as if it were yesterday standing at the schoolhouse door. You were holding a lantern up high and it showed me your face as you said, "Can I come in? I want to learn to write . . ." '

There was another silence, and in it Maria saw herself walking into that schoolhouse room. It was a bare and comfortless room, but in the middle of it was a table on which were books and papers. She had looked at them as

18

if they were bread and water and she were starving with a thirst for both.

He had told her to take a seat; and when he asked her, 'Haven't you attended this school?' she had shaken her head and said with bitterness deep in her voice, 'No; nor have I been allowed to go to the Sunday School so that I could write me name.'

When he had asked her why, he had watched her jaws tighten as her teeth came together, before she said, 'Because I would be breakin' into a fourteen or fifteen-hour day's work for me father. I am from Dagshaw's farm down the valley.'

'Have you no brothers?' he had asked.

'Huh! None. I am the only one, an' I save a man's wages, perhaps two, for they will only work twelve hours. Some prefer the mines to workin' for him.'

'Couldn't you talk to him or stand up to him?'

'You can't talk to him; he's an ignorant man. But I have stood up to him with a shovel afore now; it can't go on, though. Me mother put it to me to come to you. She said, if I could write me name and read perhaps then I would get a good position in a house, not just in a scullery. She herself was from better people than my father but they died of the cholera and she never learned to read or write.'

He had said to her, 'You should have come to school.'

At that she had abruptly risen to her feet and said, 'If I could have come to school I wouldn't be here now, would I? And if he knew I was here now he'd come and lather me all the way back. Then God knows what I might do to him, because I hate him. I would likely end up in the House of Correction, for there's murder in me heart at times. Me mother feels the same an' all.'

'But it's dangerous for you to come this way in the dark at night, and not only that, your name . . . If it was found out you were visiting me so late . . . You understand?'

19

'Aye; yes, I understand. I'd be careful though. But you're afraid, aren't you? You're afraid, an' all; an' you're a respectable man.'

He had smiled at her and said, 'Not all that respectable,' which caused her to peer at him through the lantern light and say, 'Oh aye; you must be the school teacher with the drunken wife who caused an uproar in the village?'

It was some seconds before he answered, 'Yes. I am the school teacher with the drunken wife.'

'Oh, I'm sorry. I'm sorry. It was just the carter's prattle. I thought that man lived faraway in Gateshead Fell or thereabouts, because I had heard of you as a kindly young man.'

He had smiled wanly at her as he replied, 'News doesn't travel half as quickly in Africa as it does in this quarter of the land.'

'I won't trouble you any more,' she had said, 'cos you've got enough on your plate,' to which he had replied quickly and with a smile, 'Let's risk it. Twice a week, Tuesdays and Thursdays at about this time. But should there be anyone here I shall open the curtains and you'll see the lamp-wick up high.'

After going out of the door she turned to him and said, 'I'll never forget this night . . . '

Nathaniel turned his head now to gaze up into her warm, dark eyes and, as if reading her mind, he said, 'Did you ever forget that night? Because that's what you said to me: I'll never forget this night.'

'How could I, ever?'

'But it's a long time since we have spoken of it. We hardly spoke of it at all at first, you remember? because what followed was so painful.'

He dropped his head again onto her lap and looked towards the fire. The wood had mushed itself into a deep,

20

dull, scarlet glow and in it he envisaged all that followed the night she first came to his door.

Within a month she could write her own name and copy and read aloud complete sentences. And during that month Nathaniel's wife had visited him again from her mother's house in South Shields, with the intention of staying by his side, as she had put it. But he had warned her that if she stayed then he would pack up and go, as he had done two years previously, except that this time he would leave no address. And she would have no support from him. That was the ultimatum, and she left, cursing him.

But that visit had brought him before the Board of School Managers in the Town Hall at Fellburn. They informed him that his wife had again disturbed the peace in the market place; that it was disgraceful and should another such incident happen he would be relieved of his post, because such unedifying goings-on were not to be tolerated when connected with a man in his position: a schoolmaster should be looked up to, not only by the children, but by the elders in the community, as a paragon of virtue and knowledge, a man in some ways on a level of respectability with a Minister of God. Did he understand?

He understood. And with this he had written a letter to his wife, which he knew would be read to her by the same penny letter-writer who composed her demanding scribes to himself. He told her of the situation, emphasising the fact that if she once again showed her face in the town or the nearby village, he would lose his position and consequently she would lose her support, because as he had already warned her, he would leave and she would never find him again.

But that day, when he walked out of the Town Hall, he knew he would already have lost his position if it hadn't been for Miss Netherton. Apparently the question of his conduct and dismissal had been put to a vote and it was only Miss Netherton's vote that had saved him.

Miss Netherton was a power, not only in Fellburn but also in the surrounding countryside. It was generally known that her people had owned quite a large area of the town. And even now, although she lived in Brindle House, which was no size in comparison to Ribshaw Manor, which had once been her home, she still owned a number of properties in the village as well as in Fellburn. Moreover, she was connected with big names in Newcastle, and further afield still.

He had been tutoring Maria for three months when one night their hands accidently met, and they did not spring immediately apart, but only slowly did the fingers withdraw from each other, while their eyes clung in knowledgeable confrontation of what had been happening to each of them. Even so, no word was said.

Then December came, and something happened in that month that changed their lives. Tuesdays and Thursdays were the nights for instruction. But it was on a Friday night of this particular week that she visited him. He had been to a meeting with the Church Elders. He had wanted to put on a Christmas play in which all the children would take part. The Elders were willing to countenance this, but insisted that only hymns should be sung. It was almost ten o'clock when, frustrated and irritable, he entered the house and lit the lamp; but then there was a knock on the door, and when he opened it there she was standing shivering.

He had pulled her swiftly into the room, saying, 'You're like ice. What is the matter?'

'I ... I had to see you. My ... my mother wants your ad ... advice,' she had stammered.

He had pushed her down into a chair, pulled the curtains, taken the bellows and blown up the fire. Then he had rushed into the other room and brought back the cover from the bed, and when he had put it round her, his arms remained there and, looking into her face, he said, 'How . . . how long have you been waiting?'

'An . . . an hour. It doesn't matter.'

'But why have you come?'

She had pressed him gently from her for a moment to put her hand inside her coat, and she brought out a stiff, yellowish-looking bag about nine inches long and four wide and, her voice trembling now with excitement, she said, 'We were cuttin' down wood, mother an' me. There was a tree leaning over; the wind had got it. It wasn't all that big, perhaps ten years' growth, big enough to make logs, you know, so we pulled on it and brought it down, and . . . and as I was chopping off the branches, me mother went to hack off the root. You see, it had left quite a hole where the roots had been dragged out, and as she bent over it she saw this bag sticking up at the bottom of the hole. And she pulled on it. She had to pull on it because the end seemed to be stuck; it's very sticky clay soil. Anyway, she called me and said, "Look!" And I said, "What is it? Open it." And for a moment she seemed frightened. You see it was tied at the top with a cord, but it's broken, as you see, because when she touched it it fell away; and the bag was stiff, brittle. Feel it.'

He felt it. Then her face brightened as she said, 'Guess what we found in it?' He shook his head and said teasingly, 'A fortune?' only for his surprise to be shown by his open mouth when she replied quickly, 'It could be. I don't know. But look!' and she had withdrawn from the bag a cross; not an ordinary cross in gold or silver or brass, but one studded with stones.

After gazing at it he had pulled the lamp further towards them and bowed his head over it. And then he had said, 'My God!'

23

'That's exactly what me mother said: my God! She says it may be worth something.'

'Worth something? Oh, yes; yes.'

Her hand now tightly clasping the bag, which seemed to crackle under her touch, she had then said, 'If he knew . . . Father, that's the last we would see of it. So mother said to bring it to you and ask what we should do.'

He had sat back in his chair and after a moment said, 'Well, this could be classed as treasure trove, you know, belonging to the Crown. A priest or monk must have buried this years and years ago, likely during the Reformation.'

'The what?'

'The Reformation. The breaking up of the monasteries. We must talk about that sometime. But this, I don't know. Once you let it out of your hands I think that's the last you'll see of it; I mean, of the money it might bring to the authorities. This has been known before. Or the ritual will pass through so many hands that your prize-money would be worth nothing when you got it, and it might take years.' Then after a pause he added, 'But then, there must be someone in the city who buys stuff like this. Look; will you leave it with me? I'll try and get advice. I think the best person to ask is Miss Netherton.'

'Oh, aye, yes, Miss Netherton, from Brindle House? They say she's a nice lady.'

'Well, she has helped me. But at first I won't say who you are, just that you have something you would like to sell on the quiet, and could she advise you. Will that do?'

'Oh, aye. Aye, I know you'll do your best. Oh!' She had put out her hands and touched his cheeks; then the next minute her arms were about him and his free arm was holding her, while his other was extended straight out, gripping the precious find. And thus they stood for some time before, slowly, he laid the cross on the table and, pushing the rug

24

from her, he then held her body close to his, and so tightly that they could scarcely breathe. When eventually he pressed her from him they looked into each other's eyes before their lips came together, and long and tenderly they remained so.

When it was over she leant against him as he muttered, 'Oh, my dear, dear, dear one.' And what she said was, 'I've loved you from the minute I clapped eyes on you. I knew it was only you for me. Even if your wife had not been what she is, it would have made no odds. I would have loved you in silence all me life. But now I'm yours an' you are mine for all time.'

And so it was . . .

He brought his gaze from the fire and again looking up into her face he said, 'There are fiends in this world, but thank God there are friends too. And if ever there was a friend, Miss Netherton has been one to us all these years.'

'How old is she now?'

'Oh, I should think in her early sixties, but she's still so brisk, and she has some spirit in that small frame of hers. She must have just been in her early forties when I first saw her as one of the School Managers. But I'll never forget the night I went to her with the cross . . . '

Again he turned and looked towards the fire. The embers were almost dead now, showing but pale grey and dull rose, yet in them he could see himself standing in the drawing room of Brindle House. Ethel Mead had shown him in, and Miss Netherton, on entering the room, had greeted him warmly: 'It's a bitter cold night. What brings you out in it? But first, before you tell me why you're here, would you like a drink? I can offer you port, whisky, brandy, or, on the other hand, a cup of tea or coffee.'

He had said, 'I would be pleased to have a cup of coffee, Miss Netherton. Thank you.'

25

He had watched her pull on a corded, tasselled rope to the side of the fireplace, and when Ethel Mead entered, she had said to her, 'A tray of coffee, Ethel, please'; then had said to him, 'Come and sit by the fire. But first let me have your coat.'

He had taken off his overcoat and she had laid it on the arm of an upholstered easy chair, then, sitting opposite him, she had said, 'I hope you're not in trouble again.'

'No; not this time, I can say, thanks be to God.' They had both laughed and her quick rejoinder had been, 'You must instruct Parson Mason on how to say that, because he irritates me every time I hear him drawling it out. Besides me, his Maker, too, must be tired of it.'

Again they had laughed together; and then she had waited for him to speak, but his first words caused her some surprise. 'Would you mind if I didn't tell you my business until after the coffee has been brought in?' he had said.

However, after a short pause she gave a little chuckle and said, 'Not at all. Not at all.'

Until the coffee arrived they had talked about the school and the Christmas concert and she had remarked, 'All that fuss about hymns. We get enough of hymns on a Sunday, the adults twice and the children three times. We have a surfeit of hymns. But it was six to one this time, so I thought I'd better let them win, eh?'

Looking at her he had thought what a marvellous woman she was and had wondered why she hadn't married. Some man would surely have found life at least jolly married to a woman like her.

The coffee came and a cupful was drunk before he said, 'This is very private business I want to speak about because I think, in a way, it could be illegal.'

'My! My! My! Let's hear it then. It will be a change to

deal with something really illegal and not all the little piffling things that come my way.'

'A friend of mine is in dire poverty; in fact, both she and her mother are in dire poverty and lead a life of hard work and restraint. They were pulling at a fallen tree prior to sawing it up when, underneath the roots, the mother found something that I'm sure you will think is very precious.' He now put his hand into his inner pocket and drew out the stiff leather bag, and, handing it to her, said, 'See what's inside.'

A minute later she was staring down at the cross on her palm and, strangely, she too called on God: in her case, it was: 'Dear God in heaven! How beautiful. How very, very beautiful.' Then lifting her eyes to his, she said, 'Where did you say she found it?'

'In the woodland attached to a farm. They own the farm, at least the husband does. Unfortunately, the mother and daughter are treated like serfs.'

'Oh. Oh. I could put my finger on that farm. Is it Dagshaw's? Low Meadow Farm?'

After he had moved his head slightly in acknowledgement, she said, 'Oh, yes. Yes, he's an awful man, that one. I wonder how he came by such a distinguished name, because there are other Dagshaws, you know.'

'Yes. Yes, I know.'

'And so the mother found this? Well, it is a precious find.' But then, her head jerking, she asked, 'What do you want me to do?'

'I thought you might be able to advise them what should be done. If it is treasure trove it will go to the Crown, won't it?'

'Yes, I should think so; and then that's likely the last anybody will see of it.'

'I . . . I thought as much.'

'That is until it appears in some museum years hence, or

more likely goes to a private collection. But if they were to get money for it, what would they do with it?'

'Escape, I think. I know the daughter will, and I should think the mother, too. The mother is originally from Cornwall. By what I can gather, her father was a Spaniard and there are relatives still living there.'

'But what will the daughter do?'

It was a long moment before he answered, 'She will come to me. We have discovered that we love each other.'

The small body in the chair seemed to stretch and bristle slightly. 'But you are a married man, and your wife is . . . well, you know what your wife is. Will she allow this to go unheeded?'

'All she cares about, ma'am, is that she gets enough money for her drink. But even my stipend from the school hardly supplies that. Yet it keeps her at bay.'

'You mean you intend to work all your days to keep your wife at bay?'

'Yes; if need be. I had two years of literal hell living with her; I could stand no more. I had done everything in my power to help her. When we married, I did not know that she was addicted to drink. She and her mother were very clever in that way. I lodged with them for a time, you see.'

'Oh. Oh, that is often the way: lodgers should be warned against all landladies and their daughters. I've heard of this before. Anyway, do you know what will happen to you if you go ahead and take this girl into your house, because she is a young girl, isn't she?'

'Yes. But the thing is I won't have a house in which to place her; so, if she wishes to stay with me, we will likely have to take to the road until I find other kind of work.'

'Oh.' She got to her feet, really bristling now. 'Don't let me hear you talk such nonsense! You with your brain and

28

capacity for teaching. And let me tell you, you shouldn't be teaching in that little school such as you're doing, you should be in the university taking a higher course. I have listened to you. Oh yes, when you haven't noticed, and I have seen your method of teaching. You're worth something more than a village school; and supposedly being the power behind that school, I shouldn't be saying this, but your pupils . . . what are they? what intelligence? Will any of them get anywhere? They will be able to write their names and recite the alphabet, perhaps read a little and chant Jack and Jill. But then, you don't just Jack and Jill them, do you? you drop in bits of Shakespeare and Pope. I must tell you something funny in the midst of all this seriousness. When I said to the chairman of the Board that you were a clever young man and you spoke of Pope, he got straight on his feet and cried, "That's it! We'll have no popery here." And I couldn't stop my tongue from yelling at him, "Don't show your ignorance, Mr Swindle. Pope is a great writer; Alexander Pope not Pope Alexander." God help us! Some of those men on the Board should be put to the bottom of your class. But now, back to this gem.'

As her fingers stroked the stem of the cross she whispered, 'Rubies, sapphires, diamonds. Oh my! There's a great fortune here. But who is there who might pay its worth? Take this to a jeweller, one of the less distinguished in Newcastle, and what will he offer you for them? A hundred pounds, two hundred at the most, and then sell it for thousands, perhaps even tens of thousands. I don't think you could put a price on a thing like this. Anyway, if they give it up, it will definitely go to the Crown. Oh, and I couldn't bear that. I wish I was a very rich woman.'

When his eyebrows were raised she said, 'You're surprised that I'm not. In comparison with some, yes, but in comparison with others, no. One time when my family owned the manor and houses all around and had their fingers in all

29

kinds of pies, yes; but that was when I was very young. I had a father who delighted in travelling in grand style and gambled in every city in which he stopped, and left the affairs of his estates and works to others. Is it surprising that he should come home, together with my lady mother, and find that he had been rooked right, left, and centre? And that those he had left in power and had authority to sell to advantage, had sold to his disadvantage and feathered their own nests? But still, even when the manor had to go and all the works, this house, this ten-room small establishment, remained, together with Fox's farm and a number of houses in the village and a few of more value in the main thoroughfares of Fellburn and Newcastle. I live by my rents; so, of course, I am rich compared with many people. But' – her voice sank – 'I am not rich enough to buy this. How I wish I were. Look; could you leave this in my care until tomorrow? I can promise you I won't sell it on the quiet.' She laughed, an almost girlish laugh, then said, 'There's a plan forming in my mind, but I need to work it out and make sure it is the right one for those two women; and for you, because if you intend to take this girl to yourself you will need money, whether it is yours or theirs. Will you do that?'

'Yes, Miss Netherton.'

They had shaken hands like old friends.

Maria didn't come to the schoolhouse that night, and so he was to see Miss Netherton again before he could tell her his news. And what Miss Netherton suggested the following day was, she would, in a way, buy the cross from them over a period of time. If she were to take a large sum out of the bank her agent who saw to the estate would wonder why; but it would be quite in order, owing to her generous nature, to pass over Heap Hollow Cottage and an acre and half of land, the transaction to be duly signed as a deed of gift. Also, she would be able to afford the sum of two pounds a week out of her private income, which could be divided equally between mother and daughter. And an immediate payment of twenty pounds in cash to the mother would enable her to travel to her people in Cornwall. This arrangement was to last until the whole had totalled five hundred pounds, which would cover practically five years ahead. Of course, it would be a personal arrangement and they would have to trust her; although she would put the transaction in writing herself, as it would be unwise, because of possible enquiries as to why her generosity was stretching over this period, to do it legally.

Did he think Mrs Dagshaw and her daughter would agree?

Would they agree?

When, that night, he told Maria of the arrangement she burst into tears and her sobbing became almost hysterical. What he did not tell her was what Miss Netherton had said concerning their association: Did he realise, she had said, what the reaction of people in the village and round about would be towards them should they decide to take up their abode in the cottage? Would it not save a lot of trouble if he remained at his post as a teacher and the girl lived in the cottage and cultivated the land? They could still see each other. But the way he was suggesting would bring a great deal of trouble on their heads. And to this he had replied that, be that as it may, he was determined that they should come together, and for the rest of his life he would look upon her as his true wife.

It was Maria herself who said, 'What will they do to us should we go there and live together?' And he had answered, 'Well, we'll find out, won't we?'

And they were to find out . . .

He got to his feet now and, taking her hands, he pulled her up towards him, saying, 'Come to bed. You've got a lot of

31

cooking to do tomorrow for the big tea and I've got that patch to turn over to get the frost at it. And then I've the two Fowler boys from Fellburn in the morning. They're both as thick as deep fog, but nice all the same. But they'll have to work some, and so will I if they want to get into that fancy school. Yet, why worry? Their father will buy them in if their brains won't. But it's that pit lad, Bobby Crane, I'm interested in. I hope he can cut across without being noticed after coming up from his shift tomorrow.'

'It's risky for the boy, don't you think?'

'Yes, but he wants to carry on, and that's the main thing. He's got a lot in his napper, that boy, and he wants to get out of the pit; but God help him! He'll be out soon enough if they know he's learning to read and write. Still, who's to give him away except his own lot; and there are those among them that will do just that, because they're as bad as Praggett and the owners. They think that once a man can read and write he'll never go down a shaft again; and that's true in a way, for who but a maniac would go down there if he didn't have to eat and feed his family? Here!' He handed her a spill. 'See if you can get a spark from the ashes and light the candle, and I'll lock up and put the lamp out.'

Together they walked down the deep shadows of the room to the far end where the ladder went up to the trap door and where, to the side of it, was the door of the girls' room, and opposite the one that led into their bedroom.

Within ten minutes of entering the room they were lying in bed, side by side, their hands joined as usual; and now he said to her, 'Go to sleep. I can tell when you're thinking. There's been enough thinking for one night. Good-night, my love.' He turned slightly on his side and kissed her, and again he said, 'Go to sleep.' And she answered, 'Yes, I'm almost there.'

But she was far from sleep, for she knew that he had been thinking of the past, as she had been, and, her eyes wide now, she stared into the blackness and she was back to the day when she first saw this house. And she looked upon it now as a house and no longer a cottage, because it was twice the size it had been on that day.

She could see the grass where it grew up to the window sills of the long, low, one-storeyed building, and when they had pushed the door open the smell of staleness and damp had assailed them. But she could hear Nat's voice, as he looked up to the roof, saying, 'That's firm enough. There's not a slate missing. And look at the size of the room; it must be fifteen feet long. And this other one.' He had hurried from her and through a door, then had shouted, 'This is the same length, almost.' He had then climbed the ladder, and she had heard him stumbling along overhead, and he had called to her, 'It's quite clear and there's piles of space.'

Down the ladder again, he had taken her hand and run her through the rooms to one of two doors at the far end. The first one led into a scullery-cum-kitchen, about seven feet square. Then they were out through the other door into the yard. And there, as if stuck onto the end of the house, were two byres, and beyond them a stable; and across a grass-strewn, stone-cobble yard was a coalhouse and a privy. But what was much more noticeable was the large barn. It was an old erection, and although the roof was gaping in many places the timbers were sound.

She could hear him saying, 'It's wonderful, wonderful.' And she had thought so too, but she was speechless with the promise of joy to come. But what she did say to him when they returned to the house was, 'Wouldn't it be wonderful if this could be one big room. Could you break the wall down?'

'Why not, my love?' he had said. 'Why not? We'll take the wall down and we'll make a fine kitchen of that scullery. And as for that fireplace—' he had pointed. 'Out will come that

33

small grate and we'll have an open fire, a big open fire.'

'But where will I cook?' she had said.

'You'll have a fancy oven, my love,' he had answered. 'There's a showroom in a foundry in Gateshead Fell; I've seen it many times. We'll choose a stove with an oven and a hob and a flue leading upwards, connecting with this main chimney. Oh, we'll do wonders here, my love.' And they had kissed and he had waltzed her round the uneven floor.

When at last they were outside again he said, 'Miss Netherton tells me this used to be a splendid vegetable garden; and it'll be so again. And we'll have a cow.'

'I'd rather have goats,' was her immediate reaction.

'Then we'll have goats, dear.'

How wonderful that day had been; but how they'd had to pay for it; how terrifyingly they'd had to pay for it.

Three days later, her mother had left the farm, leaving a letter for her husband, a letter penned by Nathaniel; and the irony of it was that Mr Dagshaw had rushed to the schoolmaster's house in a rage and asked him to read it. And it was with pleasure that Nathaniel had read his own writing:

'I am leaving you and going back to my people. I have known nothing but cruelty from you all my married life. I've had our child; she too is leaving you. It is no use you coming after me and trying to force me back for my people will protect me. If you remember, they never liked you. It was by chance that we met, a sorry day for me, when I visited my late cousin in Gateshead Fell. But now it is over and you will have to pay for slaves in the future. I do not sign myself as your wife because I have been nothing but a servant to you. I sign myself Mary Clark, as I once was.'

Nathaniel had said that the man had looked thunderstruck for a moment, and then had said, 'D'you want payin' for

34

readin' that?' And Nathaniel had answered, 'I do not charge for reading letters, and that one has given me the greatest pleasure to convey.' Her father, she understood, had screwed up his face and peered at Nathaniel as if he were puzzled by the answer. And it was a full two weeks before the puzzle was solved for him, and then only when he went into the market, where some toady commiserated with him about his daughter disgracing herself and going to live with the schoolmaster in Heap Hollow Cottage. And didn't he know the village was up in arms and the schoolmaster had been dismissed and the vicar had practically put a curse on them both?

Perhaps it was fortunate that the day her father confronted her, in such a rage as to bring his spittle running down his chin and his hands clawing the air as he screamed at her, was the day the second-hand dealer from Fellburn had brought his flat cart full of oddments of furniture, including a bedstead, a chest of drawers, a wooden table, two chairs, and a large clippie mat, besides kitchen utensils, and when he saw the red-faced farmer raise his hand to the nice young lass who had sat up on the front of the cart with him and had chatted all the way from the town, he had thrust himself between them, saying, 'Look! mister. If you don't want to find yourself on your back, keep your hands down, and your voice an' all.' And her father had yelled at him, 'She's my daughter and she's turned into a whore,' to which the man retorted, 'Well, if that's the case you won't want anything to do with her, will you? So be off! for I'll be stayin' till her man gets back from Fellburn where, she tells me, he's on business.'

At this her father had yelled, 'He's not her man, he's a schoolmaster who's been thrown out of his job. He's a waster, a married man.'

'Well, if that's the case, to my mind he's a nice waster, from what I saw of him yesterday. So will I have to tell you just once more to get goin'!'

35

At this her father had thrust his head out towards her as he growled, 'I'll see you crawling in the gutter. D'you hear? And I'll have the village about your ears. They won't put up with the likes of you; they'll stone you out. And you're no longer akin to me, nor is the one that bore you. Not a penny of mine will ever come your way. And you'll rot, d'you hear? You'll rot inside. You filthy hussy, you!'

And at this she had cried back at him, 'Well, as a filthy hussy I've worked for you since I could toddle, never less than fourteen hours a day and not a penny piece for it. An' the clothes on my back, an' my mother's, were droppin' off afore we could get a new rag. An' then they weren't new, were they? if you could manage to pick up something from the market stall. Even the food was begrudged us; we only got what you couldn't sell. Well, now you've got your money in the locked box in the attic, I hope it's a comfort to you, because you'll never have any other.'

She felt sure he was going to have a fit. And when she saw him turn his cold, glaring eyes on the man, she knew what was in his mind: she had told a stranger about the locked box in the attic. He would go back now to the house and move it, perhaps bury it, like the cross had been buried. At the thought of the cross she laughed inside. If he'd had even an inkling of what they had found, he would have gone mad, really mad.

She had watched him walk away like someone drunk; but after he disappeared round the foot of the hill that bordered the hollow to the right of the cottage, her knees began to tremble so much that she felt she would fall to the ground. It was only the dealer's kindly tone that steadied her when he said, 'Well, if I had to choose atween him and the devil for me father, I know which side I'd jump to. Now don't take on, lass. Get yourself inside and if there's any way of making a hot drink, be it mead with the poker in it, or tea, or a small glass of beer or what have you, I'll be thankful for it, for like yourself I'm froze to the bone. And in the meanwhile, I'll get this stuff unloaded; then we can put it where you want it.'

She had blown up the small fire in the grate, then had put a pan of water on and made some tea.

An hour later, after the dealer had gone, she pushed the bolt in the door and sat crouched shivering near the fire, waiting for Nathaniel's return. And when he came she had flung herself into his arms and cried while she related her father's visit and his last words to her. And what Nathaniel said in reply was, 'Well, it's what we expected and we've got to weather it . . .'

The onslaught began a week later when the barn was set on fire. She could see herself even now springing up in bed to see the room glimmering in a rose glow and to hear the crackling sound of wood burning. They had rushed out and made straight for the well but had stopped when, with both hands on the bucket, Nathaniel had said, 'It would take a river to put that out. A bucket is no use.' But she had cried at him, 'The sparks! They're catching here and there in the grass: if they spread, they'll get to the cottage.'

The rate at which they were able to bring up water from the well would have been of little use had it not been that the grass was still wet from rain earlier in the day.

In the flickering light they saw shapes seeming to emerge from the shadows and a voice came through the night so high and loud that, for the moment, it shut out the crackling of the burning barn as it cried, 'It'll be your house next, the whore house.' And so, maddened, Nathaniel had been about to rush in the direction from which he thought the voice had come when voices from different areas began to hoot and yell.

The following day Miss Netherton, after looking sadly on the burnt-out frame, said, 'Well, I expected something like this. But it's got to be put a stop to in some way else your

37

lives could be threatened.' And Maria remembered thinking, They're already threatened.

The following week they had brought home the first goat. She was a sweet creature, already in milk, and they thankfully drank their fill from her; at least for the next three days, before she was found with her front legs broken.

She remembered holding the poor suffering animal in her arms and crying over it as if it were a child, her first child. Nathaniel had gone to Miss Netherton's to ask if Rob Stoddart, her coachman, or the lad, Peter Tollis, could come and shoot the animal and put it out of its misery, because he himself had never handled a gun. But from now on, he said, he would learn.

The matter of the goat had incensed Miss Netherton and she had her coachman drive her into the village and to the Vicarage. And there she had told the Vicar that if he didn't stop incensing his parishioners against her tenants, as she had called them, he would in future be doing without her patronage. But, apparently, he had said that whatever she did, he would carry out God's will. So, following this, she had walked boldly into the bar of The Swan, an action in itself which caused comment, because no woman ever went into the main bar of a public inn. But there she had addressed not only Reg Morgan, the innkeeper, but also Robert Lennon, the blacksmith and his eldest son, Jack, as well as Willie Melton and his son, Dirk, who were painters and decorators, and she reminded them that of the thirty-two cottages and houses scattered around, she owned seventeen.

Next she had gone to the King's Head and there again, in the main bar, she had addressed Morris Bergen and his wife, May, and John Fenton, the grocer, and two pitmen from the nearby pit, Sam Taylor and Davy Fuller, who were known as louts and would do anything for an extra pint of ale. And addressing the latter two, she had pointedly reminded them that the owner of the mine was a friend of hers.

For the next four weeks they were left in peace. However, Miss Netherton had warned them to keep clear of the village, even if this meant going a mile or so out of their way across the fields and over the quarry-top to reach Fellburn to do their shopping, which they did in the middle of the week, so evading market day.

Then the climax came. It happened when they were walking just inside the copse that adjoined the Hill, or the Heap, as it was called, and from which the cottage had derived its name, that Maria let out such a fear-filled yell as she cried at Nathaniel, *'Don't move!'* and its effect on Nathaniel was immediate: so abruptly did he halt his step that he almost fell on his face; then she pointed to a distance not two feet away from where he was standing and hissed, 'A trap! A man-trap!'

'No!' He had stood stock-still, gasping. 'Not that. They wouldn't.'

'They would. Oh, they would.'

'That settles it!' said Nathaniel. 'I'll have the law on them. Traps are forbidden now, even for animals. And whoever set that could be having their eyes on us this minute, waiting for the screams. Will you stay there near it?' he asked her, but immediately changed his mind. 'No; I will,' he said; 'you run to Miss Netherton's and tell her. Tell her to come and see for herself. Then I'll take this matter to the Justices. I'll have a constable here and someone who can release that trap without losing a limb.'

She had picked up her skirts and run and had burst unceremoniously into Miss Netherton's kitchen and, finding no one there, had dashed into the hall, there to be confronted by the sight of the lady herself accompanied by two gentlemen. They had been laughing together but stopped, and Miss Netherton, leaving them, came towards her quickly, saying,

'What is it? What is it, Maria?' And she had spluttered, 'They've set a man-trap. Nat nearly stepped into it, he's . . . he's guardin' it. Will . . . will you come and see?'

'A man-trap!' One of the gentlemen had stepped forward. 'Where is this?'

She didn't answer because Miss Netherton was already saying, 'There is a feud going on between two friends of mine and the village. You remember the schoolmaster we talked about? I rented him a cottage, but those in the village have burnt down the barn, they have crippled his goat, and now they are aiming to cripple him or this young girl here.'

'Well, we can put a stop to that, can't we?' The man had nodded towards her, and Miss Netherton had explained, 'Mr Raeburn is a Justice of the Peace and he will settle this once and for all.'

The outcome of this and of what had come to Miss Netherton's knowledge through her coachman and the carpenter in the village, Roland Watts, relating to the person who had set the trap, was a visit from the law to the innkeeper of The Swan, the consequences being that Reg Morgan had to appear before the Justices on the 17th of March to answer the charge of unlawfully setting a man-trap to the danger of human life and limb.

Moreover, every tenant of Miss Netherton's in the village received what was then a law letter. It was written on thick paper and came from a firm in Newcastle. It indicated to the occupants that were Miss Netherton's tenants in Heap Hollow Cottage troubled in the slightest form in the future, the recipients of the letter would be given immediate notice; and it went on to indicate that it was up to them to see that the outrageous incidents against Miss Netherton's tenants ceased immediately.

So they were left alone; and they spoke to no-one except

Miss Netherton and her small household or Roland Watts in the village, and the dressmaker, Miss Penelope Smythe, should the latter happen to meet them, which was rarely.

When the twins were born they did not go to the Parson to ask if he would christen the babies. But he had a field-day in the pulpit on the Sunday, for his sermon reached the greatest length yet, an hour and twenty minutes. And Miss Netherton had laughed when later she related to them: 'He hadn't any voice left at the end of it; just enough to upbraid certain members of the congregation for falling asleep.'

A kindly parson in Fellburn had christened the children, but the record went as follows: –

> September, 24th, 1862. Oswald and
> Olan, base-born sons of Maria Dagshaw,
> begotten by Nathaniel Martell.
> Baptised October, 20th, 1862.

This entry into the church register hurt her in some strange way, for she had imagined herself to be past hurt. But she was grateful to Parson Mason and his wife, Bertha, who had been kind to them both and who had laughingly said, 'Your children being christened here makes them subjects for parish relief. But let's hope they never need it.' And Nathaniel had answered, 'They never will.'

But from the birth of her sons began the spitting. It started with the women. She'd be walking through the town. It could be on a Wednesday or a Thursday, any day but Saturday, when the town was turned over to the market, but two out of every three times she entered that town she would hear the hiss and spring aside only too late, for her skirt would be running with filthy mucus and she'd see the back of a woman or women walking away from her.

41

At this period they never passed through the village.

Annabel had followed the boys. She had been born beautiful, more so even than she herself had been. But she was of a strange nature, strange in such a way that it seemed to stretch to opposite poles within her, one to a depth of quietness and serious thinking, the other to laughter, gaiety, mimicking and quick temper. What was sad, however, at least to herself, was that her daughter, so intelligent, clever in so many ways, was still a sort of maid to Miss Netherton. When she said, 'sort of maid', she included being a companion to the older woman, for did not Miss Netherton take her shopping when she went into Newcastle, and when visiting the museums; and twice had taken her to a theatre show? She knew she should be grateful that her daughter was paying back some of the debt they owed to that very kind lady; yet, she couldn't help but have her own plans for her daughter.

And then Cherry came, and she was as fair as her father, with merry blue eyes and a tripping tongue. They were foils for each other, her two daughters. Each caused gaiety and laughter in the house where there would have been none without them, for the twins were sober young men, and Jimmy, at fifteen, was a questing boy, wanting to know the ins and outs of everything, impish in a way. And then there had been one born into life, already dead.

Her last-born was Ben. Why had they called him Benjamin? The name didn't suit him, but it happened to be the name of Miss Netherton's father. Miss Netherton had allowed that to be used, then why hadn't she let one of the girls be called Mary? for that was her name. But she would have none of it. She said she didn't believe in passing on names, it made the recipient feel fettered in some way. Nor did she believe in the role of godparents. The role of godparents, she said, was to be guardian to the spiritual life of the child. But how many godparents dare enforce their authority? She could see no spirituality in choosing a godparent for a child, only the hope by the parents that it would be a beneficiary at some future date.

She was very forthright in her thinking, was Miss Netherton. But she had constantly been a guardian angel to them all, and still was.

The payment of money for the cross had ended a year after Jimmy was born. But they had managed, because by that time they were on their feet, so to speak. The barn had been rebuilt, the wall taken down between the two rooms, a bedroom built for the girls at one side of the house and their own at the other. The vegetable garden yielded all that they needed in that way for most of the year. The apple, pear, plum, and cherry trees that had been planted in the second year now gave abundant crops. The four goats supplied them with milk and cheese, the twenty hens with eggs and a fowl for the table every now and again; and the ducks that splashed in the artificial pond that the lads had dug at the bottom of the land, gave large, greenish eggs in abundance and young ducklings by the dozen each year . . .

She turned on her side and felt the waft of Nathaniel's quiet breathing, and she told herself once again how she loved this man; more than loved him, adored him. Yet, it would be a sin to think about that if she had been a church-going Christian. No-one should be adored but God. But what were church-going Christians? Women who spat at you; men who drove their carts through the middle of narrow lanes and pushed yours into the ditch. When that had happened for the countless time Nathaniel had made a stand: We'll go through the village in future,' he said, 'straight through the middle.' And this he did, and the sight of Dagshaw's Gillyvors, as she knew they were called, brought folks running to the cottage doors and the men coming out of the inns.

But as the years went on it would seem that the villagers

took no notice of them, especially when the whole family sat upon the flat cart, while Nathaniel sat erect on the high driving seat. She always saw to it that every one of them was dressed in their best when they went through the village. And Nathaniel always drove straight down the middle of the street. One day they met the coach from the Manor. When, some way off, the coachman waved them aside, Nathaniel returned the salute in the same manner and drove his cart steadily forward until, at the last minute, the coachman pulled his horses sharply aside and drove them onto the broad grass verge.

When a head was thrust out of the coach window and a voice yelled at him, 'What in hell's flames do you mean, man?' Nathaniel had cried back, 'The public highway is for all men, and it runs through this village.'

Again this incident was brought to Miss Netherton's notice, and what she said to Nathaniel was, 'You're tilting your spear at the castle gates now, I hear. Well, you'd better keep your visor down. Still, I wouldn't worry; their arms don't stretch all that far around here. The one that bawled at you would likely be what I term the carp among the salmon. But his father is all right, quite a pleasant man really, and the younger son too. But I wouldn't say the same for his wife. There's a vixen if ever there was one. Why do nice men allow themselves to become ensnared?'

What would they have done without Miss Netherton? But oh, she wished she would do something for Anna: get her a position of some kind worthy of her brain and intelligence. She had hinted at it more than once, yet here the girl was, seventeen years old, near eighteen, and neither one thing nor the other: not quite a servant and not quite a companion. But she must get to sleep; it would soon be four o'clock in the morning.

PART TWO

～

Anna

1

Maria had cooked all day; the table was laden with her efforts: there was a currant loaf and a rice loaf, and caraway seed cakes, yule do's made from pastry and decorated with pieces of ripe cherry; there was a large earthenware platter containing two chickens, already dismembered, a bowl of pig's-head brawn; and there were moulds of soft goat cheese and a platter of unsalted butter standing at both ends of the table, besides two crusty loaves. It was a fare that would have done credit to a banqueting hall, and Maria surveyed it with pride.

She was now thirty-six years old and the little mirror in the bedroom told her that she looked her years but that she was still a beautiful woman. She hadn't lost her figure through childbearing and her carriage was erect. But there was a deep age in her eyes. How could it be otherwise, for over the past nineteen years the life of ecstatic love had been mingled with fear and humiliation not only for herself but for her brood, for they each one carried the stigma of their birth and would do so until they died. But would she have had things otherwise? Yes, oh yes. If she had been the acknowledged wife of Nathaniel her eyes would not have admitted the pain, for then she would have been the wife of a schoolmaster. And her children would have been free to wander at will from the time they could toddle, whereas they had all been kept to the boundary of the wood, the hill and the garden, and they had no friends, except for Miss Netherton.

She turned from the table as two voices hailed her from the kitchen, one saying, 'We are home, Ma,' the other, 'What can I smell?' She went quickly down the room now, saying, 'What I can smell are muddy boots and sweaty stockings. Have you left them outside?'

She was met at the kitchen door by her two sons, both in their stockinged feet, and Oswald, laughing, said, 'Oh, Ma, let's get near the fire and put our slippers on. It was actually freezing coming over the fields. I'll bet there'll be an early frost the night.'

As both young men pulled crackets from the wall to sit down opposite the open hearth, she went to a box at the side of the fireplace and, taking out two pairs of moccasin-like slippers, she threw them onto the mat between them, saying, 'You're a bit early, aren't you?'

'Yes, Ma, we've been good boys and Mr Green let us off. And we've got some news for you, too, both of us.'

'Oh! Good news?'

'Yes. What other news would we bring?' Olan smiled up at her.

'Well, will it keep till the others get in?'

The twins looked at each other, smiled, then Oswald said, 'Yes, Ma, it'll keep. Where's Dada?'

'He's in the barn with the pit lad.'

'Oh, the pit lad.' Oswald stood up, then added, 'That poor beggar. We heard in the town there's trouble at the Beulah mine. They've been routing out some of the men from the cottages, putting them on the road because they've been agitating.'

48

'I thought they couldn't do that now,' said Maria.

'Oh, they can do that, Ma. The men have only got to mention union, I understand, and they're for it.'

'God help them if they've got to live out on the moor this winter. D'you remember three years ago? There were six families out there. Four of the children died, besides an old man and woman. The young ones, I understand, eventually made it to Australia. Still' – her tone lightened – 'come and look at the table.'

'I could smell it down the road, Ma.'

Oswald punched his slender brother, saying, 'You can smell food from Land's End to John O'Groat's. But look at that.' He gazed on the table; then turned to his mother, saying, 'My! you have been busy, Ma. And where've you hidden all this stuff for the past days? It wasn't in the pantry yesterday. If it had been it wouldn't have been here today, would it?'

They all laughed now, then turned as the far door opened and Nathaniel came up the room with his youngest son by his side; and while the young boy stood, open-mouthed, gazing at the table, Nathaniel turned his gaze from it and onto Maria, saying quietly, 'You have put some spreads on that table in the past years but I think that's the best yet.'

Maria pursed her lips at the compliment, while her eyes shone with the pleasure of it. Then she asked, 'How was your pupil?'

'Doing nicely. Fine. Oh, if I could have that lad every day he would go some place, far beyond me, in what I could teach him. He just gollops up knowledge. I've never known anyone like him.'

'I golloped up your knowledge, Dada.'

Nathaniel put back his head and laughed; then looking at Olan, he said, 'All you golloped up, my son, was food.

49

And what have you got to show for it? You're as lanky as a bean pole.'

'Aye, but I'm strong with it. You can't deny that.'

'No, you're right. I can't.' And Nathaniel slapped his son on the back; then turned to Maria again, saying, 'We're going to wait until they all come, aren't we, no matter what time?'

'Of course, of course,' she said, nodding emphatically. 'But let's hope Mrs Praggett doesn't keep Cherry late tonight.'

'She should stand out for her time. She's paid for eight till six,' said Oswald; then on a laugh, 'Even if Mr Praggett decided to throw his bairns into the river or down the mine shaft. Eeh! she was funny, wasn't she, that last time she described the row he was having with his wife when she tipped the dinner over him? It's a good thing she sees the funny side of it else she wouldn't stay there five minutes.'

They were laughing again when the door of the kitchen opened and Anna came into the room. And it was her walk that brought the rest of the family to concentrate their gaze on her without giving her any greeting, because her step was slow and the pose of her head suggested hauteur, but on reaching the end of the table her manner underwent a change as she gazed along its length, but then was resumed as she addressed her father, saying, 'Mr Martell, I have news for you, and for you, Maria Dagshaw.'

'Such news, daughter, that portends a rise in your station in life, an elevated rise, into the aristocracy, say?'

'It could be so, Mr Martell. It could be so.'

'Let up, you two.' Oswald flapped his hand towards them. 'Anyway, you're not the only one that's got good news. We have too, Olan and me here, but we're keeping ours for the tea.'

50

'Oh. Oh,' she exclaimed, and laughed; then her manner returning to normal, she looked towards Oswald, saying, 'You really have good news?'

'Yes. Aye, we have.'

'Oh, I'm glad. Well, I'll keep mine an' all for tea. And Dada, when the postman brought Miss Netherton's mail he said he had a letter for you. Here it is.' She put her hand into the pocket of her short coat and handed him an envelope.

After looking at it, Nathaniel glanced at Maria. Then, turning from them, he went to the small desk that stood in the corner of the room and, picking up a paper knife from it, he slit open the envelope and read the letter.

When Maria, who was watching him, saw one hand go down to the desk as if for support, she went hastily to him, saying quietly, 'What is it?' He did not answer her, but turned his head and looked into her eyes. Then gently pressing her aside, he walked across the room and through the door that led into their bedroom, and she followed.

'Nat. Nat.' She was sitting on the edge of the bed beside him now. 'What is it? What does it say? Who is it from?'

Slowly he handed her the letter and she read it, and it was a long moment before, in a pained murmur, she said, 'No, no. She wouldn't do that. Five years. Oh, Nat.'

He was holding her close as he murmured now, 'But it wouldn't have altered their situation; they would still have been classed as . . . as gillyvors.'

She didn't pursue his statement for her mind was crying, No, but it could have altered my situation, and in other ways, too, it could have been a relief.

She lifted her head from his shoulder, saying, 'Shall we tell them?'

After a moment's thought he said, 'No. Not till after they have given us their news. They're full of it, whatever it is, and it seems good. But after the meal I will tell them.'

51

*

The meal was over, they were all replete and they had said so in their different ways and congratulated their mother on the wonderful feast.

'Now who goes first? I think ladies should have the choice, don't you, Oswald?'

As Oswald nodded down the table towards his father, Anna said, 'Mine can wait. Let Oswald and Olan tell their news.'

'As you will. As you will.'

'Well, go ahead, Oswald.'

All eyes were on the bright-faced, bulky form of the eldest of the family. And he, looking directly at his father, said, 'Mr Green has asked me if I would like to manage his other shop in Gateshead Fell.'

'Oh! Wonderful!'

'Managing a shop!'

'All by yourself?'

'Will you get more money? Double pay?'

'Be quiet. Be quiet.' Nathaniel waved them down. 'And listen. Go on, Oswald.'

Oswald took a deep breath before he said, 'Of course, it isn't as big as the Fellburn one and it's in rather a poor quarter near the river, but it's got prospects. I am to do part of the baking to begin with, nothing fancy, you know, like our present shop, just plain bread, rye, brown, and white, and teacakes, griddle cakes and yeasty cakes. Of course, the drawback is, I have further to go, yet I start at the same time in the morning. But on three times a week he is letting Olan, here, pick me up when he's on his round.'

'How much money are you getting? Twice as much?'

'No. No, Mr Moneybags.' Oswald laughed at Jimmy. 'But I'm going up to seven shillings a week and what stale bread I'd like to take away with me at night.'

52

'Stale bread!' Cherry's voice was indignant. 'There won't be much stale bread left around that quarter if it's a poor one. Anyway, tell him we don't want his stale bread.'

'You'll tell him no such thing.' Maria silenced Cherry with a cautionary hand, then went on, 'If I can't make use of stale bread for puddings then there's plenty will be glad of it, especially if we have company on the moor again, as you said earlier, Oswald.'

Oswald now nudging his brother said, 'Tell them your piece.'

'Well—' Olan ran his fingers through his hair, then smoothed each side of his cheeks as if he were straightening side whiskers, before sticking his thumbs in his braces and declaiming, 'I've been put on commission.'

'Commission? What d'you mean?' This question came from various quarters of the table; then Olan explained. 'I am to take the cart filled with trays of fancies and, as Mr Green says, break new ground. I approach private houses and inns and such like and ask them if they would be interested in placing an order with the firm of George Green, High Quality Confectioner, Established 1850. And for every order over a pound I get one penny commission.'

'A *penny*? What's a penny to brag about?' Jimmy was butting in again. 'It's something to brag about when twelve of them make a shilling, big-head,' replied Olan.

'Yes, Olan's right.' His father was nodding down towards Jimmy now. 'A shilling is something to brag about.'

'It might be, Dada, but how long is it going to take him to earn it?' said Jimmy, practically.

'Well, that remains to be seen,' replied his father. Then looking at the slightly dampened Olan he added, 'Doesn't it?'

'If the weather keeps fine I could make it in a week. Anyway, Mr Green is supplying me with an oilskin cape and cap and also covers for the trays. So he's thought about the weather.'

Jimmy was laughing now as he put in, 'But what about the poor horse?' And when Anna's hand came out and slapped him across the ear he laughed louder, and at this they all joined in.

'Well now, that's us settled.' Oswald was looking towards his sister. 'Out with it.'

All eyes were on Anna now, and she, looking up the table to her mother and father, her voice low and her mien deprived of all aping hauteur, she said, 'Dada. Ma. I'm to be a pupil teacher.'

The news brought no response for a moment; then it seemed to animate each one of them, for they all rose at once and crowded round her chair and the questions flew at her from all sides, until Maria shouted, 'Stop it! all of you, and listen.'

When the hub-bub had died down it was Nathaniel who, holding out his hand, caught his daughter's and drew her up from the chair, saying, 'Let's all go down to the fire. Good news should always be spread around the fire.'

A moment later they were all sitting or crouched round the mat, their eyes on their beautiful sister, and in what sounded like a tearful voice, she began, 'Miss Netherton took me in this afternoon. Apparently it's been under discussion for some time. I am to take up my position at Miss Benfield's Academy For Young Ladies next week.'

'The Academy For Young Ladies. Oh! Anna.' Cherry's arms were about her and the sisters were hugging.

'She never let on to you?'

Anna looked at Maria, saying, 'No, Ma; not a word. The only thing is, she has been pushing all kinds of books towards me over the past weeks, not only English and history, but ... well, things that went over my head.' She turned now and looked at her father, saying, 'Not that they would have gone over your head, Dada, philosophy and such. But, as she said, I won't need anything I've read of late in the Academy, nor for some time and with the little ones, but . . . but it may help me later on to put over my English and history to the muddle-minded minxes that grace Miss Benfield's decaying mansion.'

'Is it a mansion?'

'No, no.' She shook her head at Maria. 'It's a terraced house on two floors and has a basement with an iron grid over it.' She glanced towards her father now, saying, 'It looked as if the wash-house was below, for steam was pouring up through the grid and there was a smell of soap-suds. But up above, oh, all was different.' She wrinkled her nose now. 'Miss Benfield was dressed in black satin. She's big–' She made a sweeping motion with both hands over her chest, then she glanced at Cherry and said, 'I wanted to giggle when I first saw her. Remember that poem, The Bosom Of The World: Where all nature is unfurled . . . ?'

'Now, now, be serious.' Her father was nodding at her. 'Tell me what she said.'

'Well, it wasn't what she said, it's what she expected me to say. She just asked questions, and mostly about you.'

'Me?' He dug his thumb into his chest.

'Yes. Were your parents alive; what had they been. I said your Father had been an engineer but both of them had died of cholera.'

'What was the house like, the classrooms?'

'Oh, Dada, grim. The one room I saw upstairs was partitioned off and there were eight desks in one part. What I suppose was the drawing room is the main classroom. The dining room, too, had been partitioned off; part of it is called the music room.'

'How many teachers are there?'

'I think there are just two; Miss Benfield and another one.'

'It doesn't sound like a very high-class establishment to me.'

Anna now looked at Olan, saying, 'Nor did it to me and I'm sure it didn't to Miss Netherton. But, as she said, I have to begin somewhere. And once I get a year or so's experience I'll be able to pick and choose. I'm . . . I'm sure, Dada, it's the best she could do for me at the moment.'

Her expression was serious and so was Nathaniel's, for they both knew why it was the best Miss Netherton could do for her at the moment: a bastard and one of a family of bastards would not be classed as a fit person to instruct young ladies.

'Well now, what more news have we? Anyone else got a surprise?' Anna looked around the family.

Nathaniel still didn't say, 'I have news, surprising news.' It was Jimmy who next gave his news: 'Well, nothing happens on a farm that you could call news, except today Daisy kicked a bucket of milk over. And Farmer Billings raged about the byre, cursing. He used some words I'd never heard before and Mrs Billings chastised him, you know, how she does in that churchy voice. 'Enough! Enough! Mr Billings,' she shouted. 'Be grateful you have milk to spill; you won't find any in hell.' And you know what he shouted back at her?' He chuckled so much now that he almost choked. ' "Go and boil your head, woman! Go and boil your head!" '

Nathaniel allowed the laughter to die down before, looking down on Jimmy, he said, 'He didn't say any such thing, not Farmer Billings.'

'He did, Dada. Honest to God.'

This aroused more laughter, because Jimmy had spoken almost as Farmer Billings would have.

But Maria quickly intervened. Looking at Cherry, she said, 'Have there been any high jinks in your establishment?'

And Cherry, her face still wide with laughter, said, 'You wouldn't believe it; but it's been "My dear Florence" and "My dear Mr Praggett". They've been cooing like two doves the last few days. And I wanted to say to her, "Look, woman; don't let yourself be hoodwinked. He's no dove. You should know that by now." He's a dreadful man really. He gets so mad at times that he actually jumps. He does, he does. Like the day I told you about when I'd just hung a line full of washing out and he came rushing out the back way and straight into it and got tangled up in his wet linings and brought the whole line down – remember?'

They remembered; and just as on that first occasion, so the room was filled with laughter.

The laughter trailed away as one after another they turned their attention to the young boy who was saying quietly now, 'I'm going to be a doctor when I grow up.'

The statement, made with such emphasis, brought no response from anyone for a moment. Then his father asked gently, 'Why this sudden decision to be a doctor, Ben?' and the boy's answer was firm as he said 'Because I want to mend things, like . . . like sores on legs, Dada.'

'Sores on legs . . . ? Who has sores on legs?'

'The children that came into the wood this morning.'

'And they had sores on their legs? What were they doing in the wood?'

'Gathering blackberries, Dada. They were very small, not as big as me. They had no shoes on and their feet were dirty and they had sores on their legs.'

Nathaniel rose from his chair and picked up his son from the floor and held him up in his arms. And looking into his face, he said, 'And you will be a doctor some day, son, and heal sores on legs. God willing.'

'What if he's not, Dada?'

'What if who's not?'

'God. God willing. You said the other day you were willing to help the pit lad or anyone to read or write, but what if God isn't willing?'

A shiver ran through Nathaniel's body and he repeated to himself, Yes, what if God isn't willing? This last child of his, this small, strange and continually happy child filled him with foreboding, even fear at times.

He did not resist Anna's taking the boy from his arms and standing him on the floor again. He hadn't been aware that she had risen to her feet, but he could count on her always being there at moments such as these: when life became so frightening he seemed to become paralysed by it.

Maria was standing close to him now, saying, 'Tell them our news. It's time.'

'Oh, yes, yes, our news. We have some special news for you. But first of all I must say something to your mother that I have longed to do for the last nineteen years.' And now he took Maria by the shoulders and pressed her down into his chair. Then dropping on to one knee, he looked into her face and said, 'Maria Dagshaw; I love you. Will you marry me?'

'Oh! Nat. Nat.' Maria pulled her hands away from his and covered her face with them; and now they were surrounded by their children, all saying in different ways, 'Oh! Ma, Ma. Oh! Dada, Dada.'

'Dry your eyes, my love.' Nathaniel picked up the corner of her white apron and gently drew it over her wet cheeks. Then, sitting at her feet now, he addressed his family, saying, 'I have never kept anything back from you. You have all been brought up to face the situation that we brought upon you by our love for each other. Yet, in spite of the so-called shame, I doubt if there is a happier family in the whole of the country. So now I will tell you the news I received, that Anna brought

58

to me tonight, the news that should have been delivered five years ago. It has happened like this. My wife, as you know, was addicted to drink. In order to keep her from plaguing me, I had to find her five shillings a week for her lifetime. I used to send her a ten-shilling note once a fortnight, care of the letter-writer, the penny letter-writer, you know. Well, his letter tells me it was only by accident that he found out my wife had died five years ago. After her old mother had missed two visits to collect the money, he thought he'd better take it to the address he had been given. It was a kind of lodging house, and the landlady greeted him as if he was a relative of the poor, lonely old woman. It must have been through questioning her that he learnt my wife was already dead. The man, the letter-writer, didn't want to be implicated in anything unlawful, so he thought he had better do some explaining.'

He paused before saying, 'So five years ago I could have said the words I said a moment ago to your mother: Maria Dagshaw, will you marry me? But still' – he moved his head slowly – 'we would have been no happier than we are now, and, unfortunately, our marriage cannot erase the stain we have put upon you all.'

'Oh! Dada. Dada.' The girls were kneeling by his side, their arms about his neck, while Maria held her hands out towards her sons, and they crowded round her; and it was Olan who said, 'Whatever happens in life, Ma and Dada, I'll always thank God that I was born of you, and Oswald, being part of me, says the same, don't you, Oswald?'

'Oh, yes, yes, Ma . . . Dada.'

'And Jimmy is proud of you, too, aren't you, boy?'

And Jimmy, his voice thick, muttered, 'I don't know, being connected with you two is nothing to shout across the water. Anyway I can disown you once I can buy my farm.'

The result of this was a rough and tumble on the mat with the twins, and Anna shouting, 'Stop it! you hooligans. Look! you'll have him in the fire.'

When order was restored again, Oswald asked quietly, 'Where will you be married, Ma?'

Maria glanced at Nathaniel and said, 'We haven't got that far yet. Certainly it won't be by the Reverend Fawcett in the village. Parson Mason will do it, and gladly, I'm sure. He christened all of you.'

'Yes; your mother's right.' Nathaniel now rose and, pulling Maria to her feet, said, 'What your mother and I are going to do now is put on our coats and take a walk as far as the wood, because there's a moon out tonight and after proposing marriage one should always walk in the moonlight with the beloved.' He hugged Maria to him for a moment; then addressing his family again, he added, 'And you lot will clear the table, wash up the crocks, tidy the room, then away to bed, and by the time we come back we want to find this room absolutely clear.'

'Slavery, that's what it is, nothing but slavery.'

As Jimmy was getting his ears cuffed again, this time by Cherry, Nathaniel and Maria went out into the moonlight.

The family set about their separate duties: Oswald lifted up the large black kettle that was half crouched in the embers of the fire and took it into the scullery and poured the water into the tin bowl that Anna had already half filled with cold water.

Not until this was completed did she say to him, 'Well, what do you think about their news?'

'It's not going to make much difference to us, is it?'

She looked up sharply at Oswald, and the flickering candle-light seemed for a moment to turn him into a man, and she asked softly, 'Have . . . have you minded?'

'I wouldn't have been human if I hadn't.'

'And Olan?'

'The same; yet not quite. Well, you heard what he said. What about you?'

'Oh.' She paused for a moment and looked at her hand sluicing a piece of blue mottle soap round and round in the water; then she said quietly, 'Just now and again when I heard the word.'

'The word. Aye, it twists your guts up, doesn't it? If it were only the one word used, bastards, you'd get used to it, but somebody comes up with a new one, gillyvors, base-borns: base-born child of Maria Dagshaw and Nathaniel Martell, it says on our registration papers.'

She brought her hand out of the water, shook it, then dried it on a rough piece of towelling hanging from a nail on the cupboard door to the side of her and, turning to him again and using the pet name that her father didn't like, she said, 'I'm sorry, Ossie, but they couldn't have done anything else the way they felt. And they're wonderful people. You *do* understand?'

'Oh, yes.' He put out his hand and patted her cheek, saying, 'Don't you worry your head about what I say, Anna. Of course they are wonderful people. It's all the other buggers that are not.'

'Eeh! Ossie' – she pushed him as she chuckled – 'don't let them hear you swear. By the way, do you know the real meaning of gillyvors?'

'Yes, we are the real meaning, what else is there?'

'Well, if you break it up, a gilly is a woman of easy virtue, vor is her offspring, so there you get gillyvors or gillyflower.'

'Is that so? Well, Ma's no woman of easy virtue. Anyway, we've got this far, so I suppose we'll weather the rest, God willing. Oh–' Oswald laughed quietly – 'God willing. What do you think about Ben and his question? It shook Dada, I could see.'

61

Her voice serious now, she said, 'Ben's questioning would shake anyone; at times he seems too good to be true . . . Sh! Look out! Here they come.'

With the others now crowding into the kitchen with dirty plates and crocks, all serious issues were swamped in joke and chatter and chastising – the happy façade had been resumed.

2

‘I can't believe you'll not be popping in the door tomorrow morning. I'm going to miss you, my dear.'

‘And I'll miss you, too, Miss Netherton. Oh, yes. Yet' – Anna smiled – ‘I'm not going to the ends of the earth, not even into Newcastle, just into Fellburn, and to . . . *Miss Benfield's Academy For Young Ladies*.' They laughed together now, and Miss Netherton, putting her hands on Anna's shoulders, pressed her away, then surveyed her up and down, saying, ‘You look very smart. Your mother is a very handy woman with her needle. In fact, she is a very handy woman altogether. Do you know, I've always envied her. Yes, even in her plight and her struggles. What would I not have given to have a family, to have a daughter just like you. But there it is, man proposes and God disposes. But come; we must get away if you are to arrive at your post on time.' Her hand went out again now to Anna's head and she said, ‘How nice it is to see you in a hat. Why must the young and the old be expected to wear bonnets? I could never stand them.'

She turned now to Ethel Mead, who was standing apart, and called to her, ‘Doesn't she look beautiful, Ethel?'

Ethel adjusted her winged, starched cap, then the shoulder straps of her bibbed white apron before she said, 'Well, I've always been learned that 'andsome is as 'andsome does. So, I suppose you can say the same for beauty.'

'Oh, don't hurt yourself in your praise, Ethel.' Miss Netherton laughed, then added, 'Is that all you've got to say to Anna?'

The elderly woman now turned and looked at the slim young girl, and, her face softening, she said, 'I hope it's a good start in life for you, an' I wish you well.'

'Thank you, Ethel, thank you so much.' Yet even as she spoke she knew that whereas Miss Netherton was sorry to lose her, Ethel would be glad to see the back of her, for she was devoted to her mistress and was naturally jealous of anyone she imagined was taking her place in Miss Netherton's affections.

But in the yard, Robert Stoddart showed sincere heartiness and goodwill as he assisted her into the brake, saying, 'Up! with you then, miss, and let's get you to that school an' knock sense into those bairns. What d'you say, ma'am?'

'I say the same as you, Rob: let's get her there; but we'll never arrive on time if you stand chattering and arranging rugs. We can see to ourselves. Get up, man!'

Anna exchanged a smile with the neatly dressed, small lady now sitting opposite her, and yet again she thought, how wonderful this little woman is. How she could talk, even chatter to her servants, whom others would class as menials and beneath their notice, and yet still hold their deep respect.

There were those, however, beyond the household, who regarded her with fear, for wasn't she a property owner?

As they reached the village she told herself to sit straight and hold her head high, for they could do nothing to her when she was with Miss Netherton. Only once before had she ventured to pass through the village on her own, and she had ended up in the wood crying her eyes out, while beating her fists against the tree trunk, imagining she was pummelling the face of the blacksmith's younger son, who had made a gesture to her that she would never forget, and which she knew she dare not speak of to her ma or dada. As peace loving as her father was, she knew he would have gone into the village and taken a whip with him, for his fists would have been no match for Arthur Lennon.

Miss Netherton now leant towards her and in a raised voice to cover the noise of the wheels on the rutted road and the trotting of the horse, she said, 'There's one thing I'm not sure of, and that is how Miss Benfield will view that lovely dress.'

'Why?' Anna now drew the sides of her cape apart and looked down on the grey woollen dress while adding, 'It's plain.'

'Yes, my dear, it's plain for many occasions; but the waist is not straight. You see, it comes to a point, as does the neckline. I never thought about asking her if she had any rules on uniform. Still' – she flung her arms up – 'what does it matter? The children will like it, and they'll like you. You'll be a figure of interest. Oh, yes, compared with the other two I saw.' She chuckled now. 'I didn't ask her if she had a decent cook, but anyway, I'm sure you'll get enough to sustain you at dinner time. It is in your agreement that you get one meal. I understand that the children leave at four, but that the teachers have to tidy up the schoolrooms and check the work that has been done during the day. You will soon get into the routine. But there's going to be a snag with the winter coming on. It will be dark and although the two miles or so will be nothing to walk in the summer, it will be quite different later on. And the nights are cutting in quickly now. Have you thought . . . ?'

'There's a carrier cart leaves the market at ten past five. I shall get that.'

'Oh, well, that won't be so bad; but you'll still have the fields to cross.'

'Father or the boys will meet me; at least, someone will.'

'Ah!' And Miss Netherton sat back against the padded rail of the brake. 'We are about to enter the underworld. Sit up straight. But then, you are sitting up straight; you always sit up straight. But don't look at me, look from side to side. Keep talking, chatter about anything; look amiable, as if you were used to this early journey every day because, you know, they'll be at their doors and gates before we reach the end of the village. John Fenton will stop cutting his bacon and he'll call to his wife and his mother to come and see, and she'll say, "Where're they off to at this time in the mornin'?" '

Miss Netherton went on chatting and looking around, as she had bidden Anna to do, and she, taking up her mood, said in a light tone, 'Mr Cole is unloading a carcass from his hand-cart. There's a young man with him; I suppose it's his son.'

'That'll be Stan. Yes, that'll be Stan, the apple of his mother's eye . . . or the orange in the pig's mouth.'

Anna only just managed to stop throwing her head back and letting out a peal of laughter. Then she muttered, 'Mrs Fawcett, the parson's wife, has just emerged from The Vicarage Lane.'

'Oh, I must bow to her. How far is she down?'

'She'll be in your view within the next' – she paused – 'ten seconds, I should say.'

The parson's wife had stopped on the grass verge that surrounded the village pump, and Miss Netherton, looking as it were across Anna's shoulder, inclined her head to the woman and smiled, whilst saying under her breath, 'Just turn your head slightly. Don't smile, just glance at her, then look at me again and go on talking.'

It was like a scene in one of the little plays that she wrote for Christmas, so that they could all join in.

Miss Netherton was saying, 'By the look on her face I think she's going to have a seizure, and they will have to send for Doctor Snell. You know, I think my driving through the village is the only entertainment they ever have.'

At the end of the straggling street the road began to narrow to become no wider than a lane, and it was here that they met up with an approaching gig and Miss Netherton, standing up and looking over Rob Stoddart's shoulder, said, 'Pull into the side a moment, Rob, and pull up.'

The open carriage had been approaching at a pace, but now the horses dropped into a trot and were brought to a stop by the side of the brake. Two men were sitting in the front, and the one holding the reins touched his cap and, bending forward, said, 'Good day, Miss Netherton. You're out early.'

'Apparently I'm not the only one, Simon ... or you, Raymond.' She turned her head slightly to address the other man and he said, 'I could give you two hours or more, Miss Netherton; I've had a gallop already.'

'Oh, my goodness! You have almost done a day's work.' There was sarcasm in the tone. Then looking at the man she had addressed as Simon, she said, 'Oh, Simon, may I introduce my companion, Miss Dagshaw. Miss Dagshaw, Mr Brodrick.'

The man's eyes had widened just the slightest, and there may have been a slight hesitation before his hand went to his cap again, as he said, 'Pleased to make your acquaintance, Miss Dagshaw.'

Anna gave no reply, but inclined her head in acknowledgement. Then her gaze was lifted to the other man. He was looking at her through narrowed lids, but he did not acknowledge the introduction.

And Miss Netherton, quick to notice this, put in hastily, 'Well, we must be away or we'll be late for an appointment. Good-bye, Simon. Good-bye, Raymond.' The two men again touched their caps in salute, and Rob Stoddart said, 'Gee up! there.' And they went bowling down the lane.

It was some minutes before Miss Netherton spoke; and when she did it was to ask the question: 'Do you know who those gentlemen were?'

'Yes.'

'Oh, you've met them before?'

'No. But I've seen them in the distance when the hunt was on, or in the early morning, when one or other of them rode past the bottom of the land when making for the moor. I . . . I didn't know who they were until Dada pointed them out to me.'

'Well, if you ever write that story you are always talking about, you could do worse than set it in my previous home; you could even use our family, for you would find good material there. It wouldn't be so exciting as this present family, though, because there was no malice in it.'

'There is malice among them?'

'Oh, yes. Yes. There are very few saints in the world, Anna; we're all a mixture of good and bad. Well, those two brothers have got their share, with more good than bad in Simon, but more bad than good in Raymond; at least, that's how I see them. And from my experience, it's the good one that always gets hold of the rotten end of the stick. Simon is the younger by a year, so Raymond is in charge of the estate, the farms, and some of their business deals, such as the Beulah mine. They don't own it, but have a good share of it, and by all accounts he is a hard enough task-master. The brothers are like chalk and cheese, as brothers often are. Poor old Simon has tied himself well and truly to that house, with his mother, wife and child.'

At this point she took a long-handled umbrella and poked Rob in the back with it, saying, 'Do you purposely look out for holes in the road, man? I won't have a tooth left in my head shortly.'

Rob answered with a grunt and went on talking to his horse as he guided her over the rough pot-holed track.

Anna said, 'The mother is an invalid, I understand?'

'Yes. She broke her back while holidaying in Switzerland some years ago and has been on a spinal carriage ever since. Well, that's when she's not in bed; but she can be wheeled about on this carriage, you see. And Simon has that job most of the time; she never lets him out of her sight. But I must admit he's very fond of her.'

'The father? Isn't he there?'

'No. Arnold Brodrick travels. My own papa and he could have been brothers in their desire for travel, although in Arnold Brodrick's case it's to get away from responsibility, a sick wife and a vixen of a daughter-in-law. Now, you could get your teeth into that family for a story, as I said. Oh, yes, yes. By the way, have you written anything lately besides those little rhymes of yours?'

'I . . . I started, but the only thing I could write about with any strength of feeling was our family because, I've got to face it, I've had no experience of the world. Nor have any of us, have we?'

'Well, I won't say that. I think you've all had experience of reactions of some members of the world, and forcibly. And you know, Anna' – she now leant forward and gripped Anna's knee – 'it isn't ended. In your own particular case, and perhaps that of Cherry, it's just beginning. Men can fight the stigma in their own way. Although they feel it deeply, the male in them won't let them admit it. I've known some even to brag about it; at least, if their lineage just might have been connected with those in high places. Your mother and father, you know, and of course you do know, have defied convention, they have spat in its eye; but they picked the wrong place to do it, near the narrow confines of a village. If they had chosen to live in the city or some large town it could have passed unnoticed, or nearly so. But if one desires to be burnt alive, then I would say go and live in a village and do something that half of them would like to do but haven't the courage. Oh, it's amazing how frustrated desire can appear under the heading of righteousness. But it's been so all down the ages. I think I've said it to you before, I'm sure I have' – she tossed her head and laughed now – 'I've said so much to you. You're the only one, you know, I can talk to without keeping my tongue in my cheek. But what I am going to say now is, you must read the Greeks, more philosophy, Plato, Aristotle. Your father, naturally, hasn't touched on these except for his own entertainment. He's immersed in the later Roman period, isn't he? But you would garner wisdom from Aristotle. Well, just give it another name, common sense. Of course, you will find that philosophers, being human beings, will contradict themselves here and there, and each other. But you can blow away the chaff from the wheat and use it to your own advantage.

'A-ha!' she now exclaimed. 'Here we go into the street of learning. You know, my dear' – again she was bending forward – 'I wish I could have started you off in some better place, but I know you understand the reasons. And as I've also said, do a year or so here, by which time you will have had experience, then maybe I'll be able to talk sense and charity into one or two scholastic friends. At least, I hope so. Females, you know, are much more difficult to deal with than men. I prefer men any day in the week. In fact, I don't like women. Did you know that? I just don't like women. Of course, in your case you will have to look out for both men and women, for from the looks of you, you will have trouble with the former in one way and with the latter in more ways than one.'

Wasn't it odd, Anna thought, that this kindly, lovable benefactress should have that one flaw: she would never let her forget that she had an obstacle to surmount, that there would always be this obstacle, but it was not surmountable. However, she put out her hand and gripped the older woman's, saying, 'Whatever happens to me from now on, there won't be a moment of my life in which I will stop thanking you for what you have done for me, and not only for me, but for my family. Now, don't get up. I'll have to be on my own from today but I shall slip across tonight and tell you all my news and how I have implanted wisdom and knowledge into five- and six-year-olds, or perhaps the nines or tens . . . never the fourteens. I think I'll be a long time before I reach the fourteen-year-olds in Miss Benfield's Academy.'

'Go on with you! And my wishes go with you. You know that.' She pushed her towards the back of the brake, where Rob had pulled down the step, and as he helped her to the ground he said, 'Best of luck, miss. Best of luck.' Then leaning towards her, he whispered, 'Knock it into 'em. And I bet you'll have to do just that with some.'

'Shut up! you, and get back about your business.'

Anna gave one last look at her friend before walking towards the green-painted door and pulling on the iron-handled bell.

The brake had disappeared half-way down the street before the door was opened and a small dishevelled maid of no more than twelve years old pulled the door open, let her enter, closed it, then, adjusting a none-too-clean print cap, said, 'When you come, I 'ad to show you to the dinin' room. It's down 'ere.' She crossed the narrow hall and opened a door from which stone steps led down to the basement.

71

Anna followed her, but at the bottom step she paused for a moment and gazed in amazement at what she saw was the kitchen. But all she could take in was the rough stone floor, a black stove, a wooden table, and to the side of it a stone sink, and, at the far end was the grating through which she had seen the steam emerge. It was that grating that afforded the only light in the room.

Then the little maid was knocking on a door, and when she received the command to enter, she pushed it open and stood aside, and Anna walked into what was used as the dining-room, but which she recognised instantly was just a part of the kitchen that had been partitioned off. On the far wall was the sash window that should have given light to the whole room.

Miss Benfield was sitting at a table on which there was the remains of a cooked breakfast: there was a greasy plate in front of her which showed the traces of egg yolk. Another person was also in the room; she was standing behind a chair.

Miss Benfield looked steadily at Anna for a full minute before she drew in a sharp breath; then, as if diverted by the slight throaty noise the other woman had made, she turned to her, saying, 'This is Miss Kate Benfield, a relative, and my first assistant.'

Anna looked at the woman across the table and inclined her head and smiled, but she received no answering smile, merely a slight movement of the head.

Anna thought she had never seen anyone with such a miserable countenance, and on this admittedly slight acquaintance, she appeared to be the antithesis of her relative. The only resemblance was in their height, both women being tall, but this one was thin, so thin she looked emaciated.

'You are not suitably dressed.'

'What! Why?'

'When you speak to me, you will address me as Miss Benfield.'

'Why do you consider me not suitably dressed, Miss Benfield?' She turned her glance quickly from the big woman to the slight one because she thought she had heard her gasp. Then again she was looking at her employer, for she was saying, 'You wish to be a pupil teacher, then you should have some idea of how such a one should appear before a class of children. The uniform is as Miss Kate's here: a white blouse and a black skirt, that to reach the top of your boots or shoes.' She leant her head sideways, observing Anna's grey skirt, which was showing an inch of stocking between the hem of her dress and the black laces of her shoes.

'I'm afraid, Miss Benfield, that I do not possess a black skirt and white blouse, at least, that is, at present, but I have a dark blue dress and I will come attired in it tomorrow and until such time as I can acquire a suitable uniform.'

Miss Benfield was on her feet, her huge chest heaving as if being assisted by a pump. 'You are getting off to a bad start, young woman. Now, let me inform you there is a way to address me and there is a way not to address me. And if you wish to continue here, and rise in this establishment, you will learn that, and quickly. Your tone is anything but deferential, which manner you would be wise to adopt in future. Have I made myself plain?'

'Very plain, Miss Benfield.'

The breasts rose and threatened the buttons on the black satin blouse; then the indignant lady turned to her first assistant and said, 'You will take Miss Dagshaw and introduce her to the duties required of her today.'

The first assistant turned sharply away and made for the door and, after staring at the woman's back for a moment, Anna turned as abruptly and followed her through the kitchen, past the little maid, who was scooping ashes from the hearth, up the dark stone stairway and into the hall; thence down a passage to a room that had been partitioned off.

There were no desks in this room, but there were two long, narrow tables, each with its backless bench, and so placed one in front of the other that the children sitting at them would be facing the blackboard attached to a wall. There was a cupboard opposite the door, and this Miss Kate Benfield opened. It contained four shelves; and she started at the top. Taking down two boxes, she pointed to the pieces of cardboard inside, saying briefly, 'The alphabet. You know how to teach that, don't you? You hold them up like this.' She picked up a piece of cardboard. 'You ask them what that is; then you make them all repeat it ten times. Then, according to how far they're advanced, you do, cat, dog, rat, mat, sat, and fat. You've done this, I suppose?'

Anna made no response, so the woman put the boxes back, saying, 'That occupies the first hour.' Then pointing to the second shelf, on which there were a number of tattered-backed books, she said, 'Nursery rhymes. They'll know some of these already, having learned them at home.' She was now pointing to the third shelf. 'These trays are for clay,' she said. 'You'll find the clay in there,' and she pointed to two tin boxes. 'But you won't need these until the afternoon. They are getting tired by then. But these' – she was lifting some picture books from the bottom shelf – 'these are for the last hour in the morning. You can hand these out if they are getting restless, and ask them to tell stories about the pictures of the animals or birds. Think you can do that?'

'I should think so.' Anna's tone was cold and it wasn't lost on the woman, for she said, 'Well, you knew what you were in for, and you're starting at the bottom.'

There was something in the voice that didn't match the countenance and caused Anna to say, 'Thank you for your

74

help. You're right. I'm starting at the bottom. By the way, may I enquire what relation you are to Miss Benfield?'

'Cousin.'

'Oh.'

'Yes, cousin.' The head was nodding now and it seemed to Anna that she might have said something further about the relationship but, the hall clock striking nine, she said, 'That's fast. It's ten minutes to. The horde will be arriving at any second now,' and on this she smartly left the room.

Anna turned and surveyed the small room and the cupboard, and her thoughts were not that very soon she would be attempting to teach small children for the first time but that she would be spending the whole day in this airless, dusty little square. And when her mind touched on her home she closed her eyes for a moment as she muttered, Oh, dear God! I don't think I can stand this.

'*Quiet now! Quiet now!* Go to your rooms.' The voice brought her eyes springing wide and a hand to her throat. She was here and she must stay and put up with it. There was Miss Netherton to think about, besides her ma and dada.

'*Miss Dagshaw.*'

She started slightly as she heard her name bellowed from the hall, and she hurried along the passage, there to see Miss Benfield surrounded by eight small figures, while other children were making their way up the stairs. It would seem, though, that there was some impediment on the stairs, for a number of them stopped, so blocking the way for the rest, and they all turned and looked down on her.

Leaving the small children, Miss Benfield smartly stepped into the passage and almost hissed at Anna, 'Haven't you the sense to take off your coat and hat? Are you thinking about teaching the children like that?'

Bristling now, Anna said, 'Well, will you kindly tell me, please, where I can hang my coat and hat?'

75

Miss Benfield swallowed; then, turning to the children, she said, 'Margaret, show Miss Dagshaw where the teachers' room is.'

The small girl sidled past Anna, hardly taking her eyes from her; then ran back along the corridor, turned a corner and pushed open a door.

'Thank you.'

Anna now saw that the teachers' room consisted of two cubicles, the first holding three wooden chairs, a two-foot-by-one table, and a row of wooden pegs attached to the wall. It also had half a window and this was uncurtained. But when she pushed open the door in the partition she saw that the other half of the window was covered by a yellow-paper roller blind and that below it was a wooden frame with a hole in it, and directly below the opening was a tin bucket.

She closed the door quickly, drew in a long breath, took off her hat and hung it on one of the hooks, with her cloak under it. Her cloth handbag, in which was her purse, she kept in her hand; then, opening the door, she made for her classroom, which was but a few steps away.

The children were already seated, eight bright faces, well-washed and well-fed-looking faces, and as she returned their stares she wondered at the parents who would allow their children to be taught in a place like this.

'Good morning, children.'

'Good morning, miss.' The voices came at her one after the other. There followed a silence in which she wondered what she should say; then she was saying it. 'I am your new teacher and so I hope you will help me to get over my first day. Will you?' There was silence for a moment; then, 'Yes, teacher. Yes, teacher. Yes, teacher.' She looked at the four little children sitting upright on the first form and said, 'Now, tell me your names.' And pointing to the end one, she said,

'Yes?' and one after the other they said their names, some in a whisper, some loudly: 'Mary. Sarah. Kathleen,' and she herself, smiling at the fourth one, said, 'And I know you are Margaret.'

'Yes, teacher.'

After she had been given the names of those on the back form, she said, 'Now, shall we start with the alphabet? You usually start with the alphabet, don't you?'

'No, miss; you call the register.' It was Margaret again.

She looked helplessly towards the open cupboard. She had no register. She hadn't been told about the register.

'Oh. Well, we'll see about that later . . . '

There was no actual break until twelve o'clock, except that which the children contrived for themselves by asking: 'May I leave the room, miss?' And one bright spark caused a giggle. When coming back into the room from her excursion, she remarked, 'It stinks.'

At twenty minutes past eleven, if she was to judge by the hall clock striking the half hour and it being ten minutes fast, there were one or two yawns, so she decided to brighten things up in the rhyme section by getting the children to demonstrate the words as much as possible by the use of their hands. Looking through the book, she picked *Jack and Jill* and said, 'Now children, let's be Jack and Jill, shall we? What did they do first?'

'They went up the hill, miss.'

'All right, we'll all go up the hill.'

Eight pairs of arms followed her actions and clawed their way up the hill.

There were only six rhymes in the ragged cloth books, and when they had finished demonstrating the last: *Dickory, Dickory, Dock, The Mouse Ran Up The Clock,* and she said, 'Well, that is all,' one child called out, 'Tell us another, miss,' and this was echoed by the others, 'Yes; let us do another, miss. Please.'

She put her head back as if thinking; and she was thinking of all the nursery rhymes her father had taught them and the funny little rhymes she herself had made up, dozens of them. But she had better stick to the well-known ones . . . Which one would be good for demonstrating?

"There was a little man"? Yes, yes; she would do that one. She said aloud: 'I know a nursery rhyme. You can all act to it. It is called, "There was a little man." '

And so she began:

'There was a little man,
And he had a little gun—'

She stopped here and said, 'Well, make a gun. You know, a gun.' She used both arms stretched out now as if she were holding a gun to her shoulder. Then she went on,

'And his bullets were made
of lead, lead, lead, . . . '

'And his bullets were made of lead, lead, lead,' they repeated, then there was a chorus of, 'Bang! Bang!' Followed by high laughter, and, 'Do it again, teacher! Do it again!' So she did it again, going through the whole rhyme this time, and the responses grew louder and the laughter became higher. Then suddenly the door burst open and the first assistant appeared, her face expressing amazement.

'What on earth!'

'We are just demonstrating a nursery rhyme.'

'I heard.' It was a low whisper. Then, 'Come outside for a moment.'

In the dark corridor the woman said, 'She just needs to hear that and you'll be out of the door. Bullets through the head; I've never heard such a thing.'

'It's a nursery rhyme: There was a little man, he shot a little duck . . . '

'Well, I've never heard of it. I'm just in the next room. I couldn't believe my ears at first. Look' – her voice sank – 'if you want to remain here, stick to the rules.'

'I don't know whether I want to remain here.'

'Well, that's up to you. But I'll say this much, I think you'll work out all right, for you're the best teacher we've had for a long time. Now, take my advice and go in there and tell them they mustn't repeat that nursery rhyme, that's if they want to see you again. I'll leave it to you to work out how you'll do that. So far, from what I've heard, you seem to be able to cope with most things.'

Again Anna wanted to thank this miserable-looking woman. She also wanted to step round the corner, go into that smelly cubicle and put on her hat and cloak and go home.

And admit defeat?

She drew in a long breath and returned to the classroom.

At five o'clock Miss Benfield called Anna into the downstairs classroom and reminded her of her dissatisfaction with her apparel. She also said that, from what she had overheard, her discipline needed a great deal of improvement, and, if she did not like the meal that was provided then she had better bring her own.

To all this, and probably to Miss Benfield's surprise, Anna made no reply. She was feeling tired and weary. Moreover, she was cold. The whole house was cold. And she was hungry . . .

When she reached the market square, the carrier cart had already left, and she had never known herself to be so near to tears. She would have to walk; the twilight would soon be on her, and if she didn't hurry it would be dark before she reached the cut, which was the shortest way home. That path, at one point, passed close to the edge of the quarry, and although the quarry wasn't all that deep, she wouldn't like to fall into it in the dark. But then her father might still be waiting for her. Yet, if he saw that she wasn't on the carrier's cart, would he stay there? No; more likely he'd go back and get their own cart out.

She had been standing on her feet for most of the day, and so by the time she had left the town and had taken to the country road her step had slowed. And when she reached the cut, she wasn't surprised to find no-one waiting for her.

The cut, as it was called, ran between open green fields, through a small copse, then uphill onto the edge of the quarry, which was no more than thirty feet at its deepest point and extended over hardly an eighth of an acre. It was said that the demand for its stone had already dwindled before it was half dug out. Going away from it, the path once again ran between open fields, until it merged into the moor. At one point it crossed the bridle-path to the village. At the edge of the moor another hardly discernible path led to their own patch of woodland which, in turn, gave way to the hill and there, in its shelter, was home.

As she rounded the bottom of the hill, she saw in the distance the lights on the cart picking out Neddy's rump, and she went into a stumbling run now, shouting, 'Dada! I'm here!'

It was Jimmy who heard her first, and his voice echoed back to her: 'She's here, Dada!'

In the yard they were all about her, questioning, but her father's voice rose above the rest, demanding harshly, 'Where've you been? Why weren't you on the cart, girl?'

'Oh, Dada, let me get in and sit down. I'm worn out. One way and another, I'm worn out.'

In the kitchen Maria said, 'You've had us worried, dear. You see, you're not used to the town and . . . '

'Ma, let me take my shoes off.'

Eager hands were now at her feet and they took her shoes off and lifted her cold soles towards the blaze of the fire while rubbing them.

'May I have something hot, Ma?'

'Yes, my love, yes. It's all ready; some mutton broth.'

'What happened?' It was Oswald bending towards her now.

She turned to look over her shoulder, saying, 'Wait till Dada comes in' – she smiled wanly now – 'and I'll tell you, right from the beginning at nine o'clock this morning. No; ten minutes to, onwards.'

She had finished the soup and eaten two large slices of bread and pork fat before Nathaniel came into the room. He seemed to have taken his time unharnessing the horse and stabling it, and Maria looked at him anxiously while making a motion with her head; then he was standing in front of her, saying, 'Well! let me have it. What kept you? It was all arranged that you would come home on the cart.'

Anna let out a very audible sigh, then said, 'Do you want to hear the whole story before you eat, or after?' At this there was laughter; but when he said, 'For my part, before,' there were slight groans. So she told them exactly what had happened, from the meeting with the head of the establishment in the so-called dining room, the condition of the kitchen, what she was expected to teach, the watery stew with the grease floating on the top, which she couldn't stomach at dinner time, the first assistant for whom she felt sorry, and lastly, what had prevented her from catching the cart, which was the lecture from Miss Benfield.

'She can't go back there again, can she?' Maria appealed to Nathaniel; and he thought for a moment, then looked at his daughter and said, 'Well, it's up to you. Why not leave it until after we have eaten properly and then you can tell me what you intend to do, and I will go across to Miss Netherton

81

and give her a report, because I can see you're all in.'

'Dada.' She looked up at him and, her voice soft, she said, 'It's your fault, you know; you've made it too easy for me all these years.'

3

Anna continued to teach at Miss Kate Benfield's Academy during the remainder of September, then through October and November, and she had experience with all the children, from the five-year-olds right up to those of fourteen, who were classed as young ladies.

It should happen that Miss Benfield, the first assistant, who usually supervised the nine-to-eleven and the twelve-to-fourteen children's classes, was subject to severe bouts of head colds, during which she sniffed, blew and coughed a great deal until, hardly able to stand, Miss Benfield the elder would allow her to go to her room . . . wherever that was. Anna never found out.

When this happened Anna would take one or other of these classes on alternate mornings and afternoons and, of all Miss Benfield's classes, she liked taking those of the older girls, for she knew they enjoyed her teaching, although twice she had been pulled over the coals by Miss Benfield for taking liberties with Shakespeare. Miss Benfield had insisted that she herself would choose passages that the girls must learn by rote and from which they must not deviate.

In the course of her teaching she also had to deal with religious instruction. There was no Bible in any of the classrooms, but prior to the religious lesson Miss Benfield would hand her a copy, having marked a particular psalm or proverb that Anna must read to her class, then ask them questions about; after which they were to write a short essay on the subject.

It transpired that today she had marked the Thirty-sixth Psalm: 'Wickedness confronts God's Love'. It consisted of twelve short verses; but, of course, that wasn't enough for Miss Benfield, who had also marked the first part of the Proverbs: the Proverbs of Solomon, Son of David, King of Israel. And Anna was instructed to tell her pupils they were to write a short essay on the word 'wisdom'.

So here she was facing nine young ladies, so-called, five of the age of fourteen, four of the age of thirteen, and their faces were full of interest. She was aware that they liked her, and with the exception of one girl, she liked them. And yet it should happen that this particular girl was the brightest of them all. In fact, Miss Lilian Burrows, Anna considered, was too advanced for her age and she was sure that the knowledge she had acquired hadn't all come from Miss Benfield's Academy.

So she began.

'Well now, you are all aware what day this is' – she made a little moue with her mouth – 'and you know what lesson we have on a Friday.'

'Oh, yes, yes.'

'Oh, yes, teacher, yes.'

The scoffing retorts came from them all. They still had to address her as 'teacher' even though she had earlier pointed out they could call her Miss Dagshaw. This had caused another storm in Miss Benfield's bosom. The only one to be addressed as 'Miss' was herself. Would she please remember that!

Anna had, on that occasion, said she would try, and the bosom had swelled still further. There were many nights she caused her brothers and sisters to roll on the floor when, with a pillow pushed down a bibbed apron, her dark thick shining hair dragged up to the top of her head and her feet turned outwards, she performed a remarkable imitation of the mistress.

'Not Proverbs again, teacher!'

She looked down at the pained expression of a pretty girl sitting in the front desk.

'I'm afraid so, Rosalie; but we are having the Psalms first.'

The groans were so audible that she turned and looked quickly towards the door, then said, 'Shh! Shh!' And when quiet was restored she said, 'Now listen carefully. This is the Thirty-sixth Psalm and it is headed, "To the chief Musician, A Psalm of David, The Servant Of The Lord". Just write. "A Psalm of David." '

She waited; then after a moment she said, 'It deals with wickedness that confronts God's love.' She glanced around her, then began to read.

The transgression of the wicked saith within my heart, *that there is* no fear of God before his eyes.

For he flattereth himself in his own eyes, until his iniquity be found to be hateful.

The words of his mouth *are* iniquity and deceit: he has left off to be wise, *and* to do good.

Verse after verse she read until she reached the twelfth one. When she had finished she said, 'As you know, you

85

will have to write a short essay dealing with the wickedness that confronts God's love. Shall I read it again?'

'No, miss, no. Anyway, we read that psalm some weeks ago.'

One bright voice piped up now, saying, 'Miss Pinkerton read it on her last day here. She used to almost stutter.'

'She didn't!'

'She did.'

'She didn't! She had a lisp.'

The two combatants turned to a third girl who said, 'She didn't reign long.' Then this girl, looking at Anna, said, 'You know, teacher, you've stuck it the longest. But anyway, I hope you go on till I leave; I'm going into Newcastle at Easter.'

'Oh my! Oh my! She's going into Newcastle at Easter.'

At this point Anna rapped her ruler on her desk, saying, 'Now! now! No more chatter. Let's get on. You don't wish me to read the psalm again and so we'll turn to the essay.'

It was then that the bright spark, Miss Lilian Burrows, put up her hand, and in a high, superior, affected tone, said, 'Read us something from the Songs of Solomon, teacher, please.'

Anna's eyes widened. Here was someone who knew about the Songs of Solomon. She looked at Lilian and said quietly, 'How many of the Songs have you read, Lilian?'

'Oh' – the girl shrugged her shoulders – 'I've been through them all. I know bits and pieces here and there. Do you know them, teacher?'

'Yes. Yes, I know them.'

'Where did you learn them? In Church? Sunday School?'

'No. I have never been to Sunday School. My father taught me; he's a teacher. I have been reading them since I was quite young. They are difficult to understand at first; but they are beautiful.'

Lilian stared at Anna; then slowly she stood up, her quiet demeanour vanished and the bright bragging spark took over. In a voice belying that it was from a fourteen-year-old girl, she began,

> 'The voice of my beloved!
> behold, he cometh leaping
> upon the mountains, skipping
> upon the hills.
> My beloved is like a roe or a
> young hart.'

Anna stood amazed; her lips were following each word; in fact, keeping in time with the girl. Then she heard her own voice joining in with the words:

> 'behold, he standeth
> behind our wall, he
> looketh forth at the
> windows, showing
> himself through the
> lattice.'

She herself paused, but she couldn't stop the flow of the young girl who, head back, was oblivious to where she was as, her voice getting louder, she went on:

> 'My beloved spake, and said unto me,
> Rise up, my love, my fair one . . . '

'That's enough! That's enough!'

The rest of the girls were staring at their companion, watching her as she let out a long breath and then slowly sat down.

Now they transferred all their attention to Anna, waiting for her words of chastisement; but she couldn't chastise the girl, even though she knew she should, because what she had put into those lines had nothing to do with religion. Looking at her now, she asked her, 'Does your family pray together?'

The girl gave a loud 'Huh!' by way of answer; but then said slowly, 'No; we don't pray together.'

There was uneasiness in the room. The girls were not fidgeting but looking straight at her, and now she said, 'We shall all deal with the Song of Solomon later; now, we shall write our essays . . . '

Nothing seemed to go right for the rest of the day and when, later, during the uncomfortable ride home on the back of the cart, she saw in the distance a speck of light from her father's lantern, she felt she wanted to jump off the cart and run to him and feel the comfort of his arms and the solace of his quiet voice.

But when the cart stopped, Nathaniel had actually to help her down, so stiff was she with the cold. And the carter called to Nathaniel, 'There's snow on the way; had a flake or two way back. Glad to get home the night. See you Monday, lass.'

'Yes. Thank you. See you Monday.'

'You're freezing. Here, put my scarf round you.'

'No, no; I'm all right. Just let's hurry.'

'You'll not be able to keep this up if the weather breaks. You're shivering like a leaf. Anyway, what kind of a day have you had?'

'Awful. I'll tell you about it later.'

'By the way, we've got visitors.'

'Visitors?' When she paused in her step he pulled her forward, saying, 'Come on. Come on.'

'Who are they?'

'Two pit families. They had been on the moor; I hadn't seen them. Apparently they had been coming into the wood at night to get shelter from the wind. They had erected a kind of tent against the wood pile. That gave them a bit of support. But they must have scampered off at first light. It was Ben who brought them in; at least, he brought five bairns to the door.'

'Five?'

'Yes, five; the oldest one about seven: rags on their feet, practically the same on their backs. Your ma brought them in and gave them broth, but she said she couldn't let them stay in the house, and rightly, for their heads were walking, they were alive. Anyway, the father of two of them came down and apologised. He was a decently spoken man. I asked him how long he had been out and he said a week or more, but that they would have to make for the poor house shortly; he couldn't see his wife and bairns freeze to death out there. So I had a word with your ma and she was with me, as I knew she would be, and we told them to bring their bits and pieces down. They hadn't much; they had sold what furniture they had for grub. They did have some bedding and cooking utensils. Anyway, there's plenty of dry hay in the barn, and I lit the boiler in the tack room. We keep nothing much in there; only Neddy's harness and odds and ends. The men rigged up a kind of cooking stove, so they can eat in there and be warm. And as your ma suggested, they can have a wash down – she would, wouldn't she?' He laughed. 'She's worried about Ben being near the bairns and picking up the army from their heads. I told her Ben must have been in touch with them for days; so she'll scour him tonight to make sure.'

'Life's very unfair, Dada, isn't it?'

'In some cases it is, dear, but I must admit that many get more than their share of unfairness.'

'You did.'

'Me? Oh, no, I didn't. I've been very lucky, my dear. Your ma's had a deal of unfairness, and you and every one of you, and there's more to come, you know that; but not me. There's many a man who'd envy the six children such as I have.' He put his arm around her shoulder and pressed her to him.

'Dada.'

'Yes, my love?'

'Do you think there's anything bad about The Songs of Solomon?'

'Bad, about The Songs of Solomon? They have some of the most beautiful lines in the Bible.'

'Yes, I thought so too.'

'What makes you ask such a question?'

'Oh, something that happened today. I'll tell you about it later; all I want at this moment is my feet in front of the fire, a bowl of hot soup in my hands and Ma's fingers gently rubbing the back of my neck and her voice crying at the rest of them, "Leave her alone! Let her eat." You know, Dada, I look forward to that scene every day from one o'clock onwards. And I wouldn't exchange it for Solomon's Temple.'

Their laughter joined and their arms linked, they went into a slithering run, with the lantern swinging from Nathaniel's extended arm, and they didn't stop till they rounded the foot of the hill and saw the welcoming lamp-light from the house.

4

On the Monday morning Anna did not arrive at Miss Benfield's front door until five minutes to nine. The carrier's horse, an old and wise one, had been wary of the road and its thick coating of frost, and so the journey had been somewhat slower. But as soon as the door was opened by the little maid, she knew that this wasn't going to be an ordinary beginning to another week of repetitive lessons, and hand-clapping to keep her own and the children's fingers flexible, because the young girl, poking her head forward, said, 'She wants to see you,' her thumb jerking rapidly and indicating, 'in the big room.'

Anna went to draw the pins from her hat, but stopped; if Miss Benfield was calling her to boot in the main room, something was afoot.

'Good morning, Miss Benfield. It's a very cold . . . '

'*Be quiet!* Don't give me any of your pleasantries. I wonder that you dare show your face in my house.'

Anna stared at the woman for a few seconds before saying, 'Would you mind telling me, please, what you mean by that remark?'

'Corruption. *Corruption.*' The last word was almost yelled.

For a moment Anna thought the woman had gone mad, that she had lost her senses. But this thought didn't altogether surprise her. So her voice was level as she answered, 'I don't understand you.'

'You understand what the word "corruption" means. You have corrupted my girls.'

Now she did understand her, and immediately gave Miss Benfield her answer: 'You must be out of your mind,' and even dared to add, 'woman.'

The chest heaved twice before the woman could say, 'Lilian ... Lilian Burrows and The Songs of Solomon. Now do you understand?'

She knew both Lilian Burrows and The Songs of Solomon; but she didn't really understand, until Miss Benfield said, 'Lilian had a cousin and some friends with her on Friday evening and' – the bosom heaved again, and Miss Benfield swallowed deeply – 'when they returned home they told their mother that Lilian had recited pieces to them from the Bible, funny pieces that they hadn't heard before, and that they had giggled.' The bosom rose, and on the deep deflation, she said, 'Just imagine it. Just imagine it.'

'Yes, I can imagine it. She's a very bright girl and it would seem, Miss Benfield, that you are acquainted with the Songs of Solomon.'

'I ... I may be. I am an adult, I understand the meaning, the real meaning of the words of Solomon; but a young girl would put a wrong construction on them. And mind, not only a young girl would do so. And you have imbued this child ...'

'I have done nothing of the sort.'

'You deny it?'

'Emphatically I deny it. Lilian is well acquainted with that part of the Bible, and must have been for some time, because she can rhyme it off.'

'Yes, under your tuition, as she said.'

'*What!*'

'Don't pretend innocence, young woman. That child would never have thought of reading such things; in fact, she would have not been aware they were in the Bible, but your corrupt mind introduced her . . . '

'*Shut up!*'

Miss Benfield actually took a staggering step backwards, and her mouth opened and shut as she sought an answer; but she hadn't time to bring a word out of her froth-smeared lips before Anna cried, 'I have never read anything to my pupils except that which you dictated. Lilian Burrows is well-acquainted with the Songs of Solomon, and not with those alone, from what I judge.'

'How is it, then, that she could tell her parents that you have been reading them for years.'

'Because I told the class so. When the girl stood and recited line after line of a particular verse, the second to be exact, in which, you will remember, Miss Benfield, occur the words, "The voice of my beloved! behold he cometh . . . " '

She stopped here and Miss Benfield made no sound, but just stared at this daring, beautiful creature whom she had disliked on sight, this bastard child of wicked parents whom, she told herself, she had taken in out of pity and whom she felt had inherited some strange power, an evil power, for in her eyes there was knowledge that shouldn't be there. And, too, her bearing was such as could only be promoted by pride supplied by the devil.

A thin stream of saliva ran down from a corner of Miss Benfield's mouth. She opened her tight lips while at the same time pointing towards the door, saying, 'Get out! Leave my house! You've sullied the name of my school and I will see that you find no engagement in this town for your corrupting talents and I'll make sure that

Miss Netherton's influence will not aid you in any way in the future.'

Anna stared silently at the woman for some seconds before she said, 'This is not a school, Miss Benfield, because you have no knowledge to impart. You are an ignorant woman. The little teaching that is done here is supplied by your cousin, that poor downtrodden woman. If the school board were to examine you, you wouldn't have a livelihood, you wouldn't even be allowed to teach in a village school, because the standard there would be so far above you it would be as a university compared to this house. So, I would like you to remember, Miss Benfield, that when you are blackening my name and my ability to teach, I shall not restrain myself from giving my opinion of your establishment.'

As she turned away she thought that the woman was about to have a seizure, and when she opened the door it was to see the children coming in, but before that it was to cause the younger Miss Benfield to take a springing step away from her.

For the first time she could see what could have been a smile on the thin, worn face of the first assistant and she did not lower her voice when she said to her, 'Stand on your feet, Miss Benfield. Face up to her, because without you there would be no Academy For Young Ladies.' She had curled her lip on the last four words.

When she watched the thin, weary woman bring her teeth tight onto her lower lip, she put her hand quickly out towards her, saying, 'Do it. Make your own terms.' She took a step backwards, then said, 'Goodbye.'

The children were surprised to see their nice teacher making for the front door and the first assistant scampering after her.

Anna was on the pavement when the woman spoke, her voice coming in gasps as if she had been running: 'Thank you,' she said. 'I'm glad you came.' And again she said, 'Thank you.' And this time her head was bobbing.

Anna said nothing in reply; she could only raise her hand in a gesture of farewell; then she walked past more children escorted by very young so-called nurses and here and there a parent, who looked at the new young teacher in surprise, for she was not going into the Academy but was walking away from it, and it being only nine o'clock in the morning.

The further she walked into the town the further her anger rose. That dreadful woman. How dare she say her teaching would corrupt? Even if it had been she who introduced the Songs of Solomon, even so, how dare she!

There would be no carrier-cart going her way until twelve o'clock. She paused outside the station. She could get a train to Usworth, but then she would have as far to walk again to get home; what was more, she had never been on a train, and she didn't know how to go about it. Part of her mind told her now that she must do something about that, too, in the future.

The market-place was almost empty. She crossed it to walk down Victoria Road and past the park at the foot of Brampton Hill. Here, the shops on one side of Victoria Road petered out, but did so grandly, with the imposing structure that held the post office on the ground floor and the Registrar of Births and Deaths on the second floor.

She was actually walking blindly when the voice said, 'Oh, I'm sorry. I beg your pardon.'

The man, who had turned from fastening his horse's reins to the horse post at the edge of the rough pavement, put out his hand and gripped her arm as she almost overbalanced.

'I do beg your pardon. I didn't see you . . . Miss . . . Miss . . . you are Miss Dagshaw, aren't you?'

She blinked at the man. He was the one who had acknowledged the introduction that first day, when Miss Netherton had driven her to the school, and here on her last she was meeting him again.

'Are you all right?' He was looking into her face, and she closed her eyes for a moment before she said, 'Yes, thank you, sir; I am all right. It was not your fault. I ... I wasn't looking where I was going because' – she now forced herself to smile – 'I was in a temper, which could even be translated into the saying, blind with rage. So you see, it is my fault. But I am all right, thank you.' She made to move away, but his concern having obviously changed to merriment, she stopped, and he went on to say, 'I won't dare ask what has put you into a rage. But I understood from Miss Netherton that you were in a teaching post?'

'I was, sir, up till about' – she considered – 'until twenty minutes or half an hour ago.'

His shoulders began to shake again, and she herself laughed. The sound came out in small jerks. Then, remembering who she was, and who he was, she adopted a more sober air and her voice sounded slightly prim as she said, 'Good day to you.'

As she went to move past him he stopped her with his hand, which did not touch her but was held a foot or so from her as he said, 'Since what you say suggests that you are no longer a teacher, at least for today, may I enquire if you are on your way home?'

'Yes. Yes, I am.'

'And you mean to walk?'

'Well, sir, having no other means of propulsion except my legs, I mean to walk.'

She watched him bring his chin into his high stiff collar for a moment; and further, she noticed that the points of it did not cause a ridge of flesh to form beneath his jaws, as with most men who wore such collars. And then he said, 'You

96

know, you sounded just like Miss Netherton. Your turn of phrase and wit is a replica of hers.'

Very likely she *was* talking like Miss Netherton because she had patterned herself on her mentor's speech for many years; but as for wit, she couldn't see that she had said anything at all that could merit that word.

'Look,' he was saying now, 'I've just got to slip into the post office; I want to send a telegram. So would you allow me to give you a lift home? If nothing else, it would take the weight off' – he paused – 'your means of propulsion.'

As she looked from him to the high, two-wheeled gig with but two seats, she asked herself if it was the right thing to do to accept his offer. What would Miss Netherton have done? Oh, she would have said, let's get away. But there was a great difference between herself and Miss Netherton in relation to this man. He was one of what was termed the gentry. In his eyes, even being a sort of school-marm, she would still be considered a menial, and she didn't like that thought. She never felt like a menial. Miss Netherton had never made her feel like a menial.

'Thank you. That's very kind of you.'

'Well then, would you care to come in out of the cold and wait while I do my business?'

She had never been in this post office. When she had gone to buy stamps for her father it had been from the small office near Bog's End.

'Thank you.'

He said no more, but went a little ahead of her, and pushed open the door to allow her to pass into the large bare room that was cut in half by a counter.

'Take a seat; I won't be a minute.' He pointed to a form fixed to the wall, and she sat down and watched him go to the far end of the counter and speak to the assistant, who handed him a form on which he then wrote something before handing it back, together with some money.

There were three other customers in the post office: one was walking towards the door when, as Simon Brodrick turned from the counter, he stopped and in a loud voice cried, 'Well! Hello, you. What are you doing here at this time of the morning?'

'Oh, hello, Harry. Oh, just sending off a wire.'

'How's everyone? Haven't seen you for two or three weeks. Missed you last time when Penella came over. What about next week?'

They were near the door now. Anna had risen to her feet and Simon Brodrick put out his hand towards her, but didn't speak. He opened the door and waited for her to pass him. And when they were in the street he did not introduce her to the man but, touching her elbow, helped her up onto the steep step of the gig, then onto the leather seat, before turning to the man, who was muttering something that was inaudible to her.

Simon loosened the horse's bridle from the post and took his seat beside Anna; then looking down at the man, he said, 'Give my regards to the family,' then shook the reins as he cried to the horse, 'Gee up! there,' and off they went.

Anna didn't hear what the man replied, if he replied at all; she only knew he had all the while stared fixedly at her and that she, returning his gaze for a moment, experienced a feeling of embarrassment and unease.

They had passed through the outskirts of the town before Simon spoke, and then he said, 'Will you be looking for another situation since, as it seems, you have lost or left your present one?'

'What? I mean, pardon?'

His voice a tone higher now, he said, 'Will you be looking for another situation?'

98

'Not yet; well, not until after the holidays. In any case, I think I'll have difficulty in finding one.'

'How's that?'

'Well, firstly I don't think Miss Benfield will give me a reference, judging by our last conversation.'

'Oh, a battle of words, was it?'

'Yes. You could say that, Biblical words.'

He turned towards her and there was a note of surprise in his voice as he repeated, 'Biblical words? You were arguing about the Bible?'

'Part of it.'

'*Really?*'

She could tell by his tone that he was interested, and amused. She also told herself that he appeared to be a nice man, easy to talk to. So she heard herself saying, 'I was accused of corrupting the young ladies by allowing one of them to read a passage from the Bible.'

'Accused of . . . you mean, certain passages of the Bible touch on corruption?'

'It would appear so.'

'May I ask which?'

She looked ahead as she said, 'The Songs of Solomon.'

She saw his hand jerk on the rein and she knew that once again his shoulders were shaking, and there was laughter in his voice too as he said, 'You were teaching your pupils the Songs of Solomon?'

'*No.*' The word was emphatic. 'One of them was out to teach me. She didn't know that I was acquainted with that part of the Bible and had been since Da . . . my father introduced me to it years ago. The girl was bored with the Psalms, so she stood up and had rendered part of the second Song to the entire class before I had the wit to stop her. Then it appears that she entertained some friends at home with her repertoire.'

She drooped her head as she said, 'There was a meeting of parents and a storming of Miss Benfield.' Then after a moment her head came up as she ended, 'And I was accused of corrupting young minds.'

'The Songs of Solomon.'

'You find it funny . . . amusing?'

'Yes. Yes, I do. And you do, too; I can tell by your tone, at least now. But you were in a fury, weren't you?'

'Yes. Yes, I was. Have you read the Songs of Solomon?'

'Yes, but many years ago in my schooldays, during the period of wrong constructions and false values.'

There was a sober note to his voice now, and she said, 'Is that how you look upon youth?'

'Yes. Well, at least mine. But you, now; I'm sure that your values will be utterly right and your constructions without error.'

'I don't mind being laughed at. Dada . . . my father, oh, why do I say that when I always call him Dada?' She twisted her body in the seat as if in defiance. 'So, I will repeat, Dada often laughs at me and my ideas. I'm quite used to it.'

She was surprised when he made no reference at all to her last words and she thought, Oh, now he's recalling the gillyvor bit and Dada is the cause of it. And when, looking straight ahead, he remarked, 'You would like to be put down at the quarry end, wouldn't you?' she felt she had surmised correctly.

'How do you know that?'

'I know that you don't often travel through the village; I'm a friend of Miss Netherton's.'

'Oh. Yes, of course. And yes, I would like to be put down at the quarry end.'

About five minutes later he pulled the gig to a halt. The conversation had become desultory: he had spoken about the weather and the roads. But quickly now, he alighted from his seat beside her and went round the vehicle to hold out his hands to assist her to the ground. And when they were standing facing each other, he said, 'I must tell you something before you go, and I want you to believe that I'm not laughing at you. I'm not easily given to laughter, you know, but I haven't laughed as much as I've done this morning for a long, long time; and I would like you to know that I've enjoyed your company and our conversation to the extent that I can't look back to a time when I felt more interested in what a human being had to say. It is a great pity, at least I feel so, that I shall be deprived of such conversation in the future. Goodbye, Miss Dagshaw; and thank you.'

His hand was held out to her, and after a moment's hesitation, she placed hers in it, and as their palms touched they looked steadily at each other.

She was moving away, walking with a straight back, down the narrow path towards the quarry. She knew that the gig was still there, and she wondered why she felt so strange, that she wanted to burst into tears, when just a short while ago she too had been laughing.

'Miss Netherton will be upset.'

'No, she won't, my dear.' Nathaniel put his hand on Maria's shoulder. 'She'll understand.'

'You know, Nat, I become afraid for Anna at times. Her tongue is too ready: she comes out with things she should keep in her head, the things that you've put into her head. You know that?'

'Yes, I know, and I'm glad I've done that one good thing: I've made her think and be honest in her opinions, as well as fearless. Our children are all honest, but she is outstanding.' A smile came on his lips now and he shook his head as he said, 'Oh, I do wish I had been in on that last conversation or battle of words she had with Miss Benfield. If she said only half of what she thinks she said to that woman, then I am proud of her.'

'It'll get her into trouble some day. That's what I'm afraid of, Nat.'

'Well, my dear, if she gets into trouble it will be for a righteous cause.'

'I don't know so much. You know what she said to me about the man who came out of the post office with Mr Brodrick?'

'No.'

'She said, "He looked at me in an odd way, Ma, sort of surprised yet familiar." You see, Nat, underneath all her cleverness, she has still got to learn about life and men. I know exactly what was in that man's look because, there she was, about to drive away with Mr Brodrick.'

'It was Simon Brodrick she was with, dear. If it had been the other one, Raymond, then I would have been anxious. But Simon is a married man with a three-year-old son.'

'Yes. And you can add to that, his wife is known as a vixen. And if you are to go by the tales that Miss Netherton's Rob gets from Robert Grafton, the coachman over there, then there is hell let loose in that house at times between him and his wife. And another thing, the two brothers don't seem to get on. The Raymond one acts God Almighty, if you can believe all you hear, and he's hated at his pit.'

'Well, it isn't exactly his pit, it's his father's; at least the share that he holds; the other two owners keep out of the way. One, I'm told, lives on the South coast, at Brighton, where the life is as high as it is in London, and the other is abroad. But getting away from our dear Anna and her escort, to that poor lot in your barn. The men have gone into Gateshead Fell this morning to see if they can pick up work there. If one of them could get a job, he has a relative in the town who could house them, he says. Anyway, I shouldn't be surprised if sometime soon I shall be having a visit from one of the pit officials.'

'*Why?*'

'Oh, to tell me what'll happen to us for harbouring agitators, troublemakers, riot-rousers. One thing, they can't turn *us* out of *our* house.'

'Well, that being the case, what could they do?'

'Oh, there's all kinds of things they could do.'

'What's on your mind, Nat? What could they do? Tell me.'

'They could enclose the land roundabout, taking in the quarry.'

'That's a right of way, has been for countless years. They can't do that.'

'Possession has always been known to be nine points of the law, dear. They'll do it first, then leave us to fight it afterwards, by which time we'll have a hard job to get out of here unless we go through the village; and that means all of us and at different times. And I can't escort every one of them, not from four o'clock in the morning onwards.'

'He couldn't do that; he would be cutting off his nose to spite his face. I mean, Praggett would. Cherry wouldn't be able to get there, and Anna wouldn't be able to get to Miss Netherton's.'

'Oh, yes, Anna would. She would go through the village. And yet I couldn't see that going on long before there would be trouble. Anyway, dear, let's talk about us. Tomorrow I'm going to see Parson Mason. You know, all those weeks ago, when I went to him, I think he would have been willing to marry us then if it had been left with him. But the dear Bishop got to know about it. And through whom? None other than the Holy Reverend Roland Albert Fawcett. Were we not two wicked persons? In the eyes of God we had sinned, and grievously. We had given birth to six wonderful children, happy, well-formed, intelligent children who could more than write their own names, they could pen a complete letter, even knowing how to address the person in question. Moreover, they possessed a sense of humour and here and there a gift of wit. They were whole in mind and body. But they were gillyvors, bastards, and in the sight of God, full of sin inherited from their parents.'

Nathaniel now walked down the length of the room and stood near the window that looked on to the frost-coated vegetable garden, and he said, 'You know, I'm really of a mild nature, Maria, you know that, but on the day when I came out of the meeting in that vestry I was so burnt up with righteous indignation and rage that, just as Anna said she had the desire to hit out at that woman this morning, well, I wanted to lash out; and on that day I could see myself flailing those so-called men of God, all except our dear Reverend Mason. Anyway, his letter says the matter is settled and I go in tomorrow to propose a date.' He turned from the window now and came back to her, and he was smiling as he added, 'Do you think they'll arrange the service for midnight?'

She looked up at him and, answering his half-smile, she said, 'Could be, if they want the devil there.'

'Oh, my dear.' He pulled her up towards him, saying now, 'There is a God. I know there is, although I feel at times he is blindly furious at what goes on down here among his so-called Christian community. Anyway, let's forget ourselves; at least, let me forget myself for a moment and talk about what's going to happen to our beautiful daughter. I mean, how she is to get work anywhere near enough for her to travel home? Fellburn is out of the question. Gateshead Fell is not much better; the righteous are there too. There's only Newcastle. She could manage that on the cart in the clement weather, but in the winter, no way could she make that journey.'

'Nat, leave Anna's future to take care of itself; I've got a feeling it will. I've always had a strange feeling about our eldest daughter. I've no such worries about Cherry. But about Anna, somehow I think her future's already written down in the book.'

He stared into her face for a moment before he said, 'You're a witch; so who dare cross a witch!'

'Yes; remember that, Nathaniel Martell. Odd that' – she turned her head to the side and she smiled – 'I'll become Maria Martell. Sounds nice. Yes' – she nodded – 'I could grow to like it.'

He slapped her playfully on the cheek, then went out.

When Nathaniel crossed the yard towards the barn where the children were playing with a skipping rope, they stopped when they saw him and moved together almost into a huddle, and he went to them, saying, 'Give me the end of that rope.' After a moment's pause one of them picked up the end of the rope from the ground and, slowly approaching, handed it to him.

'There now, you take the other end and we'll see what the rest can do. Come on with you.'

When the rope was swinging, he cried at them, 'Come on! You can skip.' Then he went into the children's rhyme his pupils of years past had sung:–

> All in together, girls;
> Never mind the weather, girls;
> Lift your toes and then your heels,
> Skip high or you'll coup your creels.'

Apparently this was known to the children, for they took it up, and their giggles and laughter brought the two women from the far end of the barn to stare in open-mouthed amazement at their benefactor. This kind man, whom they'd heard for years described as the fellow in Heap Hollow who had bred a family of bastards had, to their surprise, turned out to be a gentleman. Their men said so, so he must be. Then one of them happened to turn her head and look towards the wood, with the result that she nudged her companion hard with her elbow, saying, 'Oh, look out for squalls. Look who's coming. Oh, he'll put a lid on it.'

The other woman now looked towards the approaching man and cried to the children, 'Leave go! and come on in, all of you. Come on in!'

When, startled, they obeyed her, one of the women cried to Nathaniel, 'See who's coming, mister!'

Nathaniel looked towards the man fast approaching him; then he turned to where the women were hustling the children through the open barn doors and said, 'It'll be all right. Don't worry, it'll be all right.'

He did not, however, go forward to meet the man but walked towards the house, and was standing by his front door when Howard Praggett came to a puffing standstill about a yard from him.

'You know who I am,' he began straightaway, 'and I know who you are, and you know why I'm here, don't you?'

'No, Mr Praggett; I have no idea why you're here. It is your first visit. Would you care to come in?'

'You can drop your politeness, mister. I know all about you and your tongue. I'm going to put it to you plainly; you're breaking the law, you know, in housing that scum.' He jerked his head towards the barn.

'I will answer the second part of your accusation first, Mr Praggett. I object to the word "scum". I am housing two miners and their families because you have turned them out of their cottages and they have nowhere to go but the open moor, on which at least the children would soon have perished. Now, as for the law, what is the name of this law I am breaking?'

106

Howard Praggett thrust his head first one way and then the other from the band of his collarless reefer-coat before he said, 'They are criminals, agitators, rioters.'

'If that is so, why aren't they in the House of Correction? Why haven't they been called up before a magistrate?'

The man's face had become suffused with a purple tinge and again his head jerked from side to side before he said, 'You think you're a clever bugger, don't you? But wait until Mr Raymond ... Mr Raymond Brodrick gets back from London. He'll point out laws to you. And he'll have them into the House of Correction for inciting workmen to riot, as those two did last night in the dark, going from one house to another, trying to bring the men out ... when they're quite happy and know they've got a square deal. Aye, you can sneer and laugh, but they're eatin' and they're housed and their bairns are shod.'

'Oh, that surprises me. Three of those children back there are barefoot and–' Nathaniel's tone now lost its bantering and became bitter as he ground out, 'You say they can eat and they're housed. Do you know I'd insult a pig by placing it in one of those mud-floored, stinking hovels that you call houses for the men. And the stench from that pit village can be smelt for miles. I considered Rosier's was bad enough, but your place can beat it. Now I'll bid you good day, Mr Praggett. And you can tell your master, when he returns from the big city, exactly what I have said. You can also tell him that my barn will be open to any other of his men you decide to victimise.'

The man stepped back from him as if in order to stretch his arm out and give room to his wagging finger. In a tone of voice that sounded almost like that of an hysterical woman, he cried, 'And your daughter will be out of a job. I'll see to that. She'll be one less for you to live on.'

As Nathaniel raised his arm, fists clenched, Maria's voice cried out from the open doorway, *'No! Nat. No! Don't!'*

Praggett backed away from him, shouting, 'If you start that, you'll get the worst of it. I could knock you flat because you've never done a decent day's work in your life. Flabby bastard!'

Maria was now gripping Nathaniel's arm, whispering, 'Let him go. Let him go. It would only mean trouble.'

They remained close together until the scurrying figure disappeared around the foot of the hill.

'Don't let it upset you. Come on inside. You're cold, I've made a drink.'

Inside the house, Nathaniel slowly lowered himself down into a chair and, resting his elbows on the table, he dropped his head onto his palms, muttering as he did so, 'He'll make trouble.'

'Well, we're used to that. As for sacking Cherry, his wife will have something to say on that point and she'll likely emphasise her words with the frying pan.'

He raised his head and looked up at her. 'That's what they must all be thinking, that I'm living on the children's wages.'

'That's ridiculous. They'll know, as they seem to know everything about us, that you do coaching for the children of two of the best families in the town.'

'They'll forget about that.' He sighed now as he said, 'It's been a funny week-end. The harmony of the house has been broken somehow: first, those two poor families coming in on us; then, this morning, Anna turning up out of the blue like that, and that woman accusing her; and now our latest visitor. What next, I wonder?'

'A cup of tea; it's always heartening. And I'll give Anna a shout; she's down by the wood-pile.' Maria laughed. 'She said she had to take it out on something, so she had better get a chopper and the saw in her hand.'

*

Anna had certainly taken out her feelings with the chopper and the saw. They had previously felled a tree and during the last hour she had stripped it of most of its branches and had cut them into the required lengths on the sawing block and heightened the wood-pile with them.

The wood-pile was arranged against the railings that skirted the boundary of their land. Beyond was part open rough land, part farmland, and it was very rarely that she had seen anyone crossing it except on horseback, when it was usually the Hunt. She hated the Hunt and the hunters because their beloved dog, Rover, had been killed on the occasion of a Hunt. It had become excited and jumped the fence and raced after the riders, and was trampled on. Unlike the hounds, it had not been trained to avoid horses.

She had added the last logs she had sawn up to the wood-pile when her attention was caught by the sight of a riderless horse. She put her hand across her brow to shade her eyes against the weak winter sun that cast its own particular and peculiar white light and, to her surprise, she saw that it wasn't a cart-horse but a saddled one: the reins were trailing on the ground and it was trotting gently and making towards her. Then, coming into sight from around the hedge that bordered part of the field away to the right, was another strange sight: a man was running erratically after the horse. He was calling out something; suddenly he stopped, and Anna watched his arms go up in the air as if to ward off a swarm of bees or wasps. Then, quite distinctly, she heard him utter a weird sound. It came to her like a cry for help.

As she saw the figure fall forward, she herself let out a startled cry. Within seconds she had climbed onto the pile of logs, dislodging a number as she went, and from its flat top she jumped down into the field beyond.

As she ran towards the prostrate figure the horse came towards her and she could see that it was limping. It stopped as if it expected her to do something; and as if it had spoken she shouted at it, 'In a minute. In a minute.'

As she neared the man she stopped, for he was writhing on the ground: he was lying on his back and there was foam round his lips. She noticed that his teeth were clenched but that there were two missing from the upper set. She had never before witnessed anyone in a fit but she knew instinctively that this man was suffering such a seizure. And now she forced herself to go to his side, and as she knelt down by him she took hold of one of his arms, which he was still attempting to flail and, gripping the wrist, she said, 'It's all right. It's all right.' The spasm was subsiding now; his body was rocking from side to side but slowly, as if he was spent.

She groped in the pocket of her coat, an old one that she wore when out working in the garden. There was a piece of linen in it, not a real handkerchief, but it was clean, and tentatively she went to wipe the man's lips; but her hand stayed when his lids suddenly lifted and his eyes gazed upwards. They were blue eyes, as deep a blue as you could find in the sky on a summer's day. She saw now that he wasn't, as she had thought at first, elderly but a man perhaps in his middle forties.

Slowly, he turned his head towards her and his lips moved, but no sound came from them at first; but then, after a moment, she thought he said, 'Sleep'. And she felt sure she had heard aright, for he closed his eyes and turned his head to the side.

She rose from her knees and stood looking down on him as she muttered, 'He . . . he can't stay here. It'll soon be dark.'

She turned about when she thought she heard her mother's voice calling, and looked towards the wood. The horse was standing near the wood-pile now. She again knelt down by

110

the man's side and, shaking him gently by the shoulder, she said, 'Wake up! Wake up! Can . . . can you stand?'

The eyelids flickered as if they were about to open again; then she heard him sigh, and he turned his head as if on a pillow. It could have been he imagined himself to be in bed; so, she thought, there was nothing for it, she must fly back to the house and get her father.

Rising quickly, she picked up her skirts and began to run, and she was half-way across the field when she saw her father. He was standing within the railings to the side of the wood-pile, patting the horse's muscle and she called to him, 'Dada! Dada! Come here.'

His voice came back to her asking, 'What is it?' He obviously hadn't seen her before, or the man, and as she neared him he called, 'Where has this horse come from?'

She leant against the railings, gasping, as she said, 'The man . . . the man who was riding it' – she now flapped her hand against the horse's neck – 'he . . . he had a seizure. He's lying back there in the field.'

'Seizure? What d'you mean, seizure? Did he fall off?'

'I don't know. The horse is lame; it was coming here, and then he appeared. He must have been chasing it, and then he had this . . . well, I suppose it was a fit.'

Nathaniel screwed up his face. 'A fit? How d'you know it was a fit?'

'It couldn't have been anything else. Come, please.'

As he turned hastily from her to make for the wall that abutted the railings, she said, 'Look, you can jump down here from the wood-pile. I did . . . '

As he stood looking down at the figure who had turned on his side and who was now apparently fast asleep, Nathaniel said, 'Dear, dear! God love us! Yes, he must have had an epileptic fit. There was a boy at school; after he'd had a bad one he always slept straightaway. Look, we can't leave him

111

lying here. Run back and tell your mother and bring that piece
of canvas that covers the straw. We'll have to have something
to carry him in. And another thing' – he stopped her as she
was about to run from him – 'tell the women, the pit wives,
to come; we won't be able to manage him on our own.'

Nathaniel now knelt down by the man and loosened the
cravat at his neck, and in doing so exposed a fine wool
shirt which, like the riding jacket, was of the best quality.
He was of the gentry, but from where? He couldn't recall
having seen the face before. He knew of the Wilsons by sight,
from The Hall, but they were at least three miles away. And
the Harrisons from Rowan House. And then there were the
Brodricks. He had only once seen the old man, although the
two sons, Raymond and Simon, he had passed a number of
times. This man he was sure he hadn't seen before. He must
have come quite some distance. But why, being subject to
fits, did he take to riding out alone?

It was a full five minutes before Anna, Maria, and the two
pit wives arrived, and he wanted to say to them, 'Where have
you been? You've taken so long,' for he was feeling somewhat
helpless and frustrated. But what he actually said was, 'Put a
sheet on the ground, and we'll lift him on to it.'

'Who is it?' Maria was asking the question; and when he
answered her, 'I don't know,' one of the pit women stepped
forward and said, 'I do. But however has he got this far? He
hardly goes out. 'Tis Mr Timothy, the mistress's brother.
I used to work there years ago . . . at the Manor. He was
all right once, but the fits started when he came back from
foreign parts. After the mistress was hurt with the snow
coming down on her. They thought she was dead. She might
as well be, 'cos she's hardly moved since. But, 'twas from
then they said he had his fits.'

All the time the woman was talking, they were lifting him
on to the sheet, and now, as if the pit wives had done this

before, each took up a corner of the canvas sheet near the man's head and, as if taking charge, the same woman nodded from Nathaniel to Maria, saying, 'Yous take yon end.' Then turning her attention to Anna, she said, 'And you, miss, better get a hold of that horse, he's wanderin' again. Well . . . one, two, three, and up! with him.'

There was no way of getting their burden into the wood except to walk him along its edge until they came to the gate. In the meantime Anna had run towards the horse calling to him the while; and when he stopped and waited for her, she caught at the bridle, saying gently, 'Come on with you. Come on.'

After stabling the horse and calming him down, she hurried into the house. They had laid the man before the fire, and she asked, 'Has he come round?'

'No sign of it yet,' said Nathaniel, and looking at the two pit wives, he said, 'Thank you for your help;' then spoke to Maria, saying, 'We've got to get word to the Manor because it looks as if he's going to be like this for some time. And anyway, they'll likely be worried and out looking for him by now.'

The two women were already making for the door, and the one who had done all the talking turned and said, 'Well, we'll do anything for you, mister, because you've been kind to us. But that's one thing we couldn't trust ourselves to do, nor let our men do it, I mean, go up to the Manor, 'cos we wouldn't be able to keep our mouths shut; an' the men would likely use more than their tongues.'

'That's all right. That's all right. We'll get word to them. Thanks again. Are you all right over there?'

'Oh, aye, sir, warm and comfortable, and that boiler next door is God's blessin'.'

Maria waited till they had gone before exclaiming, 'Well, *we* can't go, can we, so what's to be done?'

113

'The best thing, probably,' said Nathaniel, 'is to get word to Miss Netherton. She will let Rob drive to the house and then they can take over. Would you go there, dear, and ask her?' He had turned to Anna, and she, looking down on the man, said, 'Yes, I'll go.' And then added, 'I think he'd be more comfortable with a pillow under his head.'

'Well, leave that to me, will you?' And Maria pushed her aside. 'You get about your business and I'll see to mine.'

Outside, Anna again picked up her skirts and ran; and ten minutes later, out of breath, she was knocking on Miss Netherton's front door. And when Ethel Mead opened it she exclaimed, 'Oh, you! What's up? And look at the sight of you.' She pointed to Anna's old coat but Anna ignored her remark and said, 'Is she back yet? I mean, Miss Netherton.'

'No, but she should be any minute. It's near on dark now so she shouldn't be long; she hates being out in the dark. Sh! . . . Listen. There they are now.' Anna ran across the gravel drive and as the trap came to a stop Miss Netherton, looking down on her, cried out, 'What on earth!'

'I'll explain it later, Miss Netherton, but at the moment will you allow Rob to go to The Manor and tell them Mr . . . Mr Brodrick has been hurt and that we have him in the house.'

'Mr Brodrick?' Miss Netherton put out her hand to Rob and said, 'Hold on a minute, Rob, until I know what this is all about.' Again she said, 'Which one? Raymond or Simon?'

'Oh, not those. I understand . . . I think it's . . . well, the pit wives said it was Mr Timothy.'

'Good God! Tim. What was he doing near your place?'

'I think he was riding, but the horse went lame. I saw it running across the field, and . . . and then he came in sight. He . . . he' – she looked from one to the other – 'he had a sort of seizure.'

'Oh, God above! He had one of his fits. Look, Rob, I know it's been a longish drive but get yourself over there

114

and tell them what's happened. Was he hurt?' She was speaking to Anna.

'Not that I know of, but he seemed to want to sleep, just to sleep.'

'Yes, he would. Well, go on, Rob; don't stand there. You'll hear all about it when you get back.'

The old man said something that could have been in the nature of a grumble, but he turned the horse about; and Miss Netherton returned her attention to Anna, saying in much the same way as Ethel had done, 'Why are you dressed like that?'

'Because I've been sawing wood.'

'Sawing wood? What do you mean, sawing wood?'

'Just what I say, sawing wood. I came back this morning. I'm finished.'

'Oh, dear! Oh, dear! Let me get in and sit down.'

Inside the hall she said to Ethel, 'Get me out of this gear, will you? And I want a cup of strong tea. We'll have two cups of strong tea. And bring the decanter in, the brandy; I've had the most trying day and I need sustenance. Now, young woman, come along and tell me the reason why you got the sack, or you left, whichever it is.'

As briefly as possible Anna described what had happened. When she had finished Miss Netherton gazed at her and said, 'Well, you've done it this time. Of course it wasn't your fault, I know, but The Songs of Solomon! Let me tell you, and I could bet on it–' She leaned forward now and there was a grin on her face and a deep chuckle in her voice as she said, 'I bet those songs are Miss Benfield's bedtime reading. But having said that, she's going to make hay out of this. And she was right, you know, there isn't much chance of my getting you set on, at least in Fellburn. Anyway, the weather's terrible and for the next few weeks you'll be saved from that journey. And you may come and talk to me again. That'll make you

115

mind your p's and q's and stop you corrupting young girls.'
She laughed aloud now, and Anna with her.

When Ethel brought in the tea tray there was no decanter in evidence and Miss Netherton said, 'You've taken your time over that. And where's the brandy?'

'I didn't bring it. Remember what you said: you told me not to bring it in before seven o'clock 'cos you just go to sleep after; you don't get any work done.'

'Bring that brandy in, woman! and this minute, or you can pack your box tonight.'

'I won't bother, I'll only have to unpack it in the morning.'

When the door closed on the maid there was a look of glee on Miss Netherton's small face and she said, 'It's so nice when your servants are obliging and courteous and, more than anything else, subservient.'

Their laughter mingled again, but softly; then watching Anna pour out the tea, she said, 'Take that coat off, you look dreadful.'

'I can't take the coat off because I'm going immediately after I drink this cup of tea. I want to know what's happening to that man.'

'Oh, he'll survive. But I wonder why on earth he got on a horse; he couldn't have been on one for years. He spends most of his time in his room or in the conservatory. He grows the most beautiful orchids, you know, and he writes. And he's a very nice fellow at heart, different from the rest. You know that Simon and Raymond's mother, she's the invalid, broke her back enjoying herself in Switzerland? Never liked her. Couldn't get to like her. But there you are, I'm such a hypocrite: I go there and I talk to her and at bottom I'm sorry for her; but more so for Simon, and being married to that upstart of a vixen who's no better than she should be. And I'm sorry for the boy, too, that's Simon's son, you know, he's only three, coming up four ... What! You're

116

going now? Oh, well, I suppose you must; but come over first thing in the morning and let me know what transpired. Better still, I'll go over there and find out all about it myself, because there'll likely be the devil to pay. Raymond's valet is supposed to see to Tim, too, because Raymond spends half his time in Newcastle or Scarborough or London. It's Simon who sees to that place, and that's ruined his career. Go on with you, then. Go on. You're dying to go. But come over in the afternoon and stay to dinner. Don't answer me back. Go on.'

Anna went out smiling, and as she tucked up her skirts and ran the whole length home again, she felt a sense of well-being and happiness. Perhaps it was because she was free and tomorrow she'd be able to enjoy the company and gossip of that little woman.

At the moment, however, there was that poor man with his fits. She wondered if he was awake yet.

The man was awake, but only just. Even so, Maria took Anna to one side before she whispered, 'He seems to be a little' – she tapped her head – 'he asked where the angel was.'

'The angel?'

'Yes, that's what he said: "Where's the angel?" What did Miss Netherton say?'

'She's sending word to the Manor. She seemed to know all about him and said he was a very nice man, but unfortunately had these fits.'

'Is he touched? I mean . . . '

'She didn't seem to think so. Anyway, there'll be somebody here soon from the Manor. Don't worry.'

She went down the room to where her father was sitting in his chair by the side of the man, who certainly looked to be still asleep, and she exchanged a glance with Nathaniel before kneeling down and gently putting her hand on the man's brow, but then quickly withdrew it as the eyelids lifted. The eyes were open wide now and staring at her; and the face went into a smile, the upper lip moved and revealed the gap in the teeth as he said, 'The angel.'

She turned her head quickly and looked from her father to her mother, and Maria nodded at her, as much to say, There, what did I tell you?

The man now sighed and said in quite an ordinary tone, but slowly, 'I thought I had died at last. You are not an angel.'

'No, sir.' She laughed softly down on him. 'In no way am I an angel. Anyway, I think they are all fair-haired.'

He continued to look at her; then he asked quietly, 'Where am I?'

'You are in my home. This is my mother and my father.' She pointed to the two figures now standing to the side of her.

He looked up at Nathaniel and Maria and after a moment he said, 'I am sorry. I am sorry for troubling you. My illness is no respecter of time or . . . or place.'

He made an effort to sit up, and Nathaniel, bending quickly, put his arm around his shoulder. 'Are you fit enough to stand, sir?' he said.

'I . . . I will sit for a while longer if it will not . . . inconvenience you.'

'Not at all. Not at all. You are welcome to stay as long as you like. We have sent word to the Manor.'

The man had been looking at Nathaniel, but now he closed his eyes and his head dropped back as he said, 'Oh, dear me.'

'Would you like a cup of tea, sir?'

The head came forward, the eyes opened and his gaze rested on Maria for some time before he said, 'Tea? Oh, yes, yes; I would indeed be grateful for a cup of tea.'

'We could make you more comfortable in this chair.' Nathaniel pointed to the wooden armchair, but the man said, 'Would you mind if I sat here a little longer? I've . . . well, it is a long long time since I sat on a rug before a fire. It is very pleasant; indeed, yes.'

'By all means, sir; but we'll make you more comfortable. Pull the settle nearer, Maria, and Anna, fetch another couple of pillows.'

A few minutes later their guest was sitting propped up, supported by the weight of the settle, and with a cup of tea placed on a cracket to his side.

'Do you take sugar, sir?'

Looking at Anna, he said, 'No, I don't, but thank you. Yet I have a sweet tooth, a very sweet tooth.' Then he turned his head and stared at Maria, who was standing to the side of him and said, 'And I love sweeties.'

Maria paused as she thought: he said that just like a child, and yet he sounded sensible enough; and in her kindly way she now answered him, 'And so do I, sir, but I rarely get a chance to indulge myself, because my family are there before me whenever I make toffee.'

He smiled. 'You make toffee?' he said.

'Yes, once a week; cinder and treacle.'

'Cinder and treacle.' What he would have said further was interrupted by a voice, crying, 'Ma! Ma! It's me; I've got the push. He gave me the push, but the missis says I've got to turn up in the morning. They're going at it . . . '

Cherry's voice trailed away as she entered the room from the kitchen and she stood open-mouthed for a moment, looking at the man sitting on the mat. 'One of these days, daughter, you'll come in quietly,' Nathaniel half-grumbled at her. 'This gentleman has had a slight accident.' Then looking down on the man, he said, 'This is my daughter, Mr . . . ?'

'Oh. How do you do?' The inclination of his head was towards Cherry; but then he turned and looked at Nathaniel, saying, 'My name is Barrington, Timothy Barrington.'

And to this Nathaniel answered, 'And ours is Martell.' He glanced towards Maria as if he were saying, Well, it will be in a few days' time.

When there came a knock on the door Anna, being nearest to it, opened it and standing there she made out the figure of the man who, earlier in the day, she had laughed with and who, for no reason she could understand, had made her want to cry.

'I understand . . . ? '

'Oh, do come in.'

He stepped into the lamplit room, then turned and stared at her, shaking his head, and she had the feeling he was about to remark on this being their second meeting in one day; but then, becoming aware of others standing round the fire at the far end of the room, he apologised: 'I am sorry for the inconvenience,' he said.

'There has been no inconvenience to us, sir.' Nathaniel was coming towards him. 'Will you come in, please?'

Simon Brodrick followed Nathaniel up the room towards the fire; then stood as if in amazement, looking down onto the mat to where Mr Barrington was sitting, and said with some concern, 'Oh! Tim.'

And Mr Barrington answered, 'Oh, Simon; now don't you start. I just had to get out else I would have exploded.'

'Well, you did explode, didn't you?'

'Yes. Yes, I suppose I did, but I was going on the fact that it hadn't happened for . . . oh, weeks and weeks. Well . . . ' His voice trailed away.

Simon now dropped onto his hunkers and the two men looked at each other, and for the moment it was as if they were alone, such was the way they spoke, for Simon said, 'If you wanted to ride so badly why couldn't you have told me? I would have come with you.'

'Yes, I knew you would, but, my dear fellow, I'm sick of people; I'm sick of close proximity, even of you.' He now lifted a hand and pushed at Simon, and as Simon got to his feet he looked at Maria, and began, 'I'm sorry we've had to inconvenience . . .' only to be interrupted by Timothy Barrington saying, 'I'm not, Simon. No, I'm not sorry this has happened, because these dear people have been so kind to me and they have let me sit on the rug by the fire. How long is it since you sat on a rug by a fire, Simon?'

Simon looked down on him and said, 'As usual, you are well enough to talk and prompt an argument, but are you well enough to get on to your feet?'

'Yes. Yes. Give me your hand.'

Between them Nathaniel and Simon drew him to his feet, then sat him in the wooden chair. Once seated, he looked about him, taking in first Maria, then Nathaniel, then the small boy who was standing by his side, then the two girls who were standing together, one very dark and one very fair, and both beautiful. Then he sighed and, turning his head towards Simon, he asked, 'What did you bring?' And when Simon answered, 'The coach,' of a sudden he put his fingers to his mouth and felt the gap in his teeth, saying in some surprise now, 'I must have lost the two of them when I fell.' And now he started to laugh but stopped abruptly and, his eyes blinking, he looked at Nathaniel as he said, 'You must think it's a very queer fellow who is partaking of your hospitality. Perhaps on our further acquaintance I can prove to you that I am just odd and not all that queer.'

This brought a laugh from Nathaniel and he answered, 'Odd or queer, sir, it would be my pleasure; in fact, the pleasure of all of us, were you to partake of our hospitality whenever you feel so inclined.'

'Splendidly put. Don't you think so?' He turned his head and looked at Simon, and Simon answered, 'You wouldn't

121

expect it otherwise from a learned man. Mr Martell is a teacher, a tutor.'

'Is that so? Well, sir, I shall certainly take you up on your invitation. But now I really must go, for indeed I have outstayed my welcome.'

When, with the support of Simon, he stood up and walked towards the door, Anna noticed he didn't look as tall or as big-built as when he was lying down. His height would be about five-foot seven and, although he was thick-set, his figure was in no way bulky.

At the door he turned and said a single, 'Good-bye,' which included them all. But Simon Brodrick said nothing until, with the help of the coachman, he had placed his errant relative in the coach and had then hurried back to the door of the house, where Maria and Nathaniel were standing with the girls behind them, and here, looking first at Maria and then at Nathaniel, he said, 'I'm indebted to you. But about the horse?'

'Oh, yes, the horse.' Nathaniel turned to Anna: 'You've put him in the stable?' he asked.

'Yes. He'll be all right there until morning.'

'Thank you. I'll send for him first thing.'

'He'll have to go to the blacksmith; he sprang a shoe.'

'Likely that was the reason for . . . for the trouble. Thank you again. Good-night.'

They all answered, 'Good-night'; then they watched the driver turn the coach and make for the field gate that led on to a rough path on the edge of the open land and connected with the coach road.

When the door was closed, Nathaniel looked from one to the other and said, 'What a day! My two daughters have been sacked from their posts, I have been assailed and told that I might end up in the House of Correction, and now one of the scions of the aristocracy has an epileptic fit and ends

122

up on our mat' – he indicated the mat with a sweep of his hand – 'and further, another scion drives his coach to our door and we are thanked most graciously for our services. Do you realise, Miss Maria Dagshaw, that this day could be a turning point in our lives?'

And Maria, taking up his tone, said, 'I do indeed, Mr Martell. I do indeed. So much so that no-one must sit on that end of the mat; I'm going to cut it off and hang it on the wall.'

'Oh, I'd leave it there until the boys get in,' said Nathaniel; and Anna joined in the general laughter, even though she was thinking: Turning point in their lives? Her dada could be naïve at times; nothing could alter what they already were, what he himself had made them; not even their forthcoming marriage would or could erase the stain. And whatever condescending patronage they might receive from The Manor wasn't going to help either. Oh no. Nevertheless, she was experiencing the same feeling as she had done when, withdrawing her hand from Mr Simon Brodrick's, she had then turned from him and walked along the quarry path.

5

The news seemed to set the village on fire: those two from the Hollow had nerve to go and get married after breeding that lot. And what d'you think? Miss Netherton was there, at the church, so it was said, and also at the do they had when the lot of them returned home. And that wasn't all. Oh, no. It was unbelievable but true, flowers and fruit had been sent from The Manor. To that lot of scum! And why? That's the question, why? Oh, there was something behind this, and you needn't go very far to see the reason for it. Tommy Taylor could tell you; he saw them with his own eyes. He was picking up the letters for the second delivery when he saw Mr Simon Brodrick with that young piece. She came into the post office as bold as brass and waited for him, and then he handed her up into the gig. *He saw it.* And what was more, he saw Mr Harry Watson chatting to Mr Simon while she sat perched up there. Now, if you asked him, there was the reason for the flowers sent to the Hollow. But the nerve of that young hussy. Like mother, like daughter.

Some said they were surprised that it was Mr Simon she had caught, and him married with a three-year-old son. Now had it been Mr Raymond, they could have understood it. Yet, who could understand any decent man going within spitting distance of one of that litter. And that particular one was supposed to have been in a position of a teacher in Fellburn. Well, that surely was another cover-up, 'cos who would take her on? They would like to bet that young gillyvor had a house there, and what she taught wasn't the a.b.c.

This was the talk in the village before the end of the year 1880, but by the beginning of March, 1881, the villagers were dumbfounded by the news that that one was being taken on at The Manor to instruct the young son in his letters and such. And not only that, Mr Timothy, the one that had fits, had been seen walking across the moor with her. What next! What next! But to think the hussy had the nerve to push herself into the house, and under her mistress's very nose. But there was one thing sure, she wouldn't reign long there, not under the young Mrs Brodrick, she wouldn't. If she got wind of this, she would skin that one alive, for didn't she have a temper like a fiend? Well, there was going to be sparks flying. Just you wait.

But here and there in the village, there were those as well as a farmer or two round about, who dared to voice their doubts about this general opinion of the young gillyvor. Nobody had seen her out riding with Simon Brodrick since that day Tommy Taylor saw her. As for her walking with Mr Timothy, well, there was some talk of her finding him in the field, when he had a turn on him, and he had been taken into their house.

That couldn't be true, they were told; it was well known Timothy hardly moved out of the grounds.

Yes, that was true. But why keep on about them down in The Hollow; the couple were married now; they'd had the ceremony performed as soon as it had become possible.

Yes, they knew that, but it didn't make any difference; the bairns were still bastards.

But, said the moderate ones, you couldn't get over the fact that they were all well spoken and in decent jobs and they kept themselves to themselves.

As Miss Netherton said, after listening to Ethel, who related the gossip she had drawn out of Rosie Boyle, who came in from the village daily and acted as a housemaid, it could be that there were now two camps of thought in the village, and it wasn't before time. But she'd be sorry if the day ever came when all the inhabitants turned into kindly sensible people, to include the parson and, of course, his wife, because then she would realise they had all died, including herself.

PART THREE

The Child

1

'Must you go to this house, Anna?'

'It isn't that I must go, Ben; I want to go. I want to teach and it's an amazing opportunity that's been offered to me, practically on the doorstep, you could say. What is wrong, Ben?'

The boy took her hand as they walked across the frost-spangled ground towards the wood, and in an affectionate gesture he leant his head against her arm for a moment as he said, 'I shall miss you.'

She stopped and looked down at him. 'But it will be the same as when I was at the Academy, even better. I don't have to be at the Manor until nine and I leave again at four, and the journey will be over in a flash, because they are being kind enough to take me back and forth in the gig. You'll see much more of me than you did last year.'

His eyes were showing a sad expression, more so than usual. Suddenly, she stooped down to him and, taking his face between her hands, she said, 'What is it that's troubling you, Ben?'

'I don't know. It's just that I don't want you to go. I feel sad at your going.'

'Did you not feel sad last year when I went to the Academy?'

'No. No, I never felt sad then.'

'Oh, Ben.' She pulled him suddenly into her arms, and he pressed his head against her waist and they hugged each other; then she took his hand again and they walked in silence for some way, until she said, 'The others were happy for me when they left. Oswald and Olan, didn't they make you laugh when they dipped their knee to me? And Cherry, look how she acted the goat and said how she was going to cock a snook at Mr Praggett. And Ma and Dada and Jimmy are so glad for me. There's only you, and now you make me sad because you're so very dear to me, and you are not wishing me happiness in my new position.'

'Oh, I am, I am, Anna. I wish you to be happy. All the time I wish you to be happy, all the time I wish you to be happy.'

'All right, all right. Then don't get depressed; but what is it?'

'I don't know, Anna, just a sadness inside me.'

'Oh, Ben.' She looked down on him, troubled: Ben to say he was sad. He was the happy one, yet there was something in this small brother of hers to which she couldn't put a name. Was he fey? No, no; there was nothing pixyish about Ben. He was a boy, a highly intelligent boy. He had the power to learn so quickly. At times he surprised her, for he seemed to know the answer before half the question was put to him.

As she looked towards the wood, she could hear the sound of the axe coming from the far end. Her father was at the wood block and she must have a word with him before she went; she must say something to him that she couldn't say in front of her mother, in case it should worry her. So now, looking down on Ben, she said, 'I want a word with Dada. Look; go over to the gate and as soon as you sight the gig, come back here and whistle. Will you do that?'

130

'Yes, Anna; yes.' He ran from her and she now hurried through the wood. And Nathaniel, stopping his work at her approach, called, 'You're ready, then?'

'Yes, I'm ready, Dada. And it looks as if you've kept out of my way.'

'Perhaps you're right, dear, perhaps you're right. But now you're all ready and set to go?'

'Not quite, Dada; I want to say something.'

'Well, say it, my dear, say it.'

'I'm frightened.'

'Frightened? What about?'

'I don't really know. I'm like Ben. I asked him why he didn't want me to go to The Manor, and that's what he said: he didn't know.'

'If you feel like that, my dear, you shouldn't go. But who are you frightened of, or what are you afraid of? Not the teaching?'

'Oh, no, not the teaching, Dada. You know that. And it isn't so much that I'm frightened, it's that I have taken a strong dislike to someone.'

'Whom have you taken a dislike to? You've only been there the once.'

'Yes, I know, but that was long enough. It's the child's mother.'

'Now that doesn't augur good for your stay.'

'Oh, I don't think she'll trouble me much in the school-room. The nurse indicated that she never bothered about anything but her painting and horse-riding. And from what I gathered from the talkative old woman when I met her, the mistress took long spells in London and abroad. I also gathered that there was little love between the old nurse and the young mistress, although she's not all that young; she's over thirty.'

'What exactly has made you dislike her?'

'Everything about her: the tone of her voice, how she looks at one. I didn't tell you, but she surveyed me up and down as a farmer might a beast in the cattle-pen in the market. I fully expected her to prod me.' She gave a little laugh here and, leaning towards him, she said, 'Can you imagine the result of that action, should it have happened?'

Nathaniel laughed outright now. 'By! yes, I can, and that would be the end before the beginning of your tutoring. And you would likely have ended up in the House of Correction instead of me, and I've been threatened so many times of late. Now, my dear, whatever you do and whatever the provocation, you must endeavour to keep your temper.'

'But, Dada, I don't feel that I've got a bad temper. Well, what I mean is, not a regular bad temper. I have to be aggravated beyond endurance before . . . '

'Oh my! Oh my!' He had his hands on her shoulders now. 'Would that we could see ourselves as others see us. I am a mild man, they say – some pity me for my mildness – but there was a time last year when, if I hadn't been checked by your ma, I would surely have laid out Mr Praggett. But I am a mild man' – he shook his head at himself – 'who prefers to fight with his tongue. But none of us knows what we are capable of until the circumstances arise. It all depends upon circumstances and the feelings they arouse in one. There would be few murders if it weren't for the circumstances leading to them. We'll have to get on to that subject sometime, my dear; circumstances. Ah, there's Ben's whistle. Is that a signal that your golden carriage has arrived? Come on. Come on. And make up your mind, my dear, that the only time you will raise your voice is in laughter or in defence of someone, or extolling someone's good points.'

'Oh, Dada, shut up! Stop your preaching.' She turned to him and, throwing her arms around his neck, she kissed him, saying, 'I love you. Do you know that? You mild man, I love you.' Then, as if in embarrassment, she hurried ahead of him.

It was a young lad who was standing by the gig. He took off his cap as Anna and Nathaniel approached; then said, with a broad Irish accent, 'I'm Barry McBride, miss. I'm for to take you to the house. If you'll get up, if you're ready, we'll be away, 'cos I'm a bit late. I had a bit trouble with him.' He thumbed towards the horse. 'He's fresh.'

Anna glanced from Nathaniel to Maria, who had now joined them, and Ben who was by her side, and she said, 'I'll be away, then,' and there was just a suspicion of the Irish twang in her words which brought a twinkle to Nathaniel's eyes and he answered, 'I would, then. I'd be away with you and not keep Mr McBride waitin'.'

'Oh, sir' – the boy turned to Nathaniel – 'I'm never mistered. I'm just McBride, number two.'

'Oh,' said Nathaniel, 'number two? Why number two?'

' 'Cos I'm the second stable lad. Me brother, he's number one. He's by the name of Frank, but we're both called McBride.'

'Oh, I see, I see.' Nathaniel nodded as if the explanation had enlightened him. Then putting his hand under Anna's elbow, he said, 'Up! you go then and away.'

McBride number two now put his cap on, went round to the other side of the gig and seemed to launch himself up in one movement into the narrow seat beside Anna. As he did so the whole vehicle swayed, and when McBride number two called, 'Up! Milligan,' the horse seemed to rear slightly before turning around and having to be checked to prevent his going into a gallop.

So quickly did they leave the front of the house and make for the gate that she had no time to wave a goodbye, for it was taking all her attention to hang on to the iron rail support of the seat to keep her balance. But once on the

133

road and going at a steadier pace, she called to him, 'Why do you call the horse "Milligan"?'

'What is that you're after sayin', miss?'

Raising her voice, she cried, 'Why do you call the horse "Milligan"? It's a strange name for a horse.'

'Oh, that, miss. Well, 'tis the yard's name for him. He's really called Caster, but he's got this fightin' spirit in him. You see, miss? An' the Milligans are like that. There's three of 'em in the pit, Rosier's pit, an' two in the Beulah, an' if they're not at each other they're at anybody that passes their way, 'specially us. We're kin, you see, by birth, cousins. An' this one here is the spitting image, in his manner, like, of Michael the eldest, who kicks out at his own shadow. He shouldn't be used for the gig at all. But they want to quieten him down, they say, an' there's as much hope for that as the man prayin' for heaven while he's shovellin' overtime in hell. But what's my opinion? for it counts for little in the stableyard.'

Anna hung on tightly to her support, because her body was shaking now, and not only from the motion of the gig, as she thought, Well, whatever happens between times, I'll surely be entertained on my way there and back if I can differentiate between Michael the cousin and Milligan the horse . . .

As they bowled up the long drive, McBride number two said, 'It's me orders to drop you in the back way, miss. I questioned that to number one, you bein' a learned lady, and as usual he said for me to keep me gob . . . mouth shut, an' use me eyes an' just open me ears for orders. So it isn't me doin', miss, that you be dropped at the back door.'

'That's quite all right, Mr McBride.'

'I wouldn't be doing that, miss, as I said back yonder, I mean "mister" me; they'll scoff me lugs off.'

'Very well, I'll remember . . . McBride.'

134

'That's it, miss; give everybody his due, nothin' over and nothin' under, an' the world won't rock.'

She mustn't enter even the lower precincts of this establishment laughing, but oh, how she wished her Dada or Ma or any of them could have been on this journey with her. She looked at the red-haired boy as he helped her down on to the flagged yard, and again she had to compose her face as she imagined the effect on them all, were he sitting on the mat among them of an evening.

But, within a moment or two, there was no need for her to make an effort to compose her features, for after McBride number two had led her to the back door amidst a stoppage of work in what had been a busy yard, the door was opened by a young girl whose uniform told Anna that she could be termed a menial, and yet her features were expressing a look that didn't complement such a position, for, whether she was aware of it or not, the look on her face expressed disdain.

At first, the girl didn't speak, but walked ahead of Anna through a long, narrow boot room, then across a large scullery, before thrusting open a door and exclaiming to someone beyond, 'She's here!'

Anna stepped into the kitchen, to be confronted by three pairs of eyes, and immediately she took in the situation. The hostility was almost visible, and she met it as she meant to meet all such. Addressing the big woman in the white-bibbed apron and large starched cap, she said, 'Will you kindly inform Mrs Hewitt that I am come and wish to be shown to the schoolroom . . . ?'

As the cook said later, when seated at the head of the lower staff in the servants' dining room, you could have knocked her down with a feather. The cheek of that one, and the voice. Why! Miss Conway didn't talk like that and she was a lady's maid.

135

The cook, now addressing one of the girls standing near, said, 'Go and fetch her.'

What followed this, as the cook again said later, almost caused her to flop on to the floor, for that one dared to walk up the kitchen and cast her eyes over the array of china on the long dresser, then turn about and sort of examine the bread oven and the stove. If Mrs Hewitt hadn't come in at that moment, she would surely have let her have it.

When Mrs Hewitt came into the kitchen, she approached Anna, then looked at her in silence for a moment before she said, 'Will you come this way?'

Her tone was civil but her mien stiff.

Anna followed her out of the kitchen into a corridor, from which a number of doors led off. The end one was open and showed the outside yard, and the housekeeper, pointing, said, 'You'll go through this door when taking the young master for his walks.' Then again leading the way, she mounted a flight of stairs and, stopping on the landing, she again pointed, this time to a door on her left, saying, 'Never use that. That leads to the gallery and the house.'

She opened the other door and they now ascended a flight of stairs which led on to a wide landing, almost like a room with a sloping roof on one side. A number of doors led off, and the housekeeper, unceremoniously opening one, stepped into a room, saying, 'She's arrived, Eva.'

'Oh, come away in. Come away in.'

'How's your back?'

'Oh, the same, Mary. I can't expect any change in it now. By the way, did you see Peggy on the stairs?'

'No. No sight of her.'

'By! I'll put a cracker in that one's drawers afore I'm finished. She's been gone fully five minutes with the slops. Sit down, lass.' The nurse flapped her hand towards Anna; and the housekeeper said, 'She knows the rules'; and turning to Anna, she said, 'I've explained them to you, but they'll be put in writing. Today, though, you'll be sent for at half-past ten; the mistress wishes to see you. Is there anything more you would like to know?'

'Not at present, thank you.'

The housekeeper's bust could in no way be compared with that of Miss Benfield as regards its size, but nevertheless it followed the same action as that lady's and expressed its owner's thoughts more than words could do at the moment.

The housekeeper now turned a knowing look on the nurse, then abruptly left the room. And Eva Stanmore, looking at Anna, chuckled as she said, 'It would be advisable, lass, if you altered your tone when speaking to them above you.'

When Anna made no answer the old woman chuckled again and said, 'You likely don't consider them in that way, eh?' And when Anna again made no reply, she said, 'Well, it's up to you. Yet, I suppose if you went on your knees you couldn't change people's opinions. There's a lot of ignor . . . ramuses in this world. Anyway, the child's all ready. He's sitting in there waiting, as good as gold; not that he's always as good as gold, but he's got quite a bit up top for his age and he's interested in somebody new coming to look after him. He seemed to like what he saw in you the other day.'

'I'm pleased.'

'Aye, well, that's your room.' She pointed across to what was evidently her sitting-room. 'There's a cupboard in there for you to hang your clothes, and the master's put in the things that you'll need: slates and pencils and things like that. And, of course, the child's got his own bricks and toys.'

Anna had risen to her feet and, as she made her way to the door indicated, the nurse said, 'You're a funny lass.'

At this Anna stopped and, looking down on to the wrinkled face, she said, 'And you're a funny woman, but in a nice way,' and they smiled at each other before the old woman said, 'Go on! you.' And she went.

The schoolroom was well lit by two long windows, and standing gazing out of one was her charge.

At her approach he turned quickly, and she held out her hand and said, 'Good morning, Andrew.'

'Hello. Good morning. Did you see the horses going out? Look.' He grabbed her hand and drew her to the window, then pointed downwards, and she saw three horses being led from the yard.

'I have a pony.'

'You have? That's splendid. You like riding?'

'Yes, when I don't fall off.' His mouth went into a wide grin.

She took off her hat and coat and hung them in the cupboard, then looked round the room. It was quite comfortable. There was a wooden table on which there were books and slates, pencils and paper, already laid. An abacus was standing to the side of the table. There was another table against the far wall on which were coloured blocks with letters on them. And what struck her was everything looked new and unused. At the far end of the long room a fire was burning brightly in a small grate, which had an iron guard around it. And what she found unusual was a large leather armchair set to the side of the fireplace. Did that indicate she would have time to sit down and relax?

When she stood by the table examining the plain exercise books and those for copying scripts, the child said, 'Papa bought them, but I have a lot more, and my colouring books.'

'Show me.'

He ran to a row of low cupboards that took up part of one wall and, kneeling down, he opened one of the doors and pulled out an assortment of books, including cloth ones, and as he strewed them round him, he looked up at her brightly, saying, 'I like making pictures, not learning letters, just making pictures.'

Anna picked up one of the books and looked at the splash of colour on a page, and she nodded down at him and said, 'And yes, yes, you're very clever at making pictures. But I'm sure you'll be just as clever learning your letters. And we'll paint the letters, too, and the numbers.'

'I can count up to ten.'

'Oh, that's good. Come on, let me hear you.'

As she caught his hand he tugged her to a stop, saying, 'Will you take me for a walk this afternoon?'

'Yes, my dear, yes, if you would like that.'

'I would like that, please.'

She had the desire to stoop, sweep him into her arms and hug him. As she looked down into his face and he looked up into hers she knew she would love this child.

Betty Carter, the upper housemaid, came for her at twenty past ten. She didn't greet her in any way; she just stared at her.

A few minutes before this, nurse had called her from the schoolroom into her sitting room. There she said, 'You will have to go in a minute or so. I'm not gona say anything. It wouldn't be any use, would it, to tell you to keep your tongue still, no matter what's said to you. You're of that type, and being brought up as you have been, you're at a disadvantage, fallin' atween two stools, as it were. Well, go on; get along with you.'

Anna took no offence at the old woman's talk, for she had felt she was going to like her and that, in what she had said, she was wishing her well.

She was now on the middle landing and going through the forbidden door, and without moving her head she took in the broad corridor, with its four deep bay windows. From this, they passed into an upper hall. Here a balustrade bounded an open gallery, and from it a grand staircase led down to the ground floor.

Two corridors went off the gallery and the maid, walking quickly a step ahead of her, led her down the one to the right-hand side, which had a number of doors on one side of it, while the wall opposite was hung with pictures. They turned a corner and into yet another corridor, a shorter one this time, and at the end of which was a flight of three steps leading up to a door, and on this Betty Carter knocked twice.

There was quite a long pause before the order came to enter. And the next moment Anna found herself walking past the maid and into a large room, bare except for a long wooden table on which there was an array of jars containing brushes, a number of palettes, and a great quantity of paints. Opposite this table, some lying against the wall and some on the floor, were a number of canvasses. But standing by an easel, which was set at an angle to a long window, was the lady to whom she had been bidden to present herself.

There was also another person in the room, and she recognised him as the second man in the gig. He was standing some distance from the easel and, unlike his companion, he turned and looked at her with a hard penetrating stare. Then without speaking at all he strode past her and the maid and left the room.

Betty Carter now approached her mistress who, it would seem, was unaware of her presence, yet when the girl spoke while dipping her knee and said, 'I brought her, ma'am,' her mistress said, 'Very well. You may go.'

When the door had closed on the girl, Anna slowly walked up the room until she was about six feet from the woman; and there she stopped and waited. She watched her put her head to one side while staring at the canvas on the easel, then put out a hand and stroke some paint on to it. But it was only after she had turned completely round, placed her brush and palette on the table, then wiped her hands on a towel that was laid by the side of a bowl of water, did she turn and look fully at Anna, saying now, 'You know you are on probation?'

Anna hadn't been aware that she was on probation, but she answered, 'If you say so, madam.'

'I do say so.' It was a bawl. The woman was glaring at her now, her face suffused with temper. And Anna returned her stare, until the woman turned to the table again and squeezed some paint out on to the palette, then picked up the brush and returned to the easel. And once more she was applying the paint to the canvas. There was no sound in the room, and Anna was about to say, 'May I take my leave, madam,' when the woman said in a surprisingly quiet tone now, 'How long have you known my husband?'

The question forced Anna to screw up her face in some perplexity, as she said, 'What did you say, madam?'

'You heard what I said, girl.' The eyes were still directed towards the canvas, but the voice had changed. It was deep and seemed to have a threat in it. And, in answer, her own tone changed: she forgot the nurse's advice and admonition as she said, 'I don't understand you, madam. I have only known Mr Brodrick for a matter of months. I first saw him and the gentleman who has just left when out riding with Miss Netherton.'

'You are lying, girl.'

'I am not lying, madam. I don't lie. I have no need to lie. I have seen your husband twice since that time: the first after I left my post in Fellburn and had missed the cart and had to walk home, when your husband was on his way to the post office and he kindly offered me a lift part of the way.

141

The other time was when Mr Timothy had a seizure and we brought him to our home and your husband came to collect him. Then, I had a letter asking if I would take the post and . . . '

The woman turned to her now and held up her hand, crying, 'Enough! Enough!' Then she stood looking at her, staring into her face, which she felt to be flushed, and with an imperious movement of her hand she said, 'You may go.'

Anna did not immediately turn about, but returned the woman's stare for a moment, and when she did turn she was halted again by the voice saying, 'Girl!' and she stopped in her walk, but she did not this time turn round and the voice went on: 'You will be wise if you forget our conversation. You'll also be wise if you watch your tongue and speak only when you're spoken to, and then briefly. I hope you understand me?'

Still Anna did not turn round but walked ahead towards the door.

The woman's scream almost lifted her from her feet.

'*Girl!*'

Slowly Anna forced her body round and she wouldn't have been surprised if, like Mr Timothy, the woman had gone into a seizure as the words were flung at her like darts: 'Don't you dare! ever dare stand with your back to me when I'm speaking to you. Do you hear me? Answer me!'

'Yes, madam, I hear you.'

'Well, hear you this: you will stand there until I give you leave to go.'

Before the last word hit her she was almost pushed on to her face by the door being abruptly opened, and then a voice said, 'Oh, I'm sorry. I'm sorry. Oh, good morning. You arrived, then.'

She looked at the kindly face of Timothy Barrington, and at this moment she had the desire to burst into tears, for his

142

warm greeting coming on top of that woman's tirade was almost too much for her.

When he held the door open for her, she did not wait for the order of dismissal from her mistress, but walked past him without a word. And she almost fell off the second step into the corridor.

Some minutes later, when she reached the top landing and was making for the schoolroom door, Peggy Maybright, coming out of it with an empty coal-scuttle in her hand, exclaimed, 'Eeh! What's the matter with you, teacher? You look like a piece of lint.'

She didn't answer the girl, but went into the schoolroom and closed the door none too gently.

The child was sitting at the table and he turned and said, 'I can't count with Peggy, teacher; she's silly.'

What she should have said in admonition was, 'You mustn't call anyone silly.' Instead, she sat down opposite him and when she rested her head on her hand he enquired, 'Have you a headache, teacher?'

As she was about to say, 'Yes, dear, I have a headache,' the door leading into Nurse Stanmore's room opened and the old woman called to her, 'I'd like a word with you if you have a minute. And you, Master Andrew, keep on with what you're doing, that's a good lad.'

Reluctantly, it would seem, she rose from the chair and went slowly towards the nurse, who, still holding open the door, now closed it behind them, before turning to her and asking, 'She go for you?'

Anna swallowed deeply, then said, 'Yes. Yes, you could say she went for me.'

'What about?'

'Nothing that I can give any reasonable answer to. She . . . she just went for me. Whatever I said . . . '

'Did you cheek her?'

143

'No, certainly not. I just spoke and answered her questions.'

'Sit yourself down. You look shaken.'

'No, and I must tell you, I don't intend to stay.'

'Ah, now, come on. Come on. If it's any comfort to you we've all gone through the mill with her, some of us for no reason. She's got a temper like a fiend. The house has never been the same since the day she stepped into it. Sometimes I think she's not right in the head but' – she nodded now knowingly – 'she's all right in one direction, that's where blokes are concerned. Why, in the name of God, Master Simon took her on and didn't let the other one manage her, God alone knows; but he's dealt with her in his own fashion, and it's put years on him. If it wasn't for madam, his mother, he'd be gone long afore now. Anyway, it's about time for her trip to London. She goes up about this time of the year, sometimes stays a couple of months, going round exhibitions and things. But it's my opinion she goes around more than exhibitions. Oh aye, I know what I know. So be a good lass, and I'll bet you a shilling when Mr Simon gets word of this, she'll leave you alone. And he's concerned that the boy should be learning his letters and such. To tell you the truth, I'm glad he's taking an interest in him. He didn't seem to bother much afore, except that he told me to get him out of those petticoats and into pants. But as I said, you don't usually breech them till they're five. But you know what he said to me? In that case, by the time he was five, he'd be playing with dolls. So the poor bairn is going to be breeched shortly. Making him old afore his time, I say. But there you are, that's today. Look, hold your hand a minute and sit yourself down in that chair.'

She now almost pushed Anna into the leather chair before going to a cabinet at the far end of the room, from which she took out a bottle and a wine glass, which she then filled from the bottle and said, 'Drink that.'

144

'What is it?'

'Nothing but what could do you good. It isn't spirits, 'tis herbs. I have it made up specially, as me mother did afore her. It's a cure for most things except' – she laughed now – 'bad legs, rheumatism, and heartache. Oh, and I've known it help that, an' all. Anyway, it'll pull you together.'

The potion tasted very nice, like honey, but with a tang to it; and after draining the glass, she said, 'It's very pleasant-tasting.'

'Aye, I've always found it so meself. And you'll find it'll work on you the lower it drops into you.'

Anna rose to her feet and, looking at the old nurse, she said, 'You're very kind, and . . . and your kindness contrasts with the feeling against me I've already experienced since coming into this house.'

'Oh, take no notice. We're not all alike. But some can't help being ignorant. And there's always a mixture in every household. Now, go into the boy and give him of your best.'

Anna looked at this old woman, and again kind words were about to be her downfall, so she turned swiftly away and went into the schoolroom and began to give the boy . . . of her best . . .

It was about an hour afterwards when a tap came on the outer door of the schoolroom and after calling, 'Come in,' she rose to her feet at the sight of Mr Timothy Barrington entering the room.

'Am I disturbing you?'

As she said, 'No, not at all,' the boy jumped from his chair, saying, 'Oh, Uncle Tim, have you come to take lessons?'

'Well, I need them, Andrew, but I don't think Miss . . . Dagshaw will have time to bother with me, because you have such a lot to learn. What are you doing now?' He was looking down on to the table, then he exclaimed, 'Oh, you have drawn a dog!'

145

'No, no' – the boy laughed now – 'silly; it's a cat.'

'But where are its whiskers?'

'I haven't put them on yet, Uncle.'

'Oh, I see. Well, I think you had better, and put some legs on it, too. Then let me see what it looks like when you complete it. Go on. Do it carefully.'

As the child scrambled back onto his seat again, Timothy walked to the window, saying, 'You have a lovely view from up here, Miss Dagshaw. A most pleasant room to be taught in. I remember the schoolroom at my home: it was so dull, the windows very high. I understand they were placed so in order not to distract the pupils. And, of course, in a way, I can understand the reason. We were five young boys and three young girls, the result of my father's second marriage. His previous one had only produced my half-sister, who was past fifteen when I came on the scene . . . '

He laughed and said, 'Don't look so perplexed, but is it any wonder, the way I keep jabbering on? Madam' – he pointed now towards the floor – 'Mrs Brodrick senior is my half-sister.'

Anna nodded. 'Yes. Oh yes, I understand,' she said.

He leant towards the window and in a lower voice now, he said, 'You've had a taste of Mistress Brodrick junior's temper. One wall of my sitting room also happens to be the wall of her studio. Her high notes at times penetrate through it. I knew you had been called to the throne room; I saw you from the far corridor. I . . . I just want to say, don't let it disturb you. Simon, my nephew, will, I am sure, make things plain to his wife that it was he who engaged you, so you will not be so disturbed in the future. I . . . I am so sorry you have been subjected to this on your first day here.

'My sister would never have allowed such a thing to take place. By the way' – he glanced at her – 'perhaps you know she is an invalid, but as soon as she feels able, she would like to have a word with you.'

'Thank you for your concern, but I don't think I shall be able to stay on.'

He turned quickly towards her and said, 'Oh. Oh, give it a chance. I mean, don't let this . . . well, it will upset his father' – he nodded towards the boy – 'very much if he knows that his wife is the cause of his son's being deprived of your tuition. Do, please, re-consider. Anyway, she is leaving for London shortly. She spends a lot of her time there and' – now he smiled – 'when that happens the house returns to normal.' He leaned towards her and in a conspiratorial whisper said, 'Without exception, we all breathe easily during the respite and gather strength for the next onslaught.'

She was forced to return his smile; then, quickly changing the subject, he asked brightly, 'How is your family? And that cheery sister? I have meant to come across and visit you but . . . but I've been rather taken up with my own doings. You see, I . . . I write . . . well, I'm interested in history, but now and then I write silly stuff, like poetry.' He whispered the word, and she actually laughed as she said, 'You do? How interesting! I, too, attempt to write silly stuff.'

'That's wonderful! Wonderful! I must read some of your work.'

'Oh, no! Never. It's merely rhyme, not real poetry . . . '

'Look! Uncle . . . there.'

They turned towards the table to see the boy holding out a sheet of paper. Timothy took it, and looked at the drawing and exclaimed in admiration, 'Oh! yes. Yes; *that* is a cat.'

'It isn't, Uncle; I've changed it into a dog. Don't you know the difference?'

Timothy looked at Anna. 'I am stupid,' he said, 'I am the most stupid fellow on this earth. I must go away now and look up books and learn to know the difference between a

147

dog and a cat.' Then, turning to the boy again he said, 'You can laugh. You can laugh heartily like that, but everyone isn't able to draw like you can. I must be away now, I really must. Be a good boy. Goodbye. I'll pop in tomorrow, if I may?' He glanced towards Anna, then said, 'Goodbye, Miss Dagshaw.'

'Goodbye, Mr Barrington . . .'

She was sitting at the table again guiding the child's hand to make the capital D, while saying to herself, What a nice man. And to be stricken like he is. It isn't fair. Oh yes, it was true, as the nurse had said, there were kind people in this house.

And those same words she repeated later on that evening, while sitting with the family round the fire, telling them of her experiences during the day. However, she omitted that part of the interview with the mistress when she was asked, 'How long have you known my husband?'

There was a meaning in those words, she knew, which would have upset her parents.

'She sounds a bitch,' was Oswald's opinion, and this was confirmed by Jimmy: 'She's got that name all round,' he said; 'she doesn't care what she rides over. She went straight through the turnip field. She thinks she can do owt she likes on the land because the farm's rented from them. But Mr Billings went to the house and had a stop put to it. Some say she must drink, but I don't think so, because she's like that first thing in the morning. I've seen her riding to the moor, braying the horse with her whip as she goes, and it giving its best . . .'

Also, it wasn't until they were in bed that she said to Cherry, 'Mr Timothy asked after you,' and Cherry said, 'Did he? Did he now? Isn't that nice of him.' Then she added, 'Why didn't you say so before?' and Anna replied,

148

'Well, it would have sounded as if he was singling you out; he hadn't particularly asked after the boys or Ma or Dada. He called you cheery; I thought he was saying Cherry.'

'Ooh!'

'Now, now; don't get ideas.'

'Who's getting ideas? Don't be silly; he's an oldish man and the poor soul is . . . well, you know . . . But it was nice of him to ask after me.'

They lay quiet for a moment; then Cherry asked, 'Do you think you'll ever fall in love like Dada and Ma did?'

Again there was a pause before Anna answered, 'There are very few men like Dada about, so I doubt it. What about you?'

'I doubt it too; but I wish there were, at times, I wish there were.'

Anna didn't take her sister's words up and say, 'Yes, so do I,' she said, 'Go on, turn round and go to sleep. It's late, and the morning will be here before we know where we are.'

2

Anna had hardly begun the lesson the next morning when the door was opened unceremoniously and Simon entered. And when the child ran to him, crying, 'Oh, Papa! Papa! Have you come to take me for a ride?' He patted the boy's head, saying, 'No, not this morning. But come.' He held out a hand and drew the child towards the door leading into the old nurse's sitting room and, opening it, he called, 'Are you there, Nanny?' And when, getting up from her chair, the old woman said, 'Oh, yes, I'm here, Master Simon. And you're up afore your clothes are on, aren't you? What is it?'

'Keep the boy with you for a few moments will you, please?'

'Yes. Yes. Come here my dear, come here.'

Simon pressed the boy towards her, then closed the door and, now turning to Anna, he said, 'Good morning.'

She was standing by the table and it was a moment or two before she answered, 'Good morning,' giving as much emphasis to the words as he had done.

He walked up the room and from across the table he began to explain why he had interrupted the lesson. 'I didn't return

150

until eight last evening, when I was informed that you were subjected to some annoyance yesterday.'

'*Oh, please. Please.* It is over. Perhaps it was partly my fault. You see, I . . . I have never been in service and therefore I'm not acquainted with the procedure.'

'Oh.' The words came out on a long slow breath, and he dropped down on to the child's stool, at the same time pointing to her chair and saying, 'Sit down. Sit down.' Then, after a moment during which he gazed down on the blocks from which his son had been learning his letters, he said, 'If you are to remain here, or, I should say, come daily and teach the boy, then I'm afraid that sooner or later you will be subjected, I am sorry to say, to my wife's temper. I am speaking to you now as I would to no other member of the staff in this house. They, of course, are used to her manner, they don't need to have it explained, and so I am relieved of the embarrassment . . . '

'Please, please, don't continue. I have no wish to cause you embarrassment. I understand the situation. Should your wife wish to see me in the future I will endeavour not to arouse her ire in any way. I . . . I am not without fault; I have the unfortunate knack of speaking my mind and I have not as yet learned to be subservient.'

She watched his face now break into a smile and his head wag for a moment before he said, 'Oh, Miss Dagshaw, you will, I think, in your life achieve many things, but subservience, never. You are your father's daughter, if not your mother's, and they certainly have always been anything but subservient to opinions or gossip. And from what I gather, there's another strike impending and your father is likely to arouse the wrath of the coal gods by sheltering some of the outcasts.'

She stared at him. This family owned shares in the Beulah mine – his brother saw to the running of it, so she understood

– and yet, here he was, speaking disparagingly of it. This was a strange house, a strange family, all at odds. And she was finding it hard to understand, for she had been brought up among eight people who thought as one about most things.

He was saying, 'How are you getting on with the boy?'

'Oh, it's early days yet; in fact, merely hours, but I find him most receptive and bright, and he's a' – she paused – 'warm, loving character.'

Again his head was moving, but slowly now as he repeated, 'A warm, loving character. Strange, that.'

It seemed that the next instant he was standing on his feet, so promptly had he risen from the table.

'My mother would like to see you sometime later today,' he said. 'She is an invalid, you know, but I can assure you that your interview will be different from your experience of yesterday.'

She made no reply, and he stood looking at her for a moment before he said, and quietly, 'I'm . . . I'm glad you're here . . . I mean, to see to my son. Also that you find him of a warm and loving disposition.'

Something puzzled her about these last words as she now watched him walk towards the far door, open it and say in quite a loud voice. 'Well, back to work! young sir. Back to the grindstone!'

'Oh, Papa, Papa, did teacher show you my drawing?'

'No. No, she didn't. And Andrew' – he bent down to him – 'you must call your teacher "Miss" not just "teacher", Miss Dagshaw.'

'Miss Dog . . . shaw?'

'No; Dagshaw.'

Anna had come down the room and, looking at the child, she said, 'I think it is too much of a mouthful: "Miss" will do.'

'What is your Christian name?'

152

She paused before she said, 'Anna, Annabel. I'm usually called Anna.'

'Well' – he had turned to his son again – 'you will say Miss Anna.'

'Mis . . . sanna?'

'No. Pronounce it correctly. Not Mis . . . sanna, Miss Anna.'

The child now said on a laugh, 'Missanna.'

'Oh dear me!' He looked at Anna, saying, 'You'll have to work on that one, Missanna.'

She smiled at him, then held out her hand to the boy, and as they went up the room she heard the door close and his voice, subdued now, talking to his old nurse.

It was two o'clock when Betty Carter again entered the schoolroom unceremoniously. Standing just within the door, she looked to where Anna was sitting at the table going through some books and she said, 'Madam wants to see ya.'

Anna closed two books and placed them on top of a small pile, before she got to her feet and walked towards the girl, saying, 'Thank you. If you will lead the way.'

On the landing, before following Betty Carter, she gently pushed open a door and looked at her charge taking his afternoon nap; then, closing the door gently again, she walked towards where the girl was standing impatiently at the top of the stairhead. Once down the stairs, this impatience showed itself further when her hurrying step became almost a trot, and when Anna did not follow likewise, the maid stopped abruptly in the gallery, muttering, 'Anything the matter with your legs?'

Anna did not answer, she just looked into the narrow plain face, and with a gesture of her hand told her to go on, which in no way placated her guide, for the girl now glared at her, opened her mouth as if to let her have it, decided against doing so and went down the main staircase at a rush and so into a large hall which appeared dim even with the light from two tall windows, one at each side of a glass-framed partition, leading to what she imagined to be a vestibule and the front door proper.

The girl now nodded towards two male servants who were standing surveying them, then carried on through what, to Anna, appeared to be a maze of corridors before stopping at an embossed, grey-painted door. Having rung the bell to the side of it, the girl stood facing the door until it was opened by a woman to whom she said under her breath, 'Madam wants to see her.'

The elderly maid looked over her informant's shoulder at the slim young person standing erect; then, turning her attention to Betty Carter again, she said, 'Very well. We'll call you when you're wanted.'

The girl, after throwing a sidelong glance in Anna's direction, walked quickly away, and the older woman said, 'Will you come in, please?'

The tone was pleasant, the smile was pleasant; it was as if she had entered a different house; and this was confirmed when the maid escorted her across a hall, this too painted in a pretty grey colour, then into a small sitting-room, where a woman, dressed in a nurse's uniform, had just entered from a far door. And she stopped and looked at Anna for a moment, then said with a smile, 'Will you come this way, please? Madam will see you now.'

As she entered the large room, Anna immediately took in the furnishings: first, that there was a lot of furniture; and then that the bed was placed near the tall window at the far end; but it was the couch in the middle of the room and facing another large window that drew and held her attention. Perhaps it was not so much a couch as a bed,

154

for lying on it was a figure, with the head resting on a single pillow.

The nurse now led her to the foot of this bed and from there she looked at the pale face topped by a mass of white hair, and was immediately struck by the brightness of the eyes. They were large eyes, what she would call intelligent eyes: all the life that should have been in the body was in them. They did not move over her but were riveted on her face. And then the person spoke, and to Anna's further amazement the voice was as alive as the eyes when it said, 'Bring Miss Dagshaw a chair, please, nurse.'

A chair was brought, and Anna thanked the nurse and sat down, and once more she looked up the length of the inert body to where the head was moving slightly now, which movement brought the nurse to the bed, saying quietly, 'Would you like to be raised, madam?'

'Yes. Yes, I would, just a little.'

The nurse crossed the room to a door, opened it and spoke to someone. And now there came into the room a man in a white overall and he went straight to the head of the couch and began to wind a handle.

When the lady said, 'Three turns, Mason,' the bed slowly tilted, and now it seemed to Anna as if she and the invalid were at eye level.

'That's it. Thank you. And, nurse, will you please tell Miss Rivers that I shall need her in about five minutes.'

'Yes, madam.'

Anna was aware that they now had the room to themselves.

'How are you finding my grandson?'

'I find him an apt pupil, madam, and of a nice disposition.'

'And of a nice disposition?'

'Oh, yes, madam, a very pleasing disposition.'

'How do you intend to instruct him?'

155

Anna paused before she answered: 'Well, madam,' she said, 'I think he should become acquainted with the whole of the alphabet, and that he should be able to count up . . . but gradually, to a hundred, during which time he will be doing little addition sums and also putting his letters into one syllable words.'

'That seems very practical and will lead to when he is due to have a tutor . . . I understand you have been educated by your father?'

'Yes, madam.'

'How did he instruct you?'

Again Anna paused before she said, 'Mainly through reading, just reading.'

'Just reading?'

'Yes, madam. He is a great reader.'

'What did he advise you to read?'

'History, geography, and literature.'

'Literature? What books did you read?'

'Well, madam, the ones I remember most are those of Mr Daniel Defoe and Dean Swift. He first told us the stories, then would get the older ones in my family to read parts aloud—' her lips moved into a smile as she added, 'pretending that he had forgotten a particular section.'

'Have you many books?'

'Not as many as we would like, madam.'

'We have a good library here; you have my permission to take the loan of whatever you need.'

'Oh, thank you, madam.'

'How many are there in your family?'

'I have two brothers older than myself, madam, a sister a year younger, and two brothers younger than her.'

'You are also a friend of Miss Netherton's, I understand.'

'Yes, madam, I am honoured to be that.'

There was a long pause now while Anna had to bear the scrutiny of the bright eyes; and then the lady said, 'I am sure you will instruct my grandchild well. One last thing: should at any time you feel that you wish to speak about anything that might be troubling you while you are in this house, then I would wish you to speak to the child's father or to Mr Barrington and they will convey the matter to me. Thank you, Miss Dagshaw.'

As if a bell had rung on the lady's last words, the door opened and a young, plainly dressed woman entered, and with one last look at the seemingly disembodied lady on the bed, Anna rose and said, 'Thank you, madam,' and dared to add, 'for your kindness.' She did not dip her knee but inclined her head gravely forward. Then she took two steps back from the foot of the bed, before turning away to walk to the open door, by which the nurse was awaiting her.

The nurse smiled at her and she returned the smile; then she was handed over to the maid who had let her in and had been addressed as Wilson.

Wilson smiled at her, and she smiled back, and when the door was opened for her, Anna turned to the woman and said, 'Thank you.' And Wilson said, 'You're welcome.' And this exchange brought the waiting upper housemaid's mouth agape.

As Anna followed Betty Carter back to the nursery, she noted that the girl was no longer galloping; she also realised that having left madam's quarters, she had entered another world, and in the main, a hostile one.

Again around the fire that evening she described the events of the day, making much play of her visit to the older Mrs Brodrick. And she finished by saying, 'Well, now, that's me. What's happened to the rest of you?'

'Well,' Maria said, 'a number of things have happened; but first of all, I hear that Miss Netherton's not at all well. She's been in bed today, so I think tomorrow morning, before you take your jaunt in the gig, you should slip over and see how she is.'

'Oh yes, I will. Number two could go that way, I should think.'

Nathaniel looked at Anna and said, 'Yes; why not?' And she smiled back at him, saying, 'Why not indeed! I've just to tell my coachman to change his route and that'll be that.'

When Oswald pushed her and she almost fell off the cracket, they all started to laugh and Nathaniel put in, 'Well, he is her own coachman; and he's a comic, if ever I've heard one. But now, Oswald, tell Anna your piece of news.'

Oswald now stuck his thumbs inside the straps of his braces and waggled his fingers, then put his head on one side as he said, 'I've been offered a position.'

'I thought I knew that. You told us about Mr Green.'

'Oh, that's old stuff. Manager, I could be now, with Olan under me.'

'With Mr Green?'

'No, no. With Mrs Simpson.'

Jimmy, now bending forward in silent laughter, slapped Olan on the knee as he spluttered, 'Pies and peas, with or without vinegar.'

They were rolling on the mat again until Nathaniel cried, 'Give over! both of you. Behave. And listen. Go on, Oswald.'

'Well, it's like this, Anna,' Oswald said. 'You see, we go to this shop now and again near the river front for a pie and pea dinner; they're always good quality and it's a clean place. There used to be a man serving, elderly. Well, he was the boss and he died. The mother and the daughter did the baking and such and they had to get a new fellow in. Well, he rooked them and so the daughter went up into the shop

158

and got a lass to help her. But there's some ruffians on that front, you know, especially from the ships. Well, 'twas last Wednesday I had told Olan here that he should try servicing round that quarter, and why not try the pies and peas place? So we decided to meet at twelve when the break came, and he brought the tray in with a few odds and ends he had left. The place was a bit full and we had to wait our turn, and it should happen that two drunken fellas started to take liberties with the lass behind the counter, and when one of them leant over and grabbed the front of the lass's frock and in doing so spilt a bowl of peas, she screamed. And so I went to stop him . . .'

'Went to stop him.' Olan laughed. 'That's how he got the lump on his jaw and his black and blue cheek. It was supposed to be from a bread tray falling on him.'

'Never!' cried Maria now. 'You didn't tell me that.'

'Well, there was no need, Ma. And shut your big mouth.' He had turned to his brother, who was grinning at him. 'Anyway, when the shop was clear the mother thanked me, and then she asked me what my job was. And so I told her, and I said this was my brother, and she invited us both into the back room.'

Oswald now looked directly at Anna as he said, 'The top and the bottom of it is, Anna, she's asked me if I'd manage the shop. And I can have Olan here as an assistant. Before her man died they had been thinking about taking the empty shop next door to turn it into a sit-down place, you know. And she said, later on we could have the rooms upstairs if we wanted them. But I shook my head at that.'

There was a nudge into Oswald's side from Olan's elbow as he said, 'Tell her what she offered us.'

'Well, me twelve and six a week to begin with, and Olan, ten shillings; a rise every year and our cart fare paid for as long as we travel.'

Anna shook her head slowly as she said, 'That's wonderful, marvellous. Are you going to take it?'

'I don't know.' Oswald thumbed towards his brother now, saying, 'We thought we should put it to Ma and Dada. And, you see, I'm nineteen turned, and although Mr Green's been very good, he's got two sons and a daughter and I can never see me getting much further than the little Bogs End shop, or Olan either.'

Nathaniel smiled now at his sons as he said, 'Would you mind if I took a trip and had a look at this money-making pies and peas business?'

'Oh, yes, Dada; I'd like you to see it. And she's a nice woman. They're both nice. Apparently they've had three men in since her husband died and with the last one the takings went down by half.'

'How old is the woman?' It was Maria asking now, and her sons looked at each other; then Oswald said, 'Much older than you, Ma.'

'I'm glad to know there's somebody in the world older than me,' said Maria, and this brought forth more laughter; then Olan said, 'In her fifties. Not as old as Miss Netherton, but about fifty.'

'And the daughter?'

'Oh, she's getting on an' all.' Olan was nodding his head. 'Twenty-something, I would say. Wouldn't you?' He looked at Oswald, and Oswald said, 'I should think about twenty-four, and that's getting on for a girl; I mean, a woman.'

Maria exchanged a twinkling glance with Nathaniel, then said, 'Well, they seem stable women. But I think it's wise what your dada said; he should go and have a look at the place.'

Looking closely at Cherry, now, Anna said, 'You've been very quiet in all this. Hasn't Mr Praggett done an Irish jig on the table for you, or amused you in any way? Hasn't he thrown Janet or Lucy downstairs?'

Cherry didn't answer but her father put in quietly, 'Cherry witnessed something disturbing coming back tonight. You know the pit lad, Bobby Crane? Well, he was attacked by two other pitmen and they threatened what would happen to him if he didn't stop coming here. Apparently he wrote out a notice, well, in large printed letters, for one of the men who was pushing the union and our dear Mr Praggett found out. And two of his henchmen set about the lad. The sorry thing is one of his assailants happened to be his cousin. And my brave daughter here' – he put his arm round Cherry's shoulder – 'did some screaming, then took up a staff and actually hit one with it. I think they were so astounded at this that they went off, just aiming verbal abuse at her. Anyway, she helped young Bobby here and he's now over in the barn, sleeping I hope, after your mother's administrations.'

'Oh, I am sorry. And oh, Cherry, you were brave to stand up to them . . . Poor Bobby. What will he do now?'

'Well, he's not going back to the pit,' Cherry said. 'He's made his mind up. He's asked if he can stay in the barn tonight; but he's going into Gateshead or Newcastle tomorrow and he says he'll take anything; he might even sign on one of the boats.'

As if aiming to lighten the conversation, Ben said, 'You didn't tell them about Jimmy's bull, Dada.'

Nathaniel looked down on the boy. 'No, I didn't,' he said. 'And for once my erudite son has kept his mouth shut. But that points to a very good quality in him, because what he would have to tell would be in praise of his courage, too.'

Jimmy was now sitting with his hands between his knees, his head down and his gaze turned towards the blazing fire, and Anna, looking towards him, said, 'He's fought a bull?'

'As much as. Well, it should happen from what Farmer Billings told me, and with pride, that he had taken Rickshaw to the market. Rickshaw, by the way, is the name of the bull.

161

I always thought a rickshaw was a Chinese one-man carriage, but the bull was called Rickshaw. I wonder why.'

Jimmy's head came up and round, and he muttered, 'Because its rump swings,' then turned to gaze into the fire again for, amid laughter, his father was continuing, 'Well, the herdsman was there and he was supposed to have control of Rickshaw and to take him around the ring. Well, Rickshaw was in a pen and the herdsman opened the gate and went to lead his charge out. But Rickshaw thought differently. Apparently he must never have liked the herdsman, for he put his head down and it was the herdsman who went out.'

They were all in different stages of laughter now, some smothered, some high, some emitting squeals at their mind pictures as Nathaniel went on, 'Then Farmer Billings said there was a scattering of people all about, but Rickshaw didn't charge. He just walked forward, and my son here put his hand out, got hold of the nose piece and spoke to him, then led him quietly into the ring.'

Jimmy's head was once again turned towards his father, and he was spluttering now as he said, 'Only because I was dead in front of him, Dada, and I thought, if he was going to toss me I wouldn't go so far if I held on to his nose piece.'

Nathaniel himself was laughing loudly as he said, 'Modesty. Modesty. You used your wits and, as you've told me before, you liked old Rickshaw, and that you used to talk to him and give him titbits. He liked turnip, didn't he, and crusty bread?'

As the laughter died down Anna wiped her eyes and looked at her young brother. 'We're all laughing, Jimmy,' she said; 'but that was a wonderful thing to do. You could have been hurt, too. Anyway, tell me, is Mr Billings going to put your wage up?'

'That'll be the day for celebrations. He'll likely give me a bag of turnips, knowing that we grow our own.'

162

'Wait and see. Wait and see,' his father said, then added, 'Now we'll get to our small nightly duties, whether it's washing our face and hands or helping to set the table, and then to bed. But I myself will go to sleep tonight on the very warming thought that I have three very brave children . . .'

Anna did not rise immediately with the others, but sat gazing into the fire for a moment, seeing there the child who needed love so much, sleeping in that garret room. For after all, that's what it was, no matter how nicely furnished. Then one after another she saw those members of the household she had so far met and she reflected, in comparison with her family, how loveless they all were.

She started as her father's hand came on her shoulders and he said, 'Where were you? What were you thinking?'

She looked up at him and said, 'I was thinking how lucky we all are.' And he said simply, 'Thank you, daughter.'

3

Anna had three more encounters with the mistress before she left for London. The first one left her shaking and lying in the hedge. It was on a Sunday. She had been to see Miss Netherton, who was recovering from a very bad bout of bronchitis and had been ordered by her doctor to take a holiday, preferably in Switzerland.

This she had emphatically rejected at first, but after she was told that one of her lungs was affected, she had reluctantly succumbed to the suggestion. She had told Anna she would be leaving within the month, but in her inimitable way she had added, 'I'll be back before I get there because I can't stand foreign places. Foreigners don't know how to make tea.'

It was a very cold day, the night frost having remained on the ground, and now it was two o'clock in the afternoon. She had come along the coach road from Miss Netherton's; then after clambering up the bank and crossing the stile, she had walked along the quarry path. There had been a lot of rain before the cold spell had set in and so there were many glassy patches along the way. The rain, too, she saw had brought a fresh fall from the quarry top; soon, she thought, they would be unable to walk along here, unless the hedge was taken down.

She had just passed the part where the path narrowed to within a few feet of the quarry edge when, to her amazement, she saw in the distance a horse and rider. Towards the far end the path was bordered on one side by Farmer Billings's fields, but it eventually petered out into the moor. Because of the obstacle presented by the stile and the bank, she had never known a rider to use this path.

From this distance she couldn't make out who the rider was, but she noted that the horse had been pulled up. But then, to her utter amazement she saw that the animal was being urged into a gallop and that it was heading straight for her.

The path, although not so narrow here, still had the quarry on one side and no outlet to her right except the bramble hedge. She had no time to think, only to scream, as she fell back on to the hedge as the horse flashed past her, its smell in her nostrils and the face of the woman driving it looking down on her.

She didn't try to rise, for her weight was bending the hedge and taking her downwards, but the scream was still high in her head and it was yelling at her: She meant that! She meant it! She could have killed me. She wanted to. She's mad. Oh, my God! She's mad.

She was now lying almost prone in the bushes; the branches were entangled in her clothes and she couldn't push herself forward. She wanted to cry out now with the pain from her hands as the bramble spikes pierced her woollen gloves.

Slowly and painfully she drew herself back and into the field, and there she lay for some minutes, until she felt able to pull herself to her feet and retrieve her hat that was perched on one of the bushes.

She had adjusted her clothes and put her hat on when she heard the horse's hooves again, walking now, and she stood as if petrified, telling herself that she couldn't run across this field because a horse could easily over-take her. She was standing stiffly looking over the broken hedge when the rider drew up and stared at her. And then in an ordinary tone the words came to her: 'My horse was startled. It must have been a rabbit. Anyway, you shouldn't be walking along this path, it's dangerous. Are you hurt?'

She made no reply. She couldn't reply. She just stared back at this woman, this terrible woman, this frightening creature, who, shaking the reins, now said, 'Well, if you will walk along byways, that's your affair.'

She was still standing rigid when the sound of the horse's hooves faded away.

When she reached home and her mother exclaimed at the condition of her coat and her bleeding hands, she told her she had slipped on the ice and fallen into the hedge, and her mother seemed to believe her. But her father looked hard at her, and she returned his stare and they understood each other.

Later, when they were alone together, he said, 'Was it from the village?' and she said, 'No, Dada; it was a horse-rider and I had to jump out of the way.'

She knew he was puzzled by her answer but she didn't enlighten him further.

Their second meeting was in the schoolroom.

Simon often visited the schoolroom now and it was shortly after her visit to his mother that he said, 'I understand that you would like to borrow some books from the library, but I'm afraid' – he smiled – 'there's nothing elementary enough for school use up here.'

Then, as his mother had, he too asked, 'Have you many books at home?' and she had answered, 'Not as many as my father would like, but he *has* collected a number over the years.' And to this he had said, 'Well, if there are any he would care to borrow, you must take them.'

This morning he had visited the schoolroom early. She had just set out the books and equipment that would be necessary for the lesson. As always, the child had run to him, crying, 'Papa! Papa!' And he had stooped and picked him up, saying, 'You're getting heavier every day.' Then looking at Anna, he had asked a question: 'Everything all right?'

'Yes. Yes, thank you.'

'He is behaving himself?'

'He always behaves himself, sir.'

He had looked towards the window and remarked, 'It's a lovely day, cold, but the sun is bright.' Then he had added, 'I shall be away for the next two days, perhaps three; I'm going to London.'

Before she could make any comment the child had said, 'Will you take me to London one day, Papa?'

'Yes, yes, I hope I shall. That's if you remain a good boy and do what you're told, and learn your lessons.'

'I shall. I shall, Papa.'

He had put the child down and, stepping towards Anna, had looked her straight in the face as he said, 'Should there be anything you need, or advice, my uncle will be in the house. And, of course, there is always my mother. You just need to ask if you may see her.'

When she made no answer he had said softly, 'You understand?' And then, inclining her head, she had said, 'Yes, I understand. But I hope I won't have to trouble them.'

'I hope so too. Well, goodbye.' He had smiled at her, then patted his son's head. He had not, however, left by the door leading into the nurse's sitting room, but by that leading to

167

the landing, and there he had turned and looked at her again, his face straight, and when once more he had said, 'Goodbye,' she too had responded, quickly, 'Goodbye. Goodbye, sir.'

Why should she have felt troubled? She had sat down at the table opposite the child and when he said, 'Papa is big, isn't he?' she had said, 'Yes. Yes, he is, dear.'

'Will you take me to your house some day, Missanna?'

'I should like to, but I would have to get permission first from your papa.'

'You could ask Uncle Timothy.'

She had wagged her finger at him, saying now, 'We'll get on with our letters, shall we, Andrew?' And he, laughing, had said, 'Yes, Missanna.'

It was about half past ten in the morning when the second encounter took place. Katie Riddell, who always brought up the child his hot milk and biscuits at this time, scurried into the room saying, 'She's on her way.'

'Who's on her way?'

'The mistress of course, who else?' And the girl poked her head forward. 'At least she was making for here. She's not usually around this part in the morning, so look out.' She plonked the tray down on the table, looking at the child as she did so and saying, 'Hello, Master Andrew.' He answered, 'Hello Katie'; then she went out as quickly as she had come.

Anna felt a tightness in the bottom of her stomach: it was as if her muscles had suddenly contracted. She made herself go about her duties: she put a bib on the boy, tying the tapes into a bow at the back; then she poured out the milk from the jug into a cup, and he said, 'Why don't you have milk, Missanna?'

'Because I prefer tea.' Even whilst saying this, Anna half turned her head quickly towards the door leading into the nurse's sitting room, from where the sound of a voice was now coming, and it certainly wasn't that of the old nurse going for her assistant, Peggy Maybright.

When the door opened to reveal the figure dressed in a riding habit, had the circumstances been otherwise, Anna's thoughts would have been, She is beautiful! As it was, they were to tell herself she must keep calm, and she must keep her tongue quiet.

She noticed immediately that the child didn't jump from his seat as he would do when either his father or his uncle entered; he got down slowly to go and meet his mother, and greeted her in a most polite manner. 'Good morning, Mama,' he said.

'Good morning, Andrew. What are you doing?' She looked towards the table.

'I am going to have my milk, Mama.'

She now walked up to the table, looked down on to the tray, then turned her cold gaze on Anna and said, 'He should not be eating off a tray; a table should be set apart.'

'I shall see to it, Mistress.'

'Yes; yes, you will see to it.' She now looked around the room as if she hadn't seen it before and when her gaze was halted as she saw an easel, the child cried excitedly now, 'Papa bought that yesterday for Missanna to write on. It is called a black . . . board.'

His mother now walked towards the easel that supported the blackboard, and the child in his excitement ran to it and said, 'This is a weasel.'

'Easel.'

'Weasel. Yes, Mama, weasel.'

'Say, easel.'

'It . . . it is difficult, Mama, to say weasel.'

The eyes were turned on Anna now. 'Why haven't you done something about this?'

169

'It is an impediment of a sort, Mistress. I'm aiming to cure it, but it will take time.'

It was as if the child sensed the hostility and aimed to soothe it by saying, 'I know my two-times table, Mama, and I can count on the ab . . . a . . . cus. And Missanna says I am . . . '

'Who is this Missanna?'

'Why' – the child put out his hand – 'teacher is Missanna. Papa said I had to call . . . '

Now the voice was so loud that the child shrank back as his mother yelled at him, 'She is the *teacher* and you will call her *teacher*. You understand?' She was bending down to him, her hand tapping her skirt as she spoke. And it was a moment before the child answered, 'Yes, Mama.'

As Anna watched the woman slowly straighten her back and turn towards her, she had an overwhelming desire to respond physically to this woman – she could see her hand slapping that face – for there would be no reasoning with her.

And when she said, 'In future you will report his progress to me every week when I'm at home. You understand?' She couldn't answer her; she couldn't force, 'Yes, Mistress,' through her lips.

'I am speaking to you, girl!'

Now she was answering, her words coming fast: 'I am aware of that, Mistress; you leave no doubt in anyone's mind to whom you are speaking. Well, I am speaking, too, and let me tell you I have no need to put up with your treatment. I was engaged for this post by Andrew's father and I shall take my orders from him. Is that plain?'

She watched the colour drain from the peach-like skin; she watched the high collar of the riding-habit move in and out as if the woman was choking; and she was prepared for the onslaught. The words were fired like bullets from a gun and the report of them as loud, as she screamed, 'You insolent slut, you! You low-born insolent slut! Get out of my sight before I take my whip to you!'

'Mama! Mama! Don't! Don't smack Missanna.'

The sight of her son throwing his arms protectively around Anna's hips and pressing his head into her waist was too much. Her hands reached out and, grabbing the collar of the child's blouse, she actually flung him across the room; and his screaming died away as his head hit the skirting board and he became still.

There followed a deep momentary silence, until the door from the sitting-room flew open and the nurse hurried in crying, 'Mistress! Mistress! What have you done?'

Penella Brodrick was now leaning against the table, her hands gripping the edge, her body half over it, and she didn't answer the nurse, nor even turn her head when she heard the child begin to cry now, but seemingly having to make an effort to drag herself up straight, and with one hand held out before her as if groping her way, she went from the room.

'Missanna. Missanna.'

'I am here, dear. Don't cry, don't cry. Let me feel your head.' Anna felt the back of the child's head, where a bump was slowly rising, and as she picked him up from the floor the nurse said, 'Cut?'

'No, only a lump.'

'My God! She could have killed him. But you . . . you, lass, your tongue'll get you hung. I've never heard anything like it. One thing sure, she's never been spoken to like that in her life . . . Bring him in and lay him on the couch.'

A few minutes later, when the child was tucked up on the couch, the nurse stood beside the fire and, looking down on Anna, who was now actually shivering, she said, 'Lass, lass, you've got to learn to still that tongue of yours.'

171

'How . . . how could I? The things she said, the way she went for me.'

'Aye, I heard it all; I've sharp ears. She takes some standing, I'll admit that, by God! she does. And I'll say this to you; you know nothing of it. There's never been a day's peace in this house since she set foot in it. Of course it was her upbringing; she was spoilt from the day she was born. She was one of the Harrisons. Rotten with money they were, on their mother's side anyway; French, she was, so they tell me, and the father Irish, as mad as a hatter, died on his horse blind drunk, they say. The mother had relations in Newcastle and was married to one of the shipowners. The mistress came to a dance here with them. I remember the first time I saw her. We were watching from the upper gallery. She had all the men around her like a queen bee, but from the beginning she had her eye on Mr Simon and he on her an' all, it must be confessed. An' then in the weeks that followed, Mr Raymond an' all came into the picture. The three of them were always riding together, and be at this or that do, too. Then, of a sudden, her mother yanks her back to France; she had a Count or some such in her eye for her. But what does she do? In no time she's in Newcastle with her maid and, I understand, enough luggage that would have filled the hall here. And then started the tug of war as to who was going to get her, Mr Raymond or Mr Simon. But who did she really want? There seemed to be a tussle. Anyway, she marries Mr Simon, and mind, she could give him three years, although she doesn't look her age.'

The old woman walked towards the couch and looked down on the child, whose eyes were now closed as if he had fallen asleep; and almost under her breath she said, 'From the minute they came back from the honeymoon there was a change. Nobody knew what had happened. Nobody knows to this day what had happened.' She now glanced sideways at Anna as she added, 'A body can only guess, but it's wise to keep your guesses to yourself.'

'I can't stay here, nurse. I love the child, but you see it's impossible . . . '

'And the child loves you, me dear. He's been a different boy since you came. What company am I for a bright little lad like that? What can I learn him, or Peggy Maybright, for that matter. She can't even play with him, doesn't know how. All she's good for is fetchin' and carryin'. Look, me dear.' She now pulled a chair up and sat in front of Anna. 'She'll be gone in a day or so. Conway is skittering around, already packing, they say. The clothes that woman has, you wouldn't believe. They say she changes from her shift up twice a day. The flat irons are going in the laundry from sunrise till the moon shows up. So, me dear lass' – she patted Anna's knees now – 'stick it out. Mr Simon's for you and Mr Timothy an' all. Oh aye, Mr Timothy. And from what you didn't tell me what went on when you met madam, I understand it was pretty plain sailing down there. So you see, just give it a day or two more, perhaps a week at the most, and you won't know you're in the same house.'

'She doesn't seem sane, nurse . . . I mean, there's no reason for her attacks.'

'Oh, that's what you think. As for being sane, she's sane all right and it's the devil's saneness. And you think there's no reason for her attacking you as she does? Why, that woman is as jealous as hell of anyone Mr Simon has a good word for. She dismissed her other maid. She was a good-looking lass with a fine figure, and she came across her one day talking to Mr Simon and the lass was daring to laugh at something he had said, and out she went on some pretext or other. Now Conway, her present one, is as plain as a pikestaff, with a sour puss on her. Come on, lass, cheer up. I'll brew us a strong cup of tea. An' look' – she thumbed towards the

173

couch – 'there's somebody sitting up and taking notice. Not much the worse; but that isn't his mother's fault, because she could have brained him.'

The child now came towards Anna, saying, 'Are you hurt, Missanna?'

'No. No, dear, I'm not hurt.'

He climbed upon her knee, put his arms around her neck and, his face close to hers, he said, 'You won't go away and leave me, Missanna, will you?'

She looked back into the innocent countenance and she paused a moment before she answered him: 'No, dear,' she said; 'I won't go and leave you.'

That evening, again sitting around the fire, she did not relate the events of the day to the family, merely saying that things had gone as usual. In any case, the interest was focused on the affairs of Bobby Crane, who had been offered a job of sorts in Gateshead Fell, the terms of which were under discussion.

There was a small boat-builder on the river bank who wanted an apprentice, someone willing to learn and around the age of Bobby, who was now seventeen, but the wage was very poor, only seven shillings a week, and, as Bobby said, he could never pay lodgings out of that and live. So would Nathaniel allow him to sleep in the barn until something better came along? But he fancied this job as he would be working under the open sky. Rain, hail, or shine, it wouldn't matter to him as long as he was on top of the ground instead of under it. And the hours were good, half-past seven till half-past five with a half-hour off for dinner. He had offered to pay two shillings a week for his sleeping quarters; the rest he would need to live on.

Nathaniel had shaken his head at this point and said, 'God help him. However, I have already told him there would be no rent charged for any sleeping quarters here.

174

And Oswald, too, if he takes this job of managing the pies and peas shop, which is in his mind to do, then out of his good wage he has promised to pay for a dinner for the lad and there'll always be a bite left over here for him at night.' But her father had ended, 'What I'm really pleased about is he's more than anxious to keep up his learning, so anxious that he is determined, after he finishes at half-past one on a Saturday, he'll go around the markets and see if he can pick up some cheap books. He's got the bug all right.'

It was Cherry who put in at this stage, 'He's even speaking differently; I couldn't understand the pitmatic at first. And he looked quite nice today. Ma had given him one of Olan's coats.'

Here, Olan created the usual gale of laughter by saying, 'Olan had only two coats and now Olan's got only one.'

Leaning back against the head of the settle, Anna looked around at the fire-illuminated faces and for the countless time she told herself there couldn't be another family on earth like this one. Then that little streak of fear crept into her thinking as it had been wont to do of late: What if something happened to break it up? Yet what could happen? Nothing, except they could marry and go away . . .

Marry, did she say?

Who would want to marry them? At least, Cherry and herself. The boys might stand a better chance, but it wouldn't happen in the village or hereabouts. Oh, no, never hereabouts. But why worry about her family? they could certainly take care of themselves. What she had to worry about was that house, or the mistress of it, and the little boy who had grown to love her, and she him.

4

The mistress was leaving for London; and the bustle made itself felt on the nursery floor when Betty Carter rushed into the schoolroom and, addressing Anna in her usual fashion, said, 'Give him here! Peggy Maybright has to get him ready for downstairs; the mistress wants to see him.'

'Leave him alone!' Anna almost snapped the girl's hand from the child's arm. 'He doesn't need to be got ready except that his hands need to be washed, and I will see to that. If you have to accompany him downstairs, kindly wait outside.'

Anna watched the girl draw herself up to her full height before saying, 'One of these days . . .'

'Yes? One of these days, you were saying?'

The girl flounced out of the room, and Anna said to the child, 'Come along, dear,' and went over to the table on which stood a basin and a ewer of water, and as she poured out the water the child said, 'Why don't *you* take me down, Missanna, to see Mama?'

She paused for a moment before she said, 'Your mama hasn't asked for me. Anyway' – she was drying his hands now – 'it is you your mama wants to see. Now, be very polite, won't you? And tell your mama you hope that she has a nice holiday.'

She now took the boy to the door, where Betty Carter was standing with her arms folded and the light of battle in her eyes. And when Anna saw her thrust her hand out towards the child, she said quietly, 'You have no need to take his hand; he is quite used to walking alone. Go along, Andrew.'

She watched them as far as the top of the stairs, where the girl paused a moment before glancing back at her.

She returned to the classroom, closing the door behind her, and leant against it for a moment as she asked herself: How was it that she engendered such animosity? Surely it wasn't solely because of her birth? Could it be her manner towards people? But look how well she got on with nurse and Peggy, and how nice madam's servants were to her. And there was the housekeeper, Mrs Hewitt. She was very civil towards her . . . well, most of the time. Sometimes she appeared to be on her guard. Why this should be she couldn't imagine. Was the animosity towards her because she spoke differently? Perhaps. Well, she had her father to thank for that and she did thank him. And thinking of him reminded her of the book he said he would like . . .

It was during the child's rest hour that she decided to take advantage of the permission granted to her to use the library, for her father had mentioned that there was a certain book that he would like to read and which he had been unable to get elsewhere. She had made a note of it: Pope's translation of Homer's *Iliad* and of his *Odyssey*. They would probably be in such a library as was in this house.

She knocked on the nurse's sitting-room door and when the voice said, 'Come in. Come in, my dear,' she went in and was greeted with, 'You're just in time for a cup of tea.'

'If you don't mind, nurse, I won't have any just yet. I'm going to take the opportunity of slipping down to the library. I told you I had permission.'

'Aye, yes, you did.'

'Well, where is it? Where do I go from the main hall . . . '

'Oh, you don't have to go near the main hall. When you get to the foot of the stairs here you'll see a door opposite. Now that doesn't lead into a bedroom or such, but into a passage; then a flight of stairs leads down to the West wing, and when you land in the corridor there you'll see an oak door right in front of your eyes. It stands out from the rest for it has a rounded top. Well, that's the library, and a splendid room it is an' all; but I don't know if it's much used these days.'

'Thank you, nurse.' She was about to turn away when she recalled that there was something she had meant to ask the nurse. And so tentatively she said, 'The master. The child doesn't speak of his grandfather.'

'Huh! That's easy to explain. He's very seldom here, 'cos he travels all over the world digging up bits of crocks here and there.'

'He would be what you would call an archaeologist then.'

'Oh, would he?' The old woman's eyebrows moved upwards. 'Oh, you learned ones put names to things, don't you? Well, my explanation for what he is would be a digger up of the dead.'

'Oh, nurse.'

She went out laughing, and, following the old woman's instructions, she came to the black oak door with the arched top, and when she opened it and looked down the long room she could only gasp at the magnificence of it. It had a painted, domed ceiling, and at the far end were two long windows which apparently looked onto the garden, for she could glimpse the trees in the distance. Slowly she walked towards the highly polished mahogany-topped table that was flanked by a number of carved high-backed chairs.

She stood at one end of the table and put her hand down on the head of the animal whose curved body formed an arm of the chair, and she stroked it for a moment as if in appreciation of the workmanship. Then she turned her head first one way and then the other, and finally her gaze came to rest on the wide stone fireplace with a log fire smouldering in the hearth. The logs, she noticed, were at least four times as long as those they cut for their fire at home.

Above the fireplace two antler-headed animals seemed to be staring down at her. She looked away; she didn't like animals turned into trophies; it put her too much in mind of the cruelty of the stag hunt.

At each side of the fireplace enormous glass bookcases filled the walls, but it was the long wall opposite the fireplace that particularly held her interest. Apart from a door at the end and two small alcoves, the entire wall was made up of bookshelves holding what must be, she told herself, thousands of books.

She stood with her head back, looking upwards and wondering for a moment how anyone could reach a book from that top shelf, when she saw at the other end of the room near the door by which she had entered, a kind of double step-ladder; it was on wheels and had a platform on the top.

She smiled to herself. That's how they would reach the top shelf. Oh, how her father would love this room. She could see him spending his entire day here.

She walked to one of the alcoves. The recess was about two and a half feet deep and four or five feet wide. There was a padded bench attached to one side and a flap table at the other. The table, she saw, was hinged, and once one sat down it could be lifted up practically across the knees. The little place suggested study and she could imagine the

179

two brothers, when they were young, being made to sit here while their tutor sat at the centre table.

She ran her hand along a row of books. She must find her Dada's book and get back before the child woke and needed her. But how was she to go about finding Pope? Well, she supposed it being a fine library the books would be in alphabetical order or, at least, divided into sections.

Thinking of alphabetical order, she began to move along the shelves and soon noticed brass slots holding cards. The one she was looking at read "17th Century"; and the books here were certainly in alphabetical order. And so she moved along to the next section which, as she had expected, read "18th Century". This should be it. And yes: there was *The Essay On Man*. She took it from the shelf, and looked further along, and was not disappointed: she took down Pope's translation of *The Iliad* and his translation of *The Odyssey* in one volume. Her dada had already told her the story in the form of mythology; it was almost, to her, a fairy tale. This translation was in poetic form, and immediately she had the feeling she would never tackle reading it. She liked a straightforward story, one written by Mr Charles Dickens or Mrs Gaskell.

She wasn't sure when she actually became aware of someone talking. She rose from the seat in the alcove and looked up and down the room. Perhaps it was someone walking in the garden, but they must be talking loudly for their voices to penetrate these thick walls.

She now walked down the room towards the window and as she did so she had to pass the other door in the room. She noticed it was an ordinary door and that it was slightly ajar, and she was actually startled as she recognised the mistress's voice coming from the room beyond. She had assumed she had already left the house.

She was about to turn and tiptoe up the room when the

words that came to her halted her movement, because the voice from the other room was saying, 'You'll come over to France, won't you, darling? Promise me?'

The master had been gone from the house these last two days and now the mistress was talking to someone and using endearments.

'I promise you, my love. I promise you.'

'But what about next week?'

'I'll be up there like a shot if those damn savages behave themselves. But if they come out on strike, well, I'll have to be here, at least for a time.'

'Why can't the other two come and take their share? I've told you you should suggest it.'

'And I've told you, my dear one, I'm single-minded in everything I do, what I own, what I manage, and . . . and whom I love.'

As her mind opened to the situation presented by the words she had overheard, she turned and at a tiptoeing run reached the alcove. There, having quickly grabbed up the two leather-bound volumes that were furthest from her, she made to snatch at the Addison and Steele book; but so hasty was her action that it slipped from her fingers. Had it fallen on its edge it would have made little noise, but it landed flat on the floor with a loud plop!

She was in a panic as she stooped to pick it up, for she heard the door being pulled fully open, and, trembling, she stood up to face once again the startled but infuriated stare of Penella Brodrick.

Raymond Brodrick was at her side, and it was he who spoke. His voice light and over-hearty, he said, 'Ah! Miss Dagshaw; you are sampling the library?'

Before she could answer she watched the woman, as she thought of her, move swiftly towards her, demanding now, 'What are you doing here?'

181

'I am choosing some books, Mistress.'

'*How dare you!* Choosing some books, are you? Who gave you permission to come into this room, or anywhere near it?'

'Madam did.' She did not add, 'And your husband.'

The woman turned and said to her brother-in-law, 'Did you hear that? I ask you, did you hear that?'

'Yes. Yes, I heard.' And he looked at Anna and asked quite politely, 'Did my mother give you permission?'

'I would not have said so, sir, nor would I have dared to take the liberty of entering this room if I . . . '

'I've told you! I've told you!' Penella Brodrick cried at Raymond. 'The insolence of her! She wouldn't dare talk like that if he . . . '

'Be quiet! Be quiet!'

'I won't be quiet.' She swung around to Anna again, ordering her: 'Put those books down.'

Slowly Anna put the books on the table and immediately Penella Brodrick grabbed one up and, reading the titles aloud, she cried, 'Pope's *Essay On Man!*' She cast a glance back at Raymond, then added, '*The Iliad* and *The Odyssey!*' Then the furious look still on her face she cried at Anna, 'Don't have the effrontery, girl, to tell me that you can read or understand these books!'

'They are for my father. Madam gave me permission to take a loan of them. But yes, I could read and understand them and . . . '

'Penella! Penella!' Raymond had his hand on her upraised arm.

The books were now flung to the floor; and the words came out on spittle as the woman cried, 'You insolent bastard! And you are a bastard, every inch of you and from a litter of bastards, birthed by a whore . . . '

Anna gripped the edge of the table as she watched Raymond Brodrick almost dragging the infuriated woman down the library and through the door. She felt she was going to faint: her legs gave way beneath her. She dropped onto the alcove seat and, folding her arms on the narrow table, she was about to lay her head on them when once again she heard the voice; and now she turned a fear-filled glance towards the panelling as Raymond Brodrick's voice came to her quite plainly, almost as if he were sitting at the other side of this narrow table, saying, 'Why do you hate her so?'

'Because he's flaunting her at me.'

'You don't mean . . . ?'

'Yes, I do mean. He's never away from the nursery now, and he hardly ever went there before, and you know the reason why.'

'Penella, look at me. You say you love me.'

'I do, I do, Raymond.'

'Well, if you love me, why are you so concerned about whom he may be taking to bed? He doesn't have you, so he's bound to have someone. It stands to reason . . . You still care for him, don't you?'

'*No, I don't.* What I feel for him is hate. He's not a man. How could you expect me to feel anything else but hate for someone who's tortured me for years with his silence? He ignores me except on occasions such as when he told me to leave her . . . that bastard alone. Yes, do you know that? He's warned me what will happen if I go up there again.'

'But you never did frequent the nursery very much, did you? The child was always brought down. You've got to stop this, you know, Penella; it'll burn you out. Your body isn't strong enough to carry the hate you have for him, and now apparently for her, and your love for me. One is bound to cancel out the other.'

'It won't. *I am* strong enough. Why don't *you* hate him? You don't, do you?'

'No; I don't know. I did when he married you. And I hated you an' all, didn't I?'

'Oh, Raymond, Raymond, take me away.'

'Now, now; don't go into that again. I can't, not yet, not as long as mother is alive. When father is away the control is in her hands. Although I am the eldest she is still the boss and, as you know, every penny that passes through her books is seen to by her . . . *dear secretary.*'

'I have enough money for both of us, darling.'

'You have enough money for yourself, my dear one, and your extravagant tastes, but not for us both. Anyway, I like the life I lead. You know I do. I like to work and I like to play. Now, come on; the carriage is waiting and has been for some time now. If all goes as arranged I will see you next week-end in London, then within a fortnight in Paris. And I'll have another break in January, if you're still determined to stay away that long. Away you go now! But let me straighten your hat and kiss you once more.'

In the silence that followed Anna raised her head, then lifted her hand and pressed it tightly across her mouth as if to still the emotion that aimed to tumble from it: the amazement, the disgust, the knowledge of the situation that had been revealed to her and the fact that she was implicated in it made her feel sick. She couldn't stay in this place, she couldn't; she would have to go.

As she attempted to rise she felt dizzy, so dropped back onto the seat. It was as if she had suffered a physical attack; and she almost had. But had she done so, it couldn't have hurt her more than had the verbal one: *You bastard!* It had a dreadful sound. The word implied something bad, dirty, much more so than did gillyvor; and yet they both meant the same thing. And she had called her mother a whore . . . Ooh!

She actually sprang up, and then toppled back against the panel of the alcove as the hand touched her shoulder. She thought for a moment the woman had returned; then she was gaping up at Timothy and he was saying, 'Oh, my dear, I'm sorry I startled you. I . . . at first, I thought you were lost in reading, but then . . . Oh! my dear, come.' He held out his hand to her and his voice was light as he said, 'Just a few inches further and you would have been through that panel. It's artificial; there used to be a door there, you know.'

She turned now and gazed at the panel and she mouthed, 'A door?'

'Yes.' He was nodding at her. 'There were originally two doors leading into the other part of the library,' he pointed up the room, 'and there was only the one alcove and the boys used to fight over it when they were studying. So their father had that panel put in and the seat and the table, and that mercifully solved the problem.'

She shook her head, then took his proferred hand as he said, 'Come and sit in a more comfortable chair,' and, as if she were a child, he led her around the long table to a leather chair standing near the fireplace.

'Sit down for a moment, my dear.' He chafed her hand, adding, 'You're cold.' He took up the pair of bellows lying at the side of the fireplace and blew on the dull wood embers until the sparks began to fly up the chimney; he then drew a chair forward from the table and, after placing it by her side, he sat down and said quietly, 'Tell me what happened to upset you so.'

She was gazing down on her joined hands as she said, 'I . . . I can't explain, except to tell you that I . . . I must leave here.'

'But why? She's gone, and all tension has gone with her.' He paused. 'Did you see her before she left? I mean . . . '

Her head came up sharply and, looking at him, she said with some bitterness, 'I not only saw her I heard her and almost felt her. She was going to strike me. If it hadn't been for Mr . . . '

185

She stopped as abruptly as she had started. And when he said quietly, 'Go on,' she said, 'No, no.'

'Raymond was with her?'

When she remained silent he turned his head slowly and looked towards the alcove; then he looked down at his hands now as he said, 'You overheard them talking in the next room? That's it, isn't it? And what you heard must have amazed you; and when she knew that you had overheard . . . '

'No, no,' she put in. 'No, I don't think she knew I had overheard anything. Yet I don't know. I dropped a book and . . . and that must have told her there was someone in here, and unfortunately at any time the sight of me seems to arouse her anger, but today she . . . she did not believe that I had been given permission to take the loan of books and she called me names.'

When she stopped abruptly, he did not speak nor did he question her further, and so they sat side by side looking towards the fire until he said, 'She is a very unhappy woman; and not very intelligent. She's to be pitied, in a way. It is because you are young and learned and—' he smiled now before he said, 'beautiful'. Then he added quickly, 'Don't shake your head. I'm sure your mirror doesn't lie to you, and moreover, your straightforward and natural manner must infuriate her, for you do not act like the servant class. You are not subservient in any way because . . . well, you are an unusual girl, you know, and come from an unusual family . . . '

'Oh, yes, yes' – she nodded now – 'I come from an unusual family, and I'm never allowed to forget it . . . '

'Please. Please. I meant that as a compliment, believe me, for I admire your father and your mother and honour them for the stand they took and the way they have brought up you and your brothers and sister. You're all better educated

186

than many in the large mansions similar to this house.' Then again a note of laughter in his voice, he said, 'You must admit you're a very unusual crew.'

She wanted to smile at him. He was such a nice man, so kind. He treated her like an equal, as did Mr Simon . . . Oh, Mr Simon. And for that woman to think that she and her husband . . . She would never be able to face him now. Yet he may not know of her suspicions. What had she said? That he ignored her, didn't speak to her. Then there must be a reason. Well, didn't she know the reason? Hadn't she heard the reason? But why did they live together? Hadn't Miss Netherton said something about him being very fond of his mother, and she of him? But that surely wouldn't keep him tied to a woman like her if . . .

'That boy up there loves you.'

'*What?* Oh, yes, yes, the child. And I'm very fond of him, too.'

'Well, then, how can you talk about leaving? If I know anything, Penella will not return before Christmas, and if she decides to go to France, where she still has relatives, it could be three months before she comes back. She has stayed away as long before now. Come.' He took hold of her hand. 'Promise me you will stay with us. Anyway, what will happen to me if you go? I will only have to trudge across that moor to see you, and you know what happened on the moor the last time I trudged. And my poor horse, too, had sore feet, or a sore foot . . . '

As she rose to her feet now she did smile at him, saying, 'You should have been a diplomat; in fact, I think you are one. By the way, may I enquire how you have been feeling lately?'

'You mean the epileptic seizures? Oh . . . don't be embarrassed. I have ceased to worry about them. But, strangely, I have been free of them for weeks now. I'm on a new medicine. I had just begun taking it that day you came to my rescue and, you know, I have not had a seizure since. No; I lie. Well anyway, not a serious one, a petit mal, as it's called, once or twice, but that's all. They first started after a shock, you know. We were in Switzerland, my sister and I, and I saw the avalanche coming. It would have enveloped her, and I remember screaming a warning to her; and then it enveloped us both. But now my doctor thinks it may not be epilepsy. He has another name for it. You see, it all happens up here.' He tapped his head. 'One of the main cells decided it's not getting enough attention so hits out, and down I go fighting! And that's odd, because I'm not a fighting man. I'm a coward, an extreme coward.'

'Oh, Mr Timothy, I think . . . '

'What do you think?'

'I think you're the nicest man I've ever met.'

She watched the colour of his face change: it was as if he were blushing, and he turned from her abruptly, saying, 'Don't say that. Don't be too kind to me or I may take advantage of it.'

'I'm sorry. I didn't mean to up . . . '

He turned towards her again, saying, 'You didn't upset me, my dear, anything but. Anyway' – his tone changed – 'now that the coast is clear from dragons, dwarfs, and gingle-gill-goollies, I would like to bring Andrew across to visit your family sometime.'

'Oh, you'd be welcome. But tell me, I have never heard that word before, gingle-gill-goollies?'

'Oh, that. It's one of my home-made ones. I make up such for children's tales. Do you like fairy tales?'

'I was brought up on them.'

'Did they not frighten you?'

'Yes, some of them did.'

188

'Just some of them? Most of them did with me. We had a nanny who fancied herself as an actress and she read some of the very early ones and they are horrific. And she used to scare me to death. So I write fairy stories that have happy endings. You look surprised.'

'No. No, I'm not, because my father has told me that Sir Walter Scott wrote fairy tales.'

'Do you read Scott?'

'Not much. I . . . I'm not very fond of him. I find his writing . . . well, rather laborious. Do you like him?'

'Yes. Yes, I must confess I do like him. But then I have more time to indulge my fancy. I admit he takes some getting into.'

They were walking towards the library door now and she said, 'I would like to say thank you, Mr Timothy. You have been of great help to me.'

'Ah, well, then there's going to be no more talk of leaving?'

She sighed before she said, 'Well, not for the present.'

'That's good news. Now we can look forward to a happy Christmas, eh?'

On the drive home she wavered as to whether or not she should tell at least her mother what had transpired in the library; but then she knew her mother would surely confide in her father and the implications of that woman's suggestion would trouble them both, as it did herself. So she decided to say nothing for the time being, and she was even able to laugh at Barry's chatter as he endorsed the household's relief at the departure of the mistress.

'There's one I know'll thank God for her goin', an' that's Milligan, 'cos that poor beast's been run off his four feet. He used to duck his head every time he saw her comin' into the yard. I'm tellin' you, 'tis God's truth an' could be borne out by everybody in the stables. That horse used to back away from the door an' kick like hell. Beggin' your pardon, miss, but he did. The devil himself couldn't have used his hooves quicker than Milligan when she went to get on his back. Oh, 'tis like a ton weight off each of us; an' everyone else, too. The lasses are different in the kitchen. You can have a crack with 'em an' not be afraid of jumpin' out of your skin an' into the horse trough.'

Laughingly she enquired, why into the horse trough? to have the answer, 'Well, after the mistress's tongue has lashed out at you, you're stingin' all over. D'you know, she can swear like a trooper. She can beat our Frank. He's the first stable lad, as I've told you, miss, an' he learned from Ben Sutter. You know, he was in the Army once an' he was taught by the devil himself, who was the Sergeant Major, he said, an' there's not a word he doesn't know that you could get locked up for.'

Oh, she liked Barry McBride. He was another one she would surely miss when she left the house, as leave she must some day, and that some day would be the day that woman stepped foot in it again.

5

In the weeks leading up to Christmas, 1881, Timothy had three times brought the child to visit them: each time on a Sunday so the whole family would be present; and the boy had been enchanted with the long cosy room, but more so with its occupants and they with him. So it was proposed by Maria that Mr Timothy and the child should be invited to their usual Boxing Day party.

Oswald, Olan, Jimmy and Cherry all worked till late Christmas Eve in order that they should have Christmas Day as a holiday; as Oswald and Olan, who had now taken up their new positions in the pies and peas shop, worked up till one o'clock on Boxing Day, as also did Cherry and Jimmy. But by three o'clock they were all present, washed and changed and ready to meet their guests: besides Timothy and the child, Miss Netherton was coming and also Bobby Crane.

The lad had spent Christmas Day with them and surprised them with his ability to play the penny whistle almost as well as Oswald could play on the little flute that Nathaniel had bought him for his tenth birthday, after having heard him blowing through a reed. In consequence,

191

the get-together around the fire after Christmas dinner had been a jolly affair.

Now it was Boxing Day and party day and the room was packed. The tea had been merry and noisy, the centre of attraction being Andrew. Everybody seemed intent on making him happy and if his squeals of delight were anything to go by they had succeeded.

When at last the meal was over the family helped to clear the table, which was then pushed to the far end of the room in order to give space for some games, and the child became so excited that Miss Netherton said to Mr Timothy, 'What d'you bet me that nurse hasn't to get up in the middle of the night to somebody being violently sick?'

'No, no.' Timothy shook his head. 'If he's going to be sick I'll see that it happens before he goes to bed. But what odds? Did you ever see anyone enjoy himself as that child has done?'

As Anna and Cherry moved the two lamps into a safe place, one on each end of the mantelpiece, and put the pair of two-branched brass candelabra, holding wax, not tallow, candles, on the window sill, the child, pausing in his jumping up and down, looked about him with open mouth, then turned to Anna and said, 'It's like the story you tell me about Cinderella's palace.'

This brought a great hooting laugh from Nathaniel and a chuckle and the flapping of the hands from Maria. But Timothy, standing near the boy, looked around him, as the child had done, and said, 'Yes. Yes, you're right, Andrew. It is like Cinderella's palace. But there's more than one princess here; there are two princesses and two fairy godmothers. And then there's the king of the castle—' He extended his hand towards Nathaniel, and, turning to the laughing boys, he added, 'His sons, the princes.'

'Can we have a party tomorrow again, Uncle?'

192

'What!' This was a hoarse whisper from Timothy now. 'Do you want the king to throw us out? This is a special day; it only happens once a year.'

Gauging the moment to be right to start, Nathaniel cried, 'What game are we going to play first? "Here we go round the mulberry bush", eh? What about it, you two musicians?' And nodding towards Oswald, he said, 'You know the tune,' then turning to Bobby, he added, 'Do you? It goes . . . '

'I know how it goes, Mr Martell.'

'Then let's join hands. Come on! Come on!'

And so to the faint, sweet music of the two pipes they joined hands and danced and sang as they went:

'Here we go round the mulberry bush,
the mulberry bush, the mulberry bush,
Here we go round the mulberry bush
On a cold and frosty morning.

What do we find on a mulberry bush,
a mulberry bush, a mulberry bush,
What do we find on a mulberry bush
On a cold and frosty morning?

Nothing at all on the mulberry bush
nothing at all, nothing at all,
Nothing at all on the mulberry bush
On a cold and frosty morning.

The leaves have gone to feed the worms,
to feed the worms, to feed the worms,
The leaves have gone to feed the worms
On a cold and frosty morning.'

After they had danced and repeated the rhyme three times, Miss Netherton stopped and, panting, sat down in a chair and cried to Nathaniel, 'I've never heard that variation before.'

'No, I don't suppose you have. I made it up years ago for a little class I had when I was dealing with the making and spinning of cloth, and so on. And I discovered that the silk worms were fed on the mulberry leaves.'

'How interesting.'

'Another game! Another game! Let us play another game, a dancing game, Missanna. Missanna, like the one in the book.'

'Oh, that was a polka.'

'Oh! a polka. Not for me. Not for me.' And Timothy sat down now beside Miss Netherton, and Nathaniel, turning to Oswald, cried, 'Play us a polka.' And holding out his hand he said, 'Come on, Maria. Jimmy, you take Ben; Anna has already got her partner.' He laughed to where the child was clinging to Anna's hands. And before he had time to appoint a partner for Bobby, he saw Cherry go over to him and hold out her hand, and he noticed that the boy hesitated a moment before getting to his feet, and they all laughed when he said, 'I've got wooden legs.' And while Oswald played a brisk tune, Miss Netherton and Mr Timothy clapped in time with the music.

After one and another had dropped out exhausted and laughing, Nathaniel said, 'Well now, it's time for a little rest and some sweetmeats.' So, going to a side-table, he picked up a large box, lifted the lid and, looking around them all, he said, 'This is a gift from our dear friend, Miss Netherton.' And after they had all helped themselves to a sweet and nodded towards Miss Netherton, saying, 'Thank you, ma'am,' she said. 'Thank you all for a most happy day.'

It was Jimmy now who put in, 'Tell us a story, Dada. One of your ghosty ones.'

'Blind Man's Buff!'

They were all looking at Andrew now and laughing, and Nathaniel said, 'Well, I waive my right: the guest of honour's wishes must come first. Blind Man's Buff, it is.'

'Missanna. Missanna be blind man.'

'No; you be blind man,' said Anna, bending down to the child. And he, now gripping the skirt of her dress and attempting to shake her, said, 'No! you be blind man and catch me.'

'All right. All right. Dada, let me have a bandage.'

'Have my green muffler, my Christmas Box.'

She looked at Jimmy and, laughing now, she said, 'Oh, thanks, Jimmy. That'll do fine.'

It was as the boy scurried from the room to fetch the muffler that the sound of a horse neighing turned the attention of the party towards the door, and Mr Timothy exclaimed, 'That'll be the carriage. I said six o'clock, but it's only half-past five.'

'Oh, no, no, Uncle Timothy; we can't go home yet. Please, please.'

'All right, all right.'

It was as Nathaniel went to open the door that there came a rap on it, and when it was opened Timothy was the first to exclaim, 'Oh! Simon. What a nice surprise! Come in. Come in,' only to turn swiftly to Nathaniel and say, 'Dear me! Dear me! Here I am taking liberties. I'm so sorry.'

Nathaniel was laughing now as he addressed the man at the door, saying, 'Come in by all means, sir! And you're welcome.'

'Oh, Papa, Papa, we are having a lovely party. We have danced and sung and there are nice things to eat and . . .'

'All right, all right, I'll hear all about it later.' He patted his son's head. 'But first let me say, how do you do? to Mr and Mrs Martell and thank them for entertaining you.' At this he turned and, looking at Maria, he said, 'It is very kind of you to put up with this rowdy boy and his equally rowdy uncle,' which caused a little tentative laughter; and then he turned to Nathaniel, saying, 'Thank you, sir, not only for today, but for the kindness you have shown in the past, and mostly for allowing your daughter to impart her knowledge to my son.'

The words were very formal and for a moment they seemed to dampen the atmosphere, until Miss Netherton said in her usual imperious voice, 'Well! don't stand there, Simon; come and sit down for a moment. They are about to play Blind Man's Buff.'

He did not however obey her but, looking from the child to Timothy, he said, 'Don't you think you have both already outstayed your welcome?'

But before either of them had time to speak Nathaniel cried, 'Not at all! Not at all! We could go on all night. Just let him have one more game. Please.'

'As you wish. As you wish.' Simon was smiling now, and he went and stood near Miss Netherton's chair while Oswald, taking the scarf from Jimmy, doubled its length in four; then going to his sister, he said, 'Turn round, and no peeping, mind,' and after tying the scarf at the back he swung her about three times, crying, 'Ready! Set! Go!'

With hands stretched out before her Anna groped towards the giggles and the whisperings and, taking up the pattern of her playing the game in the nursery with her pupil, she called, 'Where is that big fellow who won't learn his lessons? Where is he? I'm sure he's over here.'

Now she turned about and made her way towards the fire. She knew this because of the heat that was meeting her. And once her feet touched the mat she swung swiftly to her left and made a dive for the armchair, and from behind it there came giggling and scampering.

And when Cherry took up the chant in which the boys joined,

'Name the one you want to catch;
name the one you want to hold,
if you dare be so bold,'

she answered,

'I name the one I want to hold:
It's Master Andrew, I make so bold.'

When she heard the child's giggle she made a little run in his direction and knew that someone had suddenly lifted him up out of her reach.

Then the chant changed:

'Move round, move round,
The blind man can't see.
Be quick! Be quick!
Or he'll catch thee.'

She could hear them all changing places, and again she was going down the room towards the fire, saying now, 'You should give me a word.' And when she heard Oswald say, 'Ma'ah! Ma'ah!' like the nanny goat, she knew he was standing near the kitchen door. She did not move in that direction but towards the big armchair again, and she knew the child was there by the suppressed little squeak he made, and she guessed he would be standing up pressed against the back of it. And so, thrusting her hands quickly out, she made a dive for him. But she had misjudged the distance, and she realised her hands were gripping the lapels of a coat. She felt them lifted from the coat she held and heard a child's voice shouting with glee: 'You've caught Papa. You've caught Papa. You've caught Papa. Not me, you've caught Papa.'

In the next second Anna had pulled off the scarf, and there she was looking into the unsmiling face of Simon. Withdrawing her other hand sharply from his and amidst the laughing and chatter, she picked up the boy from the

197

chair and forced herself to say lightly, 'Why didn't you give me a better signal?'

'I did! I did! Missanna.'

'Well, you didn't squeak loud enough.'

'Can we have another game? and then you can catch me and . . . '

'No, no.' It was his father speaking now. 'I think you've had enough for one day, and everyone has had enough of you, too. Moreover, the horses are outside and they are getting very cold, as is Grafton. And you know, when Grafton gets cold, what he does.'

'He shouts.'

'Yes, he shouts. Oh yes, he shouts.' He was smiling now, and he looked towards Timothy who, smiling back at him, said, 'And, more than shouts.'

Miss Netherton, now moving across to Simon, said, 'I've ordered my trap for half-past six, but I'd be more comfortable in your carriage if you would care to drop me.'

'It would be a pleasure indeed.'

'Well then, I'll get into my things.'

There was bustle and chatting, and then they were all crowded round the door and Timothy was saying, 'I cannot remember when I've enjoyed myself more, and I have no words with which to express my thanks. I can simply treat your kindness with impertinence by saying, may I come again soon?'

Nathaniel's and Maria's assurance that he knew he would be welcome at any time was drowned by the laughter brought about by Miss Netherton saying, 'Take my arm, you philanderer; you would make a wonderful professional beggar.' Then, turning to the family, she spoke to them as a whole, saying, 'You know what I think. I haven't this fellow's tongue, so I can simply say, thank you for a most happy time.'

198

Robert Grafton had now come forward and was swinging the lantern to show Timothy and Miss Netherton to the carriage and the child was saying his goodbyes to all in turn, shaking each hand and saying, 'Thank you. Thank you.' Then as his father lifted him the child put one hand round his neck and of a sudden, reached forward and tugged Anna towards him by gripping the front of her dress and with his lips pouted out he kissed her, an audible kiss on the mouth. For a second her eyes were again looking into Simon's, and she gave a slight gasp and tried to loosen the child's hand from her collar.

But he held on to it and said, 'I will see you in the morning, Missanna?' and she stammered, 'Y . . . yes, in the morning.'

'I love you, Missanna.'

She was feeling that even her hair was on fire. There were laughing murmurs all around her; and Simon was saying, 'You must forgive my son for expressing his feelings so publicly,' and to Nathaniel and Maria he said, 'You'll be glad when this invasion is over.'

Amid loud protestations he nodded from one to the other, then said, 'Good-night. Good-night all,' and made his way towards the carriage.

They stood and watched the horses being turned on the frost-bitten ground and they remained standing round the opened door until the side lights of the carriage had disappeared through the gate and onto the narrow road.

With the closing of the door, there was a general expression of shivering and a making for the warmth of the fire, and although they talked and chattered about the events of the day, a quietness now seemed to have descended on them, and presently Oswald said, 'It's one of the nicest Christmases I can remember, and we've had some nice ones, haven't we, Dada?'

'Yes, Oswald; we've had some nice ones, but as you say I think this is the nicest. I suppose it's because we've made a child happy and he needed to be made happy. He's had no life, no child's life, from what Anna tells us. He's to be pitied, in a way.' Then turning his gaze onto Bobby, who had his head down, he said, 'I don't retract on that, Bobby. There are many worse things than an empty belly in this world. You can't live on love, I know, but it helps a slice of dry bread to taste as if it had butter on it.'

'Oh, I know, I know, Mr Martell, I know what you mean. An' I've watched the bairn the day; it's just as if he had been let loose.'

'Have you enjoyed yourself, Bobby?' The sudden enquiry brought his head sharply round to look at Cherry, and he stared at her for a moment before he said, with a grin, 'You know, if I knew you better I would say that was a bloomin' silly question to ask me.' And this wrought a change back to laughter, his own being the loudest: but then, with a slight break in his voice, he looked at Maria and said, 'You'll never know really what you've done for me this Christmas. What you've all done for me. To me dying day I'll remember it. Whatever else happens in me life I'll remember this day.' He turned to look at Cherry again and said, 'You've got your answer.' And she laughed, her mouth wide, saying, 'I can see how they wanted to throw you out of the pit; you talk too much.'

Their reactions to something funny was back, and again there was general laughter, for the whole family had noted and remarked on how the young fellow hardly ever opened his mouth; and Anna had asked her father: 'Does he talk much when he's learning his reading?' to be told, 'It's forced in a way, but it's getting better.'

They weren't late in going to bed, and it was after the two girls had lain silently side by side for some time that Cherry said softly, 'I like him.'

200

'Who?'

'Bobby.'

This caused Anna to turn on her side and face her sister, and say, 'What d'you mean by that, you like him?'

'Just what I said.'

'Which I take it to mean, you more than like him?'

'I'm not quite sure of that, Anna; but I've never sort of felt like this about any other boy. Not that either of us have had the chance to meet boys. But there's those from the village you see now and again walking through the fields on a Sunday, in their best suits, and to my mind Bobby seems to stand out. He did, even in his pit clothes; and he's got a mind and he thinks. But . . . but I'm older than him.'

'Oh, yes, yes, a lot older, a year and a bit! What is he? Seventeen, and you're eighteen, just gone.'

'Don't laugh. It isn't right that age should be like that; the man should always be the older.'

'Don't be silly! It's how you feel, it's got nothing to do with age. Look at Miss Alice Simmons from Bowcrest, she who married last year. Remember? She's thirty-four, they said, and she married a man of twenty-five.'

'Well, that lot can make laws for themselves; the higher you're up the less it matters . . . '

'You had better not let Dada hear you talk like that; he'll ask where all your learning's gone? And I'll say this: if you like Bobby, go on liking him; but get to know him better. And anyway, you know nothing could happen for years.'

'I know that, but I can but hope.'

'Well, go on hoping, dear; it's better than no hope at all.'

She turned away and onto her side and after a moment Cherry said softly, 'There's someone interested in you an' all; but there's no hope at all in that quarter, and I feel sorry, I do.'

'What d'you mean? What d'you mean?' Anna had turned back again and was half-sitting up in bed.

'Oh, lie down, you know what I mean. You could see the way he looked at you when he was holding your hands in Blind Man's Buff. And I think I'm not the only one that noticed. Dada isn't blind to that kind of thing.'

'Cherry! Cherry Dagshaw! Shut up! D'you hear? Don't ever dare bring that subject up again, to me or anyone else. *D'you hear?*'

'All right, all right. Lie down.'

Anna lay down, and after a moment Cherry, with a big heave, turned on to her side, saying, 'If I had my doubts before how you felt, you've dispelled them now.'

Anna was for flouncing round again but she stopped herself by gripping the edge of the feather tick. She would have to leave that place; there must be no waiting.

PART FOUR

❧

The Blow

1

⚬

The winter of 1881–2 had been a severe one. There were
days when the roads were impassable because of the heavy
falls of snow; and conditions were made even worse when
the thaw set in.

She hadn't kept the promise to herself to give up her post,
telling herself that the child needed her. However, she was
relieved, yet at the same time sorry, whenever the weather
made her visits impossible.

The severest snowstorm occurred in February. It went on
for four days. Huge drifts blocked the roads, trains were
unable to run, and when eventually the thaw came the rivers
overflowed their banks, flooding much of the land in and
around the villages; only the moors seemed to escape. And
perhaps this was as well, for in the second week of March,
two pit families and a single man made their home on the
moors, at least on the edge of it and as near as possible to
Nathaniel's woodland fence, in order to get a little shelter
from the trees.

They had been there for three days before Nathaniel and
Anna, having gone down to the wood-pile to replenish the
house stock, came across them; and they were aghast at

hearing the sound of a child coughing its heart out under one of the tarpaulin shelters, three rough habitations that Nathaniel wouldn't have offered as shelter to his goats. The company consisted of three men, two women, and five children. One man had a fire going in a holed, square, tin box and had erected a tripod over it on which a kettle was swinging. And when Nathaniel spoke to them across the railings, saying, 'Dear! Dear! This can't go on,' the man said, 'We ain't takin' any of your wood, mister.'

'I'm not talking about wood,' said Nathaniel, harshly now. 'I'm talking about the conditions under which you are living and that child coughing in there.' He pointed to the tarpaulin and makeshift walls of oddments of furniture. And he said, 'You only had to come and ask. You know you could have used the barn; others before you have done so.'

The man came towards the fence now and the other two men and one of the women followed, and it was the first man who spoke, saying in a quiet voice, 'Aye, I know that, mister. You've been very good, and you needn't have been, with what they've done to you and your lot. But we didn't want any more trouble to come on you. So we'll be all right here for the next day or two, then we'll shift. We're goin' into the town. We'll get something; if not, the workhouse will have to keep us. But that'll be over me dead body. I'll swear on that. And we'll all see our day with that lot back there.' He thumbed over the moor in the direction of the mine. 'Livin' on the fat of the land, they are. We're turnin' out more bloody coal now than we ever have; three times as much as twenty years ago. I know me figures, mister. I know me figures. I'm a union man. That's me trouble, I'm a union man. The three of us here are and there's many more back there an' all. If they'd only have the bloody guts to stand up for what they think an' come out. That's why we're here, you see. We tried to get them out. Stand together, I said.

206

And what happened? That bloody keeker, Praggett, put his oar in again.'

'Why is it always Praggett who seems to have the last say in the evictions?'

'Oh, well, mister, he just works to orders an' all. There's only one there who has a good word for us and that's Taunton, the engineer; but he's got to watch his step. It's been worse since Morgansen, the second owner, come up from London and put his neb in: they should get themselves bloody well down below and see what goes on in order to let them live like lords. But I suppose Morgansen's come 'cos of his lass is goin' to marry Brodrick. An' he's lordin' it an' all since his old man died. But we'll see our day with the lot of 'em. They can do nowt about it. The union's growin' and it'll swell an' swell an' suffocate the buggers, and I hope I live to see it.'

Looking at the man, Anna could see just how he had talked himself out of his job: he was a box-thumper. And yet he had a cause, oh yes. But what was this about Mr Raymond going to marry the other mine-owner's daughter? That was something new. Oh dear, what about his brother's wife? She recalled the day she listened in to his protestations of love, so what would she do now? How would she react?

She was wintering, as nurse had called it, in the South of France; and she remembered nurse adding laughingly, 'I hope she summers there an' all,' to which she had mentally agreed, for the house was a different place without her personality. And except for the two weeks it had been in deep mourning for the loss of the master, Arnold Brodrick, the news of whose death had only reached them a week after he had been buried in some remote area abroad, the house had taken on a peaceful air. And she had felt herself to be accepted more and more by the staff, with one or two exceptions: the upper housemaid's manner, to say the least, was still offensive.

Maybe it was because she had been bred in the village and was the blacksmith's niece.

Her father was saying in a puzzled tone, 'Why won't you accept the hospitality of the barn? It is weatherproof and warm and your wives could cook in the tack room. And that child needs shelter other than that erection, if I'm to go by that racking cough.'

It was one of the other men who answered this, saying, 'We would like to, mister. He won't tell you' – he pointed to his talkative companion – 'but Praggett tells us that if any more of us are given shelter from you they can ring off the land and then you would have no way out for your horse and cart, and the only other way on foot would be through the village. And we know that you've had trouble there as well.'

Nathaniel's indignation seemed to put inches on him and his voice was loud now as he cried, 'They cannot enclose us, the moor is common land. And we are bounded on two sides by Farmer Billings's land.'

'Aye, well, you know, sir—' The man was nodding at him and in a quiet voice he said further, 'Billings only rents the farm from the Brodricks. It's their land, you see.'

'But Mr Brodrick would never allow it.'

'Aye, you would think so, but . . . but Morgansen's got a bigger slice, so I understand, of the cake, and Brodrick must be out to please him, I suppose, seein' as he is goin' to join his family. Strikes me it's a business deal as much as a marriage. Anyway, that's it, sir. We didn't want to get you into a fix like that, for they say Morgansen is tougher than Brodrick.'

'There are public rights of way that even all the Brodricks and Morgansens have no control over. Now, take down those ramshackle attempts at cover and get yourselves into the barn. You can have the boiler going in a short time and hot water and hot drinks for that child. How are you off

208

for bedding?' He was looking at the women now, and one of them said, 'Well, sir, not too bad, but it's a bit damp.'

'Then get it over and get it dried off. Look, carry your things along to the gate there. Until the weather gets better you'll have to make journeys back to the wood-pile to keep the boiler going. There's plenty of wood, so you needn't worry about that or anything else . . . Fencing us in indeed!' He turned about now and, taking an armful of logs, he said to Anna, 'Come. Did you ever hear anything like that? What will they try to do next?'

'Well, they've said it before, Dada, and they'll likely carry out their intent, and leave us to fight it after.'

'Just let them try. What a pity Miss Netherton's away! She would have gone over there and blown them up. She knows the law. For two pins I'd go myself . . .'

'Please, Dada, don't get involved any more than you need. I'll be going over tomorrow. I'll see Mr Simon; perhaps he will be able to do something, although, as he says, he washes his hands of the mine and all its business. He doesn't like what's going on there any more than you do. As for Mr Timothy, I think if he had worked there he would have been the first one to go on strike.'

On entering the house Nathaniel cried, 'Maria! Maria! Come and hear the latest.' And when Maria emerged from the kitchen saying, 'What is it now?' he told her, and she listened in silence as she stood drying her hands. Then she asked quietly, 'What if they have the authority?'

'They haven't the authority to take in common land, moorland.'

'But it must belong to somebody. They just haven't bothered to rail it in before now.'

Nathaniel looked from Maria to Anna; then going to a chair, he dropped down onto it, and again remarked, 'I do wish Miss Netherton was here. I know nothing about law.

I've been stupid enough all my life to deal in folklore and fairy tales, never getting down to the basics. I'm an idiot, a pleasant idiot, that's what I am.'

'Yes. Yes, of course you are, dear.' They were standing one at each side of him now, and Maria, stroking his hair back from his forehead, added, 'I've known that for a long time and I've wondered how I've put up with it.' Then Anna laughed and Nathaniel looked at her and said, 'She means that. Under that pleasantry she means that.'

'Yes, of course I do. And now what we all want is a nice glass of elderberry wine, heated.'

When Maria returned to the kitchen Nathaniel looked at Anna and, all the steam going out of his tone, he said, 'If we can't get the cart out, how will we manage to get the hay and animal feed in, and our groceries? And then there are the boys; if the moor is cut off they'll have a mile and a half to walk, and have to pass through the village to get on the old coach road.'

'Well, don't worry about that, Dada, they'll do it. Or they can stay in the town, you know: there's those rooms above the shop that they're always talking about. I'm sure Mrs Simpson would like them there permanently. As for Bobby, he'll tramp with them, and then there'll be less likelihood of their being set upon than if they were on their own; even though we know, and they now know, that Oswald is capable of taking on two men, as he's already proved. That leaves Cherry and me. Now, Mrs Praggett will see that Cherry gets there all right or you'll soon know what'll happen to *Mr Praggett*.' She laughed now. 'As for me, well, Dada, I'm thinking seriously of leaving the tutoring.'

'Why? Now why? I understood the child isn't to be put under a male tutor until he is six?'

'Oh, there are numerous reasons; the main one, of course, is that the mistress will be home shortly and I couldn't risk another up-and-downer with her without hitting her.'

He returned her smile and said, 'I understand'; then taking her hand, he added, 'I understand more than you know. I think you're a very, very wise girl, and I love you dearly.'

'And I you, Dada, because you are an idiot, a folklore fairytale idiot.' And bending, she put her arms round him and kissed him. And Maria, at this moment entering the room and carrying a tray holding three mugs of steaming wine, said, 'And I'll be expected to manage him after that!'

2

She always went into the house by the side door, the one which the housekeeper had told her she must use when taking the child for his afternoon walk, and on this occasion she was just about to mount the stairs when she heard the familiar voice of Betty Carter from along the passage, saying, 'The gig's in the yard. She's back.' Immediately she felt the urge to turn and confront the speaker, but told herself to get upstairs and continue to ignore that person.

She had hardly reached the landing before the nurse's sitting-room door opened and the old woman said, 'Oh, lass, 'tis good to see you again. Like a touch of spring. Come in, come in. He's all ready and waitin' as he has been every day. I told him you'd be here the day, though. Here, give me your hat and coat and let me have your news. Don't worry about him.' She thumbed towards the door. 'Peggy is with him at the moment. The thing is, we won't have to laugh else he'll be in here like a shot. Sit down a minute . . . Hasn't it been a winter? I thought after that big do we had it was finished, but then, to start again! I hear they've started fencing part of the land in. How's your da taking that?'

Anna gave the old woman a brief account of how her father was taking the latest situation, but went on to say that, otherwise, the family were all fine. But how was she faring? And what was her news?

'Oh, lass, you should have been here yesterday. There was high jinks downstairs. Her ladyship returned the previous night with luggage that would fill a train, so Betty Carter said. And her and Conway took nearly an hour to sort things out. Grayson said he had seen happier faces at a funeral dinner than was around the dining table that night. But that was nothing to yesterday. She must have collared Mr Raymond on his own and had a screaming match in the library with him. 'Tis said that Mr Timothy went down to her and she went for him an' all; then Mr Raymond came upstairs and told his man to pack a case and off he went. And all this, you know, because of his engagement. You would ask what it's got to do with her to get her boiled up. But then you needn't ask, if you know what I mean, lass.'

Anna knew what she meant, but she made no remark and the old woman went on, 'When Mr Simon came in later – he had been in Newcastle – he had word to go to madam straightaway. Well, from there he apparently went looking for his wife, and this led to another shindy, and then another black dinner, so Walters said, with poor Mr Timothy talking first to one and then the other about this, that, and nothin'. Eeh! by lass, this is a house, and all since that one came into it . . .' Here the door burst open unceremoniously and the child darted in, crying, 'Oh, Missanna! Missanna! I knew it was you. I told Peggy it was you. And she said it wasn't. Oh, Missanna, have you come to stay now the snow has gone forever?'

Anna looked down into the face gazing up at her. The boy had his arms around her thighs and his head was back on his shoulders and he looked so appealing that she wanted to bend and kiss him.

But all she did was stroke his hair back and ask him, 'Have you been a good boy and kept reading your books?'

'Oh yes, Missanna. And I have teached Peggy.'

' "Taught" Peggy.'

He gave a gurgle of a laugh and repeated, 'Taught Peggy.' Then added, 'But she is stupid.'

'Now, now, Andrew; that is very naughty. You must not say that anyone is stupid.'

'Well, she does not know the alphabet.'

'She may not, but that doesn't mean that if Peggy doesn't know the alphabet she is stupid. Now turn and tell Peggy you are sorry.'

Peggy was standing at the open doorway leading into the classroom and she smiled broadly as the child now walked towards her and, looking up at her, said, 'I am sorry I called you stupid, Peggy. But you still don't know the alphabet, do you?'

The girl laughed, the nurse laughed, and Anna said, 'Go on with you! Get inside there. You are a wily young man. When you apologise, you apologise; you don't end up by throwing a brickbat.'

'What is a brickbat?'

Laughing now, Anna said, 'It is what I'm going to take to your bottom if you are not careful.' And at this she slapped him playfully on the buttocks, causing him to squeal gleefully and run madly round the table. And as she brought him to a stop she thought to herself that her welcome in all ways at this end of the house made up for a lot. And she would miss it, because soon the fencing would cut off the road to the gate and that would mean she would have to walk, and through the village, before she could reach McBride and the gig. The walking itself wouldn't matter, but having to walk through the village would. However, it would provide her with an excuse for leaving here.

It was as the child was having his morning milk and she was about to take her cup of coffee in company with the nurse that Betty Carter appeared in the classroom; no knocking, just an abrupt opening of the door and that broad, thick twang saying, 'She wants you downstairs.'

Anna immediately paused in her walk towards the nurse's sitting-room door and looked hard towards the girl; and now she said, 'Who wants me downstairs?'

The girl wagged her head before she answered, 'The mistress.'

'And where does she wish to see me?'

'Where d'you think?' And with this the girl turned abruptly about and went out, banging the door after her.

Anna drew in a long breath before tapping on the nurse's door, and at the, 'Come away in, lass,' she said, 'I'm wanted downstairs, nurse ... the mistress wishes to see me.'

'Oh, dear, dear. Well, all I can hope for is she's in a better temper. But now, lass' – she put her hand on Anna's shoulder – 'just let her get on with it. D'you hear me? Just stand there and take it. The others do; so learn a lesson. It's a backward one for you, I know, an' it'll take some doing, but don't answer her back. And keep that chin of yours down a bit. The cut of your jib, you know, says a lot of how you're thinkin'.'

'Oh! nurse.' Anna smiled now. 'The cut of me jib! The first time I heard that was from Bobby, you know, I've told you about him, the pit lad, when he said some of the men down the pit didn't like the cut of his jib. Dada had to translate it for me. Anyway, I'll remember. I'll try.' She poked her face forward now. 'That's all I can tell you, I'll try. I'm not promising, but I'll try.'

215

'Go on with you!' The old woman pushed her, and a voice from behind them said, 'Can I come with you, Missanna, and see Mama?'

'Not now, dear,' she said; 'perhaps later. You come and sit with nurse, and—' she bent to him and in a stage whisper said, 'see if nurse can recite the alphabet? I don't think she can, not as well as you.' And she now pressed the boy towards the old woman, then went out. But at the top of the stairs she hesitated. That girl hadn't said where she would find the mistress. Perhaps she was in the library . . . or in that room next door. But why would she be there? Well, where else? she couldn't go to her private apartments. Oh! that girl. She should go and find her; but that would mean keeping that woman waiting, and that in itself could cause an eruption. And there was no-one else at this end of the house she could ask. And so she made for the library, only to find no one in the big room, or the smaller one. She stood in the corridor, thinking. She'd likely have an office down here where she would see the housekeeper and give her her orders for the day. But where would that be? The only other place she might be was in the studio. So, it was to the studio that she made her way.

She tapped on the door but heard no reply, so she waited, then knocked again, and when she wasn't bidden to enter she gently turned the handle, pushed the door open and went into the room and in one sweeping glance she took in the chaotic scene. The canvasses that she had noticed on her previous visit, stacked against the wall, were strewn over half the floor. Some just had holes in them, others were ripped across; but there on an easel near the window was a full-length canvas and on it the startling picture of a naked man. What was more startling still was that he was dripping with paint. His face was almost obliterated by it, and it had run down his chest and onto his loins. But although the face was hardly

216

recognisable, she knew it to be that of Mr Raymond.

Looking about her at the chaos the room presented, realisation came, and it was frightening, and she told herself that she must get out of here and quick before . . .

But she was too late, for through the open door now strode the enraged figure of the mistress, and Anna, swinging round and facing her, had a fleeting thought that told her she had never seen this woman other than mad, but never as mad as at this moment.

'*You! You! How dare you!* You were sent for to my office.'

She was beginning, 'I . . . I didn't get any directions, mistress, so . . .'

'Shut up! Shut that yapping, slimy mouth of yours!' She was advancing now, each step deliberate, and Anna steeled herself for the coming blow which she was sure was intended. But a yard or so from her the woman stopped, the words spewing out of her mouth: 'Legal separation and . . . and then divorce, so your bastards would be recognised. That's it, isn't it? But I'll see you in hell first! D'you hear? You brazen, black-haired bastard, you.'

The hand wasn't extended towards Anna but to the table to the side, and in a flash it slipped beneath a palette thick with an assortment of still-wet paints and although she knew what was about to happen, she wasn't quick enough in jumping aside. But the palette, missing her face, still came flat against her shoulder and chest. Then, as she screamed and thrust out her hands towards the woman, a heavy object hit her on the side of the head and she felt the liquid flowing over her face. She knew that the woman was screaming, and she was screaming too, but she was also sliding down into somewhere and the scream inside her head was telling her she mustn't let herself faint, because that woman might kill her.

217

As she felt her body hit the floor it seemed such a long time since she had first begun to fall; she knew that now there were more people screaming.

Unaware that she'd had her eyes shut, she now opened them to see the tall figure of Simon Brodrick pushing his wife against the wall. They were the ones who were screaming. She couldn't make out what either of them was yelling; but then she felt her own body jerk as she saw him lift a hand and catch his wife a blow across one side of her face, then lift it again and bring the back of it across her other cheek. She actually felt the impact when the woman seemed to bounce from the wall, and when next she saw him grip her by the shoulders and throw her onto the floor amid the torn canvasses, she again closed her eyes tightly.

A voice was crying, 'Oh my God!' Then, 'Anna! Anna! Wake up! Wake up! Are you all right? No, no; of course you're not all right. Oh, my dear.'

She opened her eyes to look into Timothy's face now; and she became aware that there was another man bending towards her and Timothy saying to him, 'Help me to get her up, Mulroy.'

Then the housekeeper's voice came to her as if from a distance saying, 'The blood's coming from just above her ear, I think, sir.'

They were leading her from the room now. There were more people in the corridor. She couldn't make out who they were: there was something spilling over her face. She seemed to be floating. She *was* floating: she felt herself rising in the air; then someone pulled her down and thrust her into some dark place . . .

She became aware that she was lying on a bed. She knew the sun was shining because it was hitting her eyelids. There was someone standing near her, speaking. She recognised the voice as Mr Timothy's. Dear Mr Timothy. She liked that man. He was saying, 'When did you tell her that?' and the answer came, 'Last night. I'd had enough. To make a show of herself like that with Raymond, and almost in front of my face . . . man, it was impossible to bear. It's been under cover too long; it was bound to come out. So I told her, a legal separation and then divorce.'

'What about the child?'

'I said she could have custody of him, but you'll not believe it, she doesn't want him. She said so openly. It was then I told her that his father should have him.'

'Oh, Simon! Simon, you didn't!'

'I did, Tim. And it was about time. I've lain under this since the day she spewed it at me during the first week of our so-called honeymoon, because I knew then I hadn't been the first. And she had the nerve to tell me who had.'

The voices were moving away. There was more muttering and then Mr Timothy's voice came again: 'Have you flaunted the girl to her?'

'No. No, definitely not.' Then more muttering and now Mr Timothy's voice, 'I am not blind; I know of your feelings towards her. Have you spoken of them to her?'

'No; not as yet, but I mean to.'

'You think, or you have the impression that she cares for you?'

Anna, awake now, waited for the answer; and then it came: 'I don't know, but I mean to find out, and soon. The fact that she's put up with that insanely jealous bitch's antics for so long gives me hope.'

'I . . . I wouldn't bank on it, if I were you. That's your ego talking, as they put it these days. There's the child. She's very fond of the child.'

'Yes. Yes, I know. Still, ego or not, we'll see what transpires in the future. In the meantime we must let her rest here. Now I must go to mother. She'll have heard about this already.'

219

There was the sound of a door closing, then footsteps approaching the bed again, and she felt a hand on her brow lifting her hair gently to the side and a whispering voice, saying, 'Oh, my dear. My dear.'

There was such feeling in the words that she wanted to cry and also to put her hand up and stroke the cheek of this kind, thoughtful man whose life was so marred.

When she slowly opened her eyes and looked at him, he said, 'How are you feeling?'

'Tired.'

'Yes, my dear. But just rest.'

'I want to go home.'

'You will later on. The housekeeper is going to prepare a bath so you can wash your hair and she is finding a gown for you.'

She opened her eyes wider now and put a hand up to her hair, then looked at the hand and asked, 'What is it?'

'It was oil, my dear, linseed oil. Fortunately nothing stronger.' He did not say it could have been turpentine.

'I shall never come back into this house again.'

'I know that, my dear, I know that.'

'She is mad.'

'Partly, partly.'

'No' – she shook her head slowly – 'not partly; all mad.'

He sighed then said, 'I told you once before she's a very unhappy woman. Spoilt women are often unhappy, I have found.'

'I would rather go home and wash there. If you could get the gig.'

'No, my dear; you're in no condition to go home yet. Do this to please me because, may I say it, we are friends, aren't we?'

She stared at him for a moment before saying, 'If you say we're friends, Mr Timothy, then we are friends.'

'Do you think you could say Tim? That would please me so much. And as you won't be in this house much longer there'll be no one to hear you . . . taking liberties.' He smiled over the last words.

She made no answer to this but found that her lids were closing again. She did feel sleepy, and weary; no, as he said, she couldn't go home like this. Perhaps later.

It was three o'clock in the afternoon. Mrs Hewitt had helped her wash her hair, and had then supplied her with a plain smock-like dress, and had also put a bandage round her head to cover the cut behind her ear; and she was now sitting in a room off the hall, her coat and hat on, and Simon Brodrick was standing in front of her. He was saying, 'I know that this is the end of your service here. The child is going to miss you, you know, miss you desperately.' Then he added softly, 'And I, more than he, will miss you. I'm sure you know that.' She looked up into his face but didn't answer him. And he said, 'If you feel strong enough, my mother would like to have a word with you before you leave. Do you think you could see her?'

He was asking if she thought she could see his mother. It wasn't an order, it was a request. She said simply, 'Yes.'

'I will take you along, then I will see you home.'

'There won't be any need; I . . . I would rather go on my own.'

They were facing each other now, and he said, 'We must talk, Anna. You know that, don't you?'

She stepped back from him and in a tone as harsh as she could make it at that moment, she said, 'No! No, I don't!'

'Oh, Anna, please don't say that. Look, we won't talk about it now, but I will come over and see you in a day or two, for you must know, you must have guessed.'

221

'*Please, please, don't say any more.*' And she again stepped back from him. 'You wish me to see your mother?'

He bowed his head for a moment, then went to the door, opened it and walked slightly ahead of her until they reached the grey door, through which he ushered her; then tapping on his mother's bedroom door, he entered, saying, 'Miss Dagshaw, Mother,' and turning back to her, he added, 'I'll be waiting in the hall.'

As she had done once before, she walked across the large room and to the foot of the bed, and again she was looking into the bright eyes, which were so like Mr Timothy's.

It must have been quite a full minute before Mrs Brodrick said, 'I am deeply sorry you have had to be subjected to such awful treatment in this house, Miss Dagshaw.'

Anna could not think of a reply, so she just remained still, her eyes fixed on the white face.

'You require an apology at least and . . . and I'm sorry it must come from me alone, as my daughter-in-law stresses the fact that you were asked to go and see her in her office, but instead you went into her studio, where she was disposing of private . . .'

'Madam, I am sorry to interrupt you, but I had no message to the effect that I was to see your daughter-in-law in her office. I was just told I had to come down and see the mistress. There was no explanation of where I must see her. I had never been to her office before. She had spoken to me once in the library and once in her studio. I went to the library first. When she wasn't there, I naturally went to the studio.'

Again there was a long pause before Mrs Brodrick said, 'I understand that the message was given to the upper housemaid and that she passed it on to you.'

'I'm sorry, madam, but you have been misinformed. Had I known I had to see your daughter-in-law in the office, I should not have gone to the library.'

222

'No, of course you wouldn't . . . Nurse!'

When the nurse appeared at her side, she said, 'Tell them to send the upper housemaid to me. And place a chair for Miss Dagshaw, please.'

The chair was brought, and Anna found she was thankful to sit down. And now Mrs Brodrick said, 'I am sorry that my grandson will be deprived of your teaching, because he has got on so well under your tuition.'

Again Anna remained silent.

'What will you do now?'

'I don't know, madam. I may find employment in the city.'

'I do hope so. And then perhaps you . . . you will marry?'

The blue gaze held hers until she said, 'I have no intention of doing so yet, madam.'

'I don't think the intention will be left with you for very long.' The face moved into a tight smile.

The door opened and the nurse brought in Betty Carter, leading her right to the foot of the bed.

The girl was definitely nervous and she dipped her knee towards the face that was looking at her. And then Mrs Brodrick said, 'Tell me exactly, girl, what order your mistress gave you when she wished to speak to Miss Dagshaw.'

The girl wetted her lips, her head moved slightly, and then she said, 'Go and tell the teacher to come to my office. I wish to speak to her.'

'And what did you say to Miss Dagshaw?'

'I . . . I told her that, madam.'

Anna had already turned her head towards the girl, and now she couldn't stop herself from saying, 'You did not. You did not mention the office.'

'I did so. But your nose was too high in the . . .' She stopped and her head drooped.

'Look at me, girl!' Mrs Brodrick's head was raised. 'I am saying to you that you are lying, that you never gave

223

Miss Dagshaw that message. You merely told her that your mistress wanted to see her. Isn't that so?'

'No. No, it isn't, madam. No, it isn't. She's lying, not me. I told her. I said, go to the office.'

'You did not, girl. You did not.' Anna almost hissed the words under her breath, and Mrs Brodrick called, 'Shh!' Then addressing the girl again, she went on, 'If you told Miss Dagshaw to go to your mistress's office, why did she first go to the library then to the studio, and during this time your mistress would have been waiting for her in her office?'

The girl's head was down again and she muttered, 'I did. I did tell her. I did.'

'You are lying, aren't you?'

The girl was looking into the cold blue eyes now and her own lids were blinking rapidly. Then she burst out, 'Well! madam, she's so hoity-toity. She never listens. She acts like . . .'

'Be quiet! girl. Nurse!'

'Yes, madam?' The nurse was standing near the head of the couch. 'Send for Mrs Hewitt immediately.'

Mrs Brodrick turned to the girl again, and now she said, 'You were aware that your mistress didn't want anyone to go near her studio this morning, weren't you? Answer me, girl.'

'No, madam.'

'Lift your head and look at me.'

The girl now lifted her head slowly and Mrs Brodrick repeated, 'You were aware that your mistress didn't want anyone to go near her studio this morning, I say to you again, weren't you?'

And now the mutter came, 'I . . . I knew she was in a temper, that's . . . that's all.'

The door opened again and Mrs Hewitt almost scurried into the room. She seemed to take no notice of anyone as she

224

went and stood beside Betty Carter, then dipped her knee to the old lady, saying as she did so, 'Madam?'

Mrs Brodrick addressed her: 'Hewitt,' she said, 'you will take this girl and dismiss her. Give her a week's wage in lieu of notice but no reference, for she has been the means of causing a disturbance in my house.'

'Oh.' It was a small sound coming from Anna: she wished to protest, Oh, don't do that. It'll only make things worse for us in the village. You don't know what it's like, how they feel about us . . .

'You were about to say something, Miss Dagshaw?'

The words were forming in her mind: perhaps I misunderstood her. Perhaps she did tell me where to go, but looking into those blue eyes, she knew she would not be believed. And so she remained silent and Mrs Brodrick, addressing the housekeeper, said, 'That will be all, Hewitt.'

Mrs Hewitt went to take Betty Carter's arm, but she dragged herself away and, rounding on Anna, she cried, 'I don't care, I can get a job anywhere, but you watch out; our lads will have you for this.'

'Get her out of here.' The voice was small now, the blue eyes were closed.

The nurse was standing by the bed holding a glass to her mistress's lips. Anna had risen to her feet and now she was following a motion of the manservant's hand as he beckoned to her. She gave one last look at the woman on the bed before following him, and as she came abreast of him he bent and whispered, 'Madam gets easily tired. You understand?'

She nodded, then went out and across the grey hall and through the grey door; then through the corridors until she entered the main hall, where Simon was standing.

Moving towards her, he said, 'Are you all right? You are so white.' And she answered, 'Yes, I'm all right; but I

225

think it has been a trying time for madam, I . . . I think she may need you.'

'I'll see you to the carriage first.'

'Please' – her voice was low – 'there's no need.'

'Need or no need, I will see you to the carriage.' His voice was as low as hers but firmer.

When the footman opened first the glass doors and then the main front doors, she thought ironically, I have never been allowed to come in through these doors but I may go out through them.

He helped her into the covered carriage, then reached over and took a rug from the opposite seat and placed it over her knees, before saying, 'I will call tomorrow and see you.'

'Please don't. I beg you.'

'Someone must deliver your dress when it is laundered, and if they cannot get it clean, you must be compensated for it.'

She turned her head away, and he withdrew his and closed the door, then gave a signal to the coachman, and the horses walked sedately forward.

Anna leant back against the padded leather head of the seat. She felt ill and tired. Her head was aching, as was the cut behind her ear where the stone bowl had struck her. Fortunately, it had only grazed the skin, so they had told her, yet at the same time, if she were to believe the valet's words, if the mistress's aim had been true it could have killed her, for the vessel that had held the oil had been a stone mortar used for pounding colour ingredients.

Well, she was free . . . But was she? He would come tomorrow, and the scene would be painful. But now she asked herself: would it have been so painful this time last week? and received from her mind the answer, no. Then why the change?

Behind her closed lids the motion of the coach rocked the picture of a man, a gentleman taking his hand and, bringing it with force against one side of his wife's face, then the back of the same hand against the other side, before knocking her on to the floor. Yet, had he not suffered at that woman's hands by deceit . . . and worse? But then, had not her Dada suffered at *his wife's* hands too. Moreover, he'd had to work and scrape for years to keep her at bay.

She looked down the years stretching ahead and she knew that her life would indeed be barren if she waited until she found a man whom she could compare with her Dada.

3

The following morning Anna was sitting in the big chair to the side of the fire, her feet on a raised cracket and a rug over her knees.

Earlier, her mother had said, 'A day in bed won't do you any harm after that experience,' and she had looked from her to her father and said, 'I'm half expecting a visitor and please, Ma and Dada, I'd be grateful if you didn't leave me alone during the time he is here.'

They both looked hard at her, and Nathaniel had answered for them both, 'As you wish, my dear, as you wish . . .'

It was around half-past eleven when Simon arrived. After politely greeting Maria and Nathaniel, he said to Anna, 'I have come empty-handed. I'm very sorry, but they can't get your dress clean. The turpentine with which they tried to clean it has itself left a stain, and I'm afraid I must replace it in some way.' Then after a pause, he asked quietly, 'How are you feeling?'

'Almost quite well, thank you.'

'Almost?' He turned and looked at Maria, but she refrained from commenting, saying only, 'Will you take a seat, sir?'

'Thank you.'

'Can I get you something to drink?'

'No, no; but thank you all the same. I'm on my way to town, but . . . but I thought I might call in and not only see your daughter' – he glanced at Anna – 'but express my regrets and concern for what happened to her yesterday.'

When neither of her parents spoke, he turned to Anna again and said, 'We have a very unruly boy on our hands this morning. I think I must see about a tutor for him straight away else he's going to get out of hand altogether.'

Anna asked quietly, 'You told him that . . . that I wouldn't be coming back?'

'Yes, I did. I thought it would be better to do so, but then regretted it at once, because we had tears and stamping of feet.' He turned again towards Nathaniel and Maria, adding now, 'I have never known him throw a tantrum like it, nor has his old nurse.'

'Children soon adjust,' said Maria now; 'with love and kindness they soon forget.'

'Well, in his case, I hope so.'

He got to his feet and, looking from Anna to Maria, he said, 'Would it be in order if, when I'm in the city, I make arrangements for a dress to be sent, or one or two from which to . . . ?'

'*No, sir.*' It was Nathaniel speaking. 'My daughter is not short of dresses, as my wife is very clever with her needle.'

'Oh yes, I'm sure she is.' Simon smiled at Maria. 'I was only thinking, that as her dress was ruined. . .'

'It is very kind of you, sir, and I understand that you might feel obliged to make good what has been spoilt, but I can assure you there's no need.' Nathaniel stepped to the side now, and it would seem it was an invitation for the guest to take his leave.

After a moment's pause Simon again looked at Anna, saying, 'I will call soon, if I may, to see how you are faring.'

She simply inclined her head towards him and he turned and went out, followed by Nathaniel. But immediately outside the door, he stopped and, facing Nathaniel, he said, 'I'm sorry if you took my suggestion in the wrong way, sir. I only wish to . . .'

'I knew how your suggestion was meant, Mr Brodrick, but you are a man of the world and my daughter is a young and vulnerable girl. So I ask you to imagine the tale that would be woven if it became known, as is everything we do in the surrounding countryside, that Mr Brodrick from the Manor is buying clothes for one of Nathaniel Martell's daughters.'

Their gaze held for a long moment before Simon, his head nodding in small jerks said, 'Yes, you are quite right, sir, quite right. However, I hope you will have no objections to my calling again?' There was a further pause before Nathaniel replied, 'It will all depend upon the purpose of your visit, sir.'

'Well, Mr Martell, I hope to make that plain within a short while, or at least when I am lawfully free to do so. You understand?'

Nathaniel stared at this very presentable man who was almost putting into words his determination to come courting his daughter, for that's what he would be doing, while still married. And if he won her heart would he even bother to get his freedom? And then would his dear, dear Anna do what her mother had done . . . God in heaven! No! That must not happen to his Anna.

He still made no comment as Simon bowed towards him and said, 'Good day to you, sir.' Nor did he wait to see him ride away. Instead he returned indoors and stood for a moment, his hand on the latch of the door, while he looked up the room to where Anna, wide-eyed, was waiting for him. Her mother was no longer with her and so he went straight to her and catching up her hand, he said, 'Do you like that man?'

230

Her gaze was unflinching as she looked back at him and said, 'Yes, Dada, I like him.'

'But do you love him?'

Now she looked away and towards the fire, and in a low voice she said, 'A few days ago I would have said yes, but now I am far from sure.'

'Why is that?'

She was again looking at him, but she couldn't bring herself to say, because I saw him striking his wife and knocking her to the floor.

The second visitor from the house was given a different welcome. Timothy came in carrying four beautiful orchids and a very daintily wrapped box. And as he handed her the flowers he said in broad dialect, 'Aal grown be me own 'and, ma'am.'

'Oh, Mr Timothy.'

'Ah! ah! ah! What did we say about prefixes? You should know all about prefixes; your father here must have knocked them into you.' He turned his smiling face towards Nathaniel, saying, 'I want the mister knocked off, sir.'

'Well, that is easily done . . . sir. But let me first say what extremely beautiful blooms. And you grew these?'

'Yes; it's my only talent,' he replied. 'I seem to be able to grow orchids. I suppose it's because I like them and I tell them so, being the silly fellow that I am,' only to have his attention diverted by the noise of Ben's running into the room, and he called to him, 'Ah, there you are, Ben. Guess what's in that box? It's really for your sister, but I'm sure she wouldn't mind you opening it. And I wouldn't either, because I can eat nougat at any time of the day.'

'Tim—' Anna stressed his name now, and she added, 'Will you please sit down; and my mother here, I am sure is dying to ask you if you would like a drink.'

231

He turned to Maria, now, saying quickly, 'Well, before you do, Mrs Martell, I'm going to say, I would indeed like a drink; you make tea better than anyone else I know.'

'Look! Look! Anna.' Ben cried out now as he exposed a variety of chocolates and nougat in the top layer of the box.

'Aren't they lovely! May I have one?'

'Of course, my dear, but first of all offer one to Mr Barrington.'

After Timothy had dutifully taken a nougat sweet, Ben pondered over which one he should choose; then, picking up a gold-paper-wrapped sweet, he said, 'I like things in pretty paper; they always give you a nice surprise.'

They watched the boy unwrap the chocolate and put it in his mouth, and when he cried, 'Oh! it's running,' Timothy said, 'You've got a liqueur. My! aren't you lucky. I love liqueurs. Now what about you, Anna?' and at this she said, 'Yes, I do, too,' although she couldn't remember ever having tasted one.

It was then that Anna asked, 'Did you come in the gig?' and when he answered, 'Yes, I did,' she looked towards her mother, saying, 'Number two will be outside, Ma. Will you give him a cup of tea?' only to be interrupted by Timothy saying, 'Number two isn't outside; I came on my own.'

Anna did not immediately take up this unexpected statement, but Nathaniel, turning to the window, remarked, 'Well, in that case I'll put it and the horse into the shelter of the barn for a while; it's spitting on to rain. Come on you, big fellow!' — he tapped his son on the shoulder — 'come help me.'

As Maria, too, left the room to go to the kitchen, Anna thought somewhat ironically, well, they didn't think she needed guarding against this man.

The room to themselves, she looked at him and said, 'Was that wise? I mean, to drive the gig yourself?' And he, all merriment now gone from his face and his voice, replied, 'I had a slight turn after yesterday's do and seeing you in that state. And, you know, it often happens that I have a free period after experiencing something that I really don't experience at all, as I'm not aware of it. Strange, isn't it? And isn't it strange, too, that I can talk to you like this about it? You're the only one to whom I speak of it. Do you know that?'

She took hold of his hand and said, 'Thank you for your trust, Tim. It . . . it means a lot to me.'

He stared into her face for a while before he said, 'And you'll never know what your friendship means to me.' Then turning his head away, he looked towards the fire as he said, 'You've had a visit from Simon already, I suppose?' And she answered 'Yes. Yes, he called.' And again there was silence until he said, 'Are you aware of his intentions?'

'Yes. Yes, I'm aware of them.'

His head jerked round towards her and he said one word, 'And?'

And Anna repeated the word, 'And?'

'Well, what I mean is, are you . . . well, there's a long way to go. He intends to divorce her. But that'll take time, even a matter of years, because he has to have proof; and the only proof he could offer at the moment is his intention of marrying someone else, and exposure might then wreck other lives. You understand that?'

'Yes, Tim, I understand that, and much more. And please, you needn't fear for me.' Then very quietly, she said, 'I am not going to do what my mother did. For one reason, I am not strong enough. Even should my feelings direct me, I wouldn't be strong enough. We are a very happy family. We always have been, but there has been a shadow over us

233

from our birth. It breeds hate and disdain. We have all, in a way, suffered from it, and still do. I know Oswald does; and, lately, I myself probably do most of all. And I wouldn't ever bring that on anyone else. Now do you understand?'

He had turned towards her again and was holding both her hands as he said, 'Yes, my dear, I understand.'

There was the sound of voices coming from the kitchen, and so, releasing his hold of her, he said in a clear voice, 'I have news for you now. I . . . I am leaving the Manor and setting up my own establishment.'

'No! Really? Where? Far away?'

'No, not all that far. It's at this end of Fellburn. You've probably seen it on your way in; you can just glimpse the house from the road. It's Colonel Nesbitt's old place. Briar Close.'

'Oh, Briar Close. Yes. Yes, I've heard it's a nice house.'

'Very nice indeed, but very small, at least in comparison with what I'm leaving. So it will only need a small staff. I've always wanted a place of my own. Strange, but I used to visit that house when I was young. My stepfather's cousin lived there then. I would love you to come and see it and perhaps advise me on drapes and such because those that have been left are rather dull; at least, I find them so. The Colonel lived there by himself for some years and the whole place will need decorating. But I am taking on most of the furniture because he had some nice pieces. I . . . I'm looking forward to the change. I'll be able to work there in peace. And there's a small conservatory where I can natter to my orchids when I have no-one else to talk to.'

'Is this a new idea?' she asked quietly.

'No, not really; but one gets tired of being a buffer. I'm . . . I'm very fond of my half-sister, you know . . . madam, but she understands and agrees with me. In any case, there's going to be changes in the house. Whether Penella goes or stays,

234

there'll be changes. I've always been very fond of Simon, and I like Raymond too, but the brothers never cared much for each other. So there was always buffeting needed. I am their uncle, but really, I never felt old enough for the position, there being only seven years between Raymond and myself. I could have been their brother. Anyway, now that Raymond is top man in the family, things have already changed. It's amazing what a little power will do.'

At this point, Maria entered the room with a tray on which were two cups of tea, and when Anna said, 'Aren't you having one, Ma?' Maria replied, 'Yes; but I'll wait until your father and Ben come back; they've gone out again. Once they get into that barn and with a new horse to fondle they forget about everything else.'

She went out smiling, and Anna, taking a cup of tea and saucer from the tray, handed them to Tim, saying, 'Drink this while it's hot.'

After sipping on the tea Tim remarked, 'It really is always good tea your mother makes.' Then putting his cup back on to the tray, he said quietly, 'I suppose by now you know that Simon is not the father of the child?'

'Yes; I gathered that some time ago. So may I ask you why she married one brother while she loved the other?'

'Oh, she married the one she loved; that was after she had made him jealous enough. Yet I shouldn't say that because he loved her too. She must have been in a panic when she persuaded Simon to elope with her. It caused quite a sensation, especially coming, as it did, only eighteen months after the accident had happened to my half-sister and me. I think if she had been mobile at the time she might have managed to prevent the marriage. But you know how she's placed, and only at that time was she beginning to accept what sort of life lay before her.'

He sighed now as he went on, 'It's been a sad union, more

235

so because she's continued to love him the while flaunting her association with Raymond, hoping, I suppose, that jealousy once again would stir him to prove his love for her. But it hasn't worked. And then there's the boy. She doesn't care for him because she sees him as the cause of all her misery. And Raymond, I'm sorry to say, couldn't care less about his parenthood. And until recently, too, Simon, the supposed father, had resented the child. Naturally. There again I've acted as a buffer, but no more. In law, the child is Simon's responsibility and he must see to his future.'

He took another sip from his cup; then smiled wryly as he said, 'Life is a strange affair, isn't it, Anna, for all peoples, rich and poor alike? The poor think if only they had money they would be happy and all their troubles would be at an end; the rich think if only they were free from responsibilities, if they hadn't to spend so much money on the upkeep of big houses and large staffs, if they hadn't to keep up appearances with their neighbours, how simple life would be. Then there are people like me who say, why have I been afflicted like this? Why should it have happened to me? But of late, I have come to think there is a pattern in life, a certain plan. You know, Anna' – his face brightened now – 'if I had never had the seizure in that field, and you hadn't been sawing wood at that particular time, we would never have met and I wouldn't be sitting here with you now. Instead, I should have gone on being aware of the emptiness in my life. But since you've come into it, my dear, and have become my friend, the whole aspect has changed.'

'Oh, my dear Tim.' She smiled at him now, and there was a little quirk to her lips as she said, 'You talk just like my father.'

'Well, I could have been.'

236

'Don't be silly.'

'There's nothing silly about it. There are seventeen-year-old fathers. You, I think I am right in saying, are nineteen, aren't you?'

'Yes, well, just about. And you?'

'Well, I am thirty-six, thirty-seven . . . just about' – and he laughed – 'so I am in a position to have been your father.'

She looked into his kind, attractive face, the wide mouth showing a row of white teeth, two of which, she knew, were detachable, the deep blue eyes, the thick brown hair, and she repeated to herself the feeling he had recently expressed: why had he been afflicted like this?

He was saying now, 'You will marry some day, and likely soon, but I would like to think, Anna, that whoever he is he will accept . . .' His voice was cut off here by Nathaniel coming into the room, followed by Ben who, running up to Timothy, cried 'It's a beautiful horse, sir. I like horses. He let me stroke him.'

'Did he? Well, you are indeed favoured because he's an old aristocrat, that one. He'll never see twenty again but he is very particular as to whom he allows to take liberties with him, such as stroke him.'

The boy smiled at him, then looked up at his father and his smile widened.

With Maria's entry into the room the conversation became general and after a short while Timothy, rising to his feet, said, 'I always outstay my welcome when I come to this house. It is unpardonable of me, yet you are all to blame. But I must away now.'

Goodbyes were said and Anna's last words to him were, 'And come back soon.' To which he replied, 'I will. Have no fear of that,' then went out accompanied by Nathaniel and the boy.

Maria went to the window and, looking out, said, 'There he goes. God help him! What an affliction to have and he such a gentleman. A life ruined and no prospect.'

'Oh, Ma, I don't think he needs to be so pitied. He writes, and he grows his orchids, and he reads a great deal.'

'What's that for a man of his standing' – she turned – 'when he'll never have a woman in his life?'

As Anna watched her pick up the tray and make her way towards the kitchen, her mind confirmed that her mother's words were true: he would never have a woman in his life . . .

Two days later, the sun was shining, the air was warm, and Maria said, 'There's a turn in the weather. If it keeps like this tomorrow we'll wash the bedding. There's nothing like it being dried in the sun.' Then she added, 'Why don't you go for a little stroll, you look peaky. Take Ben and go along the quarry road. See how far they've got with their railing us in. I wonder how your dada is faring in Fellburn, and what advice he'll get from Parson Mason. Oh, I do wish Miss Netherton was here. She has friends in the legal world. She would see to it. They expected her home last week.'

'Well, Farmer Billings might be able to do something, because if they bring the fencing any further he won't be able to get his cattle from one field to another. Jimmy said he was blazing mad yesterday.'

'Blazing mad won't help much. It's a law man we should have to see to this business. Anyway, go for a stroll. Ben's out digging his patch; call him. But I'd put a coat on, the wind can be keen along there, coming from over the moor.'

Anna made no protest. She took an old coat from behind the door, put it on and went out. Her mother, she knew, was uneasy, worried about what was going to happen when the fencing was finally completed. She wondered why Simon

238

Brodrick, knowing how it would curtail their liberty, had not spoken of it. But of course, it was his brother who was in charge and so he would likely have no say in the matter. Cherry said Praggett was acting as if he were building the Roman wall all over again. He was a spiteful man, that Mr Praggett.

'Ben! Ben!' she called. 'Are you coming for a walk?'

The boy stopped digging and looked towards her. 'Where?' he asked.

'Oh, as far as we can go along the quarry top.' She walked over to him, adding, 'They can't take that away from us.'

The boy stuck his spade into the ground, rubbed his hands on the back of his corduroy pants, then, looking up at her, he said, 'Must you?'

'Must I what?'

'Well, go for a walk?'

'No, I mustn't; but I would like to.' She smiled at him. 'But go on with your digging if you don't want to come.'

'Oh, I want to be with you, Anna. I'll come.'

As they walked towards the gate she said to him, 'You're always the one for walks; what's the matter? Aren't you feeling well?'

'I'm all right, but I was turning the ground over to set my potatoes; but it doesn't matter, they'll be set.'

'I think if you were setting them in June you would still have a better crop than Dada's. Everything you set grows. You have green fingers.'

He held out his hands towards her, saying, 'Green fingers! My nails are in mourning.'

She smiled now, saying, 'Before you were born Ma always examined our nails before a meal, and if they were dirty she would say just that: "Your poor hands are in mourning. Go and lift the blinds."'

239

They walked side by side along the quarry top, past the narrow way and on to where the quarry itself petered out with only a four-foot drop from the path, which a little further on merged into the moor.

'Look! They've stopped the fencing by the side of the beet field,' said Ben, pointing. Then suddenly he cried out, 'Look! Anna,' and when she followed his pointing finger she couldn't believe what she was seeing: 'Can't be!' she said. 'Can't be! Oh no!'

They ran now to the actual end of the path and she shouted, 'Andrew! Andrew!'

The little figure in the far distance stopped for a moment, then came scrambling towards her, and as she herself ran to meet him her mind was exclaiming, Oh my God! How has he got this far?

'Oh! Missanna. Missanna.' He was clinging to her, his face awash with tears. 'I've been looking for you, but this wasn't the way the carriage came. Oh! Missanna. Missanna. Come back. Please come back.'

'Oh my dear!' She lifted the child up in her arms and stumbled back across the uneven ground to the path. There she put him down, and said to Ben, 'We'll have to get word to the house. They'll be looking for him.'

'No; I don't want the house, Missanna. I hid from Peggy; I want to stay with you.'

'I could run to Miss Netherton's; Mr Stoddart will still be looking after the horse and trap.'

'All right. Well, let's go back, and you do that. Come on, Andrew. Come on.'

They had started out, almost at a run, when again it was Ben who stopped them, saying, 'Listen!' Then turning round he said, 'Look!' And there galloping across the moor came two riders, and it was the child who gave name to the first one: 'It is Mama, Missanna. 'Tis Mama.

240

I don't want to go back. May I ... may I stay with you?'

'Be quiet, Andrew. Be quiet.'

As the two horses drew almost to a skidding stop within a few feet of them, Anna had to grab the two children and jump back, and her arms around them, she glared up at the woman who now glared down at her, hissing, but almost under her breath, 'How dare you! How dare you! You steal my husband and now you have taken my child.'

'I have only this moment found the boy; he was wandering!' Anna yelled back at her.

'You told him when to come, and how to come.' Her voice had risen; then jerking her head to the side, she cried, 'Pick the boy up! McBride.'

As Anna watched the man jump from his horse she realised it wasn't the McBride she knew. And when he put his hands on the boy's shoulders the child kicked out at him, crying, 'No! No! I want to stay with Missanna. Please, please, Mama, I want to stay with Missanna.'

It was as the child broke free from the man and made to run to the side which would have taken him under the horse's head that Ben, quickly thrusting out his hand, pulled him away.

What took place next was hard to define: whether it was the woman cracking her whip or pulling on the horse, or the two children together startling the horse, it reared, and instinctively Anna pulled the child clear. But what happened to Ben occurred so quickly that at the time she had no comprehension of it; only later did the picture come into her mind: it seemed that Ben had remained just where he was and when the hoof came down on the side of his head and lifted him in the air and over the edge into the shallow dip of the quarry, she felt she had witnessed it all before; even to what took place next, when she sprang at the woman, aiming to

241

tear her from the saddle and the whip came down across the side of her face, blinding her for a moment. Then she heard her own voice screaming and she was struggling to get away from the man's hold. She saw the woman dismount, go to the edge of the dip and say, 'He's moving. He's only stunned.' She was still screaming when the woman remounted and the man let go of her and lifted the crying and thrashing child into his mother's arms.

When she looked over the edge of the quarry to see the still form of her brother lying crumpled among the stones, she cried, 'Oh my God!' And the man pulled his horse to a halt and looked back at her as if he were going to dismount again, then changed his mind and rode after his mistress.

She scrambled down the bank now and lifted Ben's head onto her arm, crying, 'Ben! Ben! Come on! Come on! Wake up!' She patted his cheek, beseeching him, 'Wake up! Wake up!' But when his head fell limply to the side she cried aloud, 'No, God! No!' Then standing up, she bent over and lifted the boy into her arms; but then found she was unable to climb the short bank with him. So she leant her body forward against the bank and placed him on the footpath above; then drew herself up beside him and picked him up again. And now, staggering like someone drunk, for he was no light weight, she carried him back along the path, through the gate, and there she started yelling, 'Ma! Ma!'

. Maria met her half-way across the open ground. 'God Almighty! What's happened? What's happened?'

'*She did it! She did it!* With her horse. And she's taken the child. *She did it! She did it!*'

Maria lifted her son into her arms now and ran back into the house and laid him on the mat. And she felt all over him before looking up at Anna where she was leaning against the side of a chair, still gasping, and in a low agonised voice, she said, 'My lad is dead. He's dead, Anna. Ben is dead.' And when Anna screamed and continued doing so, Maria had to lay back her son on the mat and then shake her daughter by the shoulders, while yelling at her: 'Stop it! Stop it! girl. Go and get help,' only to say in further distress, 'Oh my God! Oh my God!' for the red weal on Anna's face was oozing blood. But she pushed her towards the door, appealing to her now, 'Miss Netherton's. Go to Miss Netherton's. Go and get help. Tell Bob Stoddart to get the doctor.'

'But he's dead, Ma.'

'Go on! Go on!' Maria, half-crazy now, screamed, 'Run! Run!'

Anna didn't remember running to Miss Netherton's house. She didn't remember the doctor's coming; nor did she remember both Simon and Timothy standing before her father with bowed heads.

It wasn't until the fourth day when she rose from her drugged sleep and went into the long room and saw the coffin lying on the trestle table and looked down on Ben's face, which even in death still looked alive and beautiful, did she finally realise that he was dead.

But she remembered the following day, when she stood in the midst of her family by his grave, and Parson Mason said kind words over him. It was being allowed that he be buried in Fellburn because they had all been christened in that town, and because of the latter the parson had once laughingly said they were eligible for poor-law sustenance, as well as, it now turned out, the right of burial.

The family had come in two cabs: the carriage from the Manor holding Simon and Timothy followed, and beyond that had come another carriage in which sat Miss Netherton. It was also noted that there were half a dozen people from the village, who must have taken the trouble to come in by cart, waiting in the cemetery, only that same night to be censured by the clients in The Swan.

The bar was packed, the counter aflood with spilt beer, which took Lily Morgan all her time to keep sopped up between exchanging gossip with the customers. And there was plenty to gossip about on this particular night.

Willie Melton, the painter and decorator, and his son Neil, who was an apprentice to the wheelwright, stood together at the end of the counter. And the older man looked across to where the blacksmith was seated on a settle at right angles to the open fireplace, and he said, 'Well, I can understand old Miss Smythe following them, and Roland Watts, 'cos he was thick with 'em long afore he left here, but for John Fenton and his Gladys to go to the cemetery . . . well, that beats me. I thought they were just goin' into town to put in his order as one or t'other do every week, not both. But there they left the shop open an' his mother seeing to it and the old snipe wouldn't open her mouth to my lass at first when she asked her, just skittish like, never thinkin', would they be going to the funeral, like? No business of anybody's where they were going, she answered her, but not until she was walkin' out the shop . . . well!'

Before the blacksmith had time to add his own remarks a voice came from the other end of the bar-room, shouting, 'You'll come to me next, won't you, Willie?' And Willie Melton, his head wagging, shouted back, 'Aye, I might an' all, Dan, 'cos that was a surprise.'

'It should have been no surprise to you or anybody else. I've always said, they've kept themselves to themselves. Asked us in the village for nowt, neither bread, beer, nor baccy; nor for me to make any of them a pair of shoes. But I still maintain that no matter what name stuck to them, he and she brought them up decent and weathered some bad times. An' we could name names, couldn't we, who helped with those bad times? So I think it beholds everybody to live and let live.'

Robert Lennon took a long draught from his pewter mug, then, turning and looking at Dan Wallace, he said, 'You should talk like that to Parson.'

'I could an' all.'

'Aye, well, I'd like to be there an' hear you. An' you being made sidesman of late, strikes me you've turned your coat. What's happened to make you do that?'

'I've turned no coat. If you think back, I'm one of the few who kept me own opinion about them.'

'Well, does your opinion cover the mischief that one's done? All right, all right, the bairn was killed but accidentally, an' that's what'll come out in the court, if it comes up. But what happened up at the Manor when Mr Simon found out that the bairn was dead? He goes back and nearly tries to do his wife in, didn't he? Made a holy show of himself, if all tales be true. Yellin' at his wife, "You've killed the child! You've killed the child! Now are you satisfied? You hussy!" He called her that, an' in front of the servants. And then Mr Timothy tried to separate them, so we are told, and he couldn't manage it; it took two men to get him off her. Now that isn't hearsay, it came straight from the Manor. And why did all that happen, eh? It happened 'cos that hussy, not satisfied with tempting the husband, had tempted the bairn. It was a natural thing for the mother to go after it. And if that one went for her it was a natural thing an' all to raise the whip. I would have done it meself.'

'Oh aye, you would. There's no doubt about that,' said the shoemaker. 'Strikes me you've wanted to do it for years.'

'Now, now! gentlemen. Now, now!' Reg Morgan intervened from behind the counter. 'We all know who's right and who's wrong in this business. As Lily here was sayin' ' -- he nodded towards his wife – 'you can't light a fire without

245

a spark. And that hoity-toity miss certainly caused the spark that killed the child, because don't forget what Betty Carter said and what happened to her. Thrown out on her face she was and blamed for the teacher being covered in paint, or such. Well, as I see it, the mistress must have had cause to throw that stuff. And as Michael Carter and his lad said when Betty came back cryin', if it was left to them they would have tarred and feathered her, not just covered her with paint.'

'Aye, 'tis a pity duckin' stools and stocks have gone out of fashion. Morris Bergen was saying the other night that he remembers his dad being put in the stocks when he was a lad. It was to try and stop him drinkin' but he only got more drunk when they lifted him out.'

'Oh, so Morris said that, did he?' The innkeeper now nodded towards Dave Cole the butcher. 'Transferrin' your custom are you, Dave?'

'No, no. I just happened to drop in; I had a bit of business to do. You know, Reg, I sell meat to everybody. I'd sell it to the corpses in the graveyard if they could pay their way.'

This last brought forth guffaws of laughter, but not from the blacksmith's youngest son Arthur who, during all the talk, had said nothing but had looked from one to the other as if studying some deep point, and when he muttered something his father said, 'What's that you say?' and he replied, 'Nowt; I was just thinkin'.'

4

They were sitting round the fire as they had done each night since the day they had buried Ben. Nathaniel sat close to Maria, the two girls sat close together, the twins, with Jimmy between them, sat close too.

The sound of laughter had not been heard in the house for weeks. It would seem they were unable to throw off their loss. When they talked it would be in low tones; and after the day of the funeral Ben's name had never been mentioned among them. Sometimes they cried together, but generally they cried in private, that was until this particular night, the evening of the day of the inquest that had looked into the circumstances leading to Ben's death.

Nathaniel had not allowed Anna to go to the court. As he had said that morning, he would tell the justice that she was still very unwell, and that was no lie. Oswald and Olan had accompanied him to the courthouse but Maria had stayed at home with Anna, together with Cherry and Jimmy, for they both refused to go to work this morning.

They had scarcely eaten a bite all day, and when they talked it had been about everything but the matter foremost in their minds. But now here was Nathaniel sitting before the fire holding tightly onto Maria's hand, and the others were gathered round him. The table behind them was laid for a meal but it could wait; they wanted to know what had transpired in the court. It seemed at first that Nathaniel was reluctant to speak, and it was Anna, bending towards him, who said, 'Tell us, Dada, what happened, or let the boys.'

Nathaniel looked at his sons, and it was Oswald who, looking from one to the other, said, 'She got off.'

A quiet stunned period of some seconds followed Oswald's words; then he went on: 'The court was packed; and there she stood, that woman, looking as if she wouldn't say boo to a goose. And when she was questioned you could hardly hear her answer, her voice was so low. I couldn't hear half of what she said. But when one of the solicitor men had the stable man McBride in the box and he said to him, "Explain what you saw," well, the man seemed hesitant; but then he said, "The young master was about to run under the horse's head and the boy pulled him aside out of harm's way. It was then the horse reared and the offside front hoof caught him on the head and sent him flying." '

Oswald drew in a long breath and looked at his father as if Nathaniel would take up where he had left off, but Nathaniel remained silent, and so he continued: 'The solicitor man then asked him what happened next? And he again seemed hesitant to speak; but then he said, from what he could see the young lady went to grab the mistress and the mistress brought her riding crop down on her. Then the solicitor man suggested again that it was after the young lady tried to grab his mistress.

'And the man said, yes. And then he was asked what happened when he came on the scene with his mistress, and he said, "Well, sir, the child was clinging to the young girl, and . . ." He hesitated again, and was prompted by the solicitor man who said, "Yes; go on." And then he said, "The child was yelling he didn't want to go home with the mistress but wanted to stay with the teacher."

' "But that is not all you heard, is it?" the solicitor asked him, but McBride said, "I think it is, sir." Then the solicitor man came back at him again: "Did you not hear your mistress accuse the teacher of something?" he said. And I could see the man was upset, and he bowed his head now and wagged it a bit as he said, "There was a lot of confusion and yelling. She said something but I couldn't make out what it was." And you know' – Oswald was now looking from his mother to Anna – 'that woman had been sitting with her head bowed, and now she turned and looked towards the man and that painful look went off her face and for a moment she looked devilish. I'm telling you, she looked devilish. But no matter how the solicitor man kept on, the stable lad wouldn't say any more and he was told to stand down. Then it was the doctor's turn, and he said—' Oswald paused here and wetted his lips before going on. 'He said Ben was dead when he examined him, and Anna, Miss Dagshaw, he said, her face was bleeding from what had been a whip lash. What was more, she was demented and had to be put to sleep, and she still wasn't herself. After that the two solicitor men went up to the bench and there was a lot of talk with the justice. And the justice said it was a pity the young teacher was unable to be present as she could have thrown more light on the matter. And then he spoke to the jury. He told them that it would seem there had been no intent to harm the boy, whose action in trying to save the younger child must have startled the horse; then unfortunately he had been struck by the hoof and, according to the doctor, had suffered no pain but must have died immediately.

'It would be for them to decide. Or words to the effect. You know how they go on. The jury wasn't out very long and when they came back they said, it was . . . accidental death.'

249

Oswald now turned and looked at his father. Nathaniel was sitting with his head bowed, and Oswald's voice was very soft as he said, 'It was then that Dada sprang up and cried, "She killed my child! She killed my child!" And there was an uproar in the court and the justice said if Dada couldn't be quiet he would have to leave the courtroom. But he wouldn't. He shouted at them how that woman had tried before to run his daughter down and had attacked her and split her head open with a bowl and covered her with oil. But by this time the policemen were pulling Dada outside. And then the justice man started speaking again and he said that the woman of course was not entirely without blame but it wasn't within his province to judge her, but her reactions had led to a tragedy and it would remain with her how she viewed her conduct in the future.'

There followed a long silence until Olan broke it by remarking, 'There was nobody from the Manor there, I mean, none of the men, not her husband, or Mr Raymond, or Mr Timothy. I looked round and couldn't see one of them. But I saw her come out with the solicitor man. Anyway they said she's been left the Manor for weeks; in fact he put her out.'

'Oh, Dada.' Anna was kneeling in front of her father now, holding his hand, and he, looking down on her, said, 'It's all right. It's all right, my dear. But it was a sorry day when you went to that house.'

Then raising his head he glanced around his family, saying, 'We have never spoken of death, but I know now we must because he is still here, he is still among us. I also know that he was due to die. Ever since he was a baby and so beautiful I have felt that the saying, Those whom the gods love die young, could be applied to him. I can tell you now that I always had this fear that I would never see him grow up. And you know something, my dear family?' – he paused

250

here before adding – 'He knew that. From the things that I remember him saying, he knew that his time was short. So from now on we will speak about him. You know, I saw him last night as plain as I'm looking at you now. You had all gone to bed. I came down the room to lock the door, and he was sitting on the mat there, in front of the fire, where he always sat, his legs tucked under him, and he turned and looked at me and his smile was so serene.'

His voice now broke and the tears, welling in his eyes, rolled down his cheeks and he turned and laid his head on Maria's shoulders. She, patting his head with one hand, held up the other and warded her family off, and, her own voice breaking, she said, 'Enough. Enough. The weeks of mourning have passed. We must go on living. As Dada says, he is still here. We will talk about him as if he hadn't gone from us in the flesh. Now, not one of us has eaten today and I'm sure you boys and Dada, here too, could do with a meal. So, come on, and rest assured that nothing that can happen in life from now on can hurt us more than Ben's going.'

As Anna rose to go to the table she thought, Strange, the things people say. Rest assured that nothing that can happen in life from now can hurt us more than Ben's going. That was assuredly tempting providence and her Dada had said Ben had known his time was short, yet he had insinuated that it was she who had brought his end about by going to that house. Yes, yes, he had. He had voiced what she knew had been in his mind for weeks now, and she wasn't mistaken when she imagined she had caught a look of censure in his eyes.

251

5

It was a full fortnight later and Anna was at the wood-pile when she saw the rider coming across the moor, and she would have turned and hurried towards the house except that she knew, were he to follow her, her father would order him away, and in no small voice. She had wondered over the last few weeks how she would have taken her father's attitude to Simon if her own feelings hadn't changed towards him.

She went on sawing until he dismounted and came towards the railings, and only then she looked at him when he said, 'How are you?'

'I'm quite well, thank you.'

'Come here; I want to talk to you.'

To this she answered, 'I'd rather you didn't. We have nothing to say to each other.'

'I don't agree with you; we have a lot to say to each other. I will tether the horse here and come in by the gate.'

She saw there was no way of stopping him, and so she resumed her sawing until he reached her side, when his voice had a curt note to it as he said, 'Stop that for a moment, for goodness sake!'

She stopped, took out the saw from its cut and laid it against the wood-pile; then turned to him, saying harshly, 'What do you want of me?'

He smiled now as he said, 'That's a silly question for an intelligent young woman to ask. You know what I want of you, Anna, what I've wanted of you from the first time I saw you. You remember? The day you lost your position through the Songs of Solomon. I knew that morning that something had happened to me. You must have, too.'

'I did not.' Her words were emphatic. 'Even if you had not been married I would not have thought what you suggest.'

'Well, all I can say, my dear, is, you are much stronger than I am.'

When he put his hand out towards her she stepped back from him, saying, 'You are still as you were that morning, a married man with a child'; then she paused before adding, 'Whether he is your son or not, he is your responsibility.'

When she saw the dull red colour flood over his face like a blush, she turned her head away, saying, 'I am sorry. I am sorry, but I've got to make things plain to you.'

It was some seconds before, so it seemed, he could speak, and then he said in a low voice, 'All I'm asking is that you give me some hope, and that in the meantime until . . . until I can get a divorce we can be friends. You have no hesitation in being friends with Timothy, so why not with me?'

'There's all the difference in the world: Timothy is not asking for a closer association.'

'Oh, isn't he!'

Her eyes widened, and after a moment she said, 'How can you suggest such a thing? He is an . . . an invalid, he is . . .'

'He's a man and he's not an invalid, he is subject to fits, but so was Caesar and many other men in the past, and they had their women. And why do you think he is never off your

253

doorstep? The least excuse and he is over here. Oh, I know what I know.'

Slowly, she said, 'I'm sorry to hear you have such a low opinion of him.'

'I have no low opinion of him. You take me up wrongly. I've a very high opinion of Tim. I am very fond of him. I'm only pointing out to you that he is a man and he sees you as a beautiful girl.'

'He is seventeen years my senior.'

He closed his eyes for a moment, then said, 'I want to say to you again, don't be silly, but I won't. I will only point out to you that there's a very large number of the male population of forty or more who marry young women, many still in their teens. Why is it that a female in her mid-twenties is beginning to be looked upon as an old maid? It is because girls marry young and many seem to prefer much older men.'

Her answer was: 'Well, by my next birthday I shall have reached twenty and so I'll then be bordering on the age for old maids, and I can tell you I would prefer that state to marrying a man in his fifties.'

'Oh! Anna.' He was laughing at her again. 'I know one thing for sure, I could never lose my temper with you, I just have to laugh at you.'

She had a flashing mental picture again of his hand coming up first to one side of his wife's face then to the other, and also the tale that Cherry had brought back from Mrs Praggett's, that he would have throttled his wife on the day that Ben died if the menservants and Mr Timothy hadn't intervened.

He had taken a step towards her and she couldn't move backwards now because the sawing cradle was in the way, and his voice was very low as he said, 'I somehow got the impression some time ago that you didn't dislike me, even that we were both of a similar way of thinking, because, in spite of my wife being there, you came back, and I hoped it wasn't only because of the child. Then quite suddenly you changed. I felt it. Why? It wasn't as if the fact of my marriage had suddenly been sprung on you. You had known that all along and although no word of endearment had passed between us, I felt you knew that I'd come to care for you, and that you were aware of the obstacles but were ignoring them. What made you change towards me, Anna? Tell me.'

She stared into his face for a full minute before she said, 'When I saw you strike your wife and knock her to the ground.'

He stepped back from her, his face screwed up in disbelief. 'You mean to say, because I was outraged at the way she had treated you and perhaps could have killed you if that mortar pestle had struck you fully on the temple, and because I was angry for you and so therefore struck her *that turned you against me?*'

'No; it didn't turn me against you. I still think kindly of you, but if you were free tomorrow, I wouldn't marry you.'

There was utter disbelief in his voice as he said, 'Just because of that incident?'

'I don't know for sure, but yes, I think so. I only knew that my father, under any provocation, would never have done that. He'd had a wife, whom I am sure you have heard about, who drank and showed him up in public, so much so that she threatened his livelihood, and for years he had to work to keep her at bay. And I'm sure he had more provocation to strike her than you had your wife, at least as fiercely as you did.'

As he shook his head while muttering, 'My God!' she went on, her voice rising, 'You say you did it because you were angry at her treatment of me. That wasn't the reason. You did it because you had wanted to do it for a long time, because she had deceived you, because she had made you father of a child that wasn't yours. *That was it, wasn't it?*

255

You had never struck her before; you had just ignored her. And that's what turned her into the fiend that I knew, and made her jealous of anyone you looked at.'

There was a look of amazement on his face, but he made no effort to call a halt to her tirade, and she went on, 'I've never hated anyone in my life although I've had reason to, especially among the villagers, but I hate your wife because she killed my brother. That was no accident; the horse didn't rear because the child was near it; it reared because she pulled on the reins and dug her heels into its sides. And I know now that she had meant to turn that horse on me, not on my brother. Yet, feeling as I do towards her, I understand her reactions towards me, and in a way I feel sorry I was the cause of them.' Her voice sank at this stage and she ended, 'So now you must see that it would be foolish on your part to go on hoping that there could be anything between us, even friendship. What is more, my father could not bear it . . .'

'*Oh, your father!*' The words came out in a loud, indignant burst. 'It is always *your father*. Have you ever thought what that man has done to you? What he and your mother have done to you all? He has scarred you all for life. He has made you all the butt of the village. You are afraid to walk through it. He prides himself on educating you all, but you are only partly educated because his knowledge is limited. But the fact that he has made you all think and aware of what you are, to my mind has added insult to injury, for you know you are carrying a stigma, whereas, if he had left you like the rest of the clodhoppers in the village and round about, they would have accepted you, and laughed at you, and with you, and joked about your bastardy; no, he had to go and pump his bit of knowledge into you, which aroused your sense of awareness, and all the while priding himself that he was doing the right thing by you. Oh! don't talk to me about your father.'

256

She sidled along by the wood cradle until she was standing a good arm's length from him and, gasping as if out of breath, she said, 'No. I won't talk to you about my father, nor anything else. You have made yourself and your feelings quite plain, and I hope I have too. I'll only say this, then I'll never want to talk to you again: you would have been quite willing to act as my father did and take me as a mistress until you got your divorce, by which time, and not having the strength of my father, you would likely have become tired of me. Goodbye, Mr Brodrick. I won't expect to see you this way again.'

He didn't move away, but just remained staring at her, his jaws so tight that the muscles of his face stood out white against his skin. Then suddenly swinging about, he strode from her.

She did not wait to see him unloosen the horse from the other side of the wood-pile, but she hurried down through the trees, across the garden and into the house. And Maria, meeting her, said, 'What is it? What's the matter, girl?' And she shook her head and pressed her mother aside as she made for her bedroom. There she threw herself on the bed and burst into tears.

Back in the living-room Maria turned as Nathaniel entered from the kitchen and said to him, 'She's in a state. She's gone into her room.' And he, nodding at her, said, 'He's been. I saw him come, and I saw him go, and I saw her cross the yard. And by the look on her face, I don't think we'll see him again.'

To this Maria answered, 'Well, thank God for that'; then added, 'What did Miss Netherton say about the fencing? Has she heard any news?'

'I didn't go to her, my dear. Let them get on with it. If we are fenced in then they are fenced out. It doesn't matter any more.'

'But!' she protested now, 'what if we have to go through the village all the time?'

'Well, we'll have to do that, dear. They can only kill us.' He smiled wanly at her now, then went towards the fireplace and sat in his big chair, while she stood looking at him and shaking her head. He had become a lost man. He might think Ben was still here, but because he couldn't touch him, he had become a lost man.

6

It was on her visit during the following week that Miss Netherton once more came to the rescue, and in two ways. First, she said she would see to it that their horse-fodder and groceries were brought from the town in her trap and put over the fence at a point where they could easily be picked up. But in the meantime she was going into the matter of the law concerning the enclosure of land. Secondly she raised a more important issue. She was touching the fading scar on Anna's cheek, saying, 'It'll disappear gradually, except where it bled, and you might have two or three little spots there. But that'll be nothing,' when, turning to Maria, she asked, 'Does she know about the business of the cross?' And when Maria shook her head and said, 'No; none of them does,' Miss Netherton said, 'Well, it's about time they did. So, come, Nathaniel, and sit down; we have a little business to discuss.'

Anna saw the glance exchanged between her parents before they looked at her and walked slowly to the table.

When they were all seated Miss Netherton turned to Maria and said, 'I needn't remind you of the contract we made: I was to buy the cross from you for the sum of five-hundred pounds. Remember?'

Nathaniel nodded, and Maria said, 'Only too well, Miss Netherton, only too well. We are still grateful . . .'

'Oh, well, you might be more grateful still. Now listen.' At this point she turned and looked at Anna and said to her, 'I won't go into how all this started but your parents can enlighten you later on.' Then turning back to Maria, she added, 'I've thought: there it is, lying in my box in the bank. I had it recorded in my will what was to become of it; but on thinking further, I came to the conclusion that, being who I am and also a stubborn individual, I could go on for years, and it's now that you need more help. So, having a friend in the jewellery business in Newcastle, and he *is* a friend, and an honest man, as far as a jeweller can be, dealing with gems—' She smiled here, then went on, 'I told him part of the story as to how I had bought the cross, but not from whom, yet how it had been found, and he was more than interested to see it. So, I got it from the bank and there' – she put her hand on the table – 'I laid it in front of him and I've never before seen a man struck dumb in such admiration. He said he had seen many beautiful pieces of jewellery of all shapes and sizes but nothing like that. I then told him I wanted to sell it and to the highest bidder. And to this he said there should be no bidding in this case; that would bring it into the open. It must go to one man, someone who bought precious things like this just to possess them, and there were a number of such about, but not in this end of the country. He would have to take it to London, where he had a friend in the business who was a frequent visitor to Amsterdam and many other cities in the world looking for rare jewels. Apparently they are becoming scarcer, the real ones, so are more valuable. He asked if I would trust him with this precious and ancient thing, and I said, yes. He went to London last week, and I saw him yesterday, and he told me, in his turn, that he had never seen his friend so excited in his life, and that he was a man who

260

always kept a poker face and usually gave nothing away.'

She now looked from one to the other, but when no-one spoke she went on, 'I then told him to get on with it and let me know how much it was worth . . . No; not how much it was worth, because we will never handle the worth of that item, but I thought I might be offered as much as a couple of thousand pounds. Then he staggered me by saying that his friend knew of someone who would be very interested in an article like that and that he might get as much as six thousand for it.' She now wagged her finger at each of them in turn. 'He's my friend, I'm telling you; but if he said six thousand, being a business man, I bet the deal would be eight.' Here she pursed her lips. 'You see I know a bit about bargaining. However, I did not show any excitement at this point but said, well, he must do his best, and he said he most certainly would and that I should hear sometime this week. Now, my dear' – she placed her hand on top of Maria's, where they were gripped tightly together on the table – 'whatever the mysterious big man gives, we will share. Mind again, whatever the mysterious man offers, my friend in London will take his cut; then my friend in Newcastle will also want a cut. You understand?' She didn't wait for an answer, but went on, 'However, five per cent or ten per cent, I've worked out we should get at least two thousand pounds each.'

Both Maria and Anna made gasping sounds and sat back in their chairs, but Nathaniel did not move, and Miss Netherton said to him, 'Well, Nathaniel, aren't you impressed?'

'Miss Netherton, I am amazed, but more so at your kindness and your concern for us.'

'Well, I've always been concerned for you because I like you. I like you all, and whatever I've done for you, this girl' – she now put her hand across the table in Anna's direction – 'has repaid me with her company over the years. Without her, at times, I should have been very lonely, and there's no

261

money that can pay for good companionship. And anyway, after I knew that those devils had cut off the entry to your own place, which, don't you worry' – she again wagged her finger from one to the other – 'I am seeing to. Oh, definitely. I have a solicitor working on it; and I know what you earn as a tutor has naturally been brought to a halt because you cannot use the cart now. So I would like to think that when you get the money you will consider moving from here and all the turmoil you have had to suffer. You'll be able then to buy a nice little place in the town, or wherever you like. Should this happen, and I hope it does, I shall miss you; but then, I've always got my own transport and I can visit you frequently.'

Maria's head was already slowly shaking when she brought out slowly, 'I would hate to leave this house, Miss Netherton. We have put up with a great deal over the years in order to stay here. And the fact that you were near and championed us has been of such help that I cannot put a name to it. I don't know what Nathaniel will say about it all, but since you let us have this house I've always imagined living here until I died. And . . . and we have brought the family up here and within these four walls and our bit of ground we have been happy; that is' – she bowed her head – 'up till lately. But,' she sighed, 'we are still a united family, so close. As Nathaniel says, only death can separate us.'

'Well, my dear, it will be up to you. No, of course not, I wouldn't want you to leave, but I was just thinking of your welfare and that tribe in the village. But . . . but there is hope there; you have friends, more than you know; people who have the courage now to defend you openly in the public bars . . . Oh' – she wagged her head – 'you wouldn't believe what I hear. A poor old lady sitting in her house alone . . .'

They all smiled at this, and she joined them, then she said, 'Well, I must be off and go and see how Timothy is getting on.

262

He hasn't been well these last few days.' She nodded again. 'He had a strong exchange with Raymond over the fencing, I may tell you. But I understand that Raymond pointed out that he isn't entirely in control now, but he agrees, and yes, yes, I'm giving it to you straight' – she was nodding again – 'that you, Nathaniel, are mostly responsible for what has happened, for you *will* house the men from the pits.'

'Would you rather I saw them die, the old people and the children on the moor?'

'No. No, I wouldn't. I would have housed them myself rather than that. But then' – her head drooped – 'I was never as brave as you, Nathaniel, or you, Maria. I knew there were many, at times, on the moor but I couldn't bring myself to defy convention. I work mostly with my tongue.'

Anna now put in quietly, 'And it is a sword, and you've always used it in our defence.'

'Well, that's as may be.' Miss Netherton rose from the chair, saying, 'Now, I've got to walk back and manoeuvre that bank . . .'

'Oh, you don't go down the bank!' said Maria.

'Well, how do I get out, unless I jump the fence and trudge across the turnip fields to the nearest part of the main road, where Stoddart will have the trap? But don't you worry, my dear: I do go down the bank, but Stoddart has made a little four-rung ladder that he places there. They'll not beat us. But come along, Anna, and walk some of the way with me. The sun is shining, the May blossom is about to burst. There are things to look forward to even now.' She spread her glance quietly over the three of them, but neither Nathaniel nor Maria made any response to this.

Anna had gone down the room and picked up a shawl from the back of the settle; now she put it around her shoulders and followed Miss Netherton out.

It was as they were walking along the path that led to the stile that Miss Netherton said, 'Are you cold, girl?'

'Yes. Well ... not cold; I ... I always seem to feel a little shivery.'

'I know that feeling; it's from heartache. It'll pass. It'll pass, my dear.' They walked on for a moment in silence, then Miss Netherton said, 'Did you know that Timothy has left the Manor?'

'No. No, I didn't. I understood he was going to, but that he had to have the new place made ready.'

'Yes, that was his idea; but it would have taken another three months or more. The decorators have been in and done some work, but apparently he got himself so worked up that he ordered all his things to be moved into the new place and came and asked my assistance in choosing a small staff. And so there he has been for the last week or so. He has had a really bad turn but that hasn't deterred him. I've got him a cook, a kitchen maid and a housemaid, and a butler-cum-valet, and I vetted them all very carefully before I let him engage them. He's had to buy a carriage and horse, and Stoddart's cousin has taken on that job. Stoddart also recommended a gardener; and so, in a way, Timothy is set up. But oh dear, those turns. Poor fellow; it seems that any sort of conflict brings them on. He can apparently go months at a time, though; even forget about them. I have to ask myself why the nice people in this world have to be so afflicted. Ah, here we are; and there's Stoddart with my stepladder to heaven, or is it the other place?' She chuckled now, and as she neared the stile she pointed to the left, saying, 'If I'd only been a few years younger, I'm sure I could have slid down that bank. I've always thought what a stupid place to set a stile. But then I must remember that the road below was dug out of a field. Why, I don't know. I suppose it was to skirt the village.'

Anna helped her over the stile and then held on to the top of the short ladder until she reached the road. And from there Miss Netherton laughed up at her, saying, 'There's life in the old dog yet.'

As he was lifting the ladder from the bank, Stoddart looked up at Anna and said, 'She'll break her neck one of these days, miss, the games she gets up to.'

'What you've got to do, you old fool, is to get up on to your seat and get that horse moving.'

Anna watched the trap bowl away, before turning to walk back to the house. On reaching the small gate that led through their own fencing she stopped and looked over the landscape to where, in the distance, the hills rose. The sun was glinting through clouds, casting their shadows on the hillsides and making it appear as if they were running with rivulets of silver. Of a sudden she longed to be there on those hills and beyond, away, away, anywhere but here.

She drew the edges of the shawl tight about her throat before hurrying on, telling herself now that this was one feeling she must get rid of. They had lost Ben, so how would they take to letting her try to find a post some place far away?

Her mother had said to Miss Netherton that she wanted to die here, and during the past weeks she had seen herself going on year after year, until she too died here after a wasted life: digging in the garden, sawing wood, carrying their fodder and groceries from wherever Stoddart would drop them; sitting round the fire at night in the winter or a table in the summer, reading. As the years went on the family would assuredly disperse. The boys would marry: Oswald and Olan were forever talking about the virtues of their employer and her daughter. And Jimmy would marry. Yes, Jimmy would marry. And Cherry? Oh, Cherry's heart was already placed. Anna had guessed this some time ago, for whenever she and Bobby could be together, they were. Her father must have noticed, too, but he wouldn't be displeased with that association. That left herself.

And what was her future? What had she to look forward to here? Had she been over-critical in holding up her father as a model to Simon? She could have become Simon's mistress. Oh yes, she could have become his mistress. And what would that have mattered? At least to the surrounding countryside she was a bastard already and she would just be acting out the part again, as her mother had done. After all, a gilly was a loose woman and the vor was her offspring. If it hadn't been for her father, would she have succumbed to Simon's pleas? At this moment she didn't know; she only knew that she was lonely; she felt lost, and she couldn't help but wonder what was happening to the child. By now he would certainly have been taken in hand by the male tutor.

Her father met her at the gate, saying, 'Billy got out. He's cleared the remains of the cabbage and has taken the young carrot tops. You mustn't have put the latch on the door.'

'Oh, I'm sorry, Dada.'

'You should be more careful and pay attention.'

She stood and looked after him as he walked away. Her Dada was telling her she must take more care and pay attention. She was a little girl again, being told how to see to the animals; to put false clay eggs under the broody hens; shown how to lift the hens from the barks without them fluttering; told always to be careful how she walked in the low grass near the pond because some of the ducks laid away; how to mix crowdie, hot in the winter with boiled cabbage leaves, and plain in the summer; how never to tether the goats near the bottom field because that is where the yew tree grew, and a stomach full of their leaves could kill them.

Just now he had used the same tone to her as when he had taught her those things, the same tone as when dealing with the book learning: he would say the brain had to be fed as well as the body.

Her father would never be the same again, nor would she.

She went into the house. It seemed as if her mother was waiting for her.

'Sit down,' she said; 'I must tell you the beginning of what Miss Netherton was on about. I mean, the cross.'

As Anna listened to her mother, she was made to wonder why her Dada hadn't told all this in the form of a fairy story as they sat around the fire at night, and this made her say, 'Will you tell the others as well, tonight, Ma?'

Maria looked away towards the end of the room, then down at her hand to the fingers that were tapping the table, and she said, 'Your Dada and me had a talk about that, and we thought it best not to say anything because you never know how a word might slip out unintentionally.'

'But when you get the money, they'll want to know; you can't hide . . .'

'We've thought of that. It'll supposedly have come from my mother's people in yon end of the country. We're going to put it to Miss Netherton and she'll fix it . . . I mean explain it. But then, I don't think there'll be any need; they'll take Dada's word. And we trust you not to say anything either, because, you know, if anything of this ever did leak out, there'd be a lot of trouble. Oh yes, and we've had enough trouble, haven't we?'

Her mother was staring into her face in silence now, and it was as if she were saying, 'Whether you admit it or not, you're to blame. You know it, I know it, and your Dada knows it. Oh, yes, your Dada knows it.'

It was almost three weeks later when Timothy called. He had walked from the coach road, and after knocking on the door he had shouted, 'Anyone in?' And she had opened the door and said, 'Oh, hello. Oh, I am pleased to see you.' And she was; for, during the past fortnight at least, she had often wondered why he hadn't called and had realised that she was missing him, his talk, his voice, his parleying of words with her. He seemed to be the only one she could smile at, or with.

'I'll tell Father,' she said immediately. 'He's in the barn with Mother. They are cutting up chaff.'

'Oh, I wouldn't disturb them for a moment. Let me have a look at you. How many years is it since I last saw you?'

She said, 'I hear you've moved.'

'Oh, yes, yes, I'm established, and that's what I've come to see you about. We have been living in chaos for the past few weeks but although the furniture is now in place I am stuck about the colour of drapes. I want a suite covered and I suppose the curtains should match; in fact, I intend to get rid of all the curtains in the house. Wait till you see them. As I told you before, they are very drab, and I was wondering if you would come over and give me some advice?'

'Oh.' She shook her head now. 'I've never had any experience in choosing materials or matching colours, except for a dress or a blouse that mother would be making for me or Cherry.'

'Oh, I'm sure you've got perfect taste. Anyway, they have sent a great assortment of materials from Newcastle. I knew I could have asked Miss Netherton's advice, but you know' – he poked his face towards her now – 'her house is still dressed in the style of the fifties and I feel I want something more up to date, more modern, bright, cheerful ... Oh, the adjectives I use! Anyway, will you come?'

'I should love to, and also to see your home. Do you feel you're settled in it?'

'Oh, yes, yes. I feel different altogether.' A sombre look came over his face as he added, 'Life became unbearable up there, really unbearable. I went up yesterday to see my sister and she tells me there's going to be further changes. She doesn't know whether Raymond will bring his wife there. But between you and me, I don't think that young lady fancies being mistress of that house. Perhaps it's from what she has already heard. Anyway, her father is a widower and they have taken quite a big place outside Newcastle, and it's my opinion that Raymond will end up there. That, of course, would leave Simon in charge of the house.' He stopped abruptly, wetted his lips, then said, 'Did I tell you I've acquired a carriage? Nothing elaborate. Also a trap. I enjoy the trap so much. I've brought it today. I've tied her up at yon end of the fence on the west side. Would you like to take a jaunt back with me and see my little hut?'

'Yes. Oh yes.' She found herself smiling widely at him, for he appeared at the moment like a bright light suddenly illuminating her dull existence. And she added excitedly, 'Would you mind waiting until I change my dress? Perhaps you would like to go and have a word with Dada and Ma in the barn?'

'I'll do that. Yes, I'll do that.'

She hurried to her bedroom and after a moment of standing before the small mirror, which reflected her black dress and showed up her face as utterly colourless, she turned swiftly as if making a decision and went to the cupboard in the corner of the room. Two dresses were hanging there. She took down the saxe-blue one with a white collar attached, and after changing into it she again looked in the mirror, then turned the white collar inwards. Next, she took down a paper bag from the top of the cupboard and drew out a black straw hat, which she put on. She then opened the top drawer of a chest of drawers and took out a pair of black gloves and a white handkerchief. Lastly, she donned her black cloak. Now she was ready.

In the yard, where her mother and father were now standing with Timothy, she could see immediately that her parents had noticed she had changed her dress, and their surprise showed. But they did not comment on it, yet she knew there was censure in their eyes that after only a matter of weeks, she could shed her outward sign of mourning.

'I shall bring her safely back.' Timothy was smiling from one to the other, but Nathaniel's answer was brief: 'Drive carefully, then,' he said.

'I certainly shall.'

'Don't stay too long,' said Maria now. 'The twilight still comes early.'

'I won't.' She looked from one to the other, then turned and walked away, leaving Timothy to say goodbye to them.

As they drove away she lifted her hand in farewell to them, but received no response.

She admired the horse and she admired the trap, and she told him so as he sat on the opposite narrow seat, and she laughed at him as he said, 'Get up there! Daisy.'

'You call her Daisy.'

'Well, it is instead of lazy, because she is the laziest animal I've ever come across. Look at her stomach. She's too full of oats to work. Edward, that's the new coachman, he says we've got to cut down half her feed and stop giving her tid-bits. But I can't resist giving her tid-bits. She loves sugar and sweeties.'

'Well, in that case you mustn't grumble if she won't gallop.'

'Gallop! I don't think she's ever galloped in her life. She wouldn't know how to. She belonged to my doctor's children. They are grown up now and he didn't know what to do with her. So that's how I came by her.'

On entering the village, Anna was immediately aware that there were people standing outside the forge where a horse was being shod. Timothy was sitting sideways and so he merely glimpsed them; but she was sitting facing them and she saw the blacksmith drop the horse's hoof, then straighten his back and stare towards her. She heard him distinctly shout a name, and then, glancing sideways, she saw one of his sons come out of the forge, and although she didn't move her head any further round, she knew that they were both looking in her direction.

Next, a woman about to enter the grocer's shop turned and stared, and was joined by a man coming out. And he stared. Then two faces seemed to pop up over the rim of bottled glass that formed half of the window in the King's Head. Lastly, where the road narrowed as it left the village, two farm workers stepped from the middle of the road onto the verge to allow them to pass. One of them touched his forelock, saying, ' 'Day, Mr Timothy.' And Timothy called back, 'Good day, Roberts.' But the other man just looked at them steadily, at least at her.

After driving some distance further on Timothy said, 'It'll be all over the village tonight. Will you mind?'

'Why should I?'

'Yes, why should you? And anyway' — he glanced at her — 'they know I'm harmless, at least they consider me so . . . Poor Mr Timothy. I get annoyed, not just annoyed but angry when I hear that, because I am not poor in their sense of the word.'

She put her hand out and touched his knee, saying, 'You shouldn't let that trouble you. They are ignorant. I . . . we have all suffered from their ignorance for years, so, in a way, I know how you feel. But they would do you no harm ever, whereas us, they would like to burn us alive.'

271

'*Oh! Oh!* Don't say a thing like that, Anna. As you said, it's ignorance, just ignorance because in the main they're not cruel, just stupid.'

'I don't agree with you there, Tim. To me they are ignorant, cruel, *and* stupid. Do you know that my mother never came back from the town for years but that she had to wash her skirt?'

He turned his head quickly towards her, 'Wash her skirt?'

'Yes, wash her skirt, because they would spit on her. Was she not living in sin? – and this was the rub which annoyed them, being comfortably under the patronage of Miss Netherton, their landlady, at least of a number of them. Yet they didn't spit on the widow of a certain farmer who had died eight years before but whose place had been taken over by the wife's own brother, and she produced a child each year.'

'Oh, yes, yes.' He was nodding his head now. 'I know who you mean. But two of that family are idiots.'

'Idiots or not, they're accepted. So why should we have been tormented all these years? Can you tell me the reason? Those children on the farm are not only bastards . . . yes, I can use that word, at least to you, Tim, but they are the result of incest. But I think at the bottom of it the main reason, or one of them, is that my father educated my mother, and then they educated us as far as it was possible. We were outcasts, yet we acted as superior outcasts, and they couldn't bear that. They still can't. I . . . I' – she bowed her head now – 'I'm still afraid of the village, Tim.'

'Oh, my dear, you mustn't be; they can do nothing more. And as you said, you're under the patronage of Miss Netherton, and also, may I say so, of me, for what my patronage is worth. But that is the wrong word to use. It is my feeling of friendliness towards your entire family

272

and knowing that I have in you a very, very, special friend. Anyway, come along, smile; you cannot live with the dead, Anna. You are alive and your life is before you. Ah . . . here we are! And look.' He pointed to the horse's head. 'She knows the gate already, as she knows where the manger is and what's in it. Oh, she's a knowing girl. Get up! there with you.'

The drive was short but it opened into a large gravel square, and there stood the house. It was creeper-covered and large flower-heads of wistaria were hanging over the upper windows. He pointed to them as he drew up the horse, saying, 'That's growing on to the roof. Fletcher, our gardener, tells me we'll have to get it down if we don't want the gutters to be blocked and water to come through the ceilings. Oh, my goodness, the things that have got to be looked to when you take on a house.'

He held out his hand and helped her down from the step; then looking at the man now standing to his side, he said, 'Oh, Edward, see to her, will you? But I think you had better cut down her feed tonight.'

'Yes, sir.' The man grinned now. 'So you can give her more tid-bits, sir.'

Timothy said nothing to this but exchanged a knowing look with Anna; then, taking her elbow, he led her onto the pillared porch, through an open oak double door and into a hall. It was quite a large hall for such a moderate-sized house, and the broad stairs that went up from it were of plain oak and were uncarpeted and, pointing to them, Timothy said, 'I nearly broke my neck on them yesterday. I must get them covered; in spite of Miss Netherton. She thinks it would be a sin to cover up that old wood. Well, my dear, let me have your cloak and hat.'

He led her into a room at the far end of the hall and with a theatrical gesture he said, 'The drawing-room, ma'am.' Then added, 'It's hardly bigger than the house-keeper's room in the Manor. But it looks comfortable, don't you think?'

She stood in the middle of the room and looked around, turning her body as she did so. She did this twice before answering, 'I think it's lovely, Tim; more than that, beautiful. And I don't know why you want to replace the curtains.'

'You don't?'

'No.' She went over to one of the two deep-bay windows and, feeling the curtain material, she said, 'It's beautiful brocade.'

'But it's faded. It should be a deep rose. Look; pull open the pleats and you will see.'

'Yes. Yes, I can see from the pelmet and the fringe, but it goes with this room. I don't think you will ever improve on it.'

'But if I had new ones made in the same colour?'

'They would be new, unworn, untempered, and shouting at everything else in this room.'

He now turned slowly and looked about him before saying, 'You know, I think you're right. Yes, you're right. I never thought about it that way; one thing shouting at another. Well, well, I'm so glad you came, Miss Dagshaw. You have saved me quite a bit of money.'

They laughed together now; then he said, 'Come and see the dining-room.'

They were in the hall again when a thick-set middle-aged man approached him, saying, 'Would you care for some tea now, sir?'

'Yes. Yes, I think we would, Walters. By the way, this is Miss Dagshaw, a very dear friend of mine, and she's come to help me choose curtains. At least that was the idea, but she tells me now that I would be wrong to change the drawing-room ones.'

274

The man smiled at Anna now. He had a pleasant broad face as he said, 'I'm sure the young lady is right; they are magnificent curtains, sir.'

'But as I've said, Walters, they're faded.'

'A lot of faded things are magnificent, sir.'

'Ah. Ah.' Timothy now pointed to his butler-cum-valet with his thumb. 'I'll have to watch out for him; I've already discovered we've got a philosopher here.' And at that he left the man still smiling broadly and led her into the dining-room, saying immediately, 'Now don't tell me you like these curtains.'

She looked around the room at the mahogany table, chairs, and sideboard, and the two glass cabinets of china; then up at the glass chandelier hanging from the painted decorated circle in the middle of the ceiling, and she said, 'Yes, I like them, but this room is not so light as your drawing-room and so I think you could have a less heavy curtain at the window.'

'Ah, well, new curtains for the dining-room. Now come along and see what I would like to call the library but daren't. It is a glorified study.'

The room was about fifteen feet long and twelve feet wide and two walls had shelves from floor to ceiling and these were filled with books. The table was littered with more books, but in the middle of it was a large writing-pad. And when she looked at it he dismissed it saying, 'Scribbles, scribbles. I keep scribbling words in the hope that I may astound myself. You see, the Renaissance interests me, particularly the influence of Florence. You could say, one way and another, I waste a lot of time.' And saying so, he pointed to the French window and said, 'That leads out into a little conservatory.'

A few minutes later she was standing under the covered glass dome, and she turned to him, saying, 'Little? Why do you call it little? It must run the length of the side of the house.'

'It does, but I suggest at present I'm comparing the rooms with those in the Manor. But I'm not belittling it, oh no, because this is mine. The conservatory up there didn't belong to me, it was only loaned, and then again much against the grain of the head gardener. We didn't see eye to eye; we didn't get on together.'

Showing her surprise, she said, 'I couldn't imagine you not getting on with anyone.'

His face unsmiling, he stared at her as he said, 'Under my "be pleasant on any account" façade, if I don't think a thing is right, I'm almost like you, yes I am, I speak out. I may tell you, I wasn't loved by all the staff in the Manor. You see, as though I were an idiot, a dear idiot, I was allowed to walk and wander where I would, until some people realised that nothing escaped me, and that if you were subject to epileptic fits it didn't mean that you were mental. It took quite a time for some people to realise this; but when they did, their attitude towards me changed: I knew too much about them and their pilfering. And it was on a big scale, too, the top hierarchy working in conjunction with the outside farm staff, and the suppliers all making hay when the sun shone, and even when it didn't.

'I stopped their game; and they were afraid I would split on them. And this I told them I would do if they tried it again. For some, it must have been a gold-mine in which they had been digging for years, even before my sister was confined to her chair. I came across it, of course, when she became ill; and it angered me to know that, even in her state, she was being swindled, and by the Estate steward too. So you see, Anna, everybody doesn't love me.'

'I'm glad of that.'

'You are?' His eyebrows moved up.

276

'Yes. It makes us more on a level, say.'

'Oh, I see. Oh' – his chin jerked – 'I don't know whether I do or not. That's one we will have to talk out. But come, come on upstairs.'

The bedrooms were airy and well furnished, but when they came to two steps going off on to another landing, he stopped and said, 'That is the staff's private quarters. Cook has a room, and the girls have another which they share. Walters has a room at the far side of the hall near the kitchen; but he is in communication with me upstairs if I should need him, which' – he made a slight face at her now – 'I don't intend to for a long time, because the tranquillity of this house will act as a balm on me. Come along, now we'll go down and visit cook, and the girls, then we'll have some tea.'

The cook, Mrs Ada Sprigman, dipped her knee at the introduction and Anna thought how, at one time, she would have made the boys roll on the floor by imitating anyone dipping their knee to her. But not any more, never any more.

The kitchen maid was Lena Cassidy, trim, broad Irish, and she too dipped her knee. The housemaid was Mary Bowles and she addressed her as 'ma'am'.

What a difference from her reception at the Manor. And she couldn't help but think that these people knew who she was, and therefore all about her.

Walters brought tea into the sitting-room on a trolley. There was a choice of China or Indian tea, dainty sandwiches and small cakes, and she ate of them because she was feeling suddenly hungry and she hadn't felt so for weeks, or months, for that matter . . .

Tea over, she chose from the samples certain materials that might do for the bedroom curtains, and he made notes of her choice. When, later, they sat by the window in the drawing-room, he looked across the small space that divided them and said, 'I cannot tell you when I've enjoyed an afternoon more. Anna' – he leant towards her and took her hand – 'promise me you'll be kind and come and see me often.'

'The kindness will be on your part, Tim, because I wouldn't like anything better. You see' – she looked down at their joined hands – 'I cannot any longer talk to Dada; something died in him when Ben went. Ma is good and kind, but we never have a discussion together; she's always been only too pleased to leave that to Dada. At one time, he and I would talk for hours and he would go into a particular period of history when perhaps new thinking, new ideas were developing. Given the opportunity, you know, Tim, my father could have been a great speaker; he is so lucid and everything he talked about he made interesting. I'll never forget one conversation we had. It was many years ago, but at the time it seemed to set the pattern of my thinking. What happened today, he said, didn't really happen today, nor yesterday, nor the day before; it was born as a thought in someone's mind, then passed on by word of mouth, then word of mouth was written down and the writing was read. Another brain picked up these thoughts and worked on them. And so it went on until the effect is seen in what happens today. It may have been the declaration of a war; it may have been an assassination; it may have been the fruition of some great love; but it never really happened today. it happened days gone, perhaps weeks gone, perhaps years gone, hundreds of years gone when someone had a particular thought. All there is, he said, is thought. Without thought, what is there? Nothing, for without thought we cannot conceive anything.' She blinked, then muttered, 'Oh dear! Fancy me recalling that! Yet, that is how he used to talk. But . . . but not any more. No, not any more.'

Now he was shaking her hand up and down, saying, 'My dear, you once told me that you scribbled poetry in bits and pieces. I would say to you now, forget about your poetry, put your thoughts down. Put down what you have just said to me, and go on from there.'

Slowly she shook her head as she said, 'That would be merely simplifying things: I mean, writing simple things, because at bottom, I think simply.'

'Oh, my dear, how the world wants to read something that has been simplified. The verbiage that the so-called great minds pen is read through struggle and only by a few. A man gets a name for being a great writer and why? because to the ordinary people he is difficult to understand: he has enjoyed himself spewing out words, words, words, beautiful words, perhaps, but when analysed they are to be found mostly out of context with his subject. I have begun so many books in my time, my dear, and I have thrown them down with irritation, knowing that I was reading the outpourings of a man's idea of himself, as I can only call it, especially when he is so certain that he is right. Science has begun to move fast, and so many scientists depart from their principles to make things known; some are worse than religious fanatics.

'They fight each other for the right to be right. They stand up in lecture rooms and expound their theories, theories that within ten years might be deemed to be out of date, but at the time they are so certain that they are right in what they think, that they convince others, too; just as Catholic or Protestant will do when asserting there is only one God and He is theirs; not only will they kill others but they kill each other in the name of that God; He will be on their dying lips. Have you ever thought, Anna, of the number who have died because of God? Christ was crucified because of God, and His adherents have crucified each other down the ages, burnt each other at the stake, hanged, drawn, and quartered each other. Where is the reason in man that allows him to do this? or believe in such a God? How can anyone be sure that there is any God at all? And have you ever thought, Anna, of Christians who are strong in their faith but who are terrified of dying, and should one of their own die they mourn him, whereas, if they were following their faith they would know he was in these so-called mansions in heaven. So why mourn? Oh, my dear' – he put his hand across his eyes now – 'I'm so sorry. I'm on my egg-box; I'm indulging in my pet hate of all dogmatic individuals, when I should be remembering that I am talking to someone who has just suffered a loss.'

'Please. Please, Tim' – she drew his hand from his brow – 'I understand perfectly. And I'm with you in thought every step of the way. And don't worry about my feelings for Ben; like Dada, I don't think he's gone anywhere yet; his body's in the graveyard but his spirit's still in the house. But' – she looked to the side – 'I sometimes wish, for Dada's peace of mind, that he would move on and go wherever spirits go, for, as long as he remains or as Dada thinks he remains, he will be in a daze. And that's all I can call his present state, a daze.'

She now looked quickly towards the window, saying, 'The sun's going down; I must get home. But oh, Tim, I have enjoyed my visit, and our talk. It's wonderful to be able to talk like this again, and to listen. You say I should write, and I say you should write, but I know you do and I would love to read some of your work, some of your poems.'

'Oh, my dear, I'll have to be either very very drunk or very very ill before I let you or anyone else read my poems.'

'Well, I'll come some evening on the quiet when you're very very drunk.'

'Do that. Oh please, do that.'

280

They went out laughing.

As he drove her home she thought of Simon's words when standing near the sawing block: 'He's a man, and some of the greatest men have been epileptics.'

Be that as it may, she could never see this dear friend of hers asking any woman to marry him. He was too sensitive of his disability and the knowledge that people shied from even a child in fits, let alone from a thrashing-arms man.

281

PART FIVE

❧

The Cross

1

It was a strange summer. Towards the end of May the heat became intense; then on the seventh of June people imagined that the world must have gone topsy-turvy or that it was coming to an end, for on this day there was a heavy fall of snow, three and four inches in some places, to be followed directly by muggy and then hot weather again.

It was very noticeable that tempers became frayed. There had been other hot summers or cold winters but these hadn't seemed to affect the family. But since Ben's death so many things had happened, the latest being that Oswald and Olan hadn't returned home until well after nine o'clock the previous night. They were both very tired; they had been working up till half-past eight. It had been too hot for many people to bother cooking, and so the shop had been packed all day, as, in fact, it had been all week. And Oswald had tentatively put a proposal to his parents. Mrs Simpson had suggested that they make the rooms above the sitting-down shop comfortable where they could both sleep during the week, then come home at the week-ends. Oswald had looked from his mother to his father, then said, 'It's a long trail, Dada, when you've had a day on your feet in the heat, and the bustle! And she's doing us so well and is such a kind woman.'

Nathaniel had looked at Maria, and she had looked at the floor before she had conceded: 'Well, if you want it that way, Oswald, so be it. You're both men now and have to live your own lives. But as long as you come home and see us at the week-end . . .'

'Oh—' Oswald had put out a hand to each of them, saying, 'Of course we will, Ma; and bring our money with us.'

It was now that Nathaniel put in, 'If you are living away, son, we won't expect any money from you; at least, not what you have been giving. And I'm sure Mrs Simpson will look after you. She seemed a very respectable woman, and sensible.'

'She is, Dada; and her daughter, too; and the business is going ahead fine. Both Olan and me think there are prospects there.'

At this Maria lifted her head and said, 'What kind of prospects?' and looked straight at her son, so that he, a bit flustered, answered, 'Well, Ma, she'll give us a good rise at the end of the year; we feel sure on that. And because she's in business, she gets a discount on clothes and things and said if we ever wanted anything . . . well, we could have a ticket.'

'Very kind of her, I'm sure,' Maria said; then turned away . . .

But it was settled that the boys were to leave home, and Maria had packed up a preliminary bundle of clothes for each of them and which they would take with them the following morning, the rest to be taken on their next return journey.

From then on, for most of the week only Anna herself, Cherry, and Jimmy were at home, at least during the evenings. And then it would seem that there was a lot for Cherry to do outside, especially where Bobby Crane was concerned. However, there was no objection from either her mother or her father.

Anna now often found herself walking with Jimmy. Since Ben's going, he, too, had changed. He seemed to have lost his impishness; in fact, at times, in his talk one would think he was quite as old as the twins.

On this particular night, walking by her side through the wood, he proffered the remark, 'The house is breaking up, isn't it, Anna?'

'What do you mean by breaking up, Jimmy?' – she had stopped – 'The boys had to go into town.'

'Oh, I know that. I know that. But the next to leave will be Cherry. She'll marry Bobby.'

'How can she do that? He's still apprenticed: they'll have nothing to live on.'

'Oh, I don't think that will matter very much. They'll get through. Dada would help them. Anyway, if she doesn't get married soon there'll be trouble.'

'Oh! Jimmy.' She again stopped abruptly; and he did so, too, and, looking at her, he said, 'She's ready for marrying.'

This was her young brother, not yet eighteen. Had it been Oswald talking, she would have understood. Yet, Jimmy was a farmer, living with raw nature every day . . . But, oh dear me.

She walked on now, thinking: He said Dada would help them. Did he know anything about the money that would be coming, supposedly from her mother's people? Her parents hadn't mentioned anything further about what Miss Netherton might get for the cross or if she had already got it; and she hadn't asked them, because there seemed to be a wall growing between them. Of course, she must remember that Miss Netherton had been away for the past three weeks on holiday. She had gone down to a place on the South coast called Brighton.

287

They had been walking on, but once again she was brought to a stop by Jimmy's saying, 'I want to get away, Anna.'

Dumfounded for a moment, she could only gaze at him. Then when she managed to speak, her voice was a little above a whisper: 'Why, Jimmy? Where to? What do you mean?' she said.

He smiled at her now as he repeated, 'Why? Where to? What do you mean? Why? Because what is there here for me? You know something? I'd like to go to sea.'

'You would?'

'Yes. Yes, I would. That's where to, to sea.'

'They'd be upset if you were to leave.'

'Well, they'd still have each other, and that's the main thing in their life, isn't it? And, of course, they'll still have you. Oh! Anna' – he now put his hand on her sleeve – 'why didn't you take the chance that was open to you? That fellow would have stood on his head for you: Mr Simon.'

'*Jimmy!*'

'Oh, you can say "Jimmy" like that, but we're all bastards, aren't we? And you wouldn't have been any worse thought of; in fact, there are some who would have looked up to you, let me tell you.'

She almost pushed him on his back, so fiercely did she thrust him aside as she said, 'Well! let me tell you, as I see it, I didn't give myself the name of bastard, it was passed on to me. And I'll tell you this much an' all, I'm never going to earn it, no matter what happens. Now is that clear?'

'Oh, Anna, I'm sorry. I'm sorry. But oh, lass, the thought of you ending your days stuck back there with the pair of them. They see nobody else but themselves. You must face it; I did a long time ago. Oh, aye; they brought us up well, but drugged like with tales around the fire; the happy routine. Nothing was ever going to change. But we're no longer children, we're grown-up men and women, and the older we've grown the more they've grown back into their early days. Night after night I've sat on that mat and watched them. At one time I used to like to watch them, but not any more. They're not two people, they're just one. They could lose the lot of us as long as they have each other.'

'Jimmy! Dada's been distraught over Ben. Really! I've never imagined you thinking like this.'

'We were all distraught over Ben; and as for how I think, it shows that you haven't given much thought to me.'

'I have. I have. But I didn't think you looked on them like that.'

'Well, how do *you* look on them?'

She turned from him without answering, and walked slowly towards the chopping block, and there, placing a hand on it, she looked over the railings to the moor, and in her mind she saw riding across it a man who would have taken her for a mistress; and she also saw a man writhing on the ground in an epileptic fit.

When she felt Jimmy's hand on her shoulder she turned and looked at him, asking quietly now, 'Do you intend to go soon?'

'Aye, yes; before the winter sets in. But it's strange, because the only one I'm going to miss is you; and wherever I go I'll be thinking of you, and seeing your face, because you've got a beautiful face, you know, Anna. You're beautiful altogether.'

'Oh!' – she closed her eyes – 'don't, Jimmy. Don't.'

'Why shouldn't I say it? Right from a child I used to like looking at you, more so than at Cherry. Cherry's pretty, but you're beautiful. And where's it going to get you? Wasting away in that long room and in this square of ground from which you can't even drive out on the cart. Oh, my God! Anna, it makes me sick when I think of it.'

289

She stared at this brother of hers, this young boy: he was still a young boy but he talked like a man, he thought like a man, he was a man, as much, or even more than the twins. He was a man as Ben would never have been. He was even now a man as his father had never been. She put out her arms towards him and they clung tightly together for a moment and then he swung away from her and, as if he were aiming to leave her and them all at this very moment, he leapt the wall behind the wood-pile and ran across the open moor, leaving her with her head bowed over the wood block and moaning as if she had lost another brother, or someone, someone even closer . . . which she had.

2

Twice of late she had walked to Timothy's house. It was exactly a mile and a half away, if she went over the stile and dropped down the bank into the road, so avoiding the village. She had enjoyed the walk; and had met only one person, a man driving a farm-cart. And she had not encountered a carriage.

It was towards the middle of July, about four o'clock in the afternoon, when she said to her mother, 'I think I'll take a walk along to Mr Timothy's, Ma; I've got these books I would like to change.'

'But it's still so hot.'

'There's a breeze coming up and the road's in partial shade for most of the way. Anyway, Ma, I feel I want to stretch my legs.'

'You'll feel better tomorrow when Miss Netherton comes back; you'll have something to do then. Fancy her going all the way to Holland! She's been gone more than five weeks now. I . . . I think it might be about . . . about the other thing.'

It was the first time her mother had alluded to the cross, and she said, 'You think so, Ma?'

'Yes. Your Dada was saying a lot of such trading goes on in Amsterdam.'

'She'll have a great deal to tell us when she comes back, I'm sure. Anyway, that's one thing.'

'Oh, yes, she will, she will; and it'll likely be settled. But, money or no money, I still wouldn't like to leave here. Would you?'

She drew in a long breath and looked downwards before she said, 'Sometimes I feel hemmed in.'

'Yes. Yes, you're bound to, lass.' Maria put in quickly. 'You're bound to. And I understand. Don't think I don't. I understand. But something'll turn up, you'll see, something'll turn up.'

Anna didn't ask what her mother thought might turn up, she just said, 'Will I have to put a hat on?' and Maria smiled, saying, 'I don't see why. We've never conformed to style, have we? No; go as you are; your dress looks cool. It certainly won't rain today.' Then she added, 'We haven't seen him for a week or so. Perhaps he's had another turn.'

'Oh, I wouldn't think so. He goes to Newcastle quite a bit. I know he's researching some old books in the archives of the Literary Library; no, the Literary and Philosophical Society Library, he calls it.'

'Well, it's a good thing he's got something to pass his time with, the way he is.'

As she left the house and walked towards the stile, Anna wondered why her mother always alluded to his infirmity. She seemed forever to be pressing the point. Yet there was no one more sane and normal than Timothy, and the more often she saw him the more she would forget he was ever ill in any way.

She climbed the stile; then put down her two books on the ground and, preparatory to negotiating the bank, turned her back to the roadway and felt carefully with her right foot for

292

one of the footholds she had made, and placed her left foot in a similar one further down; then let out a scream when a hand gripped her calf and a voice said, 'Want a helpin' 'and, miss?'

When the hand pulled her feet to the lower ground, she swung round and fell against the bank, and looked into the face of Arthur Lennon, the blacksmith's son. He was a man of twenty. His hair grew long over his brow and down his cheeks, and he had a moustache trailing down each side of his mouth. His face showed one wide grin.

For a moment she couldn't speak, but looked beyond him to where another man had stepped from behind the hedge that bordered the other side of the road. There was a gap in the hedge wide enough to let a farm-cart through, and the man was holding a large tin by its handle and a brush in the other hand, and to his side stood a younger boy.

'Get out of my way!' She pressed her hands against the bank in order to rise, but the grinning face was hanging over her now, saying, 'Ask civilly.' And when next his hand came on to her breast and, half turning his head to his companion, he said, 'There's nowt in them; flat paps for a gillyvor,' she screamed, 'Take your filthy hands off me, you dirty-mouthed individual! Get out of my way, you lout!'

'Lout, am I? Who you callin' a lout, you whorin' bastard? Not satisfied with breakin' up one family, you have to go for the fitty one. How does he manage? Does he have a fit when he's at you?'

When her knee came up and caught him in the groin he jumped back, holding himself; and she was about to turn and grab her books from the top of the bank when his arms came about her and, spewing obscenities at her, he dragged her screaming through the opening and into the field. When his hand came across her mouth and her teeth bit into it, he pulled it back, bawling, then brought her a blow on the face that sent her head spinning for a moment and seemed to knock the breath out of her body. The next minute she was on her back and he had one knee across her legs and was now tearing at the front of her dress while he shouted to the man, 'Drop the can here, an' go and fetch your Betty. Tell her to bring a pilla.'

'A pilla? You don't mean the tar . . . ?'

'Aye, I do. Me da said it should have been done a long time ago. An' look! stop that bugger from scarperin'.'

The man put down the tin of tar saying, 'My God! Arthur, they'll have you up;' but he was laughing while he said it; and Arthur Lennon said, 'Just let them try. Lucky you had the job of doin' the railings. Look! get after him, quick! or he'll be at the village afore you know where you are. Bring him back here; I'll settle him.'

The man caught up with the boy and, hauling him by the collar, brought him back and thrust him to the ground beyond Anna, and her assailant grabbed him by his shirt-front now and threatened: 'You open your mouth about this and I'll cut your tongue out. D'you hear me? One word an' you know what'll happen to yer. If not that, down below something'll happen there, you understand?'

The boy made no sound but trembled visibly, as he now watched Arthur Lennon trying to pin Anna's clawing hands to her side.

'Untie the york on me legs,' Lennon growled at the boy, 'an' put it across her mouth. Go on! Untie it.'

With shaking hands the boy untied the rope from beneath the man's knee, where it had been used to hold up the trouser leg, and when he leaned over her his eyes were looking straight down into hers, and he shook his head as if to say, I can't help it. I can't help it. Then he put the rope across her gaping mouth.

The man, now taking his knee from her legs, stood up; then bending over, he put one arm between her legs and the other under her waist and with a flick, turned her on to her face as if she had been a sheared sheep. Then, pulling her arms together, he held them with one hand while he loosened the piece of rope from his other leg, and with this he tied her wrists. He then dragged off his thin necktie, with which he tied her ankles together. This done, he now turned her on to her side, and with one pull he split her dress from top to bottom, then her underskirt, then her thin summer camisole. She was now naked to the waist.

It was when Anna felt his hands on her drawers that her whole body writhed. She was screaming inside her head, praying to die now. She next felt the sleeves being torn from her shoulders, then her dress being ripped at the back; but it was after the smell of the tar filled her nostrils and the first full brush of it was slapped on her breasts, then dragged over her stomach and downwards that she knew no more. She did not hear Lennon growl at the boy, 'Stop your whimperin' else I'll strip you and lay you aside her.'

He had finished tarring her when the other man returned, accompanied by his sister, Betty Carter. She was carrying a pillow and she stood looking down on the black-streaked body with the clothes lying in strips from it, and she said, 'You did it, then, Arthur. Uncle Rob said you should an' that you would one day. An' she's only gettin' what she deserves, the bitch.'

Looking down on the black nakedness, her brother said, 'Didn't ya try her afore you tarred her? In for a penny in for a pound.'

'Split that pilla!'

When Betty Carter tried to split the pillow-case the ticking was too strong, and she said, 'Give me your knife,' and with it, she split the pillow down the middle and then puffed as the feathers floated over her. But she didn't hand it to Lennon; instead, she said, 'Let me do it.'

And so she stood over the prostrate form and shook the feathers down on to the wet tar.

'Turn her on to the other side,' she said, and both men, now using their feet, turned the unrecognisable form on to its other side, and as Betty Carter emptied the pillow-case she cried, 'You didn't put any on her hair! Have you any left?' She now took the brush from the can. 'Hardly a scrape,' she said, 'but it'll do.' And with this she drew it a number of times over the shining dark hair, then, gathering up some loose feathers that were lying round about, she finished her job. And now they all turned and looked at the boy, who was vomiting.

'He'll split,' Davey Carter said.

'My God! he won't.'

He now pulled the boy up by the hair of his head and with his doubled fist hit him in the groin, bringing him doubled up again; then warned, 'One squeak out of you, just one, an' like I do with the cattle. Understand?'

The boy gasped and made a motion with his head. 'Who's gona find her?' Betty Carter said.

'Oh, they'll find her right enough. She was likely goin' on a jaunt to the fitty one an' he was likely expectin' her. Oh aye, he would be. I wonder how much he pays her? Somethin's keepin' that lot in clover up there. Oh, they'll find her all right. Afore the night's out there'll be a hue and cry.'

'But what about when she comes round?'

'Oh, well, by that time we'll have had a drink and be givin' them a bit of entertainment in the bar, and then we'll be off. We were goin' in any case. I was due for the sack the morrow, anyroad, 'cos then old Peterson will have found out that he's a pig short. An' Davey here, he's fed up, so we had made wor plans. It was just honest luck that we came across her. By! I've been wantin' to do that to the

296

stinkin' whore for years. She'll not stick her nose in the air so much now.'

'What about me? He knows that it was me.' She pointed to the boy.

'Don't worry about that.' And taking the boy by the collar again, Lennon pulled him towards Betty Carter, pushing his face close to hers as he said, 'Look! you've never seen her in your life afore, except in the village, understand? 'Cos if you don't we'll get you. I'll get you. We're not goin' all that far away, we're just goin' to lie low for a time. But if you squeak, one of these nights I'll pick you up and I'll do what I said. Oh, an' I'd like doin' that. I've always liked doin' it and I'll like doin' it to you. Oh yes! You get me?'

The boy was so sick he could neither say anything nor make any movement, but Lennon said to Betty Carter, 'He understands all right. Don't you worry, Betty, don't you worry. But let's get some of this off wor boots. Anyway, that's what we've been workin' at, tarrin'; expect to get dabbed up a bit at this job. Oh, an' aye. Bring her books off the bank; she may want to have a read.' He laughed.

A minute later he threw the books into the hedge, then with his foot he eased her body towards them; and saying, 'Goodbye, Miss Gillyvor,' he turned to the others and thumbed towards the village, and they followed him out of the field.

The sun still shone and birds in the thicket still sang.

3

Mrs Bella Lennon stood at the bedroom window and looked down on the unusually busy village street. There was something up.

Hurrying down the narrow stairs, she went out of her front door and into the smithy, where her husband was standing in the opening talking to their eldest son, Jack.

'What's up?' she said. 'What's all the bustle?'

Her son turned to her and said on a laugh, 'The gillyvor's lost, the whorin' one. It seems that Mr Tim called in at her dear Papa's – that was around six o'clock, so they say. So, they've been runnin' like scalded cats ever since. Damn fools, them. I bet she's laid up with somebody else.'

'It wouldn't be our Arthur,' said the blacksmith on a deep guffaw, then added, 'By the way, where is he?'

'He's gone into Fellburn with Davey.'

'Fellburn? What for?'

'Well, apparently he was fed up and wanted a night out, so he says. Didn't you see him go in? Didn't he call in?'

'No, he didn't. What time was this?'

'Oh' – she shook her head – 'some time ago. He came in the back way and had a sluice under the pump. He had been down with Davey who was tarring the new railin's for Dobson; then he got changed and went out, saying as usual, "I'll be back when you see me." '

The smith now looked at his son. 'You didn't see him pass this way, did yer?' he said.

'No; and I've been outside here most of the time. Aye! Look!' He pointed. 'Here's a carriage, an' comin' hell for leather.'

As the carriage passed them, Mrs Lennon said, 'That's Mr Timothy in there and somebody else.' Then turning to her son, her eyes screwed up and her whole face one of enquiry, she said, 'You must have seen our Arthur come out of the house?'

'Ma, I'm neither drunk nor daft at this hour of the day and I tell yer he hasn't passed me.'

'Well, he surely wouldn't go out the garden and jump the wall.'

The three of them looked at each other. Then hurrying from them, Mrs Lennon went upstairs again and opened a door off a narrow landing and surveyed her son's room. It looked as it always did. But going to the cupboard, she saw his working clothes thrown into the bottom of it, together with his boots. Well, that was nothing new. But looking on the shelf above she saw that something was missing. After opening the top drawer in an old chest, she stood biting on her lip. The two shirts she had ironed and put in there just this morning, after yesterday's wash, were gone, as also were his long pants and two pairs of socks. Then, lifting the lid of a wooden box that took up the space between the chest and the wall, she saw it was empty. The oddments usually in it were no longer there, the two woollen guernseys, his other cap, a good Sunday waistcoat, and a muffler.

She took the stairs almost two at a time and, bursting into the smithy, where her husband and son were now working, she cried, 'Stop it! Stop it! He's gone.'

The hammering ceased and her husband looked at her and said, 'What d'you mean, he's gone?'

'He's done a bunk for good. He's taken his back-pack and his clothes. He must have pushed them all in there and dropped them out of the back window. That's the way he went.'

The men looked at each other; then the smith, turning to his son, said, 'Finish that. We've got to get that order out; they're waitin'; an' they don't come easy.'

And then, pushing his wife before him, they went into the house and at the foot of the stairs he said, 'The box?'

'The box? What d'you mean the box?'

'Don't be so bloody stupid, woman! The box under the bed. Have you seen to it?'

'No. No. But he wouldn't, not Arthur.'

Without a word the smith bounded up the stairs into their bedroom, pulled out a tin trunk from under the high bed, lifted the lid, put his hand down through oddments of clothes and felt the tin box. Pulling it out, he looked up at her as if in relief. Then he opened it, and as he did so his expression changed. And when they were both looking down into the empty cash box he said, 'The bugger! I'll have him. I'll get him. All twenty-seven of them!'

'You should have put it into the bank. I've told you an' told you.'

'Aye, and let the buggers know what we've got. They know too much down there already. Gold-mine, they'd be sayin' it is. But my God!' He stood up, his teeth grinding as he said, 'I'll get him! I'll find him!'

'You'll do nowt of the sort.' She pushed at his big frame. 'An' you'd better not let on to our Jack, either. You're always pulling a long face about the bills not bein' paid. He knows nowt about this, an' if his Lena got to know, we wouldn't have a minute's peace, ever. An' you expectin' him to work overtime, like the night. So stick it back!' And she thrust her foot against the big box.

'By God!' Lennon said; 'if I could get me hands on him this minute! Anyway, why the rush? He was set to finish the domino game the night. He could have wiped Willie Melton off the board and raked up a nice little pile after fourteen games at sixpence a go.'

'Never mind that. Get downstairs and put a face on to our Jack. And from now on that'll larn you. By God! it will. Twenty-seven pounds in that wild young sod's pocket.' She paused as though thinking, then said, 'D'you think he'll sign on some boat?'

'Likely; an' Davey with him, 'cos whatever he does that dumb head'll follow. An' think on, woman, what's goin' to happen when his mother finds out. She'll be along here, saying, as usual, our Arthur's leading her dear lad astray.'

'God! He went astray when he was born that one . . .'

It was about two hours later. The village street was still abuzz, with small groups here and there gossiping, when Dan Wallace came to the forge opening and asked, 'Seen anything of our Art, Rob?'

'Young Art? No. Is he lost an' all?'

'Well, he hasn't come in for his tea. And it's now goin' on eight. His mother's goin' up the pole.'

'Perhaps he's run off with the gillyvor.'

'Don't be so daft! He was helpin' Davey Carter the day, an' I can't see hilt nor hair of Davey, either.'

The blacksmith, who was now dressed in his second best suit, came out of the forge and closed the doors, and he had his back to Dan Wallace as he said, 'An' you won't. He's . . . he's gone into Fellburn with our Arthur for the night.'

'Oh. Oh, I see. Well, I wonder where the young kite has got to . . . ?'

The young kite was now sneaking in the back door of his home. And when his mother saw him she said, 'Where d'you think you've been?' then stopped and said, 'My God! What's the matter with you, boy? You sick?'

The boy opened his mouth, took in a deep gulp of air and said, 'Dad. Where's Dad?'

'Out looking for you, of course. Past eight; where've you been?'

'Get Dad. Get Dad, Mam.'

'You bad? Caught somethin'?'

'Get Dad, Mam! Get Dad.'

The woman now pushed the boy into a chair; then she turned and ran out of the house, up the village street, past the King's Head, and on past the cottages, shouting to one after another, 'Have you see Dan?' And one woman, rising from a chair where she had been sitting trying to keep cool, pointed and said, 'Just this minute turned up the alley.'

The alley led to Willie Melton's stint, where he kept his pigs, and there she saw her husband talking to Willie, who had a bucket in his hand and a crowd of pigs around him, and she called, 'Dan! Dan! He's in. Dan! come on.'

When her husband came up to her, she said, 'He's bad. Something's wrong with him, he can hardly speak . . .'

When they entered the house the boy straightaway got up from his chair and, going to his father, gripped his hand as he said, 'Dad. Dad, they said what they'd . . . he said what he would do, Arthur Lennon, but . . . but you won't let them will you, Dad? You won't let them, will you?'

'What in the name of God! are you talkin' about, boy? What did he say he would do?'

302

The boy looked at his mother, then put his hand down between his legs and said, 'Cut 'em off. Cut 'em off.'

The husband and wife exchanged looks, and his father said gently, 'Sit down, lad. Sit down and tell me.'

'No, Dad, no. You've got to go and get her.'

'Get who?'

'The young lass, the young lass. She's lyin' in the hedge.'

'Oh my God! My God!' His mother now put her hand up through her hair and let out a cry, and her husband said, 'Shut up! Shut up! Tell me. Tell me. Where's the girl? What have they done?'

'Tarred . . . tarred and feathered her, he did, he did. Tied her up. Said . . . said what they would . . . would do, an' . . . an' he will, Dad, he will.'

'*He will?*' Dan Wallace stood up now. 'He'll swing if I get my hands on him. Come on, lad; show me where she is?'

'No, Dad, no. I can't . . . I can't go. At the stile.'

'Come on, come on. Be a brave lad. Nobody'll do anythin' to you.'

'They will. They will; I was there. I was there. And Davey Carter an' his sister an' all. Aye . . . aye, she . . . she was awful, Betty . . . she was awful.'

'Come on. Come on.' Dan Wallace now led his son out into the street, but he had to keep a firm arm round him and keep pressing him forward. Then his wife, who was at the other side of him, turned and said, 'Here's the carriage comin'! It's Mr Timothy's. Stop it! Stop it! Tell 'em!'

Dan Wallace waved his hand, and when Edward pulled up the carriage Timothy put his head out of the window in enquiry and Dan said to him, 'My boy here, sir, my boy says he knows where the girl is.' He looked beyond Timothy now to the strained face of the girl's father, and Nathaniel cried, 'He does? He does? Where?'

'Sir, I think both of you . . . I think you'd better prepare yourself for somethin'. I don't know, but my boy here seems to know all about it. They threatened him.'

'Who, man? Who?'

'I'll tell you later, sir, but I think we'd better get there, wherever it is. Come on, sir.' He now took his son's arm and ran him down the street, the carriage following, and this brought people out of their houses, out of the gardens, and out of both inns, all asking questions.

Beyond the village, when they came to the gap in the hedge, the boy shrank against his father, but his father dragged him into the field and when the boy pointed, Dan Wallace muttered, 'Almighty God! Oh, Almighty God!' And a minute later, when Nathaniel and Timothy stood looking down on the tarred and feathered naked body, with its torn clothes spread like broken wings at each side of her, both, for a moment, had to hold on to each other for support. And then Nathaniel was kneeling on one side of her and Timothy on the other; and Timothy, taking her smeared face between his hands, said not a word, for his mind was screaming against the obscene cruelty that had been inflicted on this innocent girl, on his beloved Anna.

Nathaniel raised his head and looked at him and whispered, 'She's . . . she's breathing.'

They both stood up and looked about them. It seemed that a crowd of people had gathered from nowhere and were standing awestruck.

Dan Wallace said, 'She'll have to be lifted on to a cart or something.'

But Timothy's coachman said quietly, 'I . . . I wouldn't touch her, sir, until a doctor comes, and the polis.'

Nathaniel looked at the man; then he looked at Timothy; and after a slight hesitation Timothy said, 'Get into Fellburn at top speed and bring them both.'

'We . . . we can't leave her like this. We must loosen her arms and legs,' said Nathaniel, kneeling beside Anna.

Timothy too knelt and tugged at the knots, then looking around he muttered, 'A knife? Has anyone got a knife?'

At least three knives were handed towards him; then, as he cut the rope around Anna's wrist, Dan Wallace said, 'I wouldn't move her arms, sir, not for a bit. She'll be in cramp.'

When Timothy had finished there were feathers sticking to his tarred hands and somebody offered him a handkerchief; then another.

The crowd had grown now, but it was silent: it was definitely a group of frightened people, for they could surely see the outcome of this dreadful deed.

The boy was clinging to his mother now and crying openly. And when a thin voice near them said, 'Did he do it?' Mrs Wallace startled everybody by screaming, 'No! he didn't. Your bosom drinking mates did it. Arthur Lennon and Davey Carter. And aye, aye, where's his sister? Where's his sister, dear little Betty?'

Her husband turned on her fiercely now, saying, 'Shut up! Shut up! woman. That'll be seen to later.'

It was noticeable now that here and there a person moved out of the crowd and went quietly away, and one of these was the blacksmith . . .

It was exactly twenty-five minutes later when the doctor and the policeman arrived in the carriage, and after pressing through the crowd they both stood and looked down, first with amazement, then with horror at the sight of the tarred and feathered girl.

The doctor now took off his coat and rolled up his sleeves before kneeling on the ground. Putting his ear to the discoloured mouth and then roughly rubbing the sticking feathers to one side, he felt the flesh below the breast.

305

Standing up, he said, 'We must get her to hospital.'

'Hospital?' It was a whispered word from Nathaniel, and the doctor said, 'Yes. You won't be able to get her clean with soap and water, and I'm afraid she'll be ill for some time, if only with shock.' The doctor now looked at the policeman who had already taken out a notebook, and he said grimly, 'I hope you get your details right.' And the policeman said, 'I will that, sir, I will that. Never in me life have I seen anything like it. Whoever did this should swing.'

And Timothy's mind yelled at him, 'And they might yet. Oh, yes, they might yet. Oh! Anna. Anna. Oh, my dearest Anna.'

The doctor was saying, 'It's a question of how we're going to get her in. She should be laid out on something flat.'

'Can you put her in the carriage?'

The doctor looked at Timothy now and said, 'That would be very awkward, sir, especially with the mess she's in.'

'Never mind about the mess.'

A voice from the crowd shouted, 'Me flat cart an' horse is in the road, sir. It's high with hay but that can be dumped. You're welcome.'

'Thank you,' the doctor called. 'Can you back it in here?'

'Aye, if the people'll move.'

The people moved and the horse and cart was backed almost up to Anna's side, and she was lifted on to it by Nathaniel and Timothy. And when Timothy said, 'I'll sit beside her, Nathaniel,' Nathaniel raised his hand and answered quietly, 'No; you get in the carriage, sir, I'll sit beside her.' And Timothy, admitting to the prerogative of the father, went to the carriage now with the doctor and the policeman, and the carriage followed the flat cart in the long twilight as they took the road to Fellburn and the hospital, leaving a subdued and not a little fearful village behind them.

4

The following day the police arrested Arthur Lennon and Davey Carter as they were about to board a boat they had signed on at South Shields. The boat was bound for Bergen.

Later in the day a cab arrived in the village, holding two policemen and an inspector, to arrest one Betty Carter for her being implicated in a most atrocious attack on a young girl.

The village was quiet, people spoke in undertones. The King's Head was full that night but The Swan was practically empty. The blacksmith and his son, the painter Willie Melton and his son, and a number of others were all conspicuous by their absence from The Swan. There was recalled in the village the conversation that had taken place one evening in the inn about tarring and feathering, and those who laughed about it.

In the King's Head the conversation was quiet as the events of the day were gone over. It was said that all the lass's family had remained at the hospital most of the night; the younger girl hadn't been to work that day nor the boy to the farm; and Mr Timothy had been at the hospital too. It was also said that Mr Simon from the Manor had been to the hospital. It was surmised that it was touch and go for the lass. If she didn't come round it would be a hanging job for two, that was sure. As for Betty Carter, well, she only put the feathers on her so it could be just a long stretch. But whichever way it went, this village would never be the same again. Why couldn't they have left them in the Hollow, alone? They had done nobody any harm; in fact, in some ways they had done good. Look how they had taken those families off the moor. It was only four years ago that two old people and some bairns died out there. And did anybody really believe the lass had broken up the couple in the Manor? It was known as loud as the headlines in a newspaper that those two had been at each other's throats ever since returning from their honeymoon. Betty Carter herself used to bring news in on her days off. As for the lass being free an' all with Mr Timothy, was it likely, seeing he had those fits? Everybody knew he was a book-learned man and her being a teacher like her dad, well they would have something in common, wouldn't they? But young Lennon had always been a vicious type. His father and Jack . . . well, they did the talking, but give them their due, they weren't vicious. No, a voice had put in, they were just the ones that passed on the tinder to set the fire alight, and he had actually done it to their barn, hadn't he? And yes, they all agreed that was right, that was right.

And so it went on, and from day to day now, while everyone waited.

When, a week later, the news spread through the village that the lass had sort of woken up and it was thought she might live, the majority drew in long breaths and said quietly, 'Well, thank God for that! There'll be no swingin' job, no matter what else.' It only took a swingin' job to get a village a very bad name; and there were families in this village that went back to the last century, such as the Wattses . . . But then, of course, they had to leave. But Miss Penelope Smythe, her people went back a longer way, as did Dan Wallace's. And yes, the grocer's, John Fenton. Oh yes, the grocer; his wife Gladys was always yapping about ancestry. You would think they had made the village. One thing they had done, they had rooked it with their grocery charges. You could buy some of the stuff at only half the price in Fellburn. Gladys was crafty: she knew only too well you had to get to Fellburn and back, and if you hadn't a gig or a trap, that was tuppence on the carrier cart and extra if you had livestock. Oh, the Fentons knew what they were about. Still, all those in the King's Head were glad to know that the lass had woken up.

Timothy's carriage drew up outside his house, with Simon following on horseback. After alighting, they went inside together, and the first words the butler said were, 'How is she, sir?'

'She's still very low but she's holding her own.'

'That's good news, sir.' Then looking from one to the other, he enquired, 'Is it something hot or a glass of wine you'll be taking, sir?'

Timothy now looked at Simon, and Simon said, 'A brandy would be acceptable.'

'And for me, too.'

A little while later they were settled in the sitting-room and after no words had passed between them for some minutes, Simon, suddenly getting to his feet, walked to the window, saying, 'I know how you are going to respond, but I must say it: she's suffered this indignity and terror for things she hasn't done; so she wouldn't have suffered any worse if she had done them. In fact, it wouldn't have happened.'

'You mean, if she had fallen in with your wishes and become your mistress?'

Simon swung round now, saying, 'Yes. Yes, I do, Tim. That's exactly what I mean.'

'Well, she refused you, didn't she? And she'll always refuse you.'

'We'll see about that.'

'You won't! You won't, Simon. You won't.'

'Who's to stop me? You.'

'Yes, if I can.'

'You would ask her to marry you?'

Timothy's mouth went into a hard line now as he looked at the other man. 'No,' he said; 'because I wouldn't ask anyone to marry me. But she trusts me. I am her friend. She listens to what I say. And if it's the last thing I do I'll prevent her from following the pattern of her mother. However, there will be no need; she won't have you. At one time she might have had some feelings for you, in the way you imagine she still has, but I'm sure it's no more. What happened to kill it, for I think it is dead, I don't know. But something did happen: perhaps you know what, apart from your having a wife.'

Slowly Simon turned away and looked out of the window again, and Timothy now asked, 'Have you heard anything from Penella?'

'No; only that she's living in Newcastle as near Raymond as possible. Not that that's going to do her much good.'

'I've always thought you were wrong in that direction, Simon. If she had thought so much of Raymond she would have married him when he gave her the child. It was you she wanted and has always wanted. Her chasing Raymond was to stir you up. And it did, but in the wrong way. She wasn't prepared for that. And I must say this: if you had been of a more forgiving nature from the beginning, your life together would have been quite different from what it has turned out to be. The very fact that you could forgive her would have proved your love for her.'

'Oh, shut up!' Simon now reached out, took up his half-empty glass from the table, threw off the remainder of the brandy, and said, 'I must be on my way. But thank you, dear uncle, for your kind advice.'

'You are very welcome, nephew,' Timothy answered in the same vein; then added, 'You can see yourself out.'

But on nearing the door, Simon turned and, looking at Timothy, then round the room, he said, 'I envy you this place, you know.'

'I know you do; and not only that but my liberty, too.'

'Huh! You're a clever old stick, aren't you?'

'Oh, yes. Perhaps not so much clever as old, being nine years your senior.'

Simon went out on a harsh laugh and Timothy walked to the window, to see him emerge from the house and mount his horse, and the sight of the smart, lithe figure riding down the drive swept away the assurance he had assumed just a few minutes ago. Will she? he thought; and he answered himself, Yes, she might. Having suffered this indignity, this terrible indignity, she might think, What does anything matter any more? But whatever she should decide to do, life would never be the same for her again.

Anna was in hospital for three weeks and in a convalescent home for two further weeks, the latter having been arranged by Miss Netherton. Then, on the day they brought her home it was into a house full of flowers and with the long table covered with gifts, in the middle of which was a large arrangement of fruit in a high-handled decorative basket trimmed with ribbon.

There were even presents from some of the villagers, as Maria pointed out: ginger cake, jam preserve, a box of home-made toffees; then the large boxes all tied up with ribbon: some, her mother pointed out, were from Mr Simon and Mr Timothy and others from the boys and Miss Netherton. And placed among all these were pretty cards wishing her well.

311

Anna had expressed her thanks quietly and in just a few words.

This was what was troubling the family: she didn't talk any more like she used to do. It was now more than five weeks since that awful time, but as the doctor said, it could be further weeks or perhaps months before she would really be herself again. Again and again he would say she was a lucky girl to be alive at all. And if she hadn't been taken to hospital and treated straightaway she would never have survived.

Unfortunately, they'd had to cut off some of her hair; it had been impossible to get it clear of the tar. And now the ends reached only to her shoulders. Yet, if anything, it seemed to enhance her face. In a strange way, though, it didn't seem to make her any younger as such a crop usually did, for her features appeared to have aged. She could have been a woman in her thirties.

She listened to the buzz of conversation around her, but didn't appear to hear any particular thing that was being said. Her mind seemed to have undergone a change: it no longer picked up and dealt with present issues, but would wander back into the past when she was young, when she was a girl sitting in the barn learning her lessons in the summer-time; or in the winter, hurriedly clearing the long table of the breakfast dishes and spreading the books out and looking across at her dada's bright face as he would laughingly say, 'We will now call the register. Benjamin Dagshaw.'

'Pesent, sir.'

And her father would say yet again, 'As I have informed you, Benjamin Dagshaw, you may be a peasant but that "pesent" is *present*.' And there would be laughter. Then: 'James Dagshaw.'

'Present, sir, all of me.'

More laughter.

'Cherry Dagshaw.'

312

'I am not all here, sir; my heart's in the highlands.'

'Your heart will be in your mouth, madam, in a moment.'

'Annabel Dagshaw.'

'I am all yours, sir.'

Often such remarks would come later, but always they brought laughter with the lesson . . .

'What are you smiling at, dear?'

She looked up at Maria. 'Was I smiling, Ma?' she said.

'Yes, you were. You must have been thinking something nice. What was it?'

'Oh, I don't know . . . Ma?'

'Yes, dear?'

'I would like to go to bed.'

'Then you shall go to bed. It's been a very trying day.'

Timothy had left earlier, feeling that she would want to spend a quiet time with her family. Miss Netherton, too, had left with him, having said in an aside to Maria, 'I'll come over tomorrow morning. I have news for you.'

Now there were only Cherry, Jimmy, and Olan. Oswald had had to remain in the shop for, as he had said, someone must keep things going. But he had sent Anna a book by the poet Tennyson, entitled *Ballads and other Poems*.

So Maria and Cherry had helped to undress her and tuck her up in bed. And when, later, Nathaniel came in, he stood by her side and, taking hold of her limp hand, he said, 'You are home, my dear, and I hope never to leave it.'

And at this Anna closed her eyes and her mind left her childhood dreaming and leapt ahead into the everlasting future, during which time she would never again leave this house.

313

5

It was at the end of August when Arthur Lennon and David Carter, together with Beatrice Carter, were brought before the Justice in Newcastle to answer to the heinous crime that Arthur had committed against a young girl, which could have led to his being tried for the capital crime of murder had she not recovered.

His Lordship, John Makepeace Preston, sentenced Arthur Lennon to five years' hard labour, and David Carter, he who had aided and abetted him, to four years' hard labour, and Beatrice Carter, who had put the final touches on the outrageous and indecent act, three years in the House of Correction. And Arthur John Wallace, the boy who had been subjected to such fearful threats, which had now left him with defective speech not previously apparent, referred to as a stammer, the Justice commended for coming forward and speaking in detail about that which he had witnessed was being carried out by these three vicious people; and also for how he had related, albeit most painfully, the threat made to his person by the prisoner, Arthur Lennon.

There had been no response from anyone in the courtroom when the sentence was passed on Lennon, but when the

Justice sentenced both David Carter and his sister, their mother had stood up and screamed, 'They didn't do it! They didn't do it! He made them. You can't send her along the line.'

After she was evicted from the courtroom, it was noted that her son stood with bowed head and shoulders, while Arthur Lennon stood white-faced and with his eyes glaring, yet his body was trembling as if he were under shock. As for Betty Carter, it would have been expected of her that her face would have been awash with tears, but she remained dry-eyed and tight-lipped. And when the wardress held her shoulder, it was seen that she tried to shrug off her hand.

All the proceedings were related to Maria in various ways by Miss Netherton, Timothy, and Oswald. Nathaniel, Maria noted, said very little except, 'Justice has been done. For once, justice has been done . . . '

Miss Netherton hadn't come the following morning, as promised, to give them her news because her house had been stormed by the blacksmith, his son, and Mr and Mrs Carter; also by Willie Melton and his son Dirk and the landlord of The Swan, Reg Morgan, and his wife Lily, for they had all that day been given notice to quit their premises. 'Why,' had demanded Reg Morgan and Willie Melton, 'are we being made to suffer for what the Lennons have done, and the Carters an' all?'

This had caused an argument between the two groups outside the house, and when she appeared at her door with Stoddart on one side of her and Peter Tollis on the other, Miss Netherton told the Meltons that they had been included in the evictions on good authority: they had been inciters in what had happened, together with the innkeeper and his wife. And at this Reg Morgan yelled, 'You can't put us out. We were engaged by the brewery.'

'Then let the brewery find you other premises. That inn belongs to me, as do the other houses. If you feel you have been wronged, there is always the law. Go and take it up and see how far you will get.'

When Willie Melton began to plead and say he was sorry that he had opened his mouth, she stared at him, then stepped back and said to Stoddart, 'Come in and close the door.'

So the village was once more up in arms, at least in part. However, the four families found they were getting little sympathy from the rest of the inhabitants. But this did not stop the blacksmith from going into the inn that night and saying he wasn't going to lie down under this; he would go to a newspaper and get them to print why all this had happened. And why had it happened? Because, as the parson had said, those two had lived in sin and had bred a family in sin and one of them had followed in the footsteps of her mother, and it was she who had brought tragedy on the village with her antics.

But it was Dan Wallace who stood up to him again and boldly asked who had set fire to the barn all those years ago? Who had crippled the goat? Who had got together a mob to try to scare the wits out of them? And who had set the man-trap? As for him going to a newspaper, the newspapers had had a field day about the case already. What had the headlines said? 'Innocent girl near death through the spite of villagers. The first case ever to have been heard in this part of the country of a female being tarred and feathered.' And what did they predict? It could be a hanging case if she died. And it was lucky for him and his son and the other two that she had survived. And to his mind the sentences were light.

When this counter-attack brought no support for the blacksmith he had stormed out of the bar and made for the vicarage. But there his reception was cool, and this enraged the man further. He reminded the parson that last Sunday he had preached that the sins of the fathers were passed on to the children even to the third and fourth generation . . .

It was ten days later when Miss Netherton visited the house in the afternoon. The weather had changed: there were squally showers and it had turned cold. And when she entered the room where Anna was sitting in the big chair before the blazing fire, her first words were, 'Oh, isn't that a welcome sight! There's a lot to be said for the winter.' Then taking Anna's hand, she said, 'How are you feeling, my dear?'

'All right, thank you; much better.'

'That's good. That's good.' Then turning to where both Nathaniel and Maria were standing, she said, 'Sit down. Please sit down and I'll sit here next to Anna and tell you my news. At last, at last, it is settled.' And as she took her seat she added, 'Well, it was settled some time ago, but I never believe in any business deal until it is in writing, stamped with a red seal or the money is in the bank. And in this case the money is almost in the bank.' And at this she opened her beaded bag and took out an envelope from which she withdrew a letter and a cheque, which she passed to Maria, saying, 'Read that.' And when Maria had read it, she said, 'Oh, my goodness! Oh! Miss Netherton,' before passing it to Nathaniel, who gazed at it, then looked at the spruce, neat figure of his benefactress, murmuring in amazement, 'I can't believe it.' Then bending towards Anna, he said, 'Look at that, my dear.' And when Anna read the amount she slowly lifted her eyes and looked at Miss Netherton, and in almost a whisper said, 'Seven thousand, two hundred and fifty pounds! Oh, Miss Netherton.'

'Well—' Miss Netherton took the cheque from her fingers, put it back into the sheet of writing paper, tapping it as she did so and saying, 'This is the amount after all their bits and pieces have been taken off. I told you they would all get their cuts.' And again looking at Maria, she said, 'The cross was

317

sold to a private dealer in Amsterdam, so I'm told, for ten thousand pounds. You can guess what it's really worth.'

'I can't believe it. I just can't believe it.'

'Well, my dear, you can, you can. Now the agreement was we would share this. That means we should have three thousand, six hundred and twenty-five pounds each. But let me be practical. I have already given you five hundred pounds, and this deducted from your share leaves you with three thousand, one hundred and twenty-five pounds. Isn't that right? Oh, Maria, Maria, don't cry so. This is a happy event.'

'I can't believe it. And . . . and you are so good. You really needn't have done anything about it. We needn't have heard another word, yet you go to all this trouble.'

'It was no trouble. You have no idea how I've enjoyed myself over this transaction. Why, when I was in Holland I went about and saw and met people I never imagined I would meet up with in my life, and they were all gentlemen. Oh, yes, the Dutch are very courteous and so wonderfully interesting. And they nearly all spoke English, which was just as well. So, I've got a lot to thank you for because *I* didn't come across that exquisite piece of work, did I? And you, too, Nathaniel, smile please. Come on. We've had enough sorrow about lately, let us rejoice in this piece of good fortune. And you know something?' She was now wagging her finger at Maria, who was wiping her face with the hem of her white apron. 'I have never yet come in this house without within five minutes of my arrival being offered a drink of some sort, nearly always a cup of tea. And here I am bearing gifts' – she pulled a face at herself now – 'and not a drop am I offered.' The last was said in an Irish twang. And when Maria rose hastily to her feet, saying, 'Oh, Miss Netherton, Miss Netherton,' and then bent quickly towards her and kissed her on the cheek, the older woman kept swallowing for a moment before she said,

'Go on with you! Go on, I want a strong cup of tea. And Nathaniel, look, it is raining and heavily, so would you mind telling Stoddart to take the contraption into your barn, and then bring him into the kitchen for a drink. Will you?'

When they had the room to themselves, Miss Netherton, now taking hold of Anna's hand, said, 'I wish my news could have altered the look in your eyes, my dear. But no money in the world will do that. The only person who can do that is yourself. And now I want you to promise to try and put the past behind you, because never again will you be treated as you have been. I can assure you of that. And then there is your future. We shall have to think about that. Is there anything you want to do?'

Anna shook her head slowly, then said, 'I cannot think ahead. I don't seem able to think at all.'

'Oh, my dear, that feeling will pass. But we must find something for you to do. Timothy was saying that you might like to go and study in some ladies' college?'

The faintest of smiles came on Anna's face as she said, 'He said that?'

'Yes, and much more. Oh, he is indeed worried about you. You are so dear to him. Anna—' She now took hold of Anna's hand and, looking into her face, she said, 'Tim is a very special person. Do you know that? Have you yet found that out?'

After a pause Anna said, 'Yes. Yes, I have. I've never met anyone as kind as him in my life, except yourself.'

The answer seemed to make Miss Netherton impatient for a moment, for she dropped Anna's hands, sat back in her chair and said, 'Oh, dear me.' And Anna said, 'Why do you say, Oh dear me, like that?'

'Oh, it doesn't matter just at the moment. I'll talk about it later when you're feeling stronger. And you know, you're not going to get strong sitting in that chair. I know the weather is

319

inclement but there'll be some nice days ahead and you must get out and walk.'

In answer to this Anna said, 'I haven't seen Timothy since shortly after I returned home.'

'Well, you wouldn't, because he's gone to London.'

'London? He didn't say.'

'Well, he didn't tell you because you weren't in any fit state to listen to him or to anybody else when you first came home. But you see, his book's been accepted.'

'*His book?*' Anna pulled herself up straighter in the chair. 'I didn't know he had written a book; he said he just scribbled.'

'Oh, yes, he always says he just scribbles. But he's written a book on the Renaissance period. He's very interested in that period of history, and it's going to be published.'

'Really?' Anna turned her head away now, saying, 'He's never mentioned it.'

'He's a very humble person, is Tim, too humble for his own good ... too thoughtful for his own good. He deprecates himself just because of the one little handicap he's got. And, after all, it is a little handicap. The unfortunate thing about it is he doesn't know when it's going to hit him. But to my mind, otherwise it is of no great importance. So, my dear, yes, he is going to have a book published. He will likely tell you all about it when he returns. It's been in the publisher's hands for some weeks now and, reading between the lines of what he's saying, they seem to think highly of it. Not that I got much out of him about it.'

Half dreamily now, Anna said, 'Strange that he never mentioned it to me. We talked such a lot about books and authors and the Renaissance period. He used to speak of Dante, and then of the influence of Machiavelli and of the return to Classical learning. 'Tis strange.'

320

'Ah, here's that cup of tea.' Miss Netherton turned towards Maria, who was carrying in a tray holding four cups of tea, and as she put the tray down, she said, 'Nathaniel has taken a cup out to Stoddart, Miss Netherton. He said he'd better stay with the horse; it seemed rather uneasy being put in a strange place.'

After sipping from the cup, Miss Netherton said, 'I've always said, Maria, you make a very good cup of tea.' Then she added, 'Ah! there you are, Nathaniel,' as he entered the room. 'I know what I wanted to say to both of you. It's this: I don't know what you intend to do with the money, but one of the first things I would suggest is you get yourselves a horse and trap now that the fences are down. And by the way, I can tell you that both Raymond Brodrick and his future father-in-law, Albert Morgansen, have been pulled over the coals for that piece of law-breaking. John Preston got his solicitors to rake from the archives old laws and those two had to pull their horns in when they were confronted with them. There are land-enclosure laws and land-enclosure laws, and those two didn't do their homework. Of course, it was mostly Praggett's doing, I suppose. Anyway, what about the horse and trap?'

Nathaniel looked at Maria and she at him, and they both smiled and Nathaniel said, 'Yes, that is a marvellous suggestion. It will certainly be one of the first things we do.'

'And secondly, what about you both taking a holiday, away by yourselves? I can see to this young lady here, and the rest of the family are quite able to see to themselves. Of course, I know you'll have to mull over that one, but think about it. And, of course, what I must ask you is, have you any choice of bank into which you'd like to put your money? If you decide it should go into mine, then I will take you both down and introduce you to the manager. He will then explain where best it would be to invest whatever part of it you would

321

like to earn a little interest. Anyway, that will all be explained to you. So, will tomorrow be convenient for you?'

'Oh, Miss Netherton, any time, any time you care to take us in,' said Nathaniel now. 'And I can say this, neither of us will live long enough to thank you for all you have done for us.'

Miss Netherton looked to the side now and upwards as she said, 'It's odd what money can do. It's odd what locks it can oil, what doors it can open. If only everybody used it for the good. But there, it's not time for preaching and I must away.' She rose to her feet; then turning to Anna, she said, 'Remember what I told you. Get out in the air as soon as the weather changes, and walk. Walk over to my place every day. Yes, that's a good idea. I'll expect you every day.'

'I will. I will in a short while.'

Anna didn't get up from her seat but she watched her parents escort her dear friend out of the house. Then, her head dropping back, she closed her eyes as she said to herself, 'Get out and walk. Get out and walk.' She didn't care if she never walked again. She just wanted to sit still in this limbo into which she had been thrust. She couldn't see that anything which might happen in the future could arouse her interest ever again. She was dead inside. She had died when that tar brush swept down the front of her body and he had pushed it between her legs.

6

It had rained for days; then had come a muggy period: there
were mists in the morning, with the sun trying to get through
a haze, followed by damp, cold nights. Anna could not often
take a walk of any length, but she spent quite a bit of her
time now in the barn or the tack-room or in the new stable
that had been erected to house the nine-year-old horse they
had acquired, whose spruceness had made Neddy look a
very poor relation indeed, and whose harness had to be kept
burnished. The advantage of doing these chores was that in
the main she could be on her own.

Twice during short spells Timothy had brought the carriage over and taken her back to the house, and she had
enjoyed these breaks in the monotonous routine. But even
so, he had done much of the talking, telling her about
London and the publisher and making light and fun of
what the critics might say about his book, which was to be
published in the coming spring. On the last occasion he
had driven her home, and just before they alighted, he had
taken her hand and said, 'Oh, Anna, Anna, come back.'
She didn't need to ask, Come back from where? she knew
what he meant.

Today she was sitting in the tack-room rubbing a wax mixture into the harness when the door opened and Jimmy appeared, which made her say immediately, 'You're back early. Anything wrong?'

'I . . . I asked if I could come away. I've . . . I've had the runs all day and I'm not feeling too good . . . You shouldn't be doing that; it's hard work, that.'

'A little bit of hard work won't hurt me.'

'Dada or Ma always does it.'

'Yes, but they're busy.'

He sat down on an upturned box, then asked quietly, 'Have they given you any of the cash they came into from our unknown grandmother? I thought she had died years ago; and then our grandfather married again, which was why Ma couldn't lay claim to Low Meadow after he died.'

She looked at him in surprise: 'No. No,' she said. 'Why do you ask?'

'Just thinkin'. We've been kept in the dark about lots of things, while the fact of our beginnings has been thumped into us. And now this money business that they are being close about.'

'Well, you have your wage, and they take only half of it now.'

'Aye. Aye, that's right. But I must tell you, Anna, I'm leaving for sure.'

'Oh, Jimmy! Please.'

'I've got to, Anna. There's something inside of me raging to be away. Anyway, I've shot me bolt: I gave him me notice, I'm not bonded. A month, I said. He doesn't believe I've got the bellyache; thinks I'm gettin' a bit uppish because I asked to come off early.'

'They're going to be upset.' She motioned with her hand towards the door.

324

'Oh, I don't know. You know, I once said to you, as long as they've got themselves, that's all they need. And I'm more convinced of that than ever. You could have died. Any of us could have died and they would have missed us and mourned us, but if one of them were to go the other would go an' all.'

'Why do you think like this, Jimmy?'

'Don't you?'

She allowed her gaze to fall on to the harness, then said, 'You're bitter about something. You didn't used to be.'

'Aye, perhaps I am, but I can see nothing ahead here. I want to get away, escape. And there's another one that'll be escaping shortly, and that's Oswald. He's sweet on the daughter.' He laughed, but then put his hand to his stomach, saying, 'Here I go again,' and turned to leave, and she said, 'How long have you been feeling like this?'

'Oh, since the day afore yesterday.'

'You could have picked something up in the market.'

He halted at the door and turned and looked at her, and she said, 'What is it?' But he shook his head and went out.

Jimmy couldn't go to work the next day. He had bad diarrhoea and headache, and Anna said to Maria in the afternoon, 'You should call the doctor.' But Maria said, 'It's only a bout of diarrhoea; he will eat apples before they're ripe.'

'Ma, I think Jimmy should have the doctor. He's bad.'

'All right, all right, girl. You've all had diarrhoea at one time or another. It's the season of the year.'

'I thought the season for a loose bowel was in the Spring.'

'Oh, it could come any time; it all depends on what you eat, but if it will ease your mind, dear, I'll get your dada to go for the doctor . . . '

Nathaniel was lucky. He caught the doctor actually coming out of a house in the village and when he told him his boy

325

had diarrhoea the doctor had looked at him hard and said immediately, 'Well, let's get away.'

He was now standing in the kitchen, his two hands on his black bag which he had placed on the table, and he was saying, 'I'm sorry to tell you the lad's got cholera. There's one case in the village and a number in the town. And more in Gateshead Fell. It started there again. It's the water. They've built a blooming hospital for the cases, when what they should be doing is preventing anybody going into it. It's clean water everybody wants. Now, you get your water from the pump, don't you?'

No one answered him.

'Well, boil every drop of it, every drop. And let's hope the lad's a light case. Who have you got coming home?'

After a short intake of breath Nathaniel said, 'My daughter. She works for the Praggetts.'

'Well, get word to her. Tell her to stay there.'

'And tomorrow my two eldest sons come in from Gateshead. And there's a young man sleeps in the barn.'

'Oh, you must put a stop to that. Get word to them.' He now bit on his lower lip, saying, 'Well, you'd better all stay put. I myself will call at Praggett's on my way back home. Where do you say your sons work?'

When Nathaniel told him, Anna put in, 'Mr Barrington, he knows where the shop is; he would get word to them if you asked him.'

'I'll do that. I have to pass his house so I'll call in on my way. Now do what I tell you: boil the water, then wash everything that comes in contact with him. There's no need to worry; he's a strong fellow. They can get through better than some. Well, I'm away. We're probably in for another bad patch, as this has spread from the towns. I thought we had seen the last of it years ago. They've hardly got over the smallpox scare, and now this. Well, I must away.

326

I'll call in tomorrow or the next day if possible. But you can't do very much, only what I've told you.' And as he was going out of the door he asked, 'Where do you bury your slops?'

'In the cesspool at the far end of the land.'

'Any running water near it?'

They exchanged glances, and then Nathaniel said, 'There's a tinkle of a stream goes by. It comes out of a boulder.'

'Do you use that often?'

Maria now put in, 'For washing the clothes. Yes, I often do; it seems fresh.'

'Where do you take it from? Where it's running along the ground? or where it's coming out of the stone?'

She paused before she said, 'Well, some way from the boulder, where it's about three feet wide; at times it's a good foot deep.'

'Well, from now on, take it from the boulder. But boil it, always boil it. It's likely picked up less infection from its source than it will have done in passing the cesspool.'

'Oh, it isn't all that near.'

'Doesn't matter, be on the safe side. Good day to you now. And the best of luck with the lad.'

They all looked stunned, yet Anna was asking herself, Why? because she had guessed what was wrong with Jimmy when he had turned and looked at her in the doorway of the tack-room, after she had asked when he had been to the market.

'Cholera. Cholera, that's all we need now. Another affliction. Why?'

Both Anna and Maria looked at Nathaniel and he, looking at Anna, said, 'Fate never lets up, does it?'

Four days later, it looked as if Jimmy might be about to take a turn for the better: his diarrhoea had eased, he hadn't been sick once during the day. And now it was one o'clock in the morning.

Anna sat by his bedside. A candle was burning under the cover of a red glass globe, giving a warm glow to the room, which was hers and Cherry's room. For the last three nights she had sat here, sleeping some part of the day, during which time Nathaniel and Maria took over. But the strain was now showing on them, especially on Maria, for Jimmy had to be changed every two hours or so and his nightshirt and the sheets washed. There was a perpetual mist of steam in the long room, where the linen was hung round the fire which Nathaniel kept going.

The only one any of them had been in contact with, and then at a distance, was Timothy. He brought food, medical supplies and extra linen. These he put over the fence, for when he called on that first evening after the doctor had given him the news, Anna had raised her voice for the first time in weeks and yelled at him, 'Stay where you are! Don't come in! Please! Please!' And so each day he had come to the railings and left milk and oddments of food, such as jars of calf's foot jelly, a cooked chicken and fresh bread.

When Jimmy stirred, she picked up a wet cloth from a number piled on a plate to her side and placed it across his sweating brow. When his lids lifted and he looked at her she said, 'Try to sleep, dear. You'll feel better in the morning. It'll soon be over.'

'Yes, Anna, 'twill soon be over.'

'Now, now! Jimmy.'

'Anna.'

'Yes, my dear.'

'I . . . I'm going to be free.'

She said nothing but stared down into the rose-coloured palor of his face, which at the moment looked like that of an old man.

328

'I am.'

'Now, now! Jimmy. Be quiet.'

He gasped before he said, 'No time, Anna.' Then again he repeated her name, 'Anna.'

'Yes? Yes, my dear?'

'Escape. You escape, soon, or else . . . else they'll not let . . . you . . . go. They'll . . . they'll cling on.'

'Oh Jimmy, Jimmy.'

'Go . . . escape. Escape . . . they'll want someone . . . to . . . to look after them. 'Twill be you. Selfish, yes . . . yes, selfish. Get away . . . Anna.'

'Jimmy, please! You don't know really what you're saying, dear. Now go to sleep.'

'Love you, Anna. Love you.'

'Yes, and I love you, too, Jimmy. You'll be better in the morning. Doctor said you're on the turn.'

He closed his eyes and made a sound like a sigh, and she said, 'That's it. Go to sleep.'

She sat now gently stroking his square hand. The hand that had been calloused and hard up till a few days ago now seemed as soft as a child's. It lay limp in hers, and she kept her eyes on it as her own hand moved over it. For how long she sat like this she couldn't remember, but something in the hand seemed to change and caused her to look at her brother's face. It seemed unchanged, just as if he was sleeping. Yet no; his eyes were half open. She gave a gasp, then let out a low moan: 'Oh! Jimmy. Jimmy. *No! No! No!* The doctor said you were . . . Oh! Jimmy, Jimmy. Oh, my God!' She now took his face between her hands, and when she released her hold the head lolled to the side. She covered her eyes, then dropped forward over the slim, depleted body under the sheets, murmuring all the time, 'Oh! Jimmy. Jimmy.'

When finally she stood up she was amazed at the feeling of calmness in herself and, looking down on him, she said,

'You did it. You did what you wanted to do, you escaped. Oh, my dear, dear.'

Turning now, she lifted up the candlestick with the red glass shade attached and left the room to go to her parents' door. But she didn't knock. Walking straight into the room, she held the light above her head and looked down on them. They were lying face to face, and her father's hand was on the coverlet and resting on her mother's shoulder. She said quietly, 'Dada.'

She had to say his name three times before he turned on his back, looked at her, then pulled himself upwards, saying, 'What is it? What is it?'

'Jimmy has gone,' she said simply.

On hearing these words, it seemed that her mother sprang out of the bed, that they both sprang out of the bed. She watched them rush from the room, and slowly she followed them. At the door of the bedroom she put the candle on top of the chest of drawers and it showed up them both lying over their son's body.

She turned and went out and down the long room and blew the fire embers into a blaze.

'Get away,' he had said. 'Escape. Get away. Or they'll keep you here to look after them.' Well, would that be such a bad thing?

Yes. Yes! The cry in her head startled her; but she turned to see her father come staggering down the room. He was in his nightshirt and he too looked an old man. She watched him drop into a chair by the table and rest his head on his hands, and then she heard him say, 'The sins of the father indeed shall be visited on the children and the children's children even to the third and fourth generations.' Then turning his head slowly towards her, he said, 'I always knew we should have to pay. Which one will He take next?'

330

7

There was no formal funeral for Jimmy. They came in a black hearse and took him away, as they also did Stan Cole, the butcher's son from the village.

Two days later Maria went down with it and Nathaniel seemed to enter a period of madness. For four nights and days he hardly left her side. And Anna seemed to spend her whole life running between the bedroom and the cesspool. The doctor said to her, 'Let up, girl. Let up.' And his voice was harsh when he spoke to Nathaniel, saying, 'There's other things to be done besides sitting beside the bed. Your daughter will be next if she doesn't get help.' And Nathaniel, after apparently coming out of a daze, said, 'I'm sorry, I'm sorry; but I can't lose Maria. I can't lose her.'

And to this the doctor replied, 'You'll lose them both if you're not careful, and yourself an' all.'

'That would make no odds, because if she goes I go.'

It was the evening of the fourth night that he left the bedroom and came into the long room and sat at the little desk and began to write.

As Anna passed him for the countless time with the emptied pail, he stopped her and said, 'I hadn't made a will but I've written it down here. If we should go' – he didn't say, If your mother should go, or, If I should go, but, If we should go – 'the house and the money in the bank will go to Oswald and Olan. They'll look after you. Cherry will be all right; Bobby will take care of her.'

She put the pail down on the floor and stared at him, and he turned to her and said, 'What is it?'

She couldn't tell him. She couldn't say to him, 'You're leaving me in care of the boys; you're not saying to me, there is fifty pounds, or a hundred pounds, or two hundred pounds, you're leaving me in care of the boys. I am to grow old here in this house . . . in care of the boys. They could get married and come and live here. You have even thought of Cherry's future. Bobby will take care of her, you said. So you know what's been going on. But me, your beloved daughter, so I thought, you have left in care of the boys.' With a quick jerk she lifted the pail and hurried from him. And he went after her, and at the bedroom door he stopped her, saying, 'I could not live without your mother. Don't you understand?'

Yes. Yes, she understood. She understood that an intelligent, caring father could have quite another side to him. Intelligent he was, naturally, but caring was because he wanted them all around him as protection from the outer world and its condemnation. As he had bred each one he hadn't thought of their future, only of his needs of the moment. She had thought him advanced in his thinking, on a par with Timothy, but now, females still had their place, and it was subordinate to men's. She passed him and went in to her mother. On this occasion he did not follow her, but went back down the room again.

As she sat by the bed, Maria turned her head and looked at her. 'Look after your father,' she said. 'Promise me you'll look after your father. He'll need you. Stay with him.'

332

When Anna made no reply, Maria said, 'Promise me?'

Still she made no answer; and then Maria, her hand coming out and groping for hers, said between gasps. 'Don't . . . don't marry . . . that man. Don't . . . don't saddle yourself. Far better . . . take what . . . the other . . . one offers.'

Anna couldn't really believe her ears. She withdrew her hand from her mother's grasp and stood up. Her mother was saying, 'Do what I did. Don't marry a good man because he has fits.' She had the most awful desire to shout, 'I'd marry him tomorrow if he asked me, but he never will, and I know it. And I'll tell you something else. I love him and if he asked me to live with him, I'd do it. But not the other one. Never!'

Nathaniel came into the room now and, looking at her, he said, 'What's wrong? Is she worse?'

Anna stepped aside but said nothing, and Maria put her hand out to Nathaniel, and he gripped it and sat down by her side. Anna left the room and went outside into the fresh morning air. The mugginess had gone and there had been a frost in the night and she took in great gulps of air while telling herself not to let go, for she knew there was something in her head on the point of snapping.

8

Maria did not die. From that night on, she slowly recovered. Perhaps, Anna thought later, it was because she had refused to conform to her mother's wishes and she couldn't bear the thought of her beloved husband being left without someone to take care of him. Although her father had always been handy in making odd things with wood, he was more proficient in directing others to do the chores. He had never made a meal for himself, nor washed a crock nor swept a floor. And she hadn't seen him even set a fire. Either her mother had done it, or she, or one of the boys.

The first day it was considered safe for the others to return to the house was one she tried to forget, for the boys cried and Cherry cried and Bobby Crane cried, and her mother cried and her father cried, all over Jimmy's going. But *she* didn't cry, for all the while she looked at them hugging each other, she could hear Jimmy's voice saying, 'Get yourself away. Escape.' Odd, when she came to think back. Jimmy knew his parents, the other side of them, the selfish side, the side she had never guessed at. But what she tried to tell herself, and kindly, was, it was all part of one's human nature. Yet she had to force herself to feel sympathetically towards them now.

When one after another asked her how she was, she knew they were referring to her long convalescence, not to when she had been dragged up out of it and forced to be run off her feet these last weeks.

Their mother was better, their father was here. Oswald and Olan had been out of harm's way, going about their business, as had Bobby, living in the room above the boathouse; and, of course, Cherry, in the Praggett fortress. But what she was to remember about the family reunion was her father, standing at the door of the house, looking first up into the sky, then across into the far distance as he cried dramatically. 'Why had my second son to be taken when that woman over there who killed my last born is spared?' And Oswald had said, 'What Dada. She got it too?'

'Yes, I understood she got it too, and so bad she landed up in Gateshead cholera hospital. Yet she is spared and brought back to live in comfort. There's no justice.'

This had been news to Anna, which brought home the fact that there had hardly been any exchange of words, except those necessary for daily contact between her and her father, since the night he had written his will. It was as if, by her reactions, he knew he had failed her in some way.

The next visitor was Miss Netherton. She had commiserated with Nathaniel and Maria over Jimmy's loss, then when she was leaving, she said to Anna, 'Come; walk with me to the trap, I've left it at the field gate.' But once outside, she said, 'What on earth has happened to you, girl? A ghost could have more substance. Tim said he was worried to death by the look of you. He's . . . he's in London again, you know.'

'Yes. Yes, I know.'

335

'He's . . . he's been simply marvellous during this dreadful time, not only in keeping you going, which I know he has, but seeing to Penella.'

'Penella? Mrs Brodrick?'

'Yes. Apparently she had written to him from Newcastle; she wanted to see him. And when he got there he was told she had already been taken to the Gateshead cholera hospital. Well, he went there and found she was in a room by herself, but he wasn't allowed in; he could see her through a glass door. She happened to catch sight of him, so he tells me, and she put out her hand towards him. I saw him shortly after this and he was upset. As he himself said, there was nothing of the grand imperious lady left. She was a very ill woman and looked a frightened one. So what does he do? He goes to Simon and tells him. I don't know what passed between them, but I guessed it was something pretty strong. I do know, through Tim, from what he said, the doctor didn't think there was much chance of her surviving. Apparently she had lain too long without attention. So Simon went. This was over a fortnight ago, and the result was she didn't die. However, and again from what Tim says, she must have got the fright of her life, because she's a very changed individual. Oh, by the way, I must tell you, the child's got a tutor and he seems to have taken to him. He's a youngish man and, as Simon said, the first words the child always utters to him are, 'When are you going to bring Missanna back?' Apparently when he couldn't be consoled after you left, Simon told him you had gone to look after Uncle Tim.'

'That was rather a silly thing to say, wasn't it?'

'Not so silly, when you think about it. The boy was very fond of Tim and likely it was more acceptable to the child that Tim should be the reason for your not coming. Anyway, we've got to forget about other people and concentrate on yourself. Now, what I suggest is that you come over to me and stay for a week or so, and Ethel will fatten you up.'

Anna smiled softly on the elderly woman and in a low voice, she said, 'You're always so kind to me, always so good and thoughtful, but . . . but on this occasion would you mind if I left your invitation open for a while? There is something at the back of my mind that I'd like to get straight.'

'Such as?'

'Oh, well, I can't explain it yet.'

'You could if you talked about it.'

'Yes, but I want to be sure in my own mind that I can do this.'

'You're thinking about taking up a course in a college?'

'No. No, not that.'

'Then what?'

Anna's smile widened now as she said, 'If I make up my mind to do this, you'll be the first one to know about it. I can assure you of that.'

'Ah, there's a mystery here. I like mysteries. Life can be very dull without mysteries. I realised how different life could be when I was in Holland; the excitement, the meeting up with a different breed of men . . . Oh, I know. Thinking about Holland. Let me guess. Tell me if I'm right or wrong. Just give me a nod. Your father is going to provide you with enough money to start a school of your own. That's it, isn't it?'

The smile disappeared from Anna's face and her voice sounded rather cool as she said, 'No, Miss Netherton. My father has never even thought along those lines, not in any way.'

'What do you mean, not in any way? Has he not settled something on you?'

'No. No; not a penny; in fact I can speak to you about it, because you are my friend. But when he thought my mother was dying, he knew he would go, too. And I'm sure he would have, even if it meant taking his own life, because he couldn't

337

live without her. He made out a rough will' – she turned her head away – ' I can see him doing it now. I was going up the room with an empty slop bucket – at that period I seemed to have spent my whole life emptying nauseating slop buckets – and he turned to me and said, "I am leaving the house and what money there is to the boys. They will look after you. Cherry will be all right; Bobby will see to her." '

There was silence between them now. Anna watched the older woman pull the fur collar of her coat tighter under her chin and nip on her bottom lip before she said, 'I am very disappointed in Nathaniel, and in Maria, too, I must say. The boys are in good positions, by all accounts. That house should be yours and enough money with which to keep it up.' She turned and looked to the side and muttered, 'Men! Men! Nothing really belongs to women. That cross was originally Maria's. The money that I first gave them was originally Maria's. In those days everything a woman had belonged to her man; but now, as far as I can gather, they are trying to get a law passed which will allow a married woman control of her own money or property. It's to be called the Married Woman's Property Act. Anyway, I think she should have been consulted as to how it was going to be left if anything happened to them. But then' – she shrugged her shoulders – 'nobody wants to imagine that there'll come a time when they won't need what they've got; death is something that's not going to happen to them.' She put out her hands now and gripped Anna's wrists, saying, 'Don't worry, my dear. I'll see you won't be left in care of the boys, you know that.'

'Thank you, that is comforting. And I'll always remember that offer, always, on top of remembering all you have been to me over the years. I often wonder what I would have done without you.'

'My dear, that, as I am always saying, works both ways. The giver and the receiver nearly always benefit if what passes from one to the other is good. Now I will away, but' – she poked her head forward – 'I'll be racking my brains to find out what is in that top storey of yours.' She now tapped Anna on the brow. 'And I won't rest until I find out. You know me.' They parted smiling.

Anna did not return immediately to the house, but she walked through the wood and, as always, to its far end, as far as the sawing block. There she stood as she often did and looked over the moor. But today she nodded to herself as she muttered aloud, 'Wait and see what happens when Oswald breaks his news, which he will do shortly. Jimmy wasn't wrong. Propriety will go to the wind now. There'll be no waiting a year in honour of the dead. He's as ready as Cherry is for marriage.' Then turning swiftly about, she placed her hands on the block and bowed her head as if in shame at her thoughts. Yet, more and more these days they were facing her with facts, and facts, she had found out only too well over this past year, could be disturbing.

She had expected Timothy to return at the end of the week, but a letter arrived instead, saying that he had a little more business to do, but in the meantime he was enjoying himself and he had found that Walters was a very intelligent companion; and since at one time he had lived in London for five years, he was acting as a splendid guide, especially with regard to theatres. Only one thing could have added to his pleasure and that was her company. He hoped to see her soon, and he signed himself, 'Ever your friend, Tim.'

When her mother had asked whom the letter was from, she had felt like retorting, 'Why ask the road you know?' but she had answered, 'Mr Barrington.' Not Mr Tim or Mr Timothy as she usually said, but Mr Barrington, and she had stressed the name.

It was significant that her father made no enquiries with regard to the letter, although it was he who had handed it to her, having taken it from the postman . . .

The daylight was short. They were in winter now and the long evenings became a time of excruciating tension for Anna. After the evening meal, which was often passed in silence, the depleted family would sit round the fire: Nathaniel, Maria, Cherry, and herself. Often now, Bobby would be there, too, and she noticed more and more her father welcomed Bobby's presence and he would talk more to him than to anyone else. And Bobby was very forthcoming with his news. The boatbuilder had apparently appreciated his work and had promised to keep him on as a full-time hand after he had completed his two years' apprenticeship. He had also said there were prospects for him. What they were, the boatbuilder hadn't actually said, but Bobby indicated that he had his own idea of what they might be.

As Anna sat looking from one to the other she tried to thrust her mind back to the times when most of the family were rolling on the mat with laughter as Cherry imitated the antics of Mr Praggett; or when Jimmy had been describing the incidents on the farm, such as the day the bull butted the herdsman and he himself had to lead it into the ring. And then she, too, reading some of her funny rhymes while acting to them, and the quiet times, when her father would be reading aloud.

Where had they gone? What had happened? This house was now weighed down with misery.

Tonight she felt she couldn't stand any more, and so, rising, she said to her mother, 'Would you mind if I went to bed, Ma?' And Maria said, 'No. No, not at all, if you're feeling like that.' And Nathaniel, looking at her, said, 'Go, my dear. You need to rest.'

340

She nodded towards Bobby, saying, 'Good-night.' And he said, 'Good-night, Anna.'

It was a good hour later when Cherry came into the bed. She was shivering and she said, 'Are you asleep, Anna?' And she answered, 'No, Cherry.'

'Isn't it awful down there at nights?'

'Yes. Yes, it is.'

'I dread coming home.'

'I'm home all day, Cherry.'

'Oh, yes, I know, Anna, yes, I know. And you've had a rough time of it. In all ways you've had a rough time of it. I said so to Bobby, and he said he doesn't know how you got through looking after them; I mean, Jimmy and then Ma, because Dada wouldn't be much use. Well, I mean, slops and all that.'

Anna said nothing, and so they lay in silence for some time until Cherry said, 'You don't talk like you used to, Anna. You're miles away most of the time, and' – her voice broke now – 'and I've wanted to talk to you. I need to talk to you. Anna . . . Anna.'

'Yes? What is it?'

When Anna turned round in the bed, Cherry put her arms about her and laid her head on her shoulder and she muttered something, which Anna could not make out.

'What did you say?' she said.

Then when Cherry repeated it, Anna felt herself stiffen for a moment; and yet in a way she wasn't surprised. And so, all she said was, 'When did this happen?' and Cherry said, 'One Sunday when I went down to see him. It was a nice room above the . . .'

Anna pulled herself away from her sister's hold, hissing now, 'I don't want to know details; I mean, how long have you gone?'

'Nearly three months.'

341

'Oh, my God! And they don't know? I mean, Ma?'

'No, no. I've wanted to tell you. Well, we didn't seem like we used to be, but I can understand, I can understand with what you've been through. But . . . but I . . . I love Bobby, and he loves me.'

'He's so young.'

'That doesn't matter. There's only about a year between us. And he'll get on. Oh, he means to get on. And I can always work.'

'Having a baby? Who's going to look after the baby?'

Anna closed her eyes tightly and the blackness of the room was shut out for a moment by a bright light that showed herself nursing a baby, Cherry's baby, for Cherry would have to work, because they'd never be able to live on what Bobby earned. And there came again Jimmy's voice, urging, 'Escape. Escape.'

'What am I to do, Anna?'

'You know what you've got to do. You've got to tell them, and soon, and let them work it out for you. Now stop crying and try to go to sleep. You've got one comfort. Dada is very fond of Bobby, and Ma is, too. You'll have their approval, up to that point.'

'Anna.'

'Yes, dear?'

'You . . . you wouldn't break it to them, would you?'

'No, I wouldn't.'

'Oh, Anna, I'm . . . I'm frightened. I'm . . . I'm the only one that . . . well, has gone wrong and they'll be ashamed.'

'They can't be ashamed of you for doing what they did. Just look at it like that.'

'The people in the village.'

'Damn the people in the village. I've paid the people in the village for all of us. It wasn't for me alone, the degradation I was put to, it was against Ma and Dada, paying them out

342

for their daring to flaunt society, especially in a narrow village filled with narrow minds. Dada used to be always bragging that we were the happiest family in the county. That was because he had us all in this little nest; he knew that because of the stigma he had laid on us, we would never be able to fly far.'

'Oh, Anna, Anna, fancy you thinking like that. I never thought you would turn against Dada. They did what they did because they were in love, and I understand now exactly how they felt.'

'Shut up! Shut up! They only knew one kind of love. The same kind as you do. There are other kinds of love: sacrificing love; love that is shrivelled up through convention and the dirty tricks of fate and—' She stopped suddenly and muttered, 'I'm sorry. I'm sorry.' Then she turned on her side, only to turn quickly back again when Cherry said, 'It's a shame. I know you wanted to go with Mr Simon, and you should have. And you wouldn't have been any the worse.'

'Cherry' – it was a deep whisper – 'if you don't shut up, you know what I'll do? I'll slap you across the face. I won't be able to stop myself. I had no intention of ever being Simon Brodrick's mistress. *Never! Never!* Do you hear me? Even if I'd loved him desperately, I still wouldn't have become his mistress.'

'All right then; all right, you wouldn't, but I don't see now why you are blaming Ma and Dada for doing what they did. Anyway, if you want to know, people are saying the same thing about you and Mr Timothy. There! now you have it. And whether you are or not . . . '

Anna sprang from the bed, and yelled now at the top of her voice, 'I am not sleeping with Mr Timothy! or with anyone else. *Do you hear me? Do you hear me?*'

In the deep silence that followed she heard the quick steps on the floorboards. Her parents, as usual, would have been

343

sitting by the fire, hand in hand, before going to bed. And now the door burst open and her father, holding the lamp high, and from behind their mother, said, 'What is it? What is it?'

Cherry was now sitting up in bed, her arms hugging her waist and rocking herself backwards and forwards as if she already had a baby in her arms.

'What were you yelling at? What was the matter?'

It was her mother that Anna now addressed. Still in a loud voice, she cried, 'I am not sleeping with Mr Timothy. Do you hear, Ma? I'm not sleeping with Mr Timothy. I am not his mistress.'

'No one said you were, daughter. No one said you were.' Maria's voice was quiet. But Nathaniel seemed to ignore Anna's outburst for, after putting down the lamp on the wash-hand stand, he put his arm around Cherry's shoulder, saying, 'What is it, dear? What is it? What's the matter?'

When Cherry shook her head, Anna cried. 'Tell them! This is your opportunity. Tell them!'

'Tell us what?'

When Cherry still continued to shake her head, Maria came to Anna's side and said, 'What is the matter? What has she to tell us?'

'Only that she's going to have a baby. Now, is that any surprise to you, Ma?'

Anna watched her father straighten his back; she watched her mother move slowly and stand beside him, and it was she who said, 'Is this true, girl?'

And Cherry, falling back on to the pillow, said, 'Yes, Ma. Yes, it's true.'

'Well, well!' Nathaniel looked at Maria and she at him. And now Maria, putting her hand out, said, 'Come on. Get up, and tell us about it.'

Their reception of the news seemed to deflate Anna completely. She suddenly sat down on the wooden chair to the side of the bed, and her mother turned to her and said, 'Put a coat round you, dear, and come along; we must talk about this.'

A few minutes later the four of them were seated round the fire again, but now Cherry's head was resting on her father's shoulder and his arm was around her and what he was saying was, 'Don't worry, dear. The first thing we must do is get you married. There's only one problem. He's a good boy, and I like him. But you can't, as you said, go down there and live above that boathouse. What you must do is to come home. After all, this has been his home for many months now. So that's what I think you must do. Isn't that so, Maria?'

And Maria agreed. 'Yes, dear, yes,' she said; then added, 'It'll be good to have a child about the house again.'

Anna closed her eyes and there was the white light: there she was, nursing the baby, but added to the scene now was her mother talking to Cherry, and her father in deep conversation with Bobby. Of a sudden she was so tired that she couldn't even hear the voice of Jimmy's urging, 'Escape. Escape.'

But she heard Jimmy's voice loud and clear on the Saturday evening when the boys came home. She could see immediately that they were excited, and when Oswald began with, 'I know, Ma and Dada, it's not so long ago since we lost Jimmy, but you see I had me news before that to tell you. Well, it's just this; I'm engaged to Carrie; you know, Mrs Simpson's daughter, and you'll never guess what. Mrs Simpson's taken me into partnership, and Olan an' all.'

'But ... but I thought she was much older than you, Oswald?' This was Maria speaking.

'Yes, Ma, she's ... she's all of five years. But I care deeply for her and she me, and she doesn't look her age and she's

345

young in her ways. Anyway, there it is. What d'you think?'

It was his father who answered, 'I think it's very good news, excellent news, Oswald, and I'm delighted for you. And it's a marvellous opportunity you're being offered, because from what I saw of that place it should prosper.'

'It is, Dada, it is already prospering, but it will do more so. We can open up another place; we've got it all planned.'

Nathaniel now looked from one to the other as he said, 'The saying is, never one door closes but another opens. And it's true in this case. The house will know a family again, and children. Cherry's and Bobby's will be brought up here and yours when they come, Oswald, will make our week-ends bright. It's something to look forward to. Don't you think so, Maria?'

'Yes. Yes, I do, Nathaniel. ''Tis something to look forward to.'

'Well, let's drink to it. Go and bring out the elderberry, Anna.'

Anna went into the kitchen and from the floor in the stone pantry she picked up a bottle of elderberry wine and, taking it into the kitchen, she placed it on the draining board where also stood a tallow candle in a tin holder. And she stared at it for a long while before she spoke to it, saying, 'I hear you, Jimmy, my dear, I hear you. I'll wait till Monday.'

346

9

The sun was shining, but weakly. There had been a heavy frost and there was the smell of snow in the air. She had milked the goats, and then cleaned out the goat house and the chickens; she had tidied the hay bales in the barn; she had brushed Neddy; and finally had swept down the whole yard.

At twelve o'clock she joined her parents for the mid-day bite, when her father said, 'I shouldn't be a bit surprised to see it snow before the day's out, so I think there'd better be some more logs cut. Eh?' He had looked at her, and she had returned his look and said, 'I'm sorry, Dada, but I'm going visiting this afternoon.'

Maria was all attention now, but she didn't speak; it was her father who asked, 'Is he back then?'

'Yes, he was due back yesterday.'

Now Maria did speak. With her head lowered, she said, 'Wouldn't it be better if you waited for him to call?'

'Not in this case, Ma.'

'What case, daughter?' Nathaniel was looking hard at her and his voice was curt; and after a moment she said, 'There is something on my mind. I have a question to ask him.'

'Well, I've always answered your questions up to now. Can't you ask me?'

'No.' She smiled a tight smile. 'Not in this case, Dada.' As she rose from the bench at the end of the table Nathaniel said, as if to no-one in particular, 'The log-pile's going down fast. It always does in this weather, and when they come in from their work it's comforting to see a big glow.'

'Yes, it is.' She nodded at him and only just stopped herself from adding, 'So you should spend more time down on the block instead of reading.'

In her room, she stood against the closed door for a moment and muttered aloud, 'How blind one can be!' She had never realised, all these years, that her father was lazy where actual work was concerned. Of course, it was different when he was dealing with book-work, for that to him was important.

It was a full twenty minutes later when she emerged from the room, to be greeted by a gasp from Maria and her saying, 'Oh, no! Anna; you're not flaunting convention to that extent, going into grey.'

'My cloak is dark, Ma.'

'Your cloak reaches only just below your knees, girl.'

'Ma.' She walked up to her mother and, standing close to her, she looked straight into her face as she said, 'Has it ever dawned upon you that I ceased to be a girl some time ago, and only a matter of days ago stepped into my twenty-first year.'

'You are twenty, not twenty-one.'

'I said I had stepped into my twenty-first year, Ma. And one is considered to have left girlhood at twenty. I would have thought you, above all people, would be aware of that.'

'What's come over you?'

'Nothing's come over me, Ma, that hasn't come over you and Dada.'

348

'Oh, girl, you used to be so pleasant to have in the house, but not any more. Anyway, let's hope that when the baby comes you'll feel different.'

Anna's face actually stretched, and then she laughed and the sound finished on a 'Huh!' before she turned about and, saying, 'I certainly shall,' went out.

She avoided the stile road, for she felt she would never again be able to face that way. She crossed the edge of the moor, then followed the bridle path that led on to the coach road. This way put two thirds of a mile on to her journey, but she didn't mind that. Moreover, there was less chance of meeting anyone, especially at this time of the day.

When she finally turned into the drive it was to see the carriage standing in front of the house. And when Walters answered her ringing of the door-bell he exclaimed, 'Why! Miss. How d'you do? You're just in time; the master was for visiting you.'

'Oh! Anna. Anna.'

She turned quickly to look up the stairs to see Timothy descending, his hands outstretched. 'I was just about to drive to see you. Come in. Come in. Oh' – he turned to Walters – 'bring my case in from the coach, will you, Walters, please?' Then helping Anna off with her cloak, he said, 'Oh, it is wonderful to see you again. It seems years, but it's just over a fortnight. Give me your hat.'

He took the hat from her as she was about to press the hatpin back into it, and he said, 'Where do you stick this?'

'Where do you think?' She was laughing at him. 'In the hat, of course.'

'Yes. Yes, I know, but it's a felt one, madam, and it'll make holes in it, all over. Is it the back or the front? It's the back, isn't it?'

Then he turned to the maid, who was approaching across the hall and said, 'Oh, Mary, go and ask cook if she would please let us have some tea, and a cake or two.'

The girl laughed at his request for cakes, dipped her knee to Anna, then turned about. And Walters, coming back into the hall, pointed to the case he was carrying and said,

'I'll put it in the sitting-room, sir.'

As Timothy led Anna into the sitting-room she said to Walters, 'Are you glad to be home?' and he answered, 'Oh, yes, miss, though I must say I enjoyed our trip to London.'

'He would have had me there till Christmas and after.' Timothy was now thumbing towards his valet. 'Talk about night-life. Oh, I have so much to tell you. Come and sit down, dear.' He pressed her into the upholstered chair to the side of the fire; then pulling up a foot-stool, he sat down and, taking her hand and looking into her face, he said, 'Oh dear me; you . . . you still look pale. But is it any wonder! Do you know something?'

'No; tell me.'

'I think it was simply a miracle that you survived, with you in that weak condition and having to cope with that dreadful plague, and not only with one but two. I know your father was there, but men are not of much use in cases like that unless they're doctors, and then they only do the talking. But here and there during that time, I saw for myself what had to be done for those poor souls, and I've wondered at the bravery of many people, but mostly of yourself.'

'There was no bravery attached to my efforts, Tim, just necessity.'

'Did . . . did you ever think you would catch it?'

'Yes. Yes, every day.'

'That makes your efforts the more praiseworthy. Oh! my dear. My dear. When I used to look at you over those railings my heart ached for you. They are saying in the papers now it was only a light epidemic. As if any epidemic could be light! I suppose they mean in comparison with the do they had in 1853, when I was rather young.'

She laid her head back into the wing of the chair and let out a long slow breath and looked at him for some seconds before she said, 'Tell me what you did in London.'

'Oh, I shall have to write a book about all we did in London. With regard to books though, my business could have been seen to in two days ... well, two and a bit. I could have been back here over a week ago, but Walters took me to a theatre, and afterwards recommended another, and another. And we did the galleries. He's a very intelligent fellow, is Walters. I'm very lucky to have him. And what is even better, he is of a kindly disposition. And I knew that if at any time I had been in need of his ministrations he would have coped admirably. But do you know, Anna? Time and again, when I was going round the galleries and such, I thought of you and how I'd have loved you to be there. You must go to London some time. Or, come to London; I will take you to London. Yes, yes, I will.'

He shook her hand up and down now as if she had refused his invitation. And she laughed at him and said, 'All right, all right. Yes, I will go to London with you, sir, any time, any time.'

'You're laughing at me.'

'Yes. Yes, I am, and it's so good to laugh at you and with you. I haven't laughed for a long time ... I ... I have missed you.'

He stared into her face before he said, 'You really have, Anna?'

'Yes. Yes, very much. Oh, very much of late. Have you ever thought, Tim, how changeable human nature is? Do you think a character can change, really change?'

His voice was slow and thoughtful as he gave his opinion: 'Not fundamentally,' he said. 'You see, there are ingredients of good and bad, and the middling, in all of us and it depends on circumstances which bits, as it were, come out on top and dominate. Yes, it's all to do with circumstance. If life went smoothly for each of us I think our characters would remain the same: I mean the predominant facets in our characters would remain the same. But then we are often hit by circumstance. There's that word again, circumstance. To give an example. You've had your share of Penella, haven't you?' When she didn't answer he said, 'I suppose you heard that she caught the cholera. Well, it's a great wonder she didn't die. She was very ill, and so ill that I really thought she was dying and everyone else in the hospital thought so, too. This prompted me to go and see Simon. Well, what transpired between us wasn't pleasant, and not for the first time, either. Anyway, I told him it was his duty at least to go and see her. Well, by the time he went, she had taken a slight turn for the better. And I don't know what transpired between them, either, but I know when I next saw her she was a different creature from the one I had known, and who had held me in very poor esteem. She hadn't been able to bear sickness of any kind. Well, there she was, thrown in at the deep end, so to speak, and she had undoubtedly been terrified by what had befallen her. But the only way I can put it is, the experience must have acted on her like a cleansing balm, because she said to me, "Do you think he will ever forgive me?" You know, Anna, her attitude in everything she did was because she was still in love with him, and always had been. And I know at bottom he was still in love with her, while being deeply hurt and mad at her, and at his brother at the deception they had played on him. Anyway, I wasn't surprised that, when she was able to be removed, he took her home: but I must say my sister certainly wasn't

352

pleased, nor were any of them in the house. And she was aware of this. Oh, yes, she said as much to me when I saw her just before I went away. She even mentioned you.'

'Really?'

'Yes; and, my dear, don't say it like that. "That girl," she said, "must hate my very name." Of course, you cannot imagine her saying it. And I couldn't have done either at one time, but I heard her say it. And she added, "I've been insane, Tim, haven't I?" Then her next words to me told me that she thought more deeply than I had imagined, for she said, "Love is a facet of insanity, you know, Tim. I am still insane with it, but I'm harmless now. Cholera is a potent drug."'

Quietly though not subdued Anna asked now, 'Will they remain together?'

'Yes. Yes, I think so. After visiting her out of a form of duty only, the first time, I think his next visits were out of pity. And, you know, that is another facet of love. Pity is akin to love, it breeds it . . . Ah! here's Mary and Walters with the tea. And look! a cream sponge cake with preserved cherries on the top. Oh Mary, tell cook that I love her, will you?'

'Yes, sir. Yes, sir. I'll do that.' The girl grinned widely, bobbed and went out. Walters had wheeled the trolley up to the end of the couch and, looking at Anna, he said, 'Will I leave you to officiate, miss?'

'Yes; thank you.'

When the door had closed on them Timothy laughed, saying, 'Will I leave you to officiate. He's nothing if not correct, is Walters. Anyway, would you kindly pour out, madam?'

She poured out the tea; then handed him the thin, rolled bread and butter, followed by the dainty cucumber sandwiches, and lastly she cut into the sponge cake and he, leaning towards her in order to take it, said, 'It's fatal to tell anyone, especially a cook, that you are fond of a speciality

353

of hers. When she first made me a sponge cake I praised it to the skies because it was lovely, but when there's company, high, low, or middling, or she's out to tempt me from my work which, I understand from Walters, she says makes me dour, I'm presented with a cream sponge, and it puts weight on one. Still, it keeps her happy. You know, I learned from my mother years ago that the essence of a happy household starts at the oven in the kitchen. I think she was right.'

'Yes, I think so too.'

The tea over, he pushed the trolley away and was about to resume his seat on the footstool at her side when she said, 'Wouldn't you be more comfortable on the couch?'

'Yes. Yes, I would,' he said, looking towards it, 'if you would join me there.'

She sat at one end of the couch, her back in the corner, and when he sat down next to her he took her hand, but made no remark for some time; he just stared into the fire until, seeming to bestir himself out of a reverie, he said, 'It's odd, you know, the dreams one conjures up by looking into the flames. I see pictures there, but the print, so to speak, is in my mind.' And after a pause he added, 'You always have nice fires up at the cottage.'

She did not answer, and presently he turned and looked at her, saying, 'Well, don't you?' which did stir her to say, 'As you've just remarked, the prints are in your mind. Fires are only nice when the prints are nice, and the prints are only nice when people are in accord, otherwise flames can arouse anger.'

'*Oh! Anna.*' He twisted round and, looking into her face, said, 'What is it? You're unhappy. Well, I know you have been for some time, but this is different. What's happened?'

'The simple answer, Tim, would be to say I've been left out in the cold and I don't like it. But it's more than that,

354

it's a great unrest and it's been in me for a long time. I've been hurt of late, Tim, taken for granted.'

When her head drooped and she couldn't go on, he said, 'Tell me. We're friends, close friends; you can tell me anything.'

She now looked into his kindly eyes, and so she began, hesitantly at first, to tell him how she had felt over the last two years. She even mentioned the fact that she had thought she might be in love with Simon but had found she wasn't. Then she came to Jimmy, and his views on the family which had surprised her, and how he had been intending to make his escape by going to sea, and how he had almost begged her to get away. He seemed to understand their parents more than any of them did, she told him; and her voice broke when she spoke of his dying words. Then she talked of her father and of how he had changed towards her since the death of Ben, that he seemed to hold her, in a way, responsible for it because of her association with the Manor House.

What she next told him she had to tell only in part, that her mother had been left some money, a considerable sum, and at this he raised his eyebrows and he, too, said, 'Really?'

Yes, in the region of three thousand pounds, she said; and that this had come about some time before. But they had never offered her a farthing. And when she came to the night when her father had made his will, he put in, 'Oh! Anna, Anna. I want to say how I like your father. I've admired him for his mental ability, but his short-sightedness with regard to you is unforgiveable. But your mother, what was her attitude?'

She then related her mother's words when she thought she was going to die, of the promise she wanted from her and which would have tied her to the house and her father until he, too, went. But then she came to Cherry's predicament and, looking at him now, she could not keep

355

the hurt from her voice as she said, 'They welcomed it, Tim. They welcomed it because it would mean starting another family in the house. And only today my mother said that she couldn't understand the change that had come about in me of late, but when the baby came I would feel better. You see, I am to be the handmaid, the baby-minder, while Cherry keeps on her work. She and Bobby will, of course, live in the house, and as there are only two bedrooms on the ground floor they will occupy the one that is mine and I shall be relegated to one of the boys' beds in the roof. This all sounds as if I'm feeling sorry for myself. I'm not, I'm just stating facts. And one after another, the facts, of late, have been thrown at me. The latest is that my father is welcoming Oswald's engagement to the daughter of the Pie and Peas Shop owner, and who is five years older than he is, but he is welcoming this too because he is hoping for more children, as he said, to visit at week-ends. He can see the house coming alive again, and him instructing, teaching . . . teaching. Oh, I know what's in his mind. And what's more, my brothers are going to be offered partnerships. So everybody is settled and accounted for except me. Well, Tim, I'm escaping.'

'What do you mean, dear?'

'I have decided to leave.'

'Oh! my dear. Have . . . have you talked this over with Miss Netherton?'

'No; Miss Netherton wants me to go and stay with her so she can fatten me up, et cetera. But I have other ideas.'

He turned from her and leaned forward and, placing his elbows on his knees, he joined his hands together, and when he again seemed to be in a reverie, she said, 'Don't you want to know what I'm going to do?'

'Oh yes, my dear, of course.' He had turned to her again. 'Is it about entering a college? Miss Netherton and I discussed this some time ago.'

'No; it's nothing to do with that.'

'No?'

'No. I don't want to enter any college. I don't want to be taught any more except through my own reading and discussions with . . . '

She did not finish the sentence but shook her head. Then drawing herself to the edge of the couch, she pulled herself upwards and walked towards the tea trolley and there she arranged the dirty cups and saucers, moving them about as if on a chess board, while he sat in silence watching her. But when the cups and saucers began to rattle he got to his feet and walked over to her and said, 'What is it, Anna? You can tell me.'

At this she gave the trolley a push that would have sent it half-way across the room had he not grabbed it and steadied it; then taking her hand, he drew her onto the rug in front of the fire, and now they were facing each other as she said, 'I've . . . I've got a proposition to put to you.'

'Yes? Yes, well go ahead and put it.'

'Well—' She hesitated, then said, 'First of all, I must tell you one thing and I'm very, very sure of this, and have been for a long time, whether you have known it or not, and it's got nothing to do with friendship . . . I love you.'

She watched the colour seep from his cheeks. She saw his lips tremble, then mouth her name, yet no sound came from them. And so she went on, 'The proposition is this. You can either marry me or I can become your mistress.'

When he fell back from her, dropped on to the couch, put his elbows on his knees and covered his face with his hands she silently mouthed the words, Oh, my God! She had embarrassed him beyond pardon. She had thought . . . What had she thought? She was mad, for now gone, too, would be the friendship. What had she done? She was about to say, I'm sorry. Oh, I'm sorry, when his arms shot out and around her thighs and his head was buried against her stomach, and the next minute he had swung her round so that she fell on to the couch with a thump, and then they were lying on their sides looking at each other. And his words came out between gasps, 'Oh! Anna, my love. What have you said? Only what I've longed to hear, for years and years I've longed to hear those words, I love you, because I couldn't say them to you, not in the state I am in. I've always thought it would be unfair. Most women almost faint at the mention of a fit. I knew you wouldn't do that, but to offer to join yourself to me for life . . . and you said' – he was laughing now – 'you said you would be my mistress. Oh, Anna, Anna, that in a way is a great compliment; but I don't want a mistress, I want a wife. I've always wanted a wife and you as my wife . . . Don't cry, my love. Don't cry. Oh, look' – he pointed to the fire now – 'you have no idea of the pictures I have seen in those flames. Oh, my dear, dearest Anna, let me dry your eyes. And this, this is what I've seen myself doing in those flames.' And now his arms went about her and he laid his lips on hers, and the kiss was long and tender. When their lips parted they still lay and looked at each other in silence, until he said, 'There may be happier days for us but not one that I shall remember as I shall this: these last few moments. Oh! Anna. You know, I want to sing, I want to take you by the hand and run with you to some place. Oh, I don't know what I want. I think Byron's words, "Let joy be unconfined" fit how I'm feeling, although' – he laughed now – 'that had to do with the Battle of Waterloo, hadn't it?' And she, laughing too, completed his quotation: 'On with the dance, let joy be unconfined.' Their foreheads came together for a moment, then taking her face between his hands he asked quietly, 'How soon can we be married?'

'As soon as you like, my dear.'

'So be it, as soon as I like,' and when she whispered, 'Well, let it be that soon or sooner,' they fell together and laughed and rocked each other until he cried, 'Oh! I forgot. I brought you a present. Let me get my case.'

When he brought a leather case to the couch he took from it a long, narrow box tied up with a gold cord and he handed it to her, saying, 'That'll be the first of many, my dear, because I'll be at liberty now to buy you what I will.'

Inside the box were three long strands of twisted gold and she gasped as she said, 'Oh! it's beautiful, beautiful. Oh! Tim.'

'Stand up, my darling.'

She stood up, and he fastened the clasp at the back of her neck, then said, 'Come and look in the mirror,' and led her to a wall mirror in which she looked at her reflection and that of the three-strand gold necklace hanging down below her collarbone, one strand falling behind the other. Then raising her eyes to his through the mirror, she said, 'Oh, my dear, what can I say?'

Turning her towards him, he said, 'You can say those three words again that almost brought on my collapse.'

'Oh! Tim, my dear, dear Tim, they were true. I do love you and I have for a long, long time. Looking back, I think the seed was sown the day you looked at me from the mat and spoke one word; angel.'

'Well, my love, that's how I've thought of you ever since. But now' – he lifted her hand – 'you should have a ring. I have some odd bits of jewellery in the safe, but one thing I haven't got is a ring. We will go into town tomorrow and you'll have one with the biggest stone I can find . . . '

'I won't! I'll have a ring, but not one with the biggest stone you can find. I don't care for flashy jewellery.'

'You will have one, madam, with the biggest stone I can find, or else.'

'What does that mean. None at all?'

'That's right, none at all.' He bent forward and kissed her gently again; then he laughed, saying, 'I want to shout this out to someone. Shall we tell the staff?'

'You would like that?'

'Wouldn't you? Would it upset you?'

'Upset me? Oh! Tim, no, no. You are doing me an honour, and I am well aware of it because you know my history. It isn't everyone who would . . . '

He clapped his hand over her mouth, saying, 'Don't you ever refer to that. You are worth the love of any man, any man, however great he might be, and *I am honoured*. I am the one who is honoured and so very, very grateful. Oh! Anna, you don't know how grateful. You said you had felt rejected, well, I have felt rejected ever since this cursed thing struck me. I have laughed and talked and chattered aimlessly, all the while being aware of how people were even afraid to be in my company in case I had . . . one of those.' He nodded his head now. 'They were even afraid to put the word fit to it. Many a time I have left a company to prevent myself crying in front of them, because I knew they couldn't differentiate between someone who had fits and a mental defective or an idiot. No, my dear, till the day I die there will be a portion of my heart that will be indebted to you. But before we leave this dire subject I shall tell you this. When I was in London I saw the specialist who has delved into this sickness and although he said he couldn't cure me, he has come up with a pill that, although it cannot prevent the attacks, it can decrease their severity. Well' – he now spread one hand out – 'so far so good. Now, let's go and tell them.'

He led her out of the drawing-room and, seeing Walters about to mount the stairs, he called, 'Would you be kind enough, Walters, to bring in Edward and Fletcher. I have some news I would like you all to share.'

360

'Yes. Yes, of course, sir.' He stared from one to the other and smiled widely at them before hurrying out. And now, Tim, still holding her hand, led her into the kitchen, saying, 'Where is that woman who stuffs me with cream sponge cake? Oh, there you are, cook!'

Mrs Ada Sprigman turned from the table, her face beaming. 'Oh, sir, you know you are a tease,' she said. And the kitchen maid, Lena Cassidy, turned from the sink, a wide grin on her face and, bobbing from one to the other, giggled. And Mary Bowles, who was quickly wiping her mouth, likely after having had her share of another sponge cake, said, 'Is there anything you want, sir?'

'Yes, I want all your attention; Walters has gone for Edward and Fletcher. I have some news for you.'

The three women now stood side by side against the edge of the table. ' 'Tis good news, I can see, sir, or you wouldn't be looking so bright.'

'Besides being a very good cook you are a very discerning woman, Mrs Sprigman.' And at this the three women laughed. Then the back door opened and the gardener and the coachman entered, both doffing their caps. But it was noticeable that Walters didn't come in the back way, but entered the kitchen from the hallway and approached his master's side, just as Timothy, looking round his small staff, said, 'It is with the greatest pleasure in the world I am able to tell you that Miss Dagshaw has consented to be my wife.'

There was a slight gasp or two, then a chorus of 'Oh! sir. Oh! miss.'

'Oh! congratulations, sir. Congratulations, miss. We wish you every happiness, sir.'

'If anybody deserves to be happy, it's you, sir.'

'And you, miss. Oh yes, and you, miss.'

'When is it to be, sir?'

This was from Edward, and Timothy answered him, 'Well, it would be tonight if I had my way, but it will be by special licence some time within the next week or so.'

'Oh, I'll make you a spread like you've never seen afore, sir, that's if you're having it in the house.'

Timothy now turned to Anna and said, 'Well, this will be for discussion,' and Anna, looking at the cook, said, 'That would be lovely, Mrs Sprigman, to have it in this house. 'Yes' – she nodded now towards Timothy – 'we'll have it in the house.' And he, nodding back to her said, 'Very good, ma'am,' which, in the emotional circumstances, caused loud laughter all round. And now he said, 'I think a drink would be in order. What do you think, Walters?'

'I think you're right, sir. What would you like?'

'Well, toasts are usually made in champagne but I don't think we have any in our little cellar, have we?'

'No, sir. But there's a very good claret and a port, and, if the ladies would prefer it, a sherry.'

'Well, bring the three choices into the sitting room and we'll drink there. So, come along . . . '

His hold on Anna's hand was only released when, in the sitting-room, they all held a glass and in different ways the staff drank to their health. And when Tim's glass of claret touched Anna's glass and he said, 'May you know nothing but happiness, my dear, from now on,' there was a concerted chorus of, 'Hear-hear! sir. Hear! hear!'

Just before the staff left the room the cook, looking at Timothy, said, 'Would you like me to knock you up a nice dinner, sir? I had two pheasants come in this mornin'.'

Timothy now turned to Anna, saying, 'You'll stay to dinner, won't you?' And she, without hesitation, said, 'Yes. Yes, I'd be delighted to.'

'Well, that's settled, ma'am, that's settled.'

As Mrs Sprigman bobbed to her, Anna noticed that she had suddenly become ma'am and she felt an added warmth seep through her. She had entered a new world, and she'd be free in it. Oh, so lovingly free . . .

It was turned seven o'clock when they finished their dinner in the dining-room.

Anna had never sat down to such a table, nor had she ever eaten such a meal or drunk so much wine. And so, when Walters said to Timothy, 'It's snowing heavily, sir,' Timothy said, 'Oh, dear me. The carriage is going to have a job. Is it lying?'

'It's a good inch, sir, and there's a wind blowing, so there'll be drifts already.'

'Oh go out and see what Edward thinks,' Timothy said to him, 'and we'll go by that, eh?'

With the room to themselves, he murmured, 'Well now, milady, what's to happen if you can't get home?'

She smiled back at him across the table as she answered, 'I'll take great pleasure in staying the night here, sir.' And at this he laughed, and said loudly, 'Will you indeed, madam?' And she answered as playfully, 'Yes, sir, if it is your pleasure.'

'Oh! Anna, Anna. What a day! What a beautiful, delightful day! And how lovely you are! To think I shall see you every day for the rest of my life sitting across from me at our table. But seriously, would you stay the night?'

'Why not?'

And again he laughed as he said, 'Why not indeed! I shall get Mary to put a warming pan into the spare room bed. But I do feel your people should be told, so I'll ask Edward to go over on horseback. If it's only an inch or so the horse will get through all right, whereas the carriage . . . well, that's a different thing. Excuse me, my dear.'

After he had gone from the room she sat back and closed

her eyes and said to herself, 'Oh, Jimmy, Jimmy, what a beautiful escape! And what will they say when they hear the news that I'm staying the night here; that, like Cherry, I've succumbed at last to pattern? Yes, yes; that's what they'll think. And they'll be happy in a way now that I won't be able to hold my head up so high. They'll say, Why him? Why couldn't she have taken this step with the other one? Look what she's saddled herself with, a man who has fits . . . a wonderful man, a thinking man, a kind and generous man, a lovely man. Oh yes, a lovely man . . . '

Timothy came back into the room saying, 'It's all been taken care of.' Then taking her hand, he said, 'Come, my dear, we'll have coffee in the drawing-room.'

They were crossing the hall when he suddenly stopped and exclaimed, 'Christmas! We'll have a big tree in the corner there, aglow with candles, and holly and mistletoe and flowers everywhere.'

When they entered the drawing-room she said, 'How old did you say you were?' And he replied, 'You've put me into my second childhood, dear.'

When, a moment later, they stood facing each other on the rug before the fire, he placed his hands on her shoulders and asked quietly, 'Would you like children?' and as quietly she answered, 'I'd love children, Tim. Do . . . do you want children?'

'Oh, yes, yes, Anna.'

'How many would you like?' Now she was smiling at him, and he pushed his mouth from one side to the other before he said, 'Let me think. Well, ten's a round number. I like round numbers, but, all right, I'll be satisfied with five. How's that?'

'Oh! Tim.' She put her arms about him, and when they now kissed it wasn't gentle but gave evidence of the hunger in both of them. And when at last they stood apart he said, 'It must be soon, mustn't it?' And she answered, 'Yes, it must be soon.'

It was nine days later when they were married by Parson Mason in the little church at Fellburn. All her family were present, as, of course, was Miss Netherton, and also Timothy's own staff, but his two nephews were conspicuous by their absence. Nor had they received a wedding present from them. There were also present in the church Dan Wallace and his wife and son Art, Miss Penelope Smythe, the dressmaker, and Roland Watts, the carpenter, who had once lived in the village, and his wife.

It would seem that with this representation from the village, the inhabitants were wishing her well. But the village was still the village and in the King's Head there were those who reminded others that it was through her that there were two men and a girl languishing in jail and also that four families had been turfed out of their homes. Anyway, she had always lived up to her name: in fact, both lasses had, for there was one with her belly full and not married yet. And this one had stayed the night with him, hadn't she? Supposedly because the snow was too thick to drive her home. They could send a fellow on a horse, though, couldn't they? Oh, once a gillyvor always a gillyvor. And they were having the reception at the house and no honeymoon. But, you wouldn't expect them to have a honeymoon now, would you? Well, anyway, just wait and see when she sprouted the next little gillyvor, for that would give the game away. Wait till August or September; we'll see.

And there's another thing: he must have been paying for her on the side for a long time, because where did the old 'uns up in the Hollow get the money for a new horse and trap? It was also being said now that they were buying that pit lad a share in the boatyard, and he not being apprenticed to it for a year yet. Who said the wicked didn't prosper, especially when the devil took a hand in moulding them, like the new Mrs Barrington, driving here and there in her carriage and pair. Aye, the trouble that one had caused in high and low quarters alike!

It was certainly true what Parson Fawcett said: the evil that men do lives after them; but the evil that women do goes on for countless generations through their breeding.

Epilogue

~~~

There was an announcement in the 'Births' column of *The Times* and also in the local papers, which read as follows:

'On the 1st December, 1884, a daughter to Mr and Mrs Timothy Barrington of Briar Close, Maple Road, Fellburn. Joy unconfined.

THE END

12681550R20205

Made in the USA
Middletown, DE
16 November 2018